DUST & RAIN

ICEFIRE TRILOGY BOOK 2

PATTY JANSEN

CAPRICORNICA PUBLICATIONS

GET FREE EBOOKS

Visit pattyjansen.com
or scan the QR code below with your phone to sign up for Patty's
mailing list. You get four series starter ebooks for free!

CHAPTER 1

ADORIUS HAN CHEVONIAN dropped the pile of
barygraph read-outs on his desk. Pages and pages of plotted
squiggly lines slid over the wooden surface.

On top was a different sheet with a hand-drawn graph, a red line
which jumped up sharply towards the right hand side of the page. He
picked up that sheet, shook his head and frowned at the young man
who had brought him these data.

"Up by this much?"

His new student, Vikius han Marossi, nodded. Silver embroidery
glittered on the young man's white tunic, showing the insignia of the
Chevakian doga, the government assembly.

The young man had left the door open and sounds of voices
drifted in from the hall, mixed with the slapping of sandals on stone.
A breeze that carried the tang of summer ruffled the curtains and
nudged at the lingering chill in the room, a hint of the fury of hot
weather to come. As chief meteorologist, Sady knew all about the
weather; he could feel summer in his bones. And yet . . .

He looked at the graph, as if staring at it would change that
ominous red line, and shook his head again.

"What happened? When I checked a few days ago, sonorics levels
were at three motes per cube, but now they've at twelve?" Three was
normal for this time of the year; twelve was slightly above the highest
average level in the middle of winter. He wiped sweat from his upper

lip, rechecking figures in the table on the second page, in the idle hope that the attendant of the met station who had plotted the graph had misread. He hadn't.

"It looks like we're in for an interesting summer." Sonorics, the deadly rays that came from the southern land, an ice-covered plateau so mysterious that it didn't have a name, dictated the weather patterns across Chevakia.

"I'm not sure I would call it interesting. I find it frightening." Viki's tone was timid. He held his hands clasped behind his back and stared intently at the desk.

"Viki, straighten your back and look up."

The young man did as Sady told him, a startled expression on his face. Mercy, since when did the Scriptorium send him jackrabbits for students?

"Imagine you're making an important announcement to the doga. They're not going to listen to you if you mumble, and they won't take you seriously if you slouch."

"Um—I'm sorry, Senator."

"Viki, if ever you're going to be chief meteorologist, you will need to show more confidence. How else are you going to tell selfish senators that, no, their district isn't going to get an allocation of maize production, because the air current predictions are wrong and the harvest will certainly fail?"

"Um . . ." Viki went red in the face and went back to staring at the desk.

"Stand up! Look me in the eye. Tell me what you'd say to them if you were in this situation."

The young man straightened again, his eyes wide. "Um—I'd say that they were wrong asking for the allocation, Senator. I'd tell them about our high sonorics measurements and that they predict unseasonably cold weather in the south which means much less rain in the north. I'd show them the maps and show them how I calculated—"

"No, no, Viki."

The student gave Sady a startled look. "But I have to—"

"You should always keep it simple. Don't explain to them how you calculated the prediction. That not only bores them to tears, but it shows that you feel the need to justify yourself because you're not sure of your calculations."

"But—"

"Confidence, Viki. You'll need confidence in your work or the farmers and the districts will howl you down, especially those in the North. They seem to think that the sheer act of predicting is going to make it happen."

"But you can only predict rain when the circumstances indicate that there will be rain."

"Exactly, but do you think they care? Rain is money to them. If I predict rain, the doga gives them money to plant crops, simple as that. Then of course, there is no rain, the harvest fails and the meteorologist gets the blame."

"But that's . . ." Viki's eyes were wide.

"That's how things go if you're not careful." Sady sighed and shuffled the papers on his desk. He felt no patience with his student today. Those data were really too worrisome to ignore. "Have you looked at any other border stations?"

Viki pushed another bundle of papers across the table; his hands trembled.

Sady leafed through the graphs. Same results. Automated devices were all recording low pressure, and the manual measurements taken by faithful meteorology staff in the stations reported high humidity, low temperatures and out-of-season increases in sonorics. Not just one station, but Ensar, Fairlight, Mekta, all of them reporting levels of twelve, thirteen, even fourteen motes per cube.

Mercy, what was going on?

"Senator, begging your permission . . . I made this." Viki put a roll of paper on the desk. Sady frowned and unrolled it: a map, showing isobars across the country.

It was a neat piece of work, impressively detailed. He gave Viki an appreciative look. "Now that is what I call initiative. That's what I'd like to see more of."

The young man blushed.

Sady moved some papers aside and spread the map out over the table. Wavy lines ran parallel to the escarpment that formed the border with the southern plateau, a pattern that sometimes occurred in midwinter, but even then the pressure lines were usually less crowded. There was a huge low-pressure system building up.

Sady met the student's eyes.

"Any idea what it means?"

"Um . . ." The young man's cheeks went red.

Sady sighed. "Viki, this is not a trick question. I don't know either. Nothing like this has happened before. This is not a seasonal pattern. At this time of the year, we'd expect the low pressure systems to retreat to the far south and the air flow to swing around to the north."

The young man looked up, his lips forming the letter *o*. "Well, in that case, I was thinking . . . I mean . . . low pressure is usually associated with a rise in sonorics, because sonorics tends to increase the air humidity."

"Yes, but why?"

Viki hesitated. "What if . . . if the people in the City of Glass were releasing sonorics deliberately. . . ? Could they, if they wanted to?"

Sady shrugged, uncomfortable. They knew so little of the workings of the southern land and the source of those deadly rays that influenced far too much of Chevakia's weather. Some sort of machine, the classic works said, somewhere under the City of Glass. No one knew if this supposed machine was a physical thing or a myth. Sady wasn't sure the southerners themselves knew what it was. Then, fifteen years ago, after the border wars, the barriers went up and no one travelled to the south anymore. Right now, he certainly didn't want to worry about whether southerners could manipulate it, although the thought chilled him. Sonorics were deadly to Chevakians.

"Viki, please give the Most Learned Alius the message that I wish to see him." Sady didn't really expect much help from an academic who did not share his practical experience, but his old tutor had made an extensive study of sonorics and was without a doubt Chevakia's most knowledgeable expert on the subject.

"Certainly, Senator." Viki bowed and left the room at a trot.

Sady grimaced. *Really? Am I that frightening? I must be getting old.*

He shook his head. No need to worry too much over this student. After his traineeship, Viki would probably choose to move on to a career in academia—or so Sady hoped, because the youngster really hadn't the aptitude for a life as doga meteorologist.

Sady rose and went to the window.

Laid out before him in perfect geometric patterns, the splendour of Tiverius spread towards the horizon. Rows of terracotta roofs basked in the sun along perfectly straight streets, interspersed by stone buildings with columns. Trees bloomed along the roadsides, even numbers on both sides. Down in the courtyard, a man with a water truck was watering the flowers in the planter boxes.

A warm breeze stirred the curtains. A few moon cycles, and it would be midsummer, not at all the time high sonorics levels usually happened.

Sonorics levels wouldn't need to rise that much before they caused trouble. At twenty motes, it would taint the harvest, at thirty, set off the first alarms and affect exports to Arania. Chevakia couldn't afford not to harvest in the southern border provinces. The northern region was too dry to produce much more than camels and the occasional crop of maize.

He didn't want to start panic, but . . . why now? Why at the start of summer, when the annual cycle should be approaching its lowest level.

Back at his desk, he pulled out a writing pad. He scrawled on the top page, *Authorise dispensaries to start stocking salt tablets for general public use. Authorise protective suits to be taken out of storage and sent to border regions.*

This he took to his secretary in the next room, who took the note, looked at it and met Sady's eyes in a wide-eyed look.

The expression of worry cut Sady deeply. He only vaguely remembered the time of uncertainty before the barriers went up, but he had heard the tales told by older folk. The young man would have seen the barygraph readouts this morning. He would have heard the tales, too.

"Just to make sure," Sady said, hoping he exuded a confidence he didn't feel. A confidence that, following such a rapid rise, the levels wouldn't hit twenty motes per cube and trigger the lowest-level warning.

The man nodded, but similarly didn't look convinced.

Not good. Not good at all.

CHAPTER 2

Oh, morninglight, oh evenlight,
How you wake me through the night.
Oh morningstar, oh evenstar,
How do you guide me from afar?
JEVAITHI'S CLEAR VOICE faded amongst the trees, in the rustle of the wind through the pine boughs, and the singing of the birds.

She breathed the scent of grass and pine resin, letting the taste of it flow through her lungs. It was beautiful. It was strange; it was new. All her life, she had only seen the whiteness of the plains around the City of Glass, whenever her minders had deigned to take her, which wasn't often.

For the first time in all her life, Jevaithi was free. There were no courtiers telling her to behave, no ladies-in-waiting telling her to wear hideous clothes; there was no Rider Cornatan watching over her. She could dance, she could sing, she could roll in the grass.

The dress was filthy, but it didn't matter. The grass was soft and the wind was warm, although today it had been quite chilled, but she and Isandor had their furs, even if they were full of sticks and seeds and smelled of each other.

There was plenty of food and it was so easy to catch that even she, with little experience in hunting, had made two kills. Fat birds with webbed feet and funny, broad beaks. She'd learned to pluck and clean them, and cut them up for roasting. The Chevakians must keep these for eggs, because they found many of those.

There were even milking goats, although they were tricky to catch and even trickier to milk.

But it was fun. Goat's milk was tangy and smelly, but it filled her stomach.

They had seen no people.

The large house down the hill seemed empty. Once it must have been a magnificent residence, but now the paint had faded, moss covered the roof and the garden was an overgrown mess. In the fields surrounding it, the farm machines moved backwards and forwards by themselves, chug-chugging and belching steam. There was no one in those machines; Isandor had checked. How did they move?

And why was there such a large house with all these empty rooms? Why did no one look after the machines? Why were there big barns with grain just sitting there? Where were all the people to eat it? Chevakia was such a strange place, such a rich place to let all these buildings stand empty and let harvested crops uneaten.

There was the swishing of footsteps through grass.

Isandor stood at the edge of the golden wheat field, holding his hand above his eyes and squinting into the distance.

His face was so serious that Jevaithi wanted to go and hug him, but he'd been very distant ever since they had let the eagle go. He had told her that he'd wanted to be an Eagle Knight, not a leering one like the Knights who had guarded her, but an honest Knight. Of those men it was said they loved their birds more than their women. The bird that had carried them here all the way from the City of Glass had been his, briefly. As he had taken the harness off, it had flown away in the direction of the border. Isandor had watched her fly off until she became a little speck that disappeared over the horizon.

Jevaithi had asked, "Where will she go?"

Isandor had said, "Probably back to the Aranian mountains, to the mountaintops where her kin roost." And the roosts of the giant birds were said to be holy in the eyes of the Knights. Of course the eagle would go back where she could be free.

But Isandor was not free. He stood staring at the sky, with that expression of sadness over his face. The glare from the sun carved sharp angles in his face. Jevaithi didn't dare ask if he was looking for the bird to come back. Her heart—his heart inside her chest—ached with his sadness and at the same time felt warm with love. He didn't deserve sadness.

Isandor was handsome, he had the perfect royal blue eyes, black glossy hair that she loved to stroke and comb, and a few funny hairs that poked out of his chin. He tried to cut them off with the dagger and she said she liked him better with the hairs.

He didn't need to be ashamed about being a man.

She approached him through the grass and was just about to touch him when he turned around abruptly, seemed to see her for the first time, grabbed her hand and pushed her face first against the trunk of a tree.

Jevaithi barely had time to protest. "Isandor, what—"

"Shhh!" He flung his cloak over her and pressed himself against her. Under the cloak, it smelled of sweat, wet fur and pine resin. She could feel her heart beating like crazy in Isandor's chest. His arm tightened around her. All around in the forest, the birds were making alarmed noises.

"What is it?" she whispered in the darkness under the cloak, but at that moment there was a faraway cry she recognised: the plaintive, high-pitched trill that took her back to her tower room prison in the City of Glass, where she would stand with her nose pressed against the window watching the Knights soar past on their birds.

And she could almost feel Rider Cornatan's presence, always watching her. She could feel his gaze burn through her thin dress.

The eagle was surely going to see her; eagles could spot a snow fox on an ice floe from heights where you couldn't even see the rider on the bird's back. Soon, the bird would come down, and bring its mates. There was no way they could fight a couple of trained Knights. She should run, while she still could.

But Isandor's arm enclosed her like a vice, keeping her pressed to the trunk of the tree.

"Keep as still as you can," he whispered. "Eagles can only see you if you move."

Every nerve in her body was telling her that he was wrong, but it made sense. He had been an Apprentice after all. He knew eagles better than she did. She kept still, controlled her shivering muscles which were aching to run, and hardly dared breathe.

Those moments under the cloak felt like eternity, but eventually, Isandor relaxed. He retreated, leaving a cold and sweaty spot where their bodies had touched.

Jevaithi pushed the cloak off her head and squinted at the bits of blue sky peeking between the trees.

"Is it gone?" she asked.

Isandor was squinting at the sky, too. "I think so."

"It wasn't your bird, wasn't it?"

He shook his head, looking serious. "Lucky we let the eagle go. She would have given us away."

"Please do your best to hide us from them. I don't want to go back. I want to stay with you always." She hadn't thought that the Knights would find their position so quickly.

"It's not going back that worries me," Isandor said. "If the Knights catch us, why would they take you back to the City of Glass? It suits them if the Queen has had a terrible accident and won't ever come back. That way, with no Queen and no heir, they can do exactly what they want, and Rider Cornatan won't ever need to give up his power as regent. He can just call himself king. He's probably already done that."

He was right. These Knights weren't here to capture her; they were here to kill her. She had thought there was nothing worse than having Rider Cornatan in her bed, and of course she'd been stupid. There were worse things. Much worse.

"Please, Isandor, help me."

The worried expression on his face hurt her. He held her close, but another chilled wind blew through the forest, which suddenly seemed very harsh and foreign. And there was a tang in the air. If she hadn't known any better, if she hadn't been in Chevakia, she would have thought it was a flare of icefire. That couldn't be. There were barriers. She had seen them herself, felt their eerie influence, endless walls cutting through the landscape, made from metal plates set at an angle. She didn't know how they stopped icefire, but just watching them from the back of an eagle they gave her the shudders. There *was* no icefire here.

"I'm cold."

He didn't meet her eyes. Would he feel it, too, the tang in the air?

Huddling together, they studied the alien intense blue sky. The sun was much further above the horizon than it would ever be in the City of Glass, and cast harsh shadows over the grass and Isandor's pale skin.

He said, "We should probably get under cover. The door to the shed down there is open. I tested it, and there's no one in there. It will be safer, and warmer. I've found some hay that will make a nice bed . . ." He gave a wolfish grin. "Come."

He took her hand.

They gathered up whatever little things they had brought and carried the filthy bundles through the field. The grain came up to her knees and when the ears hit her legs, they tickled. She no longer laughed at the feeling. The sight of the bird wheeling in the sky had awakened a deep fear in her. Running away might work well for Isandor, but could she ever feel safe?

The shed looked rather forbidding, a structure without windows, made from a material that was grey and had countless longitudinal waves. If she hadn't known any better, she would have thought it had come from ancient times. But this was most certainly Chevakian-produced.

Isandor opened the shed door; it creaked.

Jevaithi followed him into semidarkness and a musty smell of dry grass. There was a big dark shape inside, like a big crouching animal. Jevaithi hesitated; she felt so small and nervous. "What's that?"

"It's one of their machines. I know it looks scary, but it doesn't do anything. Come over here."

Jevaithi walked past the machine, running her hand over the smooth metal and breathing its strange scent. The machine was almost as tall as a house, and was one block of metal bigger than she had ever seen before. It had a large wire cylinder on one end and stood on a set of tractor wheels. At the top was a long arm. She wondered what it was for.

Isandor had collected a couple of the strange rectangular cubes of hay as they had found stacked up in another shed. One as a table, two as chairs. A plank held treasures they had collected so far: a rusty fork, a broken pot and a couple of flat rocks for the fire. There was also the clumsy basket she had woven from straw, with three eggs, and a couple of pieces of fruit they had collected.

Isandor spread his hands. "Behold, our first home!"

She forced her worries from her mind and threw herself in his arms. He stroked her hair, but didn't say anything. He was worried, too. She could feel that in the way his heart beat in her chest.

"I think we can't keep running," she said. "We should hide instead. We should become farmers. We can keep goats and keep these funny birds."

"They're called ducks."

"Never mind. We'll look like Chevakians, and no one will recognise us."

"We don't know how to be farmers."

"That doesn't matter. The machines know how to be farmers. We can just let the machines do the work for us."

But her words had a hollow ring to it, and even Isandor would feel that they were fake. They would never be farmers. They didn't even eat anything that had come from a plant. Plants were treasures that took up important decorative positions in rich nobles' houses in the City of Glass. While her body frolicked in the grass, her mind was back in the palace.

She wondered how Rider Cornatan would use his power now that she was gone. Abuse it, rather, because she no longer watched him. And she wished she could stop thinking about the City of Glass, about how the people might suffer in her absence, because the thoughts made her feel guilty.

She had always thought that she had no power, but she did stop the Knights taking power completely, because the people wanted to see and hear *her*, not the Knights, and the Knights served *her*. But there was no point in having these thoughts, and it was not fair for those feelings to creep up on her.

"I think we will go back, one day," Isandor said softly. "It's not right, being free while the people we care about aren't."

No, it wasn't. Her room servants, those people closest to her, might be punished. They might be turned out into the street without a way to support themselves. Was that the way she wanted to reward them?

The people of the City of Glass loved her. They stood along the roads and cheered, and while she held herself proud and waved and envied them for their freedom, their love for her was very real. She challenged the Knights where she could get away with it. Even through her horrific illness and dark moods, her mother Queen Maraithe had raised her with pride. *You must always honour the people. If it weren't for the people, you wouldn't be what you are.* No she wouldn't. Without the people, the Knights would have raped and murdered her long ago.

The people in the City of Glass would miss her. They might revolt; they might be repressed by the Knights. They might accuse the Knights of making her disappear, and the Knights wouldn't take kindly to such accusations. Rider Cornatan would make sure that all those dissenters would be punished, and that would make the people only angrier, and would play into the hands of the Brotherhood of the Light and the sorcerer Tandor, whose motives she didn't understand, but who would be sure to stir up unrest. A shiver crawled over her back. Her escape might lead to the deaths of many people. She'd acted selfishly.

"Then what do you think we should do?" she asked, and she hated how discomfort laced her voice. And she hated how his words cut through the dream of being free.

"I think we'll need to hide for a while until the Knights stop looking for us," Isandor said. Which wasn't really an answer. "Then we can find somewhere to live."

She nodded, but knew it wasn't so simple. As long as she, or a child of hers, was alive, the Knights would hunt her.

His worried face broke into a smile. "Hey, don't look like that. We'll survive. I'll always be with you."

She smiled, too. "I love you."

His lips sealed on hers.

They rolled in the hay, clothes discarded along the way until they lay naked and panting, in the afterglow of lovemaking.

He whispered, "I love you so much it hurts me here." He held his hand to his chest.

She put her ear on the bare skin next to her hand. Their hearts beat in unison; she could never get enough of hearing it.

She would never leave him, never, never leave him out of sight, wherever they went.

"Love me again," she said. "Love me again and again."

He did.

But love did not solve her deeper worries.

CHAPTER 3

"THEY WEREN'T even listening!" Viki protested, spreading his hands in a gesture of frustration. His eyes, wide and brown, met Sady's, while he swerved to avoid a uniformed guard coming the other way in the corridor. They were walking back to the office from the morning's doga session where Sady had cringed through Viki's presentation on climate patterns.

"I told you that showing calculations and tables would bore them," Sady said.

"There was only one sheet of calculations and one table. You said to show the maps, so I showed mostly maps. I did what you said, honestly."

Viki was right: he had eliminated most of the calculations and dry data tables; he had made the maps bold and pretty. It was just that . . . the senators had been more interested in discussions about train lines to the north. Sady felt a deep shame about that. What a way to introduce a young man to the world of politics. *We only listen when there is something in it for us.*

"I know you did. I'm sorry, Viki. I'm not sure what I would have done differently." Would they have listened had he given the talk himself? The data was serious enough.

They went around the corner and up the stairs. Their footsteps echoed in the open staircase. Marble columns and rich wall hangings.

Carved wooden doors and leadlight windows. Splendour was everywhere.

They passed a group of senators who gave him glances that bordered on pity. *Poor Sady, who listens to him? Poor Sady, who cares about meteorology?* Some people said it was fast becoming an irrelevant discipline, that everyone already knew what there was to know, that one only needed enter a date and weather data in one of those new calculators that were being developed by the Scriptorium, and be presented with best dates for planting crops.

At the top of the stairs, Sady turned left and charged down the corridor. Viki had to run to keep up.

Someone behind him called, "Senator Sadorius, can I have a word?"

Sady stopped and turned around to see Proctor Destran mir Parkeshian behind him. Oh, mercy, that was just what he needed.

Viki said in a low voice, "Do you want me to continue to the office?"

"Stay here," Sady said. Destran would most likely want to talk about Viki's presentation.

Viki stayed, clasping his hands behind his back and tensing his shoulders. His face resembled that of a hunted rabbit.

Destran caught up and gave a customary bow. "Senator."

Sady returned the greeting. "Proctor."

From close up, Destran resembled a scarecrow. Lanky and taller than most people, he always walked hunched over, as if life were a great burden. His heavy, hooded eyelids increased that impression. His hands were like veined spiders; his neck had as many wrinkles as the neck of a very, very old turtle. Exposure to sunlight in his childhood had made his skin blotchy and age had brought the breaking out of many small, polyp-like warts over his face and neck.

The man's narrowed eyes met Sady's. "I heard you authorised the distribution of pills and suits."

"I did, for the border regions only."

"I understand you didn't ask doga permission?"

"No, I didn't. Within limits, I don't need approval." Destran would know that.

"Don't you think you overreacted?" Destran's gaze was intense.

Sady stared back. "No, I don't. Some border stations were recording sonorics levels of fourteen motes per cube."

"The warning limit is twenty."

"Yes."

There was a moment of silence. Destran continued staring and Sady continued meeting his gaze. A cold draft made the curtains behind Destran stir, and matched the icy atmosphere between them.

"I cannot see a reason for this," Destran said. "There is no evidence that we are under any kind of sonorics threat beyond what we can cope with."

"The rise is rapid and completely out-of-season."

"And the twenty motes per cube is a failsafe, arbitrary, nothing-could-possibly-happen-at-this-level kind of limit."

"My greatest worry is not the level, but the timing of it. We've never been able to test the precise effects, because, as you can understand, we are reluctant to send our people into the south. So yes, the upper limit is somewhat arbitrary, but the safety of Chevakians should be the first priority for the doga."

"Within reasonable assumptions."

"And you, Proctor, are suggesting that nothing of what you've heard today is reasonable? That the measurements my student reported are all fake? Are you suggesting that the measurements taken by our own met stations lie?"

Destran spread his hands. "No, I do not."

"Then what?"

"I think your reaction is completely out of proportion and unwarranted."

"This has the potential to become an emergency."

"So you seem to think, but tell me: who is going to pay for this extravagance?"

Ah, now they got to the real problem. Sady hated poor budgeting masquerading as policy, and Destran seemed to excel at the activity.

"Safety is more important than budgets."

"Up to a point." Destran continued, "But, to please you, I've asked for independent advice about this issue, and that's what I wanted to talk to you about."

"Independent advice?" It came out as a sarcastic remark. There was no one in the country who knew more about weather patterns than him. That's why he was Chief Meteorologist.

Then Sady noticed another man who had stayed back with Destran's aides, but now came forward.

Tall, grey-haired, straight-backed, the Most Learned Alius cut an impressive figure. As head of the Scriptorium, he oversaw academia and the tutoring of students of the arts and sciences. Sady hadn't seen the man for some time, and his dark clothing and age made him sterner than Sady remembered him. And what was with the beard?

Alius bowed and Sady returned the greeting, wondering if beards were the latest fashion in the Scriptorium. Then again, he had not known academics to take much notice of fashion. "Well met, Most Learned. You know your student, of course." Sady nodded at Viki, who stood a bit back, staring at his formal tutor.

"Oh yes, I know him." Alius smiled, and the corners of his eyes crinkled. "That was an entertaining talk, young man."

"Um . . . um . . . thank you, Most Learned." Viki's stammer was back in full force.

"I am being sarcastic."

"Ummm . . . excuse me, Most Learned. I do not understa—"

Alius shook his head. "My dear student, I turn my back on you for five seconds, and you've already become the politicians' mouthpiece."

"Um . . ." Viki opened and closed his mouth a few times, like a fish gasping in the air.

"How much time have you spent analysing these data?"

"Um . . ."

"Did you just throw them into a graph and present the results without any background research?"

"I did background research." Viki's voice spilled over into a squeak. "I'm aware of all the protocols in the Meteorological Manual—"

"That's just a silly book of rules. What do you know about sonorics? I mean—really know about it?"

"I know that sonorics are rays akin to a magnetic field, and that the source is somewhere in the south. Exposure to the rays distorts the soft tissue of the human body by collapsing the cell membranes. Sonorics increases the humidity in the air which is how we can detect

it . . . um . . ." Viki swallowed and shrank back further under Alius'
continued death stare.

Sady couldn't stand this verbal caning anymore. It was one thing
for two senators to swear at each other, another entirely for a senior
academic to tear into an inexperienced student, and one who hadn't
even made a clear transgression at that.

"I think your student did everything right," Sady said.

"*You* think so?" Alius' eyes were intense. "What do *you* know about
sonorics? Have you studied the precise properties of it?"

"Not sonorics." Sady had to concede the point. It had been Alius
who had conducted those studies, who had helped construct the
barrier that protected Chevakia. "Is there anything new to report
about sonorics that we should know?"

"At this stage, there is no need to cause panic in the public. There
is no proof that there will be any damage to the barriers below at
least fifty motes per cube and no proof that levels such as measured
in the border regions will cause harm whatsoever."

Destran nodded. "There appears no reason for your unilateral
action. I must assume that it was taken for political purposes."

"You would disagree that this rapid rise is highly unusual? That
we need to caution people in the border regions?"

"No, I don't disagree," Destran said. "We have issued travel warnings for the south."

Sady didn't make a habit of swearing, but for fuck's sake, *travel
warnings*? What good would that do? He stomped into the office after
Viki, and shut the door with a thud.

"Mercy, Viki, the day Destran defeated Milleus was a sad one. I bet
my annual stipend that Milleus wouldn't be so hesitant to take action.
What's up with him, Viki? No money, money, always the same excuse.
Well, he has all our taxes, what does he *do* with the money? Pay off his
northern supporters who keep him in position?"

They were all rhetorical questions, of course. Viki scuttled to his
temporary desk in the corner, took his maps and looked busy. He was
way too young to remember the great Milleus han Chevonian, Sady's
brother, who had been voted out ten years ago.

Milleus wouldn't have allowed Viki to have been drowned out by catcalls. Milleus wouldn't have let issues of budget stand in the way of Chevakia's safety. Admittedly, that hadn't always gone in his favour, but Chevakia had been a safe place. It had been Milleus who'd had the foresight to let Alius build the barrier that had protected the country for the last fifteen years.

Sady heaved a sigh and dropped in his big seat behind his desk. The feel of the smooth leather gave him no comfort today.

He swivelled the chair to face Viki. "Anyway, what was going on there between you and Alius?"

Viki gave him his usual startled look. "Nothing."

"Well, that looked like an odd kind of *nothing* to me. I don't recall ever being so petrified of my tutor. Why was he abusing you? *Politician's mouthpiece.* We're all mouthpieces of politics. Chevakia *is* politics."

Viki had no answer to that. He kept looking ahead of him. Avoiding Sady's eyes?

Sady sighed again. "Listen Viki, it's fine to tell me, because I can help: is there anyone at the Scriptorium who threatens you or makes you feel unsafe in any other way? Do you ever feel that you are not allowed to speak your opinion because it doesn't conform to certain opinions held by the senior academics?"

"No," Viki said, much too quickly. "No, not at all. Why are you asking?"

"Because I don't believe you. As long as I can remember, I've never heard anyone from the Scriptorium utter political comments. What is going on over there? What has gotten into Alius? What's with the beard?"

Viki looked at him, and blinked. "He's allowed to have a beard, isn't he?"

"Well, yes, but it seems strange to me. Not just the beard, but his entire behaviour. He wasn't like this when I studied—"

"Like what?"

"Like . . ." Sady shrugged, looked for words to describe his feeling, and couldn't find any that satisfied him. Aggressive, defensive, evasive, anything an academic was usually not. "Like . . . Alius always used to be more open about everything, willing to discuss. It's like he's made up his mind about this and he doesn't like being challenged."

"Well, he did build the barriers. Maybe he feels the need to defend his work to people who suggest it's not up to the job."

That was actually a really good point. And one that worried him. The academics were supposed to be impartial and non-political. And now, for some reason, Alius had decided to support Destran and consider people who opposed him an enemy.

CHAPTER 4

THE BEAR RAN across the snow-covered plain, up hills, down the other side. From the passenger seat, squashed between Tandor and Myra, Loriane could only see its bobbing back, and the reins dangling from the invisible driver's hands.

Wherever she looked in the white landscape, she could see no other people, and there hadn't been any for at least a day.

At first, when the mangled ruins of the City of Glass were still visible on the horizon, there were other refugee sleds following, families fleeing in the clothes they had worn when disaster struck, woefully inadequate for the cold. A lot of nobles, because they had sleds and could get away quickly.

But one by one, the other sleds had fallen behind until no one was left. Those sleds had to stop for the night while Tandor's bear kept going, up, down, up, down over the undulating landscape. This was no ordinary sled and no ordinary bear.

Occasionally, an eagle wheeled overhead. Loriane would cover Tandor up for fear of being recognised, but those eagles seemed to be searching only for other birds and their riders. Yesterday, she had seen a small group of them join up and make their way over the horizon in the direction of the Aranian mountains. If even the Eagle Knights abandoned the city, then what hope was there for the rest of them?

Loriane thought of the ruins, the fire and the broken bodies. The explosion she couldn't see, and the human-like shapes made of steam, one of which Myra had recognised as the father of her child. She thought of the thousands of people who didn't have sleds, and who would have been overtaken by the horror of the invisible icefire, and would have died through its burning as all those had died in the city itself.

The bear ran, the runners of the sled swished in the snow. The driver didn't pull the reins once. It seemed the animal knew the way.

Tandor's weight lay heavy against her side. Bits of his face and hands were exposed between the furs, showing peeling skin and weeping blisters. His eyes were shut. The eyelids fluttered every now and then, but Loriane's prodding didn't wake him up.

Myra was still recovering and slept a lot. Sometimes Loriane managed to wake her up to feed the baby, at other times, when the child cried, she took it to her own swollen breasts. The suckling made her stomach tense up badly, and she stopped doing it for fear of bringing on the birth out here in the snow. The baby cried a lot.

She had found out that the driver could hear her voice and that he would obey her, as long as she used Tandor's name in the requests.

They had little food. Loriane had scoured everything on the luggage rack, but she hated going through Tandor's things, fearing she'd find another horrid item like the beating heart which sat in its jar in the chest that she dare not touch.

She had only found a small box containing dried and salted meat —frozen solid—frozen fruit and cubes of a dark type of bread Loriane had never seen before. Its unfamiliar taste made acid burn in her throat. She nibbled dried meat and stayed away from eating too much snow because already she had to ask Ruko to stop the sled more often than she thought his patience allowed. Whenever she asked for a stop, he would get off the driver's seat and kick snow about, and would goad the bear until it slashed its claws at the air, and growled. The first time that happened, Loriane told him to be more careful, and Ruko threw snow in her face. She was afraid to anger him any more.

It was not to be helped; Loriane had to change Myra's bandages.

After her horrific breech birth, the girl was still bleeding quite heavily and Loriane hoped they would get wherever they were going before her supply of clean cloths ran out. The bandages needed to be rinsed, bleached and boiled, or Myra would still get sick and die of fever.

After that was done and Myra was peacefully feeding the child, Loriane would stumble off into the snow, her own baby's head threatening to burst her full bladder. There was nowhere to squat, no place to hide and after the business was done, she left an embarrassing patch of yellow in the snow, something she was sure eagles would spot. So she covered it with snow, kneeling awkwardly, but still she was sure the eagles would notice. She couldn't help it. She was tired, weary and sore, and more than anything, she wanted the roiling in her belly to stop. She wanted Tandor to wake up so that he could hear her abuse about how stupid and selfish he'd been. And then he was going to tell her what he did, and he was going to fix it before she killed him—which she should have done ages ago. He was trouble, and she'd known it all along, but somehow she thought that dangerous streak made him romantic. Stupid, stupid, stupid.

Most of all, she wanted a dry and warm place where she could rest and from where she wouldn't move until this cursed child had been born. Then she would kill that child, too, because it was part of Tandor's machinations. Fancy that—out of all the ten children she had grown inside her, she couldn't get rid of the child she least wanted.

When night came on the third day, the bear loped into a scattering of houses spread in the snow as if someone had thrown a bunch of firebricks. They were odd, blocky things spaced widely, so unlike the limpets from the Outer City which sat close together like Legless Lions conserving warmth. But houses meant people, and help, and food. Welcoming tendrils of smoke curled from chimneys; warm light radiated from windows.

Myra sat up straight, looking with wide eyes, the word *home* spelled on her face. This then, was Bordertown, the edge of the southern plateau, and as far as they could go without running into Chevakia.

Loriane was too sore and weary to be disappointed with the town's small size. Her feet were cold and she had long since given up trying to pick icicles from her hair. Her backside felt like one solid bruise, and she needed to piss again.

The bear seemed to know where it was headed.

They turned into the yard of a house as unassuming as the rest, a two-storey affair with a shed out the front. Tattered curtains covered the windows. There was light on the ground floor. As the sled came to a halt, the front door was thrown open and a woman stood silhouetted by the warm light of an oil lamp in the hall.

"Myra, be that you?"

"Ma!" Myra cried out.

Myra threw aside the furs, scooped the baby in her arms, jumped off the sled and waded through the snow.

The woman came out of the house and met her daughter in the yard, enclosing her in a hug. Myra was crying, her sobs interspersed with, "It was so awful . . . the whole city is destroyed . . . everyone is dead . . ."

The boy started crying, muffled between the two women. Myra unwrapped the furs that covered his face.

The woman gasped. "What a big boy."

"That's what the midwives said, too."

"What be his name?"

"I haven't named him yet, Ma. I wanted you and Da to be there."

The woman lifted the child from his sling, while he continued to protest loudly. Her brow was unusually heavy for a female, her nose coarse and her mouth wide. She had skin red and rough from working in the cold, and big, widely-spaced front teeth. The word *ugly* came to Loriane's mind.

A man had come to the doorway, leaning against the doorframe.

Myra's mother held the baby out to him. "Look at him, Da. Your grandson."

But the man, black-haired and unshaven, was staring past his wife and Myra to the sled, his suspicious piggy eyes narrowing when they met Loriane's.

"Where be the sorcerer?" His mouth twitched. "That be my sled and my bear."

Loriane said, "Tandor is injured. Can we please—"

"Who be you?" Eyes narrowed at Loriane. "You be the city whore?"

"Da!" Myra hissed. "Mistress Loriane has helped me. I was in pain for *three days,* not one day as you said, Ma. The baby was facing the wrong way and I did so much screaming I couldn't talk for two days. Without Mistress Loriane, I would have been dead."

The man studied Loriane's face. His suspicious look didn't vanish. "That be so?"

"Please," Loriane said. "Could you offer us a meal and a bed?"

"It'll cost," Myra's father said. He crossed his arms over his chest.

"I can pay."

"Two silver gulls?"

Loriane swallowed hard. She had no money. Never in her life had she begged for anything. "Yes." Her voice sounded unsteady. She had never lied either.

"You can't do that, Da."

"Myra, we bain't rich people. If we don't ask money from visitors, they'd ruin us."

"I didn't pay anything for her help. It's only fair that she gets to stay for free."

"Myra, get inside," her mother said.

"Why? I'm not a child anymore."

Her father said, "Ye be fifteen. Ye know nothing about money."

"But I know about what's fair. And this isn't—"

"Go inside."

"Da, you can't do this—"

"Please!" Loriane called out.

They were all silent, staring at her.

"I'm happy to sleep in the shed, but can I *please* use your outroom?" Loriane's voice cracked. A few days ago, a thin and very pregnant girl had asked the same question while standing in the warm and comfortable room of her limpet. At the time, Loriane had been angry with Tandor and had thought of refusing.

"Of course you can," Myra said. "Come, I'll show you."

Loriane pushed Tandor aside and rose slowly from the sled's seat, wincing at a stab across her belly. Neither of Myra's parents spoke although Myra's mother's eyes widened and fixed on Loriane's belly.

Myra crunched back through the snow and took Loriane's arm to help her down from the sled.

"Mother, Father, this is Loriane. She and Tandor will be staying in the upstairs bedroom. Loriane, this is my father Ontane, and my mother Dara. She has a bit of healing knowledge. I am sure that between the three of us, we can help your child into the world safely. Come."

"Leave it, Myra." Her father eyed his wife, and she shot back an angry look at her husband. "Mistress, go with my wife. She'll show ye the way."

The woman stomped off without a further word. Loriane followed her into the house, through a dark corridor with a thread-bare carpet, into a damp kitchen, where a pan bubbled on the stove. Whatever was in the pan smelled strongly of game meat, and Loriane wasn't sure if the smell made her feel hungry or sick.

The woman flung open the door at the back of the kitchen. An icy wind came in. "The outroom."

In the gathering dusk, Loriane stumbled into the freezing shack. There was a wooden plank with a hole, where she sat to do her busi-ness a few measly drops at a time. It burned. The child's head inside her pressed on her bladder and relieving herself made little difference to her discomfort.

The sound of angry voices came from the kitchen.

Loriane wriggled off the seat.

There was no jug of water to wash herself, only a stack of cloths she dare not use. The baby kicked in her ribs, hard.

Both Myra and her mother were waiting for her in the kitchen. Myra still held the child in the sling and leaned against the wall. Her mother was stirring a pan. Neither looked at the other.

"Come," Myra said into the icy silence and started up the stairs, so narrow and steep that Loriane had to support herself by running her hands along both walls.

The upstairs bedroom was tiny and freezing cold, with a hearth in the corner—empty—and just enough space around the not-quite-double bed to walk.

Loriane stood there, fighting back tears. She just wanted to go home, and not be dependent on these people who clearly didn't want her. It had not been much of a life but it had been hers: her modest limpet, the income she earned, her patients.

Isandor. She had always claimed that he was a burden to her, but at the same time, she loved him too. He was a good boy with a good heart. She hoped he was far away from the City of Glass, in a place where being Imperfect didn't matter. If it was true that he had fled with the Queen, she hoped that they were happy.

"I've got to . . . I've got to get Tandor," she said, to find the entire family standing in the doorway.

Behind them stood Ruko, carrying Tandor. Well, she couldn't see Ruko of course, but Tandor floated in the air as if carried by invisible arms.

Ontane turned to Myra. "Letting the mistress here use the room be one thing, but I don't want *him* in my house."

Loriane wasn't sure if he meant Tandor or Ruko.

Myra gave an annoyed snort. "Why do you keep going back on your promises all the time? Can't you see he's injured?"

"Ye keep out of it, girl."

Myra turned to her mother. "Ma, you heard him, didn't you? Da agreed, didn't he?"

"My agreement didn't include sorcerers and ghosts," her father said.

Her mother said, giving Loriane a prim look, "Myra, dear, ye have to understand. Our safety comes first. We still don't know what the sorcerer—"

"Stop it! Just stop it!" Loriane shouted.

Silence.

"Take him back down, Ruko—"

"No!" Myra yelled. "You call yourselves my parents? I'm ashamed of you. If you make them sleep in the shed, then I'll go there, too."

"Don't ye be stupid," her father said.

"Then he stays here. I brought them here. They're my guests. Now get out and give them some rest." Myra ushered her parents out the room and shut the door. "Put him on the bed." This to Ruko.

Tandor floated through the room onto the bed. He groaned, his eyes half open.

"You stay here and make yourself comfortable, Loriane. I'll go and get some water to wash, some firewood and make sure to bring you some food," Myra said and left the room.

Loriane dropped on the edge of the bed and sat there, staring in front of her. In a thin strip between the tattered curtains, a thick layer of ice covered the window. It was bitterly cold and her breath steamed. On a table in the corner of the room, a fur blanket moved and spread over Tandor, as if it flew by itself.

Ruko sat down on the other corner of the bed; she saw that by the way the mattress was pressed down.

"Look, Ruko," she said. "I think you better go somewhere else. These people are nervous about you." Never mind the other people, *she* was nervous about him.

By the skylights, he could kill her and she wouldn't notice before it was too late. The old king's servitors did that, according to the rumours.

She said into the silence, "You've done enough for Tandor. We can manage now. Can you wait with the sled?"

He didn't move, and she didn't know how to make him move. His cold and silent presence in the room made her shiver.

The door opened and Myra came back into the room, carrying a tray with two steaming bowls of soup and a roll of bread, still warm.

Loriane spooned up the soup. The first couple of mouthfuls were unsettling, and she wasn't sure if her stomach would tolerate the food, but then she grew comfortably warm, and wolfed down the rest, as well as the roll.

"Thank you," she said to Myra, who was busying herself lighting the fire. "You're not eating?"

Myra shook her head. "I eat with my family."

She threw a few chunks of wood—real wood—into the hearth, and started them burning. Flames licked the rough surface. Loriane had hardly ever seen wood used for furniture, let alone the wastage of it being burned.

Loriane glanced at the corner of the bed. Ruko hadn't moved. She had never seen him eat, but Myra ignored him completely, so maybe he didn't need to.

She took the other bowl of soup from the tray and set it on the bedside table. "Help me get him up."

But Myra had settled in the chair by the hearth feeding her baby, and it was Ruko who got up from his corner of the bed. His invisible hands lifted Tandor by the shoulders and propped him up against the pillows. The same invisible hands draped the cover over Tandor.

"You don't want to eat anything, Ruko?" she asked him.

"He can't eat," Myra said. "That's why he asked to be changed."

"Wait—he asked for this?"

Myra nodded. "He is one of the Imperfect children Tandor rescued from the City of Glass. There were about fifty of us living in Bordertown. He placed us with foster families."

She nodded at the bed where Ruko sat. "Ruko was unlucky to be placed with a family who only cared about the money Tandor paid them. They treated him badly. I don't exactly know what happened, but the man, a woodcutter who used Ruko as a labourer to haul his sleds, was said to be fond of young boys—"

There was a crash in the corner of the room and one of the soup bowls lay in pieces, remnants of soup oozing down the wall.

Myra shifted forward as if to get up. "Hey, don't do that. My parents are already stretching their tolerance by allowing you in here. Breaking things does not help your cause. You want to help your master? You behave!"

The corner of the bed pressed down again.

"Can you see him?" Loriane asked.

"Yes. He's sulking. He was always an angry little boy."

Loriane could stare all she wanted, but saw nothing.

"Yes, I said *little boy* and I'll say it again as long as you behave like one."

She gave a sniff.

"Anyway, then he started to grow too strong for the woodcutter to abuse, and the man stopped feeding him, and locked him in the shed and would come out at night to whip him—"

The corner of the bed moved.

Myra turned her head. "Yes, I know the whole village could hear you scream and we did nothing. I was thirteen, all right?" She glared and let a silence lapse. Then she sighed. "So because he was constantly hurting with hunger and cold, Ruko asked Tandor to take his heart so he would become a servitor."

"His heart?" Loriane thought of the beating heart in the jar in Tandor's travel trunk. She'd heard about the servitors, but had always dismissed the stories as myths.

"Yes. If you take the heart from someone with icefire in his blood, someone with Thillei blood, this person becomes trapped between life and death. He's still alive, but can't speak. He doesn't have a real body, and can walk through walls. But if he wants, he can pick up things and destroy things. You can't kill a servitor. He only dies if the master dies."

She glanced aside at Ruko, a questioning, curious glance.

Myra continued in a low voice, "We could all feel Ruko's pain on the night that Tandor did it, but afterwards he calmed and we lived peacefully—most of us with our families, but Ruko out in the snow. He doesn't feel cold. He doesn't get hungry. He's happy, as far as a person like him can ever be happy— All right, you're not happy, fine."

A cold feeling crept over Loriane's back. She didn't like this invisible angry adolescent. She'd found Isandor and his brooding moods hard enough, and he'd at least been visible to her.

"And what does Tandor want? What is his grand scheme? Do you know anything about that?"

Myra shook her head. "I don't think anyone knows. But he wanted to take the other Imperfects back from the Knights. Because the Knights came here and took all the Imperfect children into the palace, except me. So when he came to the City of Glass, he wanted to get into the palace. What he did once he was in there, I have no idea."

Eyes half open, Tandor slurped soup from the spoon Loriane held out to him.

Loriane said, "He sure did something. I mean—look at him. What's going on, why can't he talk? He must have been doing something really, really stupid." She poked Tandor's chest. "Something happened while he was down in the dungeons. The explosion was his fault, I'm sure of it."

"When he visited, he sometimes spoke of the Heart of the City and that he wanted to find it."

Loriane had heard rumours of this thing. "Do you know what it is?"

"One day, a long time back, he showed us some pictures. It's a kind of machine from way back before memory. Apparently, the people who built the glass towers played with it and it blew up on them, killing everyone who knew how the machine worked. Then the old King tried to regain the knowledge, but he only abused the power."

Loriane said, "In the City of Glass they say there was a war back in the old times, and all the people who built the city got killed—"

"And then the royal family discovered it and used its lingering rays to power the lights, the trains and the glasshouses—"

"And to make servitors to suppress the people who couldn't do anything with icefire."

"Tandor told us that the Pirosians were jealous."

Loriane felt herself get inexplicably angry. "If the King hadn't used the power badly there would have been no need for jealousy. So the Pirosians banded together and formed the knighthood—"

"Using the eagles which only grew to that size under the influence of icefire."

"That's ridiculous. Did Tandor tell you that eagles are really the souls of the dead, too?"

Myra and Loriane glared at each other.

Then Loriane shrugged. "No one knows what's true."

"And who, exactly, discouraged people to learn to read?"

"And who, exactly, has been trying to bring the servitors back?" Loriane gestured at Tandor. "He doesn't care about you. He didn't care about any of us, only about his crazy scheme, whatever it was."

Myra shuddered and clamped her hands around herself and went on in a more gentle tone, "I think he wanted to breed us Imperfects. He would come in occasionally and bring all of his children together in the guesthouse. The last time he did that, it was very different. He no longer had toys for all of us, but he'd give the older boys things like necklaces and told them to give them to girls they liked. And then he gave us drinks . . . you know, the kind parents wouldn't allow us to have. And then it turned out he had rented the entire top floor of the guesthouse and said we could all stay the night, and . . . you know . . ." She glanced at the baby. "That's how he happened."

"It's all Tandor's machinations. He wanted you to have that baby. He wanted me to have my baby."

Myra frowned at her. "When is your baby due?"

"The baby *was* due days ago. I don't think this is a normal child."

Tandor stirred and mumbled but his words were inaudible.

Myra stared at Loriane, her eyes wide. "Are you sure?"

"I'm not sure about anything until this child is born. Listen, I want you to do something for me. In my bag you'll find a pot of salve. I want you to put it in." Lucky she'd had her healing and midwifery bag with her when the city exploded.

"Put it . . . in? Inside you?"

"You wanted to be a midwife? You can start with me."

CHAPTER 5

*P*AIN.

Pain was all around.

Tandor heard women's voices, but the meaning of their babble floated outside his range of hearing. He couldn't see who the women were, but one of them had to be Loriane. Lovely, down-to-earth, *Pirosian* Loriane. The other was probably Myra.

He couldn't see where they had taken him, but after days in the cold on the sled, they were now inside. Myra's house, probably.

Ruko was there, too, a glowering presence on the edge of Tandor's vision. His figure was a mere silhouette, a dark form soaking up all icefire.

Tandor tried to move, but he couldn't. Cords of icefire bound his hands to some ethereal substrate that he couldn't feel.

"Get these off me."

Ruko came to stand next to him, looking down, his hands behind his back. The recalcitrant lock of hair obscured one of his eyes. One corner of his mouth curved up.

"Who put these bonds on me?"

"I don't know why I believed that you could control all that power unleashed from the Heart. I thought you were a sorcerer, but you're just a simple weakling."

"You're not answering my question." Why not? Ruko was a *servitor*. He should obey his master's command. On that subject, why was he speaking? Unless Tandor had also entered that space between life and death occupied by servitors and other magical beings.

"I can see no point in answering stupid questions. Whoever put the bonds on you was a smart person."

"How dare you talk to me like that?"

"I will talk to you however I like. You broke your promise. You told me that we would free Peonie."

So it was all about a girl? "I can't do anything about that until you untie me."

"No." Ruko trailed an ice-cold hand over Tandor's neck. "It's too late to change your mind. I think I'll have great pleasure killing you." He closed the hand around the base of Tandor's throat. His black eyes burned with anger.

Ruko's touch felt like burning fire, but Tandor laughed. He didn't know how he still could laugh, but he did.

"I'll remind you: you're a servitor. If you kill me, you die as well."

"Then I will have died a worthy death."

"Oh, just stop it with the rubbish. Untie me, and we'll go and find this girl of yours."

"No. I don't believe you anymore. I'm going to kill you, and all the people you care about, in the same way you took Peonie away from me."

"And how do you think the girl will love you when you're dead?"

"I'll be dead, anyway. She was the only one who cared for me, ever. You turned her into a murdering monster."

"It was nothing to do with me. It was the Knights who put sinks in the Imperfects' bodies. They caused this disaster to happen."

"You lie, you lie!"

"I don't, and if you take these bonds away, I can show you. There are ways in which I can turn her back to normal."

"You lie. I have believed you far too long."

"But you want her to join you?"

Ruko hesitated. His dark eyes looked suspicious.

"Anyway, supposing you would kill me, and you'd survive, do *you* have a plan how to rescue her?"

Ruko's lips twitched.

"See? You have no idea. You can't do it. If you take away these bonds—"

"Shut up!"

"—I can show you—"

"Shut up! I don't believe you anymore."

"Cut these bonds."

"No!"

"Cut them, I said. You're my servitor. Obey me."

Ruko folded his arms across his chest.

Tandor yanked, but his arms would not come free. He tried to call icefire, but it would not come.

He could see his own shape on the bed. He could see two vague figures of the women, but they couldn't hear him. His bond to Ruko was a bright blue strand of light, and Ruko sat, clear as life, on the corner of the bed. He wanted to sever the stream, but he couldn't. He wanted to scream at the women for help, but he couldn't.

And he couldn't show Ruko how scared he was.

"What are you going to do with me?" he asked.

Ruko smiled, not a pleasant smile. "That's better. From now on, *I* am the master."

Tandor snorted. "Most people can't even see you."

"No, but that can be fixed."

By the skylights. His travel chest contained the jar with Ruko's heart. He could, if he knew how, or had access to someone who could bend icefire, turn himself back into an independent person.

CHAPTER 6

$\mathcal{W}$ITHIN A FEW very long days, Sady went from being a senator too academic to warrant much discussion to being one of the most-discussed senators in the city of Tiverius. Everyone knew about his distribution of salt pills. Everyone had their opinion, too, mostly unfavourable. Budget problems were bad enough already, they said. He should have asked for permission, they said. Maybe he should have, but it had been within his spending limit without having to ask permission.

Destran then halted the distribution of those pills, at which border regions which hadn't yet received supplies sent a veritable avalanche of telegrams asking why they didn't get the pills while the neighbouring district had received them.

With his distribution program cut short and half the southern districts angry at him, Sady asked for funding to visit those southern regions to measure and map the changes in sonorics himself, and to quell the anger. Because he wasn't every senator's golden boy right then, the application was refused.

Every time certain senators passed him in the corridors of the building, they felt it necessary to make sneering comments. That he wanted to draw attention to the Meteorology office; that he talked up the sonorics crisis just so that he could have more staff and money. An anonymous person sent him a table of data showing effects of various levels of sonorics on humans.

Sady read the report, feeling increasingly sick. The experiment had submitted people with no natural tolerance to as much as three hundred motes per cube. The work was littered with comments like, "Subject showed severe nausea, disorientation and bleeding from nose and gums," or "Subject died after three months." Yes, it also showed that maybe Chevakian sonorics safety standards were a little on the cautious side, but mercy, this table meant that someone had actually done this work on human subjects. On Chevakians. He thought of all those girls who had been abducted from the border villages, none of whom had ever returned.

He was unable to trace the origin of the report, although he strongly suspected that it was a translation from a southern document, and that it must have come from some dark corner of the Scriptorium library.

Meanwhile, Viki's reports of the levels at border stations inched very slowly in the direction of the twenty motes, but not convincingly so, and each time he presented the figures to the doga, Destran asked for a second opinion from the Scriptorium, which either failed to arrive or spoke in very vague terms, and offered Destran an excuse for not spending money or resources on the problem.

The more time passed, the clearer it became to Sady that he couldn't afford to be caught in whatever political reason Destran and Alius had for not acting. Something needed to be done, and needed to be done urgently, while Chevakia still had the opportunity to act.

So one morning, he sent out Orsan, the faithful leader of his personal guard, with a message to a lady he hadn't seen for many years.

When Orsan returned, he was informed that the Lady Armaine wasn't interested in seeing anyone. The note she sent him was quite rude, but it made him smile. Lady Armaine might be old, but she certainly hadn't lost any of her bite. There was a fair chance that the old hag secretly relished the attention.

Everyone in Tiverius, or at least everyone in the inner city, knew the house of the merchant family whose oldest son had married the haughty southern beauty. Her dark-haired children, now well into middle age, were features of the district. Girls both, they had inherited every bit of their mother's pride, and married into well-off merchant families themselves.

Sady had been only a small toddler at the time the woman had arrived in Tiverius, but he remembered the gossip, especially since she had come into the city alone and pregnant, had given birth while staying in the merchant's house, and had subsequently married her host, a man more than twenty years her senior.

Sady remembered her son, an arrogant, sleek, black-haired youth with the bluest eyes he had ever seen. He came to Sady's school when Sady was in the highest grade, and caused a lot of fights by being an incredibly rude and outspoken little creep of a kid. Sady was never quite clear what became of the boy after he left school, save that his mother had taken him on an extended trip to the south when he was about sixteen or seventeen. By that time, Tiverius was in a full-scale diplomatic conflict with the City of Glass over the Knights' kidnapping of women from the towns on the border. The surly teenager had taken over some unidentified part of his stepfather's business and had been one of the few people who regularly travelled between Tiverius and the City of Glass. Not needing protective suits was no doubt a great advantage for him. He would be able to blend in perfectly in the City of Glass.

He used to be on the doga's books as a spy, but as far as Sady had been able to trace, hadn't delivered reports for many years. How the family lived was anyone's guess, because their merchanting business didn't appear to be bringing in a lot of money. They had no physical office, no shops, no warehouses, and yet they were still considered one of the wealthiest families in Chevakia.

The merchant had long since died of old age. Sady hardly ever saw the son anymore, but the woman's two daughters, the ones resulting from the marriage to the merchant, and their mother, still lived in the family house and Sady decided to pay them a visit in person.

Like most merchant houses, the residence was a huge sprawling affair, comprising several buildings, courtyards, pools and other such extravagances in Tiverius' dry climate.

The merchant had built it back from the street on a hill. A solid wall surrounded the land, with a forbidding fence attended by a doorman in family colours.

Sady introduced himself. "Senator Sadorius han Chevonian from the doga. I'd like to see the lady of house."

The guard's eyebrows rose. "The Lady Rosane?"

"Armaine." Such southern names, too. For the life of him, he couldn't remember the son's name, the arrogant little creep.

The guard's eyebrows rose further. "You're sure you mean to see the mistress' mother? She is very old and hasn't left the house for months."

"Yes, it is her I wish to see."

The man gave him a weird glance. "We have a standing instruction not to let anyone talk to her."

"I wrote to her and she should be expecting me." He held out the letter.

The man raised his eyebrows. "Doesn't it say here that she doesn't want to be disturbed?"

"Has the lady ever welcomed anyone? Yet doesn't she complain when people don't consult her? I'm about twice your age; I am familiar with her tricks."

"Fair enough. Come along, then. But don't blame me if she starts swearing at you. She's got a temper and is not exactly accommodating these days."

"I'm willing to give it a try."

The man led Sady through a magnificent garden where water burbled in ponds with fat yellow fish, and shrubs were neatly clipped into miniature shapes depicting birds and bears, similar to the plants he had seen in the houses of the rich in the City of Glass. The garden beds in between the bushes were paved with pure white stones, so it looked like snow on the ground.

He became overwhelmed with memories of his two trips to the City of Glass, the pristine whiteness and the scents of cooking meat —almost the only thing southerners ate. The absolute bitter cold that no one in Chevakia would have experienced before. The claustrophobia of being stuck inside a suit for days on end. The smell of the inside of the suit. The feeling that everyone in the City of Glass was on edge and you could get arrested for the simplest transgression.

They went up the stone steps into a wide and airy hall with mosaic floors, large double doors and stained glass windows.

The guard knocked at one such door and stuck his head in. "A senator from the doga is here to speak to you, mistress."

Sady couldn't hear the reply, but it sounded sharp. He was

expecting to be refused, but the man stepped back and opened the door fully. "You're in luck. She's in a good mood today."

Sady entered a magnificent high-ceilinged drawing room with a mosaic floor and plaster friezes on the walls. An elegant row of pillars supported the roof. The doors into another garden were open and let in the breeze, which billowed up the curtains. The cold edge to the breeze didn't seem to bother the woman who sat at a solid wooden desk in the middle of the room.

Sady hadn't seen her for years, and she looked much older, her face lined with deep wrinkles. Her hair was now snowy white, and tied in a loose bun at the top of her head. Over her thin shoulders she wore a heavy embroidered robe, too hot for Tiverius, but something that would not have looked out-of-place indoors in the City of Glass.

She was writing something in a thick book, her hand gnarled with age and corded with veins. Sady glanced at the curly script, wondering how many people in the south could read and write. Not many, he thought. During his visits, he had never spotted any scripts.

She looked up from her work. The eyes that met his over the rim of her glasses were cloudy with age, but still dark blue.

"Forgive me, lady, for interrupting you," Sady said. "The matter at hand is quite urgent."

"You have already interrupted me. We might as well get it over with." Her voice was educated, with the slightest of accents. Sady had almost forgotten what a southern accent sounded like.

"I'm here as a representative of the Chevakian doga," Sady began. "My name is Sadorius han Chevonian."

"Oh yes, I remember you." She cocked her head. "Weren't you one of those pesky kids who used to tease my son? What was it you used to call him? Mudhead?"

Mercy, did she really have to dig that up? To be honest, the kid's behaviour was asking for it; even the teachers said so. At some stage, Sady must have participated. Not something he was proud of.

"So, you've become a politician, like your useless brother." She chuckled. "Yes, yes, I think this talk will be interesting. Sit down there, young man. I cannot stand having to look up at people."

Sady sat, meeting her blue eyes. "Just to clear up any misconceptions, I'm not here for any political purpose."

She laughed. "That's what they all say. I am sure, senator, that once we get to the real reason you've come here, we can get the discussion to political subjects in no time. But do tell me, because I'm interested now, what makes you so insistent on seeing me?"

Sady bit his tongue. He had secretly hoped she might have mellowed with age."My question is simple, Lady. Are you aware of anything that is happening in the City of Glass?"

Another cock of her head. "Why do you ask me? You know I am not in contact with the City of Glass on a daily basis. I was a refugee, as you are certainly old enough to remember. They killed my family."

No, she certainly had lost none of her bite. "I understand, but at the moment, we have no one else to turn to. I am the doga's chief meteorologist. We have recently measured a recent sharp rise in the level of sonorics. Under the influence of the cold air streams, there is a huge supercell developing over the southern continent, a storm the likes of which we haven't seen for many years. You see, low pressure systems can be induced by a rise in sonorics and we are afraid that—"

"Yes, yes, you don't need to spell out all the details for me. I know. I wasn't born yesterday, you know?" She laughed at her own joke.

Sady met her eyes, wondering how much she knew about this subject. There were rumours that some people in the south had formulae to calculate the energy carried by sonorics motes, and that they did so in order to predict how many people they could kill and how many buildings they could destroy with it. And that brought his thoughts back to that uncomfortable piece of research circulated by unknown sources in the doga. *Subject died after three months.* Imagine the pain and suffering encapsulated in that simple line.

He asked, "Do you know then why this is happening?"

She laughed. "Don't your machines give you the answers you need?"

"Our sonorics metres and barygraphs tell us the patterns, but we need to understand what causes them, and what we can do about it."

"What you can do?" She laughed. "Once the Heart roars, watch and see glory return to our land. The process has been set in motion; there is nothing you can do, except buy our marvels, when they become available."

"Wait—this increase is the result of something people have done?"

"What do you think? That we are as helpless as you?"

"But the power cannot be controlled. When I visited the City of Glass, the Eagle Knights told me—"

"Knights!" She laughed. "They wouldn't know anything. They pretend the whole thing doesn't exist. It is they who spread these rumours—rumours which you Chevakians have been oh so quick to believe—that this power is magic and uncontrollable. Did you think anyone could derive real power out of a myth? That you could run heating and trains from something that's magic? The Knights have been trying to stifle it, for the only reason that *they* cannot see it, or do anything with it. Out of sheer jealousy, they condemned our land to poverty. But when the Knights couldn't stop the Heart working, they dragged it down under the ground as far as they could. You thought your barriers worked so well? Ha, no, that's because the Heart has been sheltered by layers and layers of stone for many years."

Sady knew that to be a lie. The Most Learned Alius had done a lot of work on the barriers, and they were effective; measurements proved that. But the suggestion that this machine could be made to emit more of the deadly rays worried him deeply. If it was true, it would be a disaster.

"Then what has changed now? Did they uncover the machine?" He didn't believe any of this, but it was always easier to get what you wanted out of people if you agreed with them. One of the despicable sides of diplomacy.

"No, not them. The Knights thought that only when they eliminated all the elements that supported the royal family could they seize complete control over the south, but they forgot that people have memories, people have books, even in the City of Glass. Some people travel to all the corners of Chevakia and Arania to find these illegal books that were smuggled from the City of Glass at the fall of the king."

Sady glanced at the book on her desk, and remembered stalls of dusty old books in the marketplace, and the great libraries: the multi-storey treasure of the Scriptorium, and his brother's extensive library. And some dark place that housed the book with the horrible experiments. He regretted that he'd never had much patience for study out of dusty books.

She continued, "Books have become quite valuable in certain

southern circles recently, initially as curiosity. Those old, forbidden books show a City of Glass none of the current population recognises. In those books, they will see the trains. They will see the comfortable houses, heated glasshouses with lush plants, and they will ask: why can't we live like that anymore, if it means no more hunger and cold? And then they find out that some people have been using the remaining power of the Heart, and have been practicing the knowledge of the old royal family and want to rid the land of the ignorance perpetrated by the Knights—see we're already into politics." Her eyes twinkled.

"I didn't ask about politics. I want to know about what is causing this rise in sonorics."

"I told you: the touch of the royal heir has woken the Heart of the City again. A time of justice and glory is coming."

"You call that glory? My whole country is under threat of this thing!" He spread his hands in a gesture of frustration.

"Tut, tut, tut." She gave him a sharp look. "Do you think we would not consider you, our valued neighbours?"

Sady hadn't meant to shout in an esteemed lady's presence. This was not a doga session. He let his hands fall back to his sides. "Sorry." Then he sighed. "I care a lot about Chevakia. I'm sure you understand why this doesn't make me happy."

"I see no reason for you to be unhappy. Once the Eagle Knights are gone from the City of Glass, Chevakia will gain a very wealthy trading partner. Relationships between the City of Glass and Chevakia are already much better than those we have with Arania. It would be wise to capitalise on that, once the City of Glass starts exporting—"

"But sonorics are dangerous to us!" How many times did he have to say this?

She cocked her head. "At high levels, yes, but no one is suggesting that any Chevakians move to the City of Glass, although, with medication being developed now, I would not rule that out in the future."

"Medication?" There was nothing other than salt pills, and they were not particularly effective; they merely helped restore any damage from low-level exposure. They did nothing about long-term effects.

"Yes, you should ask your academics about it."

Alius. A piece of the puzzle fell into place. That was why the Most Learned cared so little about sonorics. But why keep such an important discovery secret?

He started to wish he'd come here much earlier.

Also, how long had these revolution plans in the City of Glass been going on? Who was involved? Obviously the old royal family and the Eagle Knights, but what side did the citizens support?

"Who is currently the ruler of the City of Glass?"

"The Queen, as normal."

"This is not Maraithe, but her daughter?" He remembered being made to kneel for the fragile wisp of a woman, wearing gauze-thin garments and seated on a throne made of carved glass. He remembered how hot it was in the room—and inside his suit. He remembered that she barely spoke a word, but that a Knight did all the talking.

"Mar-ay-the," she corrected him. "The daughter's name is Jevaithi."

It was the first time that Sady had heard the name. "She is—how old?" He remembered a toddler girl with golden hair being snatched away from him by her minders. He had only been told that she was the crown princess much later.

"Sixteen."

"You cannot be serious about a girl that age having any influence."

"No, she doesn't have any influence at all. The regent is an Eagle Knight by the name of Rider Cornatan. Jevaithi is a puppet queen, a prisoner of the Knights. Her birthday has passed, and she should by rights have ascended the throne, but the Knights are holding on to power. To the people of the City of Glass, the royal family is sacred, even the old king, twisted a man as he was. They will not be happy to see the Knights continue to rule the country. And now, thanks to the books, they understand how the Knights are denying them prosperity. The citizens are angrier and angrier. They are getting ready to fight and take back what is theirs."

The last southern king was said to have been a figure of unspeakable evil, and the Chevakian government at the time had been glad to see him gone. Sady remembered his parents talking about it at dinner. They saw the royal family of the City of Glass as a *threat*.

"This development worries me." He could already see the reaction of panic in the doga. "If the doga hears about this, the senators will ask for all army units to be mobilised, in case the conflict spills over into Chevakia. If history is anything to go by, that is highly likely."

"It won't happen this time. Unlike the old kings or the Aranians, we're not interested in war, or expansion of territory."

"And when . . . do we get to know about this change in regime?"

"The revolution is being taken care of as we speak. With as little violence as possible. My son will have more information once he returns."

"All right. I'll speak to your son." Mercy, that would be an exercise in cringing. "Meanwhile, and until we have this medicine, do you have anything I could tell the Chevakians about the situation? 'The south has increased sonorics so they can have a civil war' doesn't quite do it."

She gave him a sharp glance. "You don't believe a word I say, and are making fun out of me."

"I reserve the right not to believe anything until I can verify it."

Another hard stare. "All right." She pulled a little book across the desk and picked up a pen.

Sady watched her veined, paper-skinned hands as she scribbled something on a page that looked like . . .

She ripped the page out of the book and handed it to him. "Here, maybe that will convince you of my sincerity."

Yes, a bank draft indeed.

Sady put it back on the desk. "I couldn't possibly accept this."

"So, you don't want to visit the southern regions to measure sonorics and map weather systems and to reassure the people?"

How did she know about his request? "It would be seen as a political bribe."

"From whom to whom? I'm an old woman, and I can spend my inheritance any way I like. See it as a gift to those who worry about the effects of struggles in my country."

"But . . ." She was right; senators often received donations from rich patrons for projects that the doga wouldn't fund.

"I know the rules. We will ask nothing in return. There are no secret deals. It's simply a sign of goodwill."

Sady opened his mouth to protest, but she continued. "While you're there, in the south, of course . . . I agree that this current

Proctor is an indecisive incompetent ignoramus. So, with our blessing, visit whom you intended to visit and if you find him amenable, return to Tiverius with someone who is not too scared to make the hard decisions. It is my guess that it was already your plan to visit such a person."

She gave him a long stare over the rim of her glasses. Those blue eyes penetrated into the depth of his soul. Mercy, how could she guess that he had been thinking about asking Milleus to come back?

"One other thing, senator. Let's do away with this nameless southern land thing. The Knights banned the land's true name, and no one could ever think of a suitable alternative. My country will no longer be The Country That Shall Not Be Named. Its true name is Peria."

Seated behind his desk opposite Sady, the most Learned Alius raised his bristly grey eyebrows and folded his hands while regarding Sady with a calculated expression. "She told you that?"

"Yes. Is it true? Are you working on such a medicine?"

He sighed. "I would really have preferred her to have kept quiet about this."

"But such a medicine would be a great breakthrough." Sady recalled Alius saying, many years ago when he had been a student himself, that such a medicine would be impossible.

"Yes," Alius said, and he folded his hands on the table.

Sady glanced at the table against the far wall, filled with equipment and trays of glass cylinders each exactly one cube in volume, that would be sealed with a glass lid on one side and a gel-covered paper on the other. When placed in a heat chamber, the gel absorbed any sonorics-charged motes, which showed up as brightly lit spots in a strong beam of light. "Then why not tell the doga about this medicine? Why involve southerners, and no Chevakians?"

"There are Chevakians involved, from a range of backgrounds. Also southerners, for obvious reasons. Every participant was asked to keep it quiet."

"But why?" Sady was almost screaming with frustration.

"Academics do not work well in the public eye. The ideas behind the project are . . . pretty controversial. The financial backers of the project didn't want to cause a storm unless we were certain that it would work."

"And does it? Work, I mean?" He had an uncomfortable thought about that report on sonorics studies on people.

"Yes."

"Then why not make it public?"

"We're not ready yet. There are tests still to be done."

"How long? We could really use this medicine right now."

"I understand completely. We will do our best to get it ready as soon as possible."

Sady rose to leave. He had not specifically asked Alius about the Lady Armaine's implication that he had received southern money, but it seemed that it had been used to fund good work, and Alius obviously had no problems accepting it.

Still, the bank draft burned in Sady's pocket.

On the way out, he wandered through the Scriptorium library, but the books about the south were in a special section which he could easily access as senator, save that his visit would be recorded and he wasn't sure what signal that would send. Foreign relations were not his responsibility; the senator who was responsible for them might object to his invasion of his turf and Sady already felt the pressure of general opinion on him.

"What do you mean, 'What's wrong?' " Sady asked.

"You've been really grumpy the last few days," Lana said.

Sady faced the other across the wooden table in the kitchen, in the manner they ate their meals every night—Sady in his work shirt and Lana still wearing her apron.

"Have I?" Sady asked, rubbing his hand over his face.

"Yes. It wasn't Serran's fault that the neighbour's ducks got into the garden."

"He is the *guard.*" Mercy, he hated to see the mess the birds had made in his pretty private space where he often sat to read and enjoy the sunshine. And he was more annoyed that no one had noticed the birds before the kitchen staff.

"Guarding the gate. For *people*. The ducks flew over the wall."

"He's the guard and should have noticed. And if he's too busy at the gate, he should have organised someone else to do it."

"Still, he's upset that you got angry at him." Lana got up from the table carrying both their empty plates. "You want more soup?"

"No, thank you."

"See, there you go. You're grumpy. You never refuse my soup, and I've made soup for you since your father gave me this job."

"Oh, don't you go like that on me. You're starting to sound like my mother." But she was right. Lana was always right when it came to judging people.

Sady sighed and let a silence lapse. "Suppose I *am* grumpy. I just don't know what to do about this sonorics situation. It isn't bad enough for an emergency, but I want the doga to prepare. Instead, it's like no one wants to make any decisions. I don't have anything to back up decisions I'd *want* them to make."

"No additional data?"

"No. Sonorics have been stable."

"But that is a good thing."

"It would be, if I didn't suspect it's only temporary, and if the level weren't so high. After I spoke to Lady Armaine, I don't think anything about the south is random anymore. We're getting a reprieve, but no one can take advantage of it. And I can't tell anyone that I got my information from her." They'd laugh in his face. "Seriously, Lana, there is only so much I can make of this low depression and building storm. I can make it sound as bad as I can, but in the end, it's only weather, never mind that it usually goes hand in hand with high sonorics."

He sighed again and stared at the table. "No one takes meteorologists seriously. They'll only hear the predictions they like to hear. I can predict disasters, but all they want to know about is their crops and whether the neighbouring district gets a higher cropping allocation."

"Poor, poor Sady." She ruffled his hair.

He smiled at her. She'd been his housekeeper for as long as he could remember, but she was more like his friend. She knew everything about him.

❄

Destran pushed approval for another road-building scheme through. Viki fumbled through another presentation which showed no significant increase or decrease in sonorics levels. People started to get angry with Sady for ordering resources be put into distributing the tablets and suits. If stored in suboptimal conditions, the tablets had to be replaced yearly at great cost to the doga.

No one made any moves towards appointing southern informants. Lady Armaine's son did not return.

A strange kind of tension built in the doga. Sady wasn't sure what caused it. Maybe Viki's rather emotionless reports of relentless higher-than-usual sonorics started to grate on people, the levels just short of twenty motes per cube. Whenever any issue remotely related to the border regions or the south or cropping was raised, senators expected Sady to speak up, but when he didn't and said that he couldn't, because he had no reliable data or the particular subject wasn't his field of expertise, one or two suggested he go on a trip to the border regions. Most notable was that one of those was a northern senator, who was also the first to mention the big V-word: vote of confidence. In Destran, that was. Destran, who kept sidestepping the issue of sonorics by saying there was no problem, which there wasn't—yet. Destran, who continued to claim lack of money.

By the end of the fifth day of these antics, with no sign of the low pressure cell evaporating or sonorics going down, Sady went to see the northern faction leaders. He really wanted that southern trip, so that he could assess how feasible it would be to strengthen the barriers and, failing that—because there was no way such a major undertaking could be done quickly—how quickly they could evacuate the region in the case that might prove necessary. And he was determined not to use the Lady Armaine's money to fund the trip. That meant he needed northern money.

He disliked doing regional deals for favours, and knew this had the potential to blow up in his face, but without their support, the doga would kill itself debating roads and train lines and the fairness of allocations for education, and whether northern children should get special allowance when coming to Tiverius to study. . . . Vote of no confidence indeed.

❋

"We are sick of Destran's paralysis," the northern senator Shara said in the comfort of her top floor office. Firelight played tricks with the folds of her northern region dress and on the gloss of her skin, black as obsidian. She fiddled with her glass, not meeting Sady's eyes while she went on a rant about all that was ill in politics, which included things Sady agreed with, and things he did not.

Here, under the roof of the building, they should feel the heat radiated through the roof, a sign of the fury of summer to come, but the weather had turned unseasonably cold.

"If we are to challenge Destran, now seems a good time to do it."

"Who is we? Who do you propose in his place?" Sady asked, feeling slightly uncomfortable. He didn't like using this regional voting to his advantage. It was exactly what he had always agitated against. That way, the meteorologist position was not bound to any region, and the positions of power were usually held by central region delegates. Like himself, like— "Milleus?"

She shook her head. "We want you to stand."

"Me?" They had to be kidding. "I don't have any support. I don't want the job."

"I don't think anyone ever wanted that job, Sady. It's not much of a job, but someone has to do it."

What she said was certainly true. Most Proctors had the job thrust upon them through circumstances. But most of them had been flamboyant, outspoken, strong characters. Everything he was not. He shook his head. "I wouldn't be any good at it."

"I think you will be."

Mercy, no. "I'm not standing and that is definite. It will be Milleus or no one."

Shara met Sady's eyes, intense. The northern senators knew they didn't have the numbers to field a candidate of their own. They were too divided for that.

"I don't know, Sady," she said.

Sady said, "We both know the doga can't go on like this. We're paralysed with indecision. Not just about this issue, but every time someone has a good plan, the group of doubters scuttle it with committees and requirements to draw up plans and have them approved. The only thing that happens is that the stacks of paper grow ever higher, but nothing is ever decided. And if something by chance does make it through, there is never any money to implement it."

"But by asking Milleus to return, you are also asking the senators to vote against every step forward the doga has made in the last ten years."

"Like what? All the doga has achieved in the last ten years is a division between the northern and southern provinces. So the provinces have more autonomy. What has that achieved except more political bickering over roads and trains? More indecision and building projects caught up in endless streams of bureaucracy. We need the unity more than ever." That was not quite true. Destran had put Milleus' rampantly negative budgets back into line, but he seemed to have taken that a bit too seriously recently.

"But . . . bring back Milleus? Are you serious? He's an old man."

"He is decisive. He steered us through the Aranian war." *And he will steer us through a southern war, if one happens.*

Sady saw his brother at the head of the victory procession through the streets of Tiverius. How had the people cheered him. Arania had attacked, but they had been well and truly defeated.

"Times are different now," Shara said.

"Not as different as you'd think."

"Have you asked Milleus if he even wants to come back?"

"I know my brother. He'll say no, but if we present him with a majority vote in the doga, he will." *Or at least he had better.* Sady set his glass down and leaned back in his chair. "Chevakia will need his experience. Whatever happens with the weather, we're facing a crisis, because we've already delayed putting in some crops too long. There will be shortages. The current senators know nothing about how to run the country in a crisis, especially one generated by a country we know so little about. Remember the fear the Eagle Knights struck into the hearts of the border regions? Remember all the young girls who were lost? Milleus was a senator then."

Shara sipped, and gave a little shudder. Most of the girls would have died from sonorics sickness soon after arriving in the City of Glass if they hadn't died at the hands of raping barbarians before that.

And then some sick mind had gone to write a report about it, as if taking the girls to the City of Glass was an experiment.

"That was all before my time," Shara said.

"It's before almost everybody's time, including mine." Milleus was fifteen years his senior. "We need the experience."

For a while, he stared into the leaping flames.

Shara continued, "Sure, not everybody is happy with Destran's achievements. With the right campaign, I think someone else could have the numbers to topple him."

Sady nodded. "Destran's support is not as strong as it was when . . ."

Another uncomfortable memory. Shouting in the benches of the amphitheatre in the doga assembly hall. Senators fighting like street urchins. And his brother standing silent and defeated at the dais. Moments later, he had thrown off his cloak, and walked out, never to return. When Sady came to the Proctor's house later that day, his brother had already been packing.

"I know when I'm not wanted and this is it, Sady. A man can only take so much. I've worked my entire damn life for this. I've. . . ."

The slam of a lid on a box had been accompanied by the shattering of porcelain.

Milleus stared at shards of pottery on the floor. "Suri loved that vase."

Suri. Ever since her death, Milleus had not been the same. Yet, he had never noticed how lonely she was. Poor Suri. For years, Sady had watched her become unhappy, knowing that she might have been better off with him than with his brother.

He should have done something. He should have told her how much he loved her.

Tears stung in his eyes.

"So what do you suggest?" Shara's voice shattered the painful memories.

Sady made a decision. "I'm travelling to Ensar in the morning."

"What? I thought you were still trying to get funding for that approved?"

"I've found some alternative money." He thought of Lady Armaine's bank draft on the corner of his desk. "I'll travel through some towns on the way. I think I can garner support for Milleus in the south of the country."

She nodded. "That is reasonable. Dangerous, though. Destran will know you're doing it. It'll only take him a short time to find out where you've gone."

"It's the only thing I can do. He's going in for the battle. He knows he's flailing and that something is up. Right now, he's probably at a meeting of his supporters."

"Probably," she agreed.

"So, let's get to business. What are the feelings amongst your northern colleagues?"

"Without calling a meeting, I would guess that Destran probably still has the numbers amongst them, but people are smarting because the northern irrigation project has been delayed for so long. If . . . someone came in and promised some set dates on it . . ."

Typical regional politicking. There wasn't enough water for all districts to get as much as they thought they needed. Yet, he couldn't say the obvious truth; he needed the North's support. Never mind that it would come to haunt him, because this was going to be a bad year for the north.

"I'm sure Milleus would hear your concerns." *Or he had better.*

"We don't want an audience; we want a decision about projects we've applied for. My constituents are sick of coming off second best."

"There is a more immediate threat to Chevakia."

"Only to the south, don't forget that. The northern regions are sick of propping up the south. The people haven't forgotten that when we had the great sand storms, which were a threat to the north, we had to beg for assistance and even then it was slow in coming."

"That was Destran's doing. You might point that out to your faction."

She nodded, slowly, but still didn't look entirely convinced.

"Sady, I still wish you would put forward a different candidate. You might as well know. Milleus was not well loved amongst my regional colleagues. He was a selfish, discriminatory pig, and what happened in his personal life was plain unacceptable to many of us."

"What happened in his personal life is none of the doga's business."

Shara fixed his gaze, her mouth twitching. "It was unacceptable nevertheless."

"So you would vote against?"

She shook her head, slowly. "I don't think we have an option. Our faction doesn't have a candidate with enough support across all regions. No faction does. If you would only stand—"

"No."

"But we would demand some sort of apology from him—at least the female delegates."

Sady nodded. Suri. He'd hate to broach that painful subject with Milleus, but it had to be done. There were just too many rumours about what had happened. Not even he knew the full extent of the story except that Suri had killed herself—there was no doubt about that—but no one knew why.

She went on, "Out of the two—Destran or Milleus—Milleus would have more clout. Yes, he has the experience, and I'm sure you'd get a much higher support for him if he has clear plans. If you're asking for Intention to Vote, then I would give it, providing he clears up the air on his personal business."

"I am asking." And there was no time for committees to be looking into Milleus' private life. It still would have to be addressed after the crisis.

She went to the desk in the corner, pulled out paper and a pen. For a while, the only sound in the room was the popping of the fire and the scratching of the pen on the paper. Then she passed him the note. *Intention to Vote.*

"Thank you. I appreciate it." He folded it in his pocket.

Not much later, he was on his way home, but having visited the leaders of all regional factions. In his pocket, he held the Intentions of five of the factions, about fifty votes in all.

The house was dark when he came home, and he spent some time rustling about with pots until Lana stuck her head around the door.

"Sady, what in the heavens' name are you doing?"

"Cooking. I'm hungry."

She sighed. "Sady, Sady, didn't I ever tell you that you can always wake me up? That's what I'm here for."

"But . . ." he started to protest, and then she smiled at him, and the tension faded.

"Sit down." She went into the cold cellar and retrieved some soup, which she heated up with a fat slice of bread. "Now tell me, how come your work is more important than having a proper dinner?"

"I'm travelling to Ensar in the morning."

She sucked in a breath of air. "I thought there was no money."

"I . . . found some."

He wished she wouldn't look at him like that. Questioning, one eyebrow raised. "It's all right. It's political money. I'm going to see Milleus." Mercy, Milleus had better be worth the trouble. He did *not* like lying to Lana.

"You're not going to ask him to return?" Her eyes were wide.

"Well, actually . . . I am."

"I never thought I'd see the day. That is good news." Her eyes twinkled. She had never made a secret of her fondness for Milleus.

The vote would be tight, and he hadn't been able to sway everyone he'd hoped to convince, but Sady was sure that if he could get Milleus to come out of retirement and back to the capital, more people would follow. People had not forgotten how his quick decisions had won the war against Arania, and how well he had taken up the command of the Chevakian army, how he had used Chevakia's balloons not just to repel the Aranian invasion, but to follow the fleeing army home and take their capital. In the doga building hung a banner with the crest of the Aranian king, taken from the palace by the victorious soldiers. Tables had turned. The attacker had become the attacked. Thanks to Milleus, the people of Chevakia slept well at night.

They would not have forgotten.

Thanks to Milleus, they would again sleep well. As for Sady, he never slept too well, and the next day, he was up annoying the household staff before dawn, packing his travel bags and his instruments, leaving Viki to mind his office in Tiverius, all fingers and toes crossed that the next few days would be boring and routine on the meteorology front and that whatever bugged Viki about Alius wouldn't come to a head.

CHAPTER 7

THE ENGINE PUFFED and chugged and thumped. Goats bleated, jostled each other and nosed around in the feed trough.

Hoses vibrated. The pipe spewed sloshes of milk into the vat; first a gush, and then a steady stream, which slowed to a mere trickle.

There. The next lot done.

Milleus pulled the release. A hiss of steam escaped the vent on top of the compressor. Suction pads disengaged from udders and flung back to their positions under the arm of the milking machine. As one, the goats lifted their heads from the feeding trough and bolted for the gate of the milking pen.

"Mercy! Be calm, the lot of you. Just *what* is wrong?" Milleus straightened, squinting against the glare of sunlight and the shimmering air. He scanned the edge of the wood up the hill, across the golden field of grain.

Only a few days ago one of his prize kids had disappeared, a female, too, born from one of his best milkers, which would have fetched a nice price at market. Milleus had taken his carbine, and scoured the woods, but had found no trace of it, not even a half-eaten carcass. The goats had been nervous ever since.

A *shadow* fell over him. Huge, dark, blotting out the sunlight. Just a heartbeat, and then it moved uphill, over the golden grain field.

Mercy!

A bird, no, a *bird* circled above him, a stark silhouette against the blue sky, with powerful wings of such size as Milleus had never seen. As fast as his old bones allowed, Milleus scrambled to the gate, pushing through the mass of jostling goats.

Over the gate, into the hot darkness of the shed, past the flickering lights of the milking machine. Up there, on the shelf. His hand closed on metal.

Thank goodness for the gun.

Hands trembling, he found the magazine of bullets and clipped it into the holder. Outside the shed, a mass of goats assailed him, having somehow found their way over, or through, the gate.

The bird soared over the forest, wings perfectly still.

The shadow passed over once more, way out of range of the gun. Milleus tracked the dark shape with the barrel, his heart thudding. The eagle wheeled, gaining height. A few lazy wingbeats and then it was gone over the crest of the hill. Milleus stood there, watching. The eagle didn't return. The sky was deep blue, without a single cloud.

Well, that was one explanation for the disappearance of the goat. Fancy that, a southern eagle. They were native to the mountain range between Arania and the south, but the largest ones, the really large ones, big enough to carry a man, lived only in the Eagle Knights' eyrie in the City of Glass. Such beasts were said not to be natural, and this was a beast like that. Riderless.

Someone lifted the latch on the gate.

Milleus whirled, aiming his gun, cursing himself.

At the gate stood an olive-skinned man with salt-and-pepper hair, in a long red robe dusty from travel.

Milleus lowered the gun. "Sady?"

"It's me all right. Milleus, you old billygoat." Sady let the gate fall shut and rushed across the milking pen, his arms spread.

Milleus set the gun next to the milking machine.

They met each other amongst the goats. Milleus revelled in his brother's hug and returned pats on the shoulder. It was so long since he had seen Sady, all the way in Tiverius where he'd sworn never to return.

"What's with the gun?" Sady asked.

"Tell you the truth, brother, I just got the biggest fright. There was a southern eagle scaring the goats. Did you see it?"

Sady shook his head. "I just came from the station. An old guy gave me a lift to the gate."

That would have been Andreus, the old nosey always ready for a chat. "Look at you, Sady. Not a day older. What in all the heavens are you doing here? The meteorology stations playing up?"

The laughing crinkles faded from around Sady's eyes. Grey-flecked brows lowered. "Don't tell me you haven't heard."

Haven't heard what?

"Sonorics levels have risen all along the border stations."

"How much?" By rights, Milleus *should* have heard, but he hadn't, because he hadn't been into town, because he'd been avoiding talk, and finger-pointing, and gibbering women.

"Much more than usual for this time of the year. We're sitting at an average of seventeen to eighteen motes per cube."

"Hang on, Sady. This time of the year sonorics levels usually go *down.*"

Sady nodded and stared over the field in a moment of reflection. There was more to the story, much more. Something serious was happening.

"Come to the house," Milleus said.

Not much later when they sat over tea and biscuits in the kitchen, Sady told his story, about sharply rising sonorics, about the rising measurements from all border stations, about the increased sonorics levels Sady had measured in this region.

"And also, there are rumours of an uprising against the Eagle Knights in the City of Glass."

"Really? Who told you that? Didn't think Destran kept any of our southern spies on the doga's books."

"No, but that doesn't mean there are none to be found."

Milleus eyed him and Sady met his gaze squarely.

"Don't tell me you've asked *her.*"

Sady expression closed.

"All right, so you *have* asked her. You know who is she is, right?"

"The old king's daughter-in-law."

"Too right. Anything she says will be coloured through a thick layer of revenge."

"I'm not trusting her." Sady sounded defensive.

"No, and make sure that you do not *ever* trust her."

"It's just that we have no one else to give us information. At least she won't feed us southern propaganda. She hates the Eagle Knights' regime as much as we do."

"Yes, but that's propaganda, too. We hate the Knights for the border raids, which they may well have recognised as a grave mistake by now. From memory, no one was too friendly with the old royal family either. It's been a relief to most Chevakians that they haven't had to tell their children scary stories about *magic* since he was disposed."

He met Sady's eyes squarely. Sady wouldn't remember any of that fear, but Milleus did. The time of Chevakian ignorance about sonorics, the time before Alius and his barrier. "Do not trust her, Sady. Do not, under any circumstance, accept any of her favours. Do not believe what she says. Find another informant. It's not as if there are no southerners at all in Tiverius."

Sady folded his hands around his teacup and stared at the table. Milleus read the signs.

"You've already gone in too deep with her?"

"I needed the money for this trip. The doga wouldn't sign for permission."

"Pay her back immediately."

Sady gave him a *what with?* look.

"Mercy, Sady, Destran gets his taxes. The situation can't be as bad as all that?"

Sady spread his hands. "That's the way it seems to be."

"Who of us is going to say 'I told you so'? Destran is a dithering fool trying to please everyone and pleasing no one in the process."

Mercy, he was angry. Milleus did *not* want to hear about Destran. The doga had voted him in. He was *their* problem. He met Sady's eyes, more irritated than he should be. He was done with politics.

"Let's talk about something else, Sady. I'm sick of this subject. How are you?"

Sady shook his head. "I'm here to talk about this. It's serious." Sady's eyes were pleading. "Something needs to be done."

"Good. Tell Destran that. What would the doga propose to do? What is causing this rise? Hasn't anyone investigated that? What does the Scriptorium have to say about it?"

"Not much, and that's the odd thing. Alius is acting strangely—"

"He's always been strange—" Academics, Milleus had no patience for them.

"Not like this. He's evasive." He hesitated, as if he deliberated on saying something and decided against it. "And ever since I've raised the issue, Destran is stalling on giving me extra funds for sonorics testing and safety measures. I've sent out some scouts, and some balloons, but no one has yet come back with an answer. I need more funds for better equipment and more people."

"My guess is Destran probably doesn't have any funds. All spent on his roads projects and other things to appease the districts. Doesn't keep a free reserve for emergencies. He can't withdraw any of his money streams for the fear of losing votes. Districts have been voting through their wallets the last few years. Sady, you don't have to tell me all this. Is there anything I don't already know that's not going to make me fume with anger?"

"Yes. This." Sady placed something on the red- and white-checkered tablecloth. A folded envelope. "Although I hope you deserve it."

Milleus took it, frowning. He knew what it was before he opened the envelope, but he opened it anyway, his hands trembling. It was indeed as he had feared: a petition from more than fifty members of the doga—for Milleus han Chevonian to come back to the capital and once more stand for the position of Proctor.

Oh mercy.

His life flashed before him: his quick ascendancy as popular senator. His appointment as senator responsible for the army. The Aranian invasion and the crushing defeat of the Chevakian troops which were but poorly organised, poorly equipped and poorly motivated. His lobbying with the Scriptorium and the young student who had developed an air ship. His speech in the doga. *We are going to build these things. We are going to win.* How had they all cheered. How had they lined up to volunteer for service. How had they hammered, sewn, trained. The magnificent sight of seeing the air ship fleet take off. And then the victory of that first battle. Milleus had gone on the airships to show his commitment.

Meanwhile, the south had assumed that since Chevakia was busy, they wouldn't miss a few girls from their border regions. The balloons had gone after the eagles, and young and brilliant Alius had designed the barrier, and no Eagle Knights had ever come back.

After the war, when concerns turned from freedom to taxes, that's when things started falling apart. When governing the country became a series of monotonous, mindless tasks to do with stupid trivialities. So the doga wanted a younger leader, someone who liked that sort of stuff.

"I can't." Milleus let the paper fall.

Sady watched him, his face unreadable.

Fifty signatures. Mercy.

"You have to, Milleus. Destran might be a good administrator, but he's hopeless in a crisis. If Destran carries on like this, it will be too late to do anything when we need to. You're the best hope we have. The south is up to something. Arania is nervous. There could be war. The *army* wants you."

"They don't vote in the doga."

"I know, but they want you anyway."

Milleus didn't know what to say. Couldn't say anything. Silence fell between them and stretched on for uncomfortable moments. Sady expected a "yes", that was clear. Milleus picked up a spoon and scraped the bottom of his empty cup to gain time for thinking. Found some strands of reason. There were many capable men in Tiverius both younger and more loved than he. He would be held to glorified incidents that hadn't been so glorious even at the time they happened. War was dirty business. Properly preparing a country for one meant discounting a lot of people's voices, running straight over their very valid objections like some sort of army general.

"I have the farm now. I'm happy here."

Sady spread his hands, and rolled his eyes at the kitchen. Pots and pans teetered on shelves. Most of Milleus' pantry was on the kitchen bench, as were the plates he used regularly. Dirty clothes spilled from a basket jan the corner. "Happy? You call this dust bowl happy? This outpost? You, who always were in the thick of it all? I ache to see you so, brother. You have no one even to talk to. Ever since you've come back here to live, you've been alone. This place is run-down, a pale shade on what it used to be like as the Proctor's country estate. It needs painting, the garden needs weeding, the roof needs cleaning. This was once a lovely house, back then."

Milleus glared at his brother. One word about Suri's death, and about how he should visit his sons more, and he'd bash his brother's face in. His jaw moved stiffly when he spoke. "After a life in the doga, I happen to like being alone, so I don't have to listen to all these nattering voices around me."

Sady harrumphed. "Take a look at yourself, brother, covered in mud and shit. I'm used to seeing a proud man, not a lowly farmer. And when I look at you, brother, I still see a highborn man, not a farmer. I see a highborn man hiding from the world, just because once, and I mean *once*, forces conspired against you."

"What? Are you calling me a quitter? I have worked this land with my own hands and turned it from a dust bowl into a profitable farm."

He glared at Sady and his brother glared back.

Milleus blew out a sigh and leaned back in his chair. "Honestly, I've done my bit for the country. I'm too old."

"The doga needs you."

"Trust me, Sady, the doga does *not* need me. I'm nothing but an old man who's run out of ideas." He put a dirt-stained hand on his brother's shoulder. "Do me the favour and stay the night before you head back, but talk to me as my brother Sady, and not as Sadorius han Chevonian, politician and mouthpiece of the doga. You are welcome at my table, brother, but understand one thing: however much you talk, and whatever has happened, I will not come back to Tiverius with you. I'm done with politics, and that is my final word."

CHAPTER 8

$\mathscr{L}$ORIANE WOKE UP in a soft grey light.

Her first thought was that she was not in her own bed at home. The second realisation was that a warm body lay nestled against her, which a glance confirmed to be Tandor, still on his back. But his arm had shifted and now lay over his chest. His breathing was regular. He was definitely getting better.

The third realisation was that some ruckus seemed to be going on outside the window, with people shouting. The fourth realisation, as she heaved thick furs aside, was that she'd been asleep for a long time and that, despite the salve Myra had put on, her pains hadn't started. The bandage had shifted and the salve, slimy and warm, was leaking onto her left inner thigh.

By the skylights, was this child ever going to budge?

Loriane stumbled to the window and shifted the sides of the curtain apart.

By the feeble light from the not-quite dawn, she could make out people in the yard, outside the shed where Tandor's sled still stood. There were men and women, standing around a sled talking. The sled's bear lay in the snow, its head resting on its paws.

Loriane didn't understand who those people were and what they were doing here, so she dropped the curtain and turned back to the room. She was so weary.

The thought of another day of having to cope with Myra's bickering parents and being away from her comfortable home made her eyes prick.

Where was she going to live now that she couldn't return home? Not here, that was certain. What was she going to do with this child she didn't want?

Tandor gave a startled snore, as if he had heard her.

"Tandor?"

His lips moved, but no sound came out.

"Tandor, can you hear me?"

A bottle hovered through the air—Ruko was still in the room—and was pressed to Tandor's lips. He drank the water in big gulps, spilling some over his cheek.

"Tandor, I know you can hear me. Can you stop this nonsense and talk to me?" She wanted to shake his shoulders, but something grabbed hold of her hand, a hard, ice-cold grip that closed around her wrist like a vice. Ruko.

She tried to wrench herself loose. "Oh, by the skylights, let me go. I'm not going to harm him." Or at least not until he told her what he'd done and how to fix it.

The grip loosened.

She grabbed her clothes off the chair in front of the hearth, which had almost died and only gave off the merest glow of heat.

Harsh voices sounded outside, a group of men arguing. She went to the window again, but the group was behind the barn and she could only see their sleds and bears, steam rising from their backs by the light of the street lamps.

Loriane slipped on her clothes and winter cloak and left the room. Everything in the house was still dark. As quietly as she could, she crept down the stairs, through the quiet corridor, the dark kitchen, and out the back door. First, the outroom.

While she sat there on the cold slab of wood, the shouting between the houses intensified: men's voices, the words just out of hearing; the swish of sled runners in the snow; the growl of a bear.

She hoisted her clothes back up and went outside.

Fresh snow had fallen overnight, covering the yard with a pristine layer of white. The sky was never completely dark at this time of the year, but it was dark enough for a couple of stars. There was a single lantern in front of a house opposite the road, and by its light, she could see silhouettes of people walking past. People with sleds, people carrying packs. Many more people than lived in this small town. Bears snorted clouds of steam into the air.

There was a group of men camped in front of the shed doors. One was shouting at another group of people in the street. She feared going up to them—what would they do when they discovered that she had food and had slept in a warm bed?—but maybe she could hear what they were talking about from inside the shed. When would it be safe to go back to the City of Glass? How many people had died? Whatever news she could snatch.

The shed door was open. The air inside smelled of straw and animals. It was pitch dark and Loriane inched ahead foot by foot. On a bench she found a lamp and a lighter, and a bit of fumbling later, the tiny flickering flame lit the hay shed.

A sound such as Loriane had never heard before issued from somewhere in the dark corners. A growl—not quite aggressive. More like a call made by mating Legless Lions.

In the corner, in a box surrounded by wooden planks and filled with straw, stood a most unusual animal. Much, much taller than a bear, on knobbly, spindly legs, with a long neck curved upwards, a body strangely out of proportion, bearing a flabby hump on its back. The fur was shorter than the bear's, brown, shaggy and moulting in clumps. The animal had an elongate head, with large, mournful eyes and long eyelashes like a pleasure-house girl. Its nose was soft, with slits for nostrils. The animal lifted one side of its soft lips, showing huge yellow teeth, and stretched its neck up in a curious way.

She had often heard Tandor speak of a camel. Was this such a beast? She heard people rode on them. This one didn't look very friendly.

The straw behind her rustled.

Loriane whirled around, but could see nothing.

"Ruko?"

There was no reply; it must be him. By the skylights, he creeped her out. Myra had said he could walk through walls. He could just pick up a knife and kill her and no one would be any the wiser, and no one would ever catch him. The time of the old King must have been frightening for his enemies, and she was fortunate indeed that she didn't live in his time, never mind the trains and other marvels. Icefire was evil, and she wanted nothing to do with it.

A strip of flickering light came in between the shed doors. The shouting had stopped, but there were still a lot of voices.

Loriane pressed her face against a crack between the doors and peered outside onto an area where at least six sleds had stopped, sheltered from the wind by the shed walls. There were families with children, elderly people, a man with nobility tattoos on his face caring for someone injured, an elderly woman, she thought. They had made a fire in Ontane's yard, and built a rough igloo out of snow. Three bears were tied to the lamp post in front of the house, which was a laughable sight, because the animals could easily rip the post out of the ground if they wanted, but they were resting, shaggy heads on their paws. The poor things were probably exhausted.

Loriane listened, but whenever the people said something, they spoke of boring things, like, *Can you fill this with clean snow?* Or, *Has your brother come out of bed yet?* That sort of thing.

She was getting cold when over the general noise of the camp, someone shouted,

"This be my house. I want all of ye gone by morning. There be plenty of room at the inn and they cook for ye, too."

Loriane cringed. Ontane.

Some men laughed.

A woman closer to the shed said, ". . . annoying old bear. Easy to talk for him in his big house and nice fire." She spoke in a city accent. "Come, help me, it's getting light now. Let's see if we can open this door, so gramma and the little ones can be out of the wind."

Loriane just stepped back in time when someone pushed hard against the doors of the shed, but the bar that locked it was heavy and the wood new, so it didn't give. Until they came back with something heavier, or found an axe. Desperate people did desperate things.

Meanwhile, more sleds arrived, swishes in the snow. Shouts of women, crying children. Reunions of families with their loved ones. Loriane caught snatches of conversation.

". . . just a wall of steam. It came over the house and it exploded, just like that . . ."

". . . and when we left, there was this incredible, horrible sight. Do you know that the entire Outer City is on fire?"

"... No ... I haven't seen anyone who looks like that. A man and two little girls?"

"Twins. My husband."

"My husband says the icefire is coming this way."

"Yes, her husband is one of the Brothers of the Light." This voice was sneering.

"Well, say what you want, but I'd rather travel with her husband than with people who have no idea what they're fleeing. Tell me— what did your husband say?"

"He's a minion for the old royal family, that's what, and it's them that caused this trouble."

"Oh, do us a favour and shut up. Don't listen to her. Tell me what your husband knows."

Loraine stood there, staring into the darkness.

This was just too frightening. Tandor had sometimes spoken of the Brotherhood of the Light. He'd said they were poor, ignorant idiots with good intentions. All she knew was that they ran schools and orphanages. And did mysterious calculations. The orphans they raised often became successful merchants, because they were good with numbers. Some of them also disappeared. Malicious rumours said that the Brothers sacrificed these children, but a more likely rumour had it that they left the country.

She wanted to go out and ask why these people blamed the Brotherhood for whatever had happened, but she had no idea how many people were outside the shed and was too frightened to open the door, lest the shed be overrun by refugees.

And if the people found out Tandor was in the house, they would lynch the man who had caused their misery. Once she had asked Tandor about his relationship with the Brothers and he had said there was none, and she had asked him about rumours that some members of the old royal family were still alive and he said that if she meant Thillei, yes, they definitely were, else why would there still be Imperfects, and they'd gone into a long discussion about what to do about icefire: use it or ignore it, and it wasn't until later that she realised how deftly he had avoided answering her question. And she also realised how much she didn't care about a conflict that happened more than fifty years ago. And how much she should have.

There were heavy thunks outside, like an axe hitting wood, and then a shout, "Hey, ye city folk, keep yer hands off my fence." Ontane again.

A man replied; Loriane couldn't hear the words, because the thunking continued unabated.

Ontane swore, and there was a hard bang, and then the sound of footsteps coming into the back door of the shed.

Loriane stiffened, but it was Ontane, his face red from the cold, snowflakes in his hair and the fur collar of his cloak. He stopped a few paces inside the door, held his storm light up, and looked around. In his furs, he looked like a malformed bear waddling on its back legs.

"Mistress, what d'ye be doing here?"

"I heard the noise. I wanted to know what was happening."

"Ye tell me; they all come from the City of Glass. Ye know what be going on there better than I, why they all need to come out here like they own the place."

"I suspect they have nowhere else to go," she said, her voice soft. "There is nothing left of the City of Glass. They're tired, cold, hungry and scared."

She met his eyes and he looked away. He *had* taken her in, even though Myra had a lot to do with that, but she suspected that underneath that blusterous attitude, he did have a heart.

His shoulders slumped. "Let's go inside. It be warm there. Dara will have some breakfast. Ye look like ye could use some."

But when he pushed open the back door it was to find a big group of people at the door of the house and Dara, bewildered, in the doorway.

"Anything you have," a woman shouted. "We'll pay. I have two young children to feed."

"We need blankets!" another woman shouted.

"My father broke his leg. Do you have a medic in town?"

Dara just stood there, while people at the back of the crowd were jostling each other for space.

"Oh, the blighting freeloaders," Ontane muttered. He shut the shed's side door, produced a key from under his clothes and locked it. "Come, mistress." He ploughed through knee-deep snow towards the crowd. "Ye lot, stop harassing my wife!"

Everyone in that crowd turned to Ontane and started shouting at him.

Ontane yelled over their voices, "Dara, get inside and shut the door. Ye lot, it be the end of winter and we have no food to share. Go out there in the forest and hunt your own. There be rabbits and moose—"

There was a shout across the street, at a neighbour's house. A woman had come outside with a crate of bread.

As one, all the refugees ran across the street, pushing to get through Ontane's gate. Young men vaulted the fence. At least a hundred people crammed into the neighbour's yard, and soon fights broke out.

Loriane followed Ontane to his house, through the trampled snow.

She was angry. "You could have shared some of your food. Those people are hungry and desperate."

"Precisely. They be desperate and we don't have enough to feed all of them, not even the ones who have money—" He stopped in the doorway and stared. "Quick, inside. There be a lot more coming."

He shut the door and shoved two bolts shut. They stood there, staring at each other.

"What can we do?" Dara said. Her plain face was wide-eyed. "They'll swamp the town. They'll ruin everything, like the Knights did."

"We go elsewhere," Ontane said. "Let's hide at Zany Peak."

"But they'll wreck the house if we bain't here."

"We'll lock it up. In any case, it be better than let the mob kill us." He looked at Loriane. "Sorcerer awake yet?"

"Not when I last looked."

"How be he?"

"Not so good, I'm afraid. He's alive, but barely conscious."

"Let's go see him." He started up the stairs.

In the upstairs bedroom, Tandor was still asleep. Loriane folded back the bloodstained cover. The low light showed up the burned blisters like ugly sores. Weeping skin glistened. A muscle in his neck twitched.

Ontane's throat worked. "He be able to ride?"

"Like this? He can't even sit up. And I don't think I could take any more fleeing."

"Ye have to, mistress. See that?" He flicked aside the curtain.

Loriane looked.

By the feeble blue light, she saw hundreds of black specks on the snow plain, thousands even. "Are they all. . . ?"

"They all be refugees wanting to eat. By midday, there be hundreds of 'em outside, and some of them been talking . . . I dunno. A wall of steam coming after them. I don't like the sounds of this, mistress. Ne'er liked the Queen's magic much, and him over there . . ." he nodded at Tandor ". . . he knows more about this magic than he let on, doesn't he? He went out there looking for the magic and it looks like magic found him instead, didn't it?"

Loriane had nothing to say to that. She was out of ideas, and too sore and tired to care.

"If we . . . go, how long will that be for?" She shivered at the thought of having to give birth somewhere in the snow, or some cramped hut, with Ontane watching.

"Not long. The wife will be with us, and we have food. You be comfortable, mistress."

Loriane shrugged. She was far from convinced, but it seemed like they didn't have a choice. She took Tandor's hand and stroked the feverish skin. Tears blurred her vision. She was so tired.

CHAPTER 9

SADY SPREAD the map out over the camp table.

The automated barygraphs hadn't lied. He had half-hoped that the devices, such as the one that stood at the base of the telegraph pole in the forest clearing, had malfunctioned, and that the massive dip in air pressure some instruments had recorded yesterday was the result of a mere error. But the protective glass was intact, and so was the tiny bellows that contracted and expanded with the air pressure, which was inversely driven by sonorics, and the thin needle, precision-mounted on a rod of crystal, which didn't expand much with heat. The crystal acted like a seesaw; the bellows pushed or pulled one end of the needle, and the other, longer, end went up or down, touching thin copper wires set at intervals. Each time the needle passed such a wire, it would send a signal down the line. Most of the barygraphs Sady had visited in these few days had the needle stuck well below the lowest sonorics reading. With all the will in the world, he couldn't call this an error.

If nothing else, the sky confirmed the low-pressure reading, with scudding clouds which looked, for all he could think, like it was going to snow any minute.

Mercy, snow in summer. There was a massive low-pressure cell building up over the southern plateau. Thankfully, sonorics had remained stable. Too high, but still stable.

"Senator, are you ready to go?" a soldier behind him said.

Sady turned around, both annoyed and appreciative of the men who had offered to help him in Ensar, after he'd come back from his private and useless trip to see Milleus and found the train delayed. Typical, the local official said, and he'd gone into a diatribe about how the doga needed to give the district more money for trains.

Money, money, everything was about the lack of money.

"The balloon's almost ready," the soldier said. "Waiting for your directions."

He was holding these men up, and they had better things to do than hang around waiting for him. "Have you been able to contact the Tiverius office?"

"Yes, briefly, although the line has a lot of static."

"Any important news?"

Sady had wanted news from Milleus, that he had changed his mind; but so far, the old bear had been completely silent.

"Vikius han Marossi sent a couple of missives for you. He says they're urgent."

Sady took the paper from the soldier. In irregular block letters, the man had written out Viki's message, *Senator Sadorius han Chevonian, please confirm meteorology handbook rule 23 and confirm that I can apply it.*

Sady shook his head. Had Viki truly never sent a telegraph and didn't he know that every character added cost?

Rule 23 regarded the collection of rooftop rainwater for human consumption. The quota system that allowed residents to keep a certain amount for their gardens wasn't easy to explain in a few words. If more water had been collected than necessary in a citizen's tank, then that house could use the excess water for ornamental gardens.

The next sheet said, *Senator Timmonian won't give me access to the city's water storage.*

Oh, mercy, what had happened in Tiverius while he'd been away?

Sady groaned. *Viki, Viki, what have you done?*

He had hoped to hang around here a few days so that he could still pick up Milleus if he changed his mind at the last moment, as Milleus was wont to do.

But now . . .

No, he couldn't stay. His duty lay in Tiverius. Viki's clumsiness was causing an avalanche of disasters. Milleus could find his own way there, although by now, Sady felt it would be unlikely he would. What then? Nominate himself to stand against Destran? Was there another option?

He let his gaze roam over the campsite. The soldiers had packed their tents into the balloon's basket and spent most of the past hour inflating the massive air bubble which now towered over the trees. Squally winds tugged at the gasbag. The balloon was weighed down with bags of pebbles, each bearing a stencilled image of the two crossed guns over a gear blade, the sign of the Chevakian army. Little boys would scour the woods looking for these ballast bags and return them to the nearest authorities for a small payment.

Sady sighed and rolled up the maps. He wished he had more time to take measurements, but his current understanding of the situation would have to do.

The soldiers folded the camp table as soon as Sady had removed the maps.

Sady clambered into the gondola and sat down at his usual spot at the back, out of the way of the crew, who were now throwing off ropes, rolling them up and stowing them.

"Where to next, Senator?"

"We head straight back to Tiverius."

Sady considered that balloons were pretty handy and, given the grim situation, he felt almost guilty for enjoying his balloon ride.

One day, when all this trouble blew over, he would have to wrest designs from the army and start a civilian balloon transport service. Much nicer than the smelly train he'd taken out here.

Thanks to the soldiers who had taken pity on him, poorly dressed as he was in an unexpected snap of cold, and waylaid by a train malfunction, he was now back in Tiverius two days early, and had been able to take sonorics measurements at height as a bonus.

Now, though, as the buildings of the city tracked under him, and the soldiers who manned the burners were letting air out to make the balloon sink to the ground, his feet itched to get back to the doga and deal with all the disasters he would find there. And the inevitable confrontation with Destran.

And before that, his impending admission of failure to his supporters. He could not tell the fifty senators who had signed intent to vote that his mission to bring back Milleus had been unsuccessful. If he did, *he* was a failure and they would never trust him again. Yet he did not want to stand for Proctor. He did not, he did not. He was not the right kind of person, not flamboyant enough. They would compare him with his brother; they would sneer about the fact that he had never married, that his brother's poor ways with women had rubbed off on him. They would say that he was his brother's mouthpiece. No Chief Meteorologist had ever challenged. He didn't even represent a district. It was a recipe for disaster. But was there an alternative?

A northern candidate would never get enough votes. There were no suitable southern candidates. Destran's cronies were out of the question.

His thoughts were going around and around in circles.

Sady caught the train from the army barracks. The city, which would normally be basking under a blue sky at this time of the year, was shrouded in heavy cloud. The citizens on the train were talking about it, and one man shared Sady's feeling that those looked like snow clouds.

He alighted from the train at Tiverius' central station and, from there, walked across the city's central square, perfectly paved, with trees planted at equal intervals. The columned, marble doga building basked in a flash of brilliant sunlight that peeped between the clouds. A gust of wind tore through the young leaves, sending a flurry of flower petals over the pavement.

Sady held both sides of his cloak together with one hand and ran up the steps. He felt lonely, abandoned and insignificant.

The wind was not as strong in the courtyard, but here his footsteps echoed eerily. Where was everyone? Sady went into the tall columned main entrance of the building and up the steps to the second floor corridor where his office was.

He was about halfway up the steps when he heard the agitated voices. A man was shouting. Someone else replied.

He turned the corner and found himself at the back of a crowd in the corridor.

Oh, mercy, they weren't standing in front of *his* office, were they?

"You can't do this!" a man shouted. "We need to be notified of any change in cropping schedule in advance."

Heart beating fast, Sady shooed people aside. "Excuse me, excuse me, can I get through?"

Some people in the crowd turned.

"Senator Sadorius!" someone shouted. More people turned.

"Senator, what's this about the change in cropping schedules?" someone else asked.

"Do you authorise the change?"

Someone else yelled, "He says we can't use water collected from our roofs anymore. So what are we supposed to do?"

Someone at the back of the crowd added, "Yeah, whose stupid idea is this?"

Change in cropping schedules? "Wait, wait, wait!" Sady advanced into the group. "Can someone tell me please what is going on?"

"He did it!" a man shouted, and pointed at the door of Sady's office, where Viki stood, red-faced, clutching a bundle of notes.

To his credit, Viki straightened and answered with a clear voice, "I did nothing unauthorised. I'm following the doga's protocol and the meteorology handbook."

"It's irrational!" a man shouted and others agreed.

Sady raised his voice. "Quiet, calm down!"

They did, glancing at each other from the corners of their eyes.

Sady looked around the group. There were men he recognised as regional representatives, and even merchants. Mercy, he'd hoped Viki wouldn't create some sort of disaster in his absence, and it looked like the young man had done just that. On top of everything else that had happened.

"Viki, would you care to explain?"

"Well, I—" He glanced nervously at all the people demanding his attention.

Sady jerked his head at the office door. "Inside."

When the onlookers grumbled, Sady added. "I'll be back shortly."

Viki disappeared into the room, and Sady followed, shutting the door behind him.

He took a step towards his desk, and stopped.

Every flat surface in the office had been covered with curling snakes of data read-outs, maps and papers. Some had spilled onto the floor.

"What in the heavens has happened here?" Sady grabbed one, glancing at the data, but needed time to fully make sense of it.

"I haven't done anything," Viki said. "I was just following—"

"Please start at the beginning."

By now, Sady had an ominous feeling about where this was going. The unseasonable cold wind was not as innocent as it seemed. The massive low pressure spikes he had measured had made it even to the capital.

Viki swallowed. "Well, after levelling off, sonorics levels suddenly went up after you left, and they crossed the twenty motes level in the border regions. First in the Fairlight district, so I used the doga's protocol to stop exports from there—"

"Viki, you can't just do that one-sided . . ."

Viki turned around and handed Sady a readout. "I can't? Look at this. I followed protocol, from the handbook!" His voice spilled over with emotion and his eyes glittered.

Sady looked at the graph Viki held up. The plotting machine had skipped up to a larger scale so that the red line hadn't risen off the page. Twenty motes, twenty-seven, thirty-six. Fifty-nine. And still, the direction of the plotted graph was up. Mercy. Blood rose to his cheeks and ears while he looked at the graph. He licked his lips. "This is a verified measurement?" The readings were nothing short of horrific.

"Look at the others. They're all close. One measurement I could discount as a transmission error, but all the measurements are like this."

Mercy. Out went his prepared words for scolding Viki. It seemed Sady himself would have acted every bit as the young student had—perhaps with more authority, but still. While he'd been away, the Fairlight district had been bombarded with sonorics. "Have you heard if the barrier is still holding with this strain?"

"It is, according to the latest news."

Sady's heart was thudding against his ribs. The town of Fairlight was very close to the border. There were thousands of people in the district, a fertile agricultural area. "Do we still have a telegraph line to Fairlight?"

"Fairlight is hard to get on the line at the moment. Too much static. But the line hasn't gone completely. We can try. Any message you want me to send?"

"Yes." Then he hesitated, knowing that what he did wish to say, *get your backsides out of there*, would cause a flood of panic and outrage. "I'll deal with it in person."

But by the time Sady had dealt with the chaos outside his office, and he had made his way to the telegraph offices, the link had been severed.

Worry rising in him, he went to the Scriptorium to ask Alius about that new medicine, because he had a feeling it would be needed soon. However, Alius wasn't in, and he had to contend with leaving a note. He made the text as urgent as he could, but figured there was a good chance he'd have to chase it up, given Alius' recent record of replying to his messages. Damn, if only he could understand why the man had decided to hate him so much.

After a brief bite to eat in the building's canteen, where he was besieged by senators wondering where Milleus was and other senators still smarting over Viki's dealing with the situation, he prepared for that afternoon's doga session. A quick glance at the agenda had him shaking his head with frustration. Funding for bridges and a new Scriptorium in regional towns was all very well, but there was no mention of the crisis, except in the section *Questions raised by members*, and he noted, with a sense of satisfaction, that it had been Viki who had entered the question *How will we deal with rising sonorics levels at our borders?*

Mercy, maybe the young student had more courage than he had given him credit for.

He gulped his food and too-hot tea while outside the window, over the administrative wing of the building, snow clouds gathered.

The signs were bad, and the doga was wracked with indecision and paralysed by a body of senators who didn't like to hear bad news and were all too happy with Alius' strange *don't worry* message. If there was a new medicine, Alius had better turn up with it soon, or he was going to evacuate. In fact, he scribbled a note which he asked Orsan to take to the stationmaster, to send any free trains to Fairlight for evacuation, his lack of funds be damned.

Folding the note, Sady rose, and as he pushed his chair back under the table, he made a decision. He owed Viki and Shara. He owed his long-dead parents; he owed Milleus. He owed Suri and her sons, and the love he had never been able to give her. He owed this city. For years, his family, friends and colleagues had taken the burden of looking after the country. It was his turn. It might destroy or kill him, but he was going to challenge.

CHAPTER 10

MILLEUS SHIFTED the van into "brake" and it rolled to
a stop just before it hit the fence. A cloud of steam
burst from the pressure vent in an angry hiss. He flung the door open,
dropped out of the van and slammed the door after him, as if it was
to blame for his mood.

Mercy, mercy on his brother if ever he got his hands on the blabbermouth.

In his mind, he could still see the town shopkeeper's smiling face,
hear his voice, "So it is true, then, you will be standing as Proctor?"

He had wanted to wring the man's neck, wanted to shout, *Who in
the blazing wastelands has told you such nonsense?*

But two of the man's customers had been standing in the corner
of the shop, wide-eyed. Next thing the whole town would be talking
about him returning to the doga, no matter that he had told the shopkeeper there was not a shred of truth in the rumour.

*If a politician says he won't stand for an election, it probably means he's
about to win it.* He'd said this himself so many times.

Well, not him. Return to the doga—pfa! They'd voted him out well
enough. What had gotten into the brain of Sadorius han Chevonian
to suggest they'd wanted him back?

*Fifty signatures, that's what. That's almost half the doga, almost a
majority.*

He blinked, staring over the golden fields of grain, fruit of years of dogged labour, but saw instead the chamber of the doga, the men and women who debated Chevakia's future seated in rows of benches. Facing him. Listening to him. They each had their copies of plans spread out before them. Not the precise details, oh no, never that, but enough to see what the army had in store for the unsuspecting Aranian attackers. Balloons. Air attacks.

The senators were loving it. From the moment he brought out those plans, he had ridden on a wave of support all the way into the Aranian capital.

Pfa, enough of this. His time in politics was over. Leave an old man to his retirement.

Peace. Quiet. Harvest time.

Milleus stomped into the control shed. Flung the door open. Lights flashed on panels on the wall. The harvester . . . He pressed a few buttons and returned to the shed's entrance to look up the hillside. Over there, beyond a copse of trees was a shed that housed the machinery. In a moment, the door would open and the harvester would come out in a cloud of steam, followed by the bin truck, ready to cut and collect the grain and bring it to the storage bins next to the house. The bin truck would chop up the straw and bundle it into bales which would keep the goats comfortable in winter. A marvel of modern technology.

He *loved* being here, being one with the farm, the fields, the goats. Anything that threatened the farm . . .

Rising sonorics levels. Sady was right. As Proctor, he *would* have done something, and Destran should act. He should be organising emergency supplies. He should be writing a letter to the southern Queen demanding an explanation. He should be sending delegations, and spies.

Milleus sighed. It wasn't *his* problem. Destran had wanted the leadership; Destran had called him incompetent. Well, let Destran find out the new meaning of incompetent.

The field was still empty.

Where was the harvester?

He went back to the panel and found all lights flashing orange. A malfunction. He pressed the reset button, and tried again. Immediately, the lights flashed orange again.

Mercy, what a day.

Well, there was nothing for it, he had to go look and hope it wouldn't require a mechanic, because he hadn't the time for waiting for parts to turn up; and with this unseasonable cold spell, it might rain and the grain would get too moist.

He jumped into the van and revved it up the hill, leaving behind a cloud of hot steam.

The door of the harvester shed was closed. Possibly jammed. Well, that wasn't hard to fix. He jumped out of the van and entered the shed through the side door . . . into the point of a knife.

"Mercy!"

Holding the knife was a wide-eyed, longhaired youth, about fifteen or so, with intense blue eyes and unruly dark hair. He wore an odd garment made from—of all things—empty seed bags.

He was not alone. Milleus caught a flash of someone else in the shed, movement under a heap of fur.

In one practiced swoop, he hit the knife from the youth's hand. *See, don't play with an old man. I'm tougher than you think.*

The boy went sprawling. Fell hard on his backside. A wooden leg shot out from under him.

Oh mercy, I've just hit an invalid.

A defensive invalid, though. The boy scrabbled in the straw, dirty hands searching.

Milleus kicked the knife aside and put his foot on the blade. Slowly, keeping his eye on the youth, he picked it up. "I'm sorry, but what are you doing in my barn?"

The youth said nothing, but stared at Milleus with those intense blue eyes.

He was too thin. Not a fighter, too young to be a trained soldier.

He had set up quite a neat camp here, with a box for a table, bales of straw for a bed—so that's where the bales from the hay loft had gone—and furs for sitting. Right in the harvester's path. And that was why it wouldn't come out.

The furs stirred. A pale face peeped out between them, then vanished again. A girl, Milleus thought.

"Don't be afraid. I won't harm you. I just need to get my harvester out." He gestured, wondering if the youths understood his words. With their furs and pale skin, they looked awfully foreign. They looked *southern.*

The girl had now lowered the furs. She was about the same age as the boy, had honey-coloured hair, grey eyes, and only one hand. Her face, pale as moonlight, wore a scared expression. She spoke a few words to the boy, equally scared, to which he replied in a soft voice.

Oh mercy—they were just runaways. Milleus stepped further into the shed, holding out his hands. "My name is Milleus." He didn't know if they understood, so he bowed his head to show he didn't intend harm.

The girl threw the furs aside and rose, arms by her side. A skinny thing, she was, with arms thin as sticks and legs with bony knees. Her skin was deathly pale.

"We thank you, farmer." Her voice sounded awfully formal. "We apologise that we have not asked permission to lodge in your shed."

Milleus would have laughed if there hadn't been that chilling tone to her voice, that self-assured toss of the head.

"Who are you?"

At this, the boy stepped between her and Milleus, holding a protective arm around her.

"We will go if we can't stay." His accent was much stronger and rougher.

Go, where? Into the forest? "No, no. I'm not telling you to go. I just want to know who you are, and how you got here, and what you're doing in my barn."

Did they have family in Chevakia he could notify? Were they planning on going anywhere?

"I am Isandor," the boy said, taking another step closer to Milleus. He was a hand's width taller than Milleus.

"And what about your friend?"

"Does not matter." His voice was abrupt.

"Just her first name. Seeing where you've come from, I'm not going to contact the authorities in the City of Glass, am I?"

A hostile look. Then a flick of the eyebrows. "Nila."

"What?"

"Her name is Nila. No more."

"All right."

Well, maybe they *were* involved in some shady thing in the City of Glass. Maybe the girl's rich parents wanted her back. Mercy, what was he to do with them?

"And what did you intend to do here? Do you have any family?"

"Can work," the boy said, showing a white-skinned arm corded with muscles.

Well, that could be a temporary solution. Milleus did have a large pile of firewood to be chopped, and his back did happen to have developed an aversion to wood chopping. Not to mention gardening.

Besides, the guest wing to the house had been empty since he had last entertained the collected ambassadors here . . . he couldn't remember how long ago. He carried the keys in his pocket. Everything would probably still be there.

"All right. You can stay here until I find another place for you. One thing, though, I will promise you: if you are in any way involved in a crime against a person or property either here or in your home country, you are asking the wrong person to help you. I will find out, and I will pass you onto the authorities. So you better be honest and swear you haven't killed anyone or stolen anything."

"We would never do such a thing, farmer," the girl said.

Farmer. What did she think he was?

"My name is Milleus han Chevonian," he grumbled. "Milleus for short." *Retired Proctor of Chevakia, so you better watch it.*

Then again, his name didn't mean anything to her, or if it did, she didn't show it.

"Nice to meet you, Milleus. We are grateful for your help."

Milleus turned away. He was too old to take this formal talk from someone barely a quarter his age.

You're just a grumpy old man, Milleus, who has stopped caring. "Now if you will take your stuff out of the way, I can get the harvester to work."

The youngsters shifted their possessions which included straw-covered furs, eggs, the old pot which he used to feed the ducks—so that's where it had gone—and some women's underwear. He chuckled at that and wondered what Andreus' wife would have made of her bloomers disappearing.

He pressed the manual button to open the large shed door. The boy gave a frightened squeak when the mechanism hummed into action.

The girl said something to him, and he relaxed, but still watched the door until it stopped moving.

"Come. I'll take you to my house."

For once, Milleus let the harvester do its work by itself. He took all of the youngsters' possessions—their furs and some clothes almost too dirty to touch—and put them in the van. It took a lot of coaxing to get the boy anywhere near it. He pointed vehemently that he wanted to walk, and continued to do so after Milleus had turned off the engine, but Milleus told the girl in no uncertain terms that he would not have *her* walk all the way to the farm; that was not the way Chevakians treated their women, and she spoke to the boy in their strange language, and eventually his stance softened.

Milleus wanted to help the girl into the van, but the boy had evidently decided he was not going to let her out of his sight. An arm around her side, he helped her to the van, speaking in a strange language, and then he squished himself in the front seat next to her, his long limbs at odd angles.

"There's a seat in the back, it's much more comfortable," Milleus said, while climbing in the driver's seat.

"I sit here," Isandor said in his intense way. He held onto the girl's shoulders and hand.

Oh mercy, have it your way.

Milleus started the van and drove back to the homestead, accompanied only but the puff of the engine. The boy held a white-knuckled hand over the girl's fingers. The girl stared at the various gauges, the pressure-metres, the water level metres, the temperature of the engine. At times, Milleus thought her lips moved, as if she wanted to ask a question, but she didn't. She puzzled him, much more composed than her flighty companion.

They arrived at the house and he pulled up at the front door. The youngsters got out, staring wide-eyed. Yes, Milleus knew the doors needed painting and the straw roof supported a veritable botanic garden of native succulents. Some were even flowering, pink daisies that moved their little heads with the sun.

Milleus opened the back door to get the filthy bundles of cloth from the back, and when he shut the van, the boy had closed his arms around the girl, nuzzling the skin in her neck. She spoke a few soft words; he smiled, his eyes all dreamy.

Milleus remembered a day too long ago, when the most beautiful woman he had ever seen waited in the garden surrounded by both their families. Music played and people laughed, but he only had eyes for her. Suri, *his* Suri in her beautiful dress, flowers in her hair.

"Come." He stomped into the cool hall, not sure why he was so angry, and wishing he weren't. He dumped the dirty clothes in the laundry and returned to the youngsters in the hall. They still held each other, hands intertwined.

"You live here alone?" the boy asked.

"Yes." *Do you have a problem with that?* "Come. I'll show you the rooms."

He pulled his key ring from his pocket and found the age-blackened key to the guest quarters. The door creaked when it opened and a waft of stale air spilled out. He half-expected some ghost of the past to come flitting down the corridor, Dena or Horus or any of the other long-gone servants. But his footsteps sounded hollow as he went into the linen room. The sun slanted through dirt-streaked windows.

"You'll want some sheets."

He had to yank the door to the cupboard hard, but the sheets inside were still neatly folded, although the bunch of herbs Dena used to put on them had fallen to dust with age.

Two sheets each, a pillowcase. Blankets were on the beds as far as he remembered. He hoped nothing had eaten them. He put everything in a pile and led down the corridor.

The first room . . .

Mercy, the Aranian ambassador used to stay here. Ghosts of the past flew by. The scent of tobacco, the chesty laugh, the rough voice. *Milleus, surely you will join me for a drink?*

The room was musty and empty, but a folded blanket lay on the bed, an empty pitcher stood on the table by the window—mercy, the cobwebs! Milleus cleared his throat.

"Isandor, you can sleep here." He dumped two sheets and a pillowcase on the bed. "And you . . ." He left the room again.

Suri's mother's room had an elegant couch, a table, a marble fireplace, a large four-poster bed with frilly curtains that were—or used to be—pink. Sunlight had faded the fabric, as well as a patch on the carpet, which used to be dark red, and was now dirty yellow. Mercy, the dust.

But the girl stood in the doorway taking it all in, letting her strange grey eyes roam. Her expression showed neither approval nor disapproval.

"This will be your room," Milleus said into the uncomfortable silence. "There is a bathroom at the end of the corridor if you want to get freshened up. You'll find some clothes in the cupboard. I hope there's something that fits you." Mercy, some of those were Suri's clothes. "I'll be in the kitchen. I'm afraid the fare on the farm is pretty simple—"

"Thank you so much."

Milleus nodded, and left.

In the kitchen, he busied himself with the fire in the stove, and then unpacked the seldom-touched items from his pantry onto the table, after clearing this morning's plates. Mercy, mercy. What did he have to feed two hungry children? He could not really use that stock powder anymore. It looked suspiciously mouldy.

Soup? Some bread? Well, that wouldn't last more than a day. He'd have to go into town to buy more. And he must buy some vegetables, too. At least he had plenty of meat and milk and cheese.

He set a large pot to boil with bones and herbs. Fresh soup would be good, never mind the powder.

There was a small noise. Milleus looked up to see the youngsters at the door, still holding hands. In Sady's hunting gear, Isandor had gained about ten years in age. Yes, Milleus was not mistaken—he did have dark fuzz on his chin.

But the girl . . . Nila, although he didn't for once believe that was her name . . .

No. You can't wear that dress.

Suri whirled around so that the pretty frills formed a full circle around her thin waistline. *Oh Milleus, thank you. It's so pretty!*

He laughed and scooped her up in his arms, stroking the soft belly that did not yet show the child within.

A pretty house needs a pretty woman.

The girl—Nila—had just such a thin waistline. Her hair, done up in a delicate bun, was straight and very southern, but the dress fitted her. *No, not that dress.* Milleus turned, cleared his throat and put the soup on the table.

"There's no fancy tableware, I'm afraid." Yes, there was, in the cupboard in the dining room, equally unused and probably dusty beyond redemption.

"It doesn't matter," the girl said. "Thank you."

Milleus scooped soup into bowls and distributed big chunks of bread. Isandor gulped the soup, holding his spoon in his clenched fist like a farm worker, and ate like someone would run off with his plate.

Nila sat up straight like the highborn girl Milleus was sure she was. She held the spoon in her dainty hand, and ate slowly, pulling little pieces off the bread before putting them in her mouth.

Milleus took his own plate and sat down. Isandor had taken Milleus' usual spot and he had to sit at the head of the table.

"Now, about you two. You came from the City of Glass?"

"From the south," Isandor said.

All right. He wasn't answering the question. "How did you get here?" The City of Glass was a long way away. The mountains across the border were pretty high and as far as he knew no one lived there.

"We had . . . we had a bird."

Oh. Milleus saw. The bird he'd seen a few days ago. But then again . . . "You let it go?"

"The bird is free."

"Is anyone after you?"

Isandor glanced at Nila. "Maybe."

"Maybe or surely?"

"Maybe. Don't know."

"And those people who are after you, who are they?"

"You ask many questions for a farmer," Nila said.

"I am giving you lodging. I think I have a right to know such things. Especially if they could lead to trouble."

"No one will harm you. It is us they want."

"And you didn't commit a crime?"

"No. I swear by my heart." She picked up a knife and held it, point to her chest.

"Oh, no, no." Milleus eased it from her hand. "We don't do that sort of thing here. We just promise."

"I promise."

Milleus normally lived and ate in the kitchen, but there was only one comfortable seat, so he told the youngsters to go to the adjacent room while he cleared the dishes.

When he entered the room, Nila sat in one of the chairs, half-asleep, her cheeks flushed, but Isandor stood at one of the many bookshelves.

"You have . . . many books."

"Yes. They're all big volumes about boring things."

A boy this age would hardly have interest in politics, philosophy and statecraft. Even he hadn't touched most volumes for many years. Who knew why he even kept all this stuff. Isandor's blue eyes roamed the titles. Big leather-bound volumes covered in dust.

He pulled one book off the shelf.

Military strategy in the Aranian war.

Mercy, how had he and the Aranian ambassador discussed this tome—until they were both red in the face and so drunk they fell asleep on these couches. Anything better than to disturb Suri's sleep and provoke her wrath.

"You read this?" Isandor asked.

"Long ago." Hah! He helped *write* it.

Isandor flicked through pages of diagrams and tables. "You use balloons in war." It was not a question, and something about the way he said it made Milleus stop cold.

"Yes, the Chevakian army uses balloons."

"Balloons better than eagles. Eagles carry one rider. Bows, arrows, maybe gun. Nothing heavy."

"But an eagle is fast and you can use a knife or the bird's claws to cut a balloon."

"You use nets. Riders can't cut. Not many have guns. I say if you have balloons you win the war." Again, it was not a question. He shut the book and put it away.

Mercy, the boy had *military* training.

A Knight? A deserter? A spy?

But his smile was too disarming. If he was a real spy, he wouldn't mention this so freely. And he would be much older. Yet Milleus made sure he locked the door to his sleeping quarters that night.

CHAPTER 11

FLAMES LEAPED in the night, against the backdrop of forest, unfamiliar dark shapes that were *trees*, where creatures hid and rustled and hooted. The sky above was dark and full of stars like the sky in the City of Glass at low-sun.

As someone new to lands devoid of snow, Carro found his senses were all askew. The smells, the sounds, the feel of the ground under his feet, everything was different. And even the nights were so incredibly *warm*.

A shiver crawling over his arms, Carro finished rubbing his eagle and put the brush back in his kit bag. So neat and tidy it was compared to those of the hunters. They had non-standard bags, and non-standard saddles. Jeito wore a harness, but the other two didn't. They'd laughed when he asked about their uniforms.

Farey knelt by the fire, using a fearfully sharp knife to slowly pull the skin off the animal Nolan had shot. Carro had seen him do it. A single shot from a Chevakian gun, from the back of a plummeting eagle, not wearing a harness.

And Rider Cornatan wanted him to *control* these hunters? That had to be his idea of a joke.

It brought up memories of the abuse at the hands of his fellow apprentices, and the eyrie he was glad to have left. It made him think of the promise he'd made to his father. *Bring them back, dead or alive, but preferably dead. Avenge the Pirosian house.* The medal that hung on a

93

chain under his clothes burned against his chest. He was no heroic soldier.

"Hey, Carro." Farey jerked his head at the pile of wood Nolan had collected. His hands shone with grease and blood.

Carro needed no more instructions. Tend to the fire. It wasn't an order so much as a task. Everyone else was busy, too. They were all pieces of the puzzle that formed the achievements of a well-oiled team. Trying to command would be useless at best, at worst would earn him disrespect. You did not order these men.

He knelt inside the pool of warm orange light and poked the burning logs into a pile.

Farey's knife worked at the carcass. His muscles cording in his arms, he was hacking the head off the animal. Bones cracked.

Nolan just returned from the creek with a bladder of water, some of which he poured into a pot. Teeth flashing, Farey grinned and threw the head of the animal across. Splash, in the pan.

"Oy!" Nolan shouted. "You wanna get me shirt all messed-up?"

Farey snorted and rose. With his long face and yellowish skin, he looked part-Aranian. Long black hair hung on either side of his face. He looked nothing like he had in the palace, yet this image was the real Farey. Had Carro met him in another life in the streets of the Outer City, he would have walked around the block.

Farey oozed danger, in his smile, in his intense look and in the way he went to stand behind Carro and breathed over his shoulder so close Carro could feel the warmth of his body, and he didn't dare breathe for fear of being stripped of his pants and raped. That's what happened to junior apprentices, after all.

Farey laughed. "The pup is scared, huh?"

"No," Carro said, but it came out as a strangled sound.

"Oh, quit that, Farey," Nolan said. "He's been a good replacement for that idiot we lost."

"Yeah, he's not half-bad," Farey said, tracing Carro's shoulder with a hand glistening with grease and blood. Carro's heart thudded in his chest. "You fancy him, huh?"

"Quit that, I said."

"Yeah, you fancy him." Farey let his hand drop. "All right. You can have him." But before he turned away, he pulled Carro against him. Carro could feel his cock through two layers of clothes.

"Hey, come and help me," Nolan said.

Carro stumbled to the fire, his heart still thudding and blood roaring in his ears, and, embarrassingly, in other places.

"Thanks," he mumbled to Nolan.

"Look after the fire for me," Nolan said, his eyes meeting Carro's in an intense look.

He transferred the pot to the fire, hanging it up on a wire frame. "Don't make them flames too high, or you can scrub the soot off."

Carro nodded, and pushed the logs a bit further apart.

Farey had pushed a stick through the carcass and hung it above the fire. He sank down with a sigh of satisfaction, wiped his hands on his trousers and pulled a bottle from his pocket.

"Want some?" He held it out to Carro, who took it from his bloodied hands.

The spirits were strong and burned in Carro's throat. He wiped the mouth of the bottle and passed it to Jeito, who was studying a map. His long hair hung forward over his shoulder. Jeito's fingers traced lines on the map. Long fingers with rings. Sometimes, when Jeito raked hair behind his ear, Carro thought he looked feminine. He was certainly not tall and lanky like Farey, or strong-jawed and stubble-chinned like Nolan.

But he'd seen Jeito with a knife, and he'd felt the strength in the grip of those fine-boned hands, and he'd seen how Jeito set fire to a farmhouse with an entire family locked inside. More than anyone, more even than Farey, Jeito scared him.

"Where are we, then?" In the group tasks were strictly divided, and it seemed talking was Nolan's task. He was perhaps the youngest of the three, and with his soft honey-coloured curls and hazel eyes, he must have a lot of Chevakian blood.

Jeito grunted. "We've searched this area." He circled a spot on the map. "Tomorrow, we're going here." He pointed at the map. His shirt hung open at the front, showing soft, hairless skin. "They're around here somewhere." Jeito's finger circled the district on the map. There was a small farming village, and a larger town called Ensar.

Yesterday, they had spotted a riderless eagle, circling high. They tried to follow the animal, only to find that it was heading back over the mountains and that it had neither a harness nor listened to whistles. A wild bird? It might have been a coincidence, but they expected the Queen to be around here somewhere. Any further north and it would have been too hot for the eagle.

Carro nodded. "I think they've hidden somewhere in these hills." He tried to sound authoritative. "I wouldn't be surprised if they let the bird go, since it will give away their position. I think we—"

"Don't think too much," Farey said. His teeth flashed a warning.

"I know Isandor better than all of you. We grew up together." That was why Rider Cornatan had sent him on this mission, wasn't it?

"What you know would fit in a brain the size of the nail on my little finger," Farey said.

"Whoa, calm down," Nolan said. "What Farey means is that obeying orders is not the way we do things here, with us. We're hunters, you know, and we don't like being bossed around like you . . . would be used to."

"Shut your trap, blabbermouth. I don't need you to explain what I said. The pup's got ears. We'll have him along, if he doesn't fuck up, but I don't want him to get any illusions about commanding us."

"You're as blunt as the sword smith's hammer."

"And your mouth's gonna kill you one day."

But Farey gave Nolan an affectionate smile as Nolan handed back the bottle, and a cracking slap on the shoulder. Nolan threw himself on Farey and the two rolled back in the grass. Carro jumped up, ready to discipline his team, but they were laughing, pushing away each other's hands until Farey lay on his back and Nolan on top of him, having pushed Farey's arms flat on the ground.

Nolan grinned. "Who's the pup now?"

In a flash, Farey got his legs under him and bucked up, sending Nolan flying in the grass. He jumped up and ran into the darkness.

"Cut it, idiots, will ya?" Jeito snapped. Then his shifty glance met Carro's. "Oh, sit down, academy boy. They're just stirring each other up."

Branches cracked and Nolan came back out of the forest.

"Stop teasing the pup," he said to Jeito, picking grass out of his hair. "I was like him just two years ago."

"That long already, feels like two moons." Sarcasm dripped from Farey's voice. "Hey. You think there is any hope for this one?"

"You gotta be fair. He can't help who his family is."

Jeito raised his eyebrows.

An uncomfortable silence fell. Nolan blushed.

Eventually, Jeito said, "Family?"

Nolan shrugged and met Carro's eyes. He mouthed *sorry*. "You don't have to tell everyone if you don't want to. Me and my big mouth."

"You can say that again," Farey growled. "If you shut your trap more often, we'd be in a lot less shit."

Carro looked down in an uncomfortable silence. *You don't have to tell anyone if you don't want to.* With these young men, nothing but the total truth would do. He spoke, still looking at the grass.

"I found out . . . before I came on this mission . . . that the people who raised me, an Outer City merchant and his family, were paid to do so. My real family . . ." He licked his lips, didn't know what else to say, or how to say it, and pulled the medallion of the Pirosian house from under his tunic.

Three pairs of eyes fixed on it. One grey, one blue, one brown.

"Oh frolicking skylights," Jeito said. "You're Rider Cornatan's son?"

Carro nodded.

Farey whistled between his teeth. "That's some name to live up to. What'd you do?"

"What do you mean—what did I do?"

Nolan explained. "Well, the Knights normally send us poor boys when they misbehave in the Knight's training. You know—to toughen them up."

Oh.

"They usually don't stick around for long," Jeito said. "Can't hack it."

"Hey, but you're not too bad," Nolan said, meeting Carro's eyes. "But tell us—what did you do?"

Carro shrugged. He didn't do anything, as far as he was aware. Maybe that was the problem, or maybe even his father thought he was worthless and wanted to stick him away, somewhere he couldn't do any more damage than he'd already done. The shame of the Pirosian house, a blot on his family.

"He speaks Chevakian, that's what he did," Farey said.

"Oh." Nolan looked disappointed. Then he shrugged, took the

bottle again and drank deeply. "Want some?" The skin around his eyes crinkled. Something about that look unsettled Carro.

Farey used the sleeve of his tunic to pick up the stick and turn the meat. Fat dripped into the fire, hissing into the flames. Jeito sat next to Farey, and whispered in his ear. Farey smiled. Jeito slapped Farey's chest in a playful gesture.

The next thing they were kissing, a deep, passionate kiss that made Carro all hot and uncomfortable in certain places.

Farey's hands moved down Jeito's shoulders. Jeito sank slowly onto his back into the grass until all Carro could see was Farey's back, and Jeito's long-fingered hands.

Carro took the bottle, meeting Nolan's eyes. "Don't mind them," Nolan said. "They're always clowning."

Carro shrugged. He couldn't take his eyes off that scene. Firelight flickered over Farey's back, and the rings on Jeito's hands, their bodies rubbing against each other, totally absorbed.

He swallowed and asked, "So . . . why are you here?"

"Isn't that obvious? I speak Chevakian, too."

"Your mother is Chevakian?"

Nolan nodded. "Yes. Before you ask me, I'm one of the slave children, born from a kidnapped woman. Never fitted into the City of Glass, so . . . I became a hunter, a spy."

You don't need to be half-Chevakian not to fit in.

"You've been doing this two years?"

"Sure have."

"Is it good?"

"You kidding? Best job I ever had. Better 'n playing cook in the Knights' mess, I'd say. No, the worst job I had was washing up and cleaning the kitchens. What about you?"

Carro shuddered.

"Doing my . . . my stepfather's accounts . . . all through the night. I was so cold. And when I complained . . . he would bring me more work." He stopped because his voice choked up. He stared into the fire, but Nolan said nothing, and he continued. "All night, I would sit there. He wouldn't feed me until I finished, and if I fell asleep, he would bring me more work. I was cold, and it was scary in the warehouse in the dark . . ."

"Hey," Nolan said. There was warm sympathy in his voice. He

reached out, and when Carro didn't react, put his hand on Carro's shoulder.

"They treat you bad, huh?"

The fire swam in Carro's eyes. He blinked and blinked, afraid to cry. If the Knights at the Eyrie heard that he, Carro, had cried . . . if his father heard it . . .

"You know, we all been hurt," Nolan continued. "That's really why they put us here. None of us fit in. Farey's half Aranian, Jeito . . ." He shrugged. "Well, he speaks for himself. They hurt us and poke us, and hope that we grow into tough men. And you know? We don't. Because we're too hurt, too cut up inside. But us, we look out for each other."

Carro nodded. He wiped furiously at his eyes, aware that Farey and Jeito looked at him, haunted looks on their faces. Not one of them laughed.

Jeito lifted the bottle to his lips and drank deeply. "Nolan blabbers too much, but he speaks right. It was no place for any of us, the City of Glass."

They all fell silent.

Somehow, Carro didn't care as much as he should. The City of Glass was far away and the warm wind in his hair was far too enjoyable. And what was more, ever since they had crossed the border, he had suffered no more debilitating flashbacks.

He lay back in the grass, staring at the star-dotted sky. The cooking meat made hissing and sizzling noises and spread the most delicious smell. The drink glowed comfortably in his belly. *We look out for each other.* No one had ever looked out for him. No one perhaps except . . . Isandor. But Isandor was the other side, now. He understood; Isandor was Thillei, a sorcerer, kidnapper of the Queen, to be exterminated. He could never be a friend.

"You all right?" Nolan said.

"Yeah."

Nolan's hand found Carro's shoulder, caressing the skin through his clothes. Carro lay still, his heart thudding.

"Hey, relax," Nolan said. His hand wandered down Carro's chest, to his belt.

Carro jerked away.

Nolan withdrew his hand, and raised himself on one elbow, meeting Carro's eyes.

"It's all right," he whispered. "We never hurt each other."

But . . .

The firelight played on Nolan's face. His eyes were sincere. He'd taken off his shirt. There was a bulge in his pants.

Carro stared through the haze of confusion. Were they all male lovers? Was he one? Whenever the Knights had violated him, he'd always become aroused. He'd had Korinne, but he hadn't really *loved* her, had he?

Long moments passed. Nolan reached out again, took Carro's hand and placed it on his bare chest. "Feel it."

Nolan's heart thudded under his fingers, through the warm and sweaty skin. He bent closer, his breath tickling in Carro's neck. Carro wanted to give in, wanted Nolan to fuck him. But that was what the Knights did to apprentices for punishment. It hurt. Nolan nibbled the skin under his ear, and ran a hand over Carro's shoulder. His lips moved up Carro's jaw line.

Men don't kiss.

Carro jerked back.

"Does it scare you?" Nolan asked.

Carro nodded. He disengaged from Nolan's touch and rolled on his back.

"It's all right," Nolan said softly. "I can wait."

Carro nodded again. But he was rock hard and wanted to go somewhere private to relieve himself. No, he wanted someone else to do it. He lay there, looking up at the stars, his heart thudding.

"Look," Nolan said.

A short burst of light tracked through the sky.

"Quick, make a wish."

They were silent for a bit.

Then Nolan asked, "What did you wish?"

"I'm not saying. It's supposed to stay a secret, otherwise it isn't a wish." But Carro didn't know what to wish. He would have wished for himself to do well so his father would love him. He might have wished for his hallucinations to stop, but they seemed to have stopped of their own volition since crossing the border. Now, he just wanted to be free of the guilt he felt about his hot, naked desire.

"Well, I wish I had loads of money and a big palace with swimming pools and all that stuff they have in Chevakia." Nolan pushed himself up. "Better go and check the food."

Before he could stop himself, Carro raised his hand, as if he wanted to say, *wait.*

Nolan hesitated, and sat back down, and leant over Carro. "So you do want it?"

Carro panicked. He wanted to scream, *No!* But he was so hard it hurt.

Nolan whispered, "About your wish." The skin around his eyes crinkled with his smile. "You didn't happen to be thinking of me? You've been ogling me for days."

Nolan reached up and felt for Carro's hand. Warm flesh met warm flesh. Something connected. Nolan shifted closer and as if it was the most natural thing, folded Carro into his arms. His curls smelled like saddle oil and unwashed hair, but very male. Nolan lifted his face, and the next moment his lips met Carro's. Moist, hot and eager.

Carro had never been kissed like this. He'd forced himself on a girl, he'd been forced to kiss when he didn't want to, and had other boys force themselves on him, and there was that incident, in the Eyrie where he had felt compelled to punish his patrol, that he didn't even want to think about.

None of those times were anything like this.

Nolan's hands were tender and questing. His callus-hardened hands warm under Carro's shirt. His breath was heavy in the gathering darkness. Nolan took off his shirt, but Carro shied away when Nolan reached for the fastening on his pants.

"What?" Nolan whispered. His lips glistened with moisture.

Carro shook his head.

"Why not? I want to fuck you."

Carro shook his head again.

"There's no need to be scared. Although . . . I was scared, too, the first time. Everyone tells you it's wrong."

Carro said nothing. He was breathing deep, panting breaths. His heart was thudding against his ribs like crazy, but his cock was hard as rock and dribbling slime into his pants. "I'm not—"

"A male lover? No, we're not. Those words are for men who are too scared to do what their heart tells them. We call ourselves wolves.

We move in a pack and if ever we need to be with the wolverines, we fuck them fast so they can get on with the breeding and they don't bother us anymore."

Carro grinned. Wolves. He liked that. Moving in a pack, no obligations to nagging women, and their parents wanting payment for offspring. No need to let himself become trapped in a marriage for the sake of appearance. He'd be independent, like his real father, and not a limp dishrag like the merchant.

"All right," he whispered, his voice hoarse. "Show me."

Nolan did.

They were beyond the reach of the glow of their fire and found each other purely by touch. There was nothing Carro hadn't seen or done before, but Nolan was gentle, and Carro forgot his doubts. He even forgot what those doubts had been.

Some time later, when the sky had gone black as midwinter night in the City of Glass, he lay in Nolan's arms in the grass staring up at the flicker of firelight on the tree trunks. The branches made ghostly shadows which jumped about like a bunch of those other horrid things Chevakia had and the City of Glass did not: bugs.

Farey called out into the night, "Hey, you two, stop clowning. Look at this!"

Nolan let go and raised himself, pulling up his trousers. Carro pushed himself up and scoured for his pants and shirt on the forest floor. He shook leaves off and jumped about on one foot while getting into his pants. He stumbled into the clearing a bit after Nolan did.

Jeito pointed at the horizon.

"What is it?" asked Nolan, staring where Jeito pointed.

"There's . . ." Jeito's eyes were wide.

They all stared at the horizon, which, as far as Carro could see, looked just as it had before. But a cold chill went over him with a breath of icy wind. He heard faint echoes of voices in his mind. If he couldn't see it, but he could hear the nagging voice of his stepfather, then it could only be . . .

Nolan whispered, "Icefire."

Icefire here in Chevakia?

CHAPTER 12

$\mathcal{S}$ADY SPENT most of the next few days talking to fellow senators, mostly in factions, because there wasn't the time to do it individually. Four trains had left for Fairlight, and he needed a decision before they could return. So he was going to challenge at the next session, because the authority to send trains wasn't his to make unless he won.

Over the years, the doga senators had developed a ritual for these canvassing meetings. It meant he announced his visit to the owner of the office some time in advance. The faction leader or senior senator would call in all the faction members, and the potential challenger would sit at the senator's desk while everyone else stood around the perimeter of the room. Sometimes, there would be food.

Over all his years in the doga, Sady had attended several of those canvassing sessions. They happened with disturbing regularity. He had always been in the audience, always somewhere at the back, closest to the door. He had always disliked the backstabbing and had often wondered why the backstabbers couldn't just get on with their work and leave the leadership to do theirs.

He saw that attitude in quite a number of his listeners, those who leaned against the wall, arms crossed over their chest. They were probably happy enough with Destran's performance and saw no reason for a challenge, or they didn't care. They thought a challenge was a waste of time and resources. He knew; he'd thought the same so often.

But this time was different. This time, the country was at stake.

Then again, he wondered if those challengers hadn't thought exactly the same thing every time they challenged. With all the abuse for not much of a stipend, certainly senators did this for the love of the country, and they challenged because they believed the current Proctor's hold on the situation was broken.

Some challenges had been successful, some not, but all challengers had believed they were doing the right thing. And for all of them, life had never been the same. There was no way he could go back to being a quiet senator after this.

So he watched the preliminary votes, or intention-to-votes, in a detached numbness. Destran still had many supporters. Too many, if he had to be honest.

He spent a long time before the meeting staring at his account balance, as if the action of staring at it would somehow increase it to a level high enough to pay for the sending of the trains if he failed to gain office.

"So what happens after the meeting?" Viki asked, in a low voice, when walking through the corridors to the doga session where he had planned to make his move.

Everyone knew it was coming, and senators scrambled out of his way, or gave him pitying looks.

"I win or I lose. Either way, you will be the Chief Meteorologist." Sady felt tight as a wound spring. If he won, funding for his projects would be a battle, but if he lost, he'd have to cut Viki's stipend to pay for the trains before resigning in disgrace.

Viki nodded, his face determined.

Sady hurt inside. He could be cutting short the young man's career as meteorologist, just now when Viki had become a lot more confident at handling requests and no longer fell apart when a senior senator asked a tricky question.

"You'll surely win," Viki said in that disarming way of his.

"I don't think so. I don't feel confident at all."

"But if you lose, what will you do?"

"I can't go back to being a quiet senator. There would be constant distrust surrounding me." At least he had never taken up the offer to live in doga-owned accommodation, but still, his stipend would be gone, and he'd need another way to pay for himself, never mind the staff. He could teach meteorology at the Scriptorium, or maybe in Arania . . . "I might join my brother on the farm."

He'd said it as a joke, and he tried to convince himself by laughing, but it came out wrong. Mercy, he was tense. It wasn't just his situation that worried him. He worried about the consequences to the country if he lost.

They arrived at the hall, Sady in front and Viki walking behind him, clutching his notes with more worrying meteorological data. No one had been able to raise Fairlight on the wire. Communication with Mekta was patchy at best. There was too much crackle on the lines so that not even the automated barygraph readings could be trusted. Because of the line outages there had been no reports of sonorics measurements, which had to be taken in person by the local meteorology officer. Sonorics in the border might well have spiked, but there was no way of knowing.

The senators at the hall's entrance stepped back to let Sady and Viki through into the richly wood-panelled hall. There was a broad stairway leading down into the hall, with the senator's benches on both sides. Men and women who had been talking to each other on the stairs stopped and watched Sady and Viki walk past. Others, already seated, stopped talking, too, and by the time Sady sat down in his usual bench, almost every senator was looking at him, including Destran, who sat on a chair behind the dais, nervously shuffling through his notes.

Sady pretended to ignore the attention. He made a show of studying the meeting's agenda, in an outwardly calm way. Inside, his nerves raged. He had never imagined what Milleus had felt when he took over, although he remembered that day well. It was in the middle of the Aranian war, when senator Milleus had taken up his former position as army lieutenant, and he and his balloon squads had taken the first victory against the western invaders.

Proctors were rarely elected at term. The Chevakian people usually re-elected whoever was in charge until that person's colleagues staged a coup. The challenges were the subject of much gossip and street theatre. Tomorrow, his name was going to be all over the gossip circuit. He'd heard some rumours already. *Who did you say was going to challenge? You have to be kidding.* Tiverians were said to be staid and calm, but they loved their political bloodlettings.

Everyone in the hall took their places.

Destran rose from his seat and opened the meeting. He listed the agreed agenda points and asked for emergency items to be added. This was a formulaic requirement normally read without much enthusiasm. It was also an invitation for a challenge.

At this point, everyone fell quiet and looked at Sady, and Sady rose, as if in a dream, a very bad dream.

"I have a point to add."

Destran glared at him. Standing here in the spot of light coming in from the ceiling, he looked very old and tired.

"I want a vote of no confidence."

The entire hall broke out in cheers and shouts.

Destran hammered the dais and eventually a semblance of silence returned. He continued glaring at Sady. "And why do you think that the doga will vote against me?"

Destran had been challenged a few times before, and had always won comfortably. If nothing else, he was surprisingly tough to unseat. Because he divided his opposition.

Sady ploughed on. "A good number of senators have become distrustful of your handling of the sonorics crisis. By pretending it doesn't exist, you—"

"And Alius continuously confirms that there isn't half as much a crisis as you say there is," a senator yelled at the back of the hall. "You're all making this up for your own advantage."

"Alius is not coming forward with any kind of solution about this, even though I've asked him, even though he promises that we will have medicine. But that aside. Alius is not a meteorologist. He does not see the large patterns and the looming food shortages. We cannot wait any longer. We don't like this situation any more than anyone else here does. Ignoring the facts does not make them go away. I want this country to survive. I want every person in Chevakia to be safe."

He looked all around the hall. "Destran continues to play down the danger. The truth is, the earlier reprieve we had from rising sonorics has been brief. The truth is that levels are rising rapidly. The last-measured level of sonorics at Fairlight was seventy-three motes per cube. Last measured. We have lost contact with Fairlight. These levels may well pour so much energy into the barrier plates that they will shatter. The truth is that a massive low-pressure cell is building over the southern plateau. There will be a snowstorm like none of us have seen in our lifetimes. I have taken it upon myself to send four trains for the evacuation of Fairlight. The drivers have risked their own lives to volunteer for this job. I have risked my life to visit the border regions. There are as yet unconfirmed sighting of eagles in the region. My sources report civil unrest in the City of Glass. That is what we're facing, and this situation will not go away by ignoring it. Are you willing to go on with a Proctor who stands by and does nothing?"

The hall descended into shouting and yelling, until Destran hammered on the dais, and by the time a measure of silence returned, a group of senators at the back of the hall were chanting, "Vote, vote, vote."

They were mostly Sady's supporters, and he noted with unease that a lot of other senators didn't yell support.

"Senator Sadorius han Chevonian, are you challenging?"

"I am." Never had two words meant more for Sady, not when Milleus said them, not when Destran said them. A trickle of sweat ran down his back. "I am challenging for the sake of Chevakia, because I want our land to survive and defend itself."

A lot of senators cheered.

"So, we vote." Destran's voice had gone flat and emotionless. "All those in favour of the challenger, Sadorius han Chevonian."

Hands went up. Not as many as Sady had hoped. He noted several of the senators who kept their hands down had stood at the back of the room during canvassing meetings. Destran's support was still strong.

People started moving around to lobby others to change their vote, both ways. The arbiters shouted for people to stay seated, but still, there was so much chaos in the hall that counters had to recount three times before the result was announced.

"Sixty-three in favour."

This was followed by shouts from the audience.

Any vote for Proctor needed a two-thirds majority, which he clearly didn't have. Which Destran didn't have either.

Senators already lined up to negotiate with him. More money for alternative industry to reduce the central region's dependency on mining. Sady could agree to that. There would have to be the revival of a lot of military industry, which would benefit the central region, because of the mines.

More money for education in the south. That was harder to promise, because no one knew what the immediate future would bring for the south. He sent Viki to the telegraph office for the latest news. The response was erratic, with reports that would take a lot more time to appreciate, and still no news from Fairlight. The wildly fluctuating sonorics levels prompted some to say that the barygraphs were broken.

While this was going on, factions were convening on the floor, and changing their votes to stand in blocs. Message boys delivered their requests to the rival candidates.

The north demanded its railways if they were to vote in favour— Sady cursed at that. But he desperately needed the north's support, so he made some sort of half-hearted promise on the damned train lines.

Mercy, he hated these kinds of votes-for-money deals, and they didn't stop with the demands from the north. The east wanted better telegraph lines. The west wanted export regulations to Arania to be relaxed. Mercy, mercy. Even if he agreed to some, there were always other demands, and other senators claiming unfairness because senator so-and-so got their wish. They were all like little children around the honey pot. And he was the bee stupid enough to have been caught in the frenzy.

The more the process wore on, the more he wished he could follow the one senator who walked out in disgust.

At the end of the afternoon, there was another vote which delivered a grand majority of two . . . in favour of senator Sadorius han Chevonian. So in the still-noisy hall, he walked down the stairs and took the ceremonial cloak and hammer from Destran, whose face twisted in a sneer. Whose face reminded Sady of Milleus' when that same fate befell his brother. He wanted to say sorry, except he was not, really. He didn't dislike Destran as a person, and his likes and dislikes had nothing to do with politics anyway. Besides, Destran looked furious.

He hissed through clenched teeth, "You and your family are all the same. Enjoy it while you can. It won't last." He turned abruptly and stormed out, leaving Sady to stare at his retreating back, feeling the literal and figurative weight of the Proctor's cloak on his shoulders.

Mercy.

What had he done?

CHAPTER 13

$\mathcal{D}$ARA AND MYRA spent a long time packing, far too long for Loriane's liking. She had nothing to pack and, with more and more people streaming into the town, wanted to be gone as soon as possible.

She carried her meagre possessions into the shed, where the bear was snorting nervously and the camel stood chewing peacefully and Ruko sat atop Tandor's chest. Well, she couldn't see him of course, but something threw a ball of twine into the air and caught it again and again.

"We can use Tandor's sled," Loriane said when Ontane stumbled into the shed after her, carrying a heavy travel chest.

He put his load down. "Where we be going we can't use a sled. Snow stops quickly down the side of the platform."

"Then how are we going to get to this hunting shack?" By the skylights, she hated the idea of another trek.

"We walk, and take the camel and a cart."

He pulled a rough cloth off a strange contraption in a corner of the shed. It was completely made out of wood—it had to be worth a fortune—and moved smoothly on the ground on two round things on either side.

"What, ye never seen wheels, mistress?"

Loriane shook her head. Like the sled, it had a tray and two beams on which to tie the animal.

"Cart." She repeated the strange Chevakian word.

He slapped his hand on the tray. "We'll put all our things here and your man on the saddle."

Loriane was going to say that he wasn't *her* man but couldn't muster the energy. She went up the stairs, ignored the piercing stare from Dara in the kitchen, and tried to get Tandor to sit up. He mumbled some incoherent words, but wouldn't open his eyes more than a sliver. His face looked horrible, half-covered in caked blood. Most of his long hair was gone. But for all she could see, his injuries were superficial.

"Come on, Tandor, stop behaving like this and help me." She shook his shoulders. His eyelids flickered, but he did not otherwise react to her. "Tandor, come on. I can't move you by myself. I've had enough of this. I know you can hear us, so help me, by the skylights."

But her words made no difference.

Slowly, she dressed him in his filthy overclothes. She had scrubbed some of the caked and dried blood and mud out of his cloak, but the furs smelled terrible.

His eyelids flickered and his eyes seemed to gain focus.

"Come on, Tandor, talk to me."

He opened his mouth, but at that moment there was a rushing sound and she was roughly pushed aside so that she fell into the chair that stood before the hearth.

"Hey, watch out!" she yelled at Ruko, who was now lifting Tandor off the bed. "Tandor, tell him that he's rude."

But Tandor had gone back to being non-responsive.

Ruko carried him down the stairs, and Loriane followed, glad for his assistance, because she wouldn't have gotten him down. In the shed, Ontane had put a saddle on the camel and was lashing a pack to the cart.

Dara strode into the shed carrying another pack, which she added to the pile already waiting to be put onto the cart. Ontane heaved the pack his wife had given him onto the cart.

"There be something you wish to take, mistress?" Ontane asked.

Loriane glanced at Tandor's chest on the sled. It was much too big to fit onto the cart with all the packs Dara had brought. Yet she couldn't leave it here. They might not come back. The refugees might destroy it. Tandor never travelled without it.

"I . . ." She walked to the chest, fingering the lid.

"It be clear that we can't take that entire thing," Dara said, before she turned away and left the shed, no doubt to get more packs from the kitchen.

Yes, Loriane could understand that, but why did this woman have to be so rude about it?

If she left Tandor's things here, vital information could be lost. She should at least take something. The books, at least.

Yet she shuddered at the idea of going through Tandor's things and finding goodness-knew-what. Like that horrid beating heart in the jar. She couldn't even blame rude and simple-minded Dara for not wanting to take that. What would she do with it?

She braced herself and pushed the lid—

—*No,* Tandor screamed in his mind, *don't take it.*

Ruko laughed. "They won't hear you. They're stupid, meaningless people."

"They saved me."

"They prevented you being saved. They are stupid."

"Why are you talking like this? You are meant to listen to me. What are you doing here? I thought I told you to guard this town."

"I'm not going to listen to a weakling like you. There's no point staying here. You don't command me, and the others don't command me. I'm going with them to Chevakia."

"You can't. You'll vanish as soon as you cross the border."

"Then I'll just have to return to my normal form, won't I?"

—the lid opened.

Dara walked past again with another look at Loriane. "Take some of his clothes, but we'll have to leave the rest of that thing here."

"I'd like to take all of it."

Dara's eyes widened. "Don't you see there be no room? We need food and blankets and the tent. We have no room for silly things like books."

"I have hardly anything to take. This can take the space for both of us."

"But we can't—"

"Look!" Ontane said.

Tandor had stiffened. His eyes were wide.

Loriane said, "See? He knows we're talking about him. He doesn't want his things to be left behind. There is important information in Tandor's books."

"And I'm saying that everything on that cart is for all of us. Food, blankets, tent—"

"I have to take it, or I'll never find his family—"

Ontane stepped between them. "Ladies, ladies, stop the fight—"

—"I forbid you to return to your normal form!" Tandor called in that place between life and death.

Ruko laughed. "You forbid? You have no say over me anymore. Never had any, coward. I've had enough of hanging around in this stupid village."

"And you'll have to hang around here some more. I want you to see what happens with all these refugees here—"

"I'm coming. Watch me." He went to Tandor's travel chest.

—Myra screamed, "Look, Da!" and pointed.

The clothes that lay atop the contents of the chest moved by themselves. Then the invisible hands rummaged through the contents underneath, pushing aside underclothes and books, and unearthed the glass jar with its grisly contents.

Lifted it. The jar stopped in mid-air.

Ontane stood watching, his eyes wide.

Myra came up behind him. The baby in a fur sling across her chest gave out muffled cries.

Ruko, for it must be he holding the jar, turned to her and held it out to her. The contents of the jar pulsed with blue glow. Myra's eyes widened.

"Da? Mistress Loriane? What's happening?"

"I think he wants you to take it," Loriane said.

"What is that thing? It's . . . disgusting." She shrank back.

When Myra made no attempt to take the jar, Ruko retreated. The jar went up, and before anyone could do anything, Ruko had smashed it on the ground. Myra screamed. Even Tandor uttered a cry.

Shattered glass lay in a heap in the straw, and amongst it, the pulsing heart.

Ontane muttered, "By the skylights, it be alive."

But Myra was still staring at the spot where Loriane suspected Ruko to be, in the middle of the barn.

"What?" she whispered. "What do you want me to . . ."

She knelt on the ground.

Her mother shouted, "Myra, don't touch it—"

—Tandor jumped forward, but his virtual body was insubstantial and his real body still refused to obey his will.

He grabbed hold of Ruko's arm, but his hand went straight through it. Ruko laughed.

"You have to learn how to be a ghost."

"What are you going to do in Chevakia?"

"I'm going to offer my services to this mistress of yours, because she seems to have more backbone than you."

"She's my *mother*, by the skylights, and she's a horrible old woman. She cares only about revenge, no matter who gets hurt."

By the skylights, he did not want his mother to get her hands on Ruko—

—But Myra had already picked up the pulsing heart in her hands. She rose, holding it out. The fluid from the jar dripped off her hands and spread a pungent odour through the shed.

The heart vanished, as if eaten up by the air.

—Tandor lunged.

He fell straight through Ruko's body and landed hard on the floor, next to his body. He scrambled up, called strands of icefire and lashed them around Ruko's upper body, even while the heart vanished into his chest.

Ruko twisted and snapped the strands, but as his body oozed icefire and faded from the in-between world, one strand hit him in the back of his head and looped around his neck. The strand stretched and grew thinner and thinner—

—There was a flash of light. Myra screamed. Loriane clapped her hands over her face.

When Loriane uncovered her eyes, a young man stood in the middle of the barn. He was longhaired and filthy, dressed in a ripped shirt and trousers held up only by a piece of string, clothes far too small for him. He was skinny and his arms were covered in bruises and scratches.

Dara was staring at him. She whispered, "Ruko? Is that you?"

He said nothing, just stood there. Like Isandor, he had only one foot, bare and red from the cold, the other leg ending in a wooden stump. His eyes were black and hollow.

"Ye always said he be gone, here's yer proof that he didn't," Ontane said. "I always seen him, every time the sorcerer brung him in here. Believe me now, woman?"

Dara snorted. "I don't know that he be real. He don't look too real to me. Hey—you, say something." She stepped up to stare into the boy's face.

"Hey, can you hear me?"

—Tandor laughed. "You thought you could get away from me?"

Ruko's voice was distant, his form in that in-between world little more than insubstantial mist. "Fuck you. I'll get you. Your control over me is only weak."

—He said nothing. His face was impassive and menacing, Loriane thought.

"Hey!" Dara poked him in the chest. "An adult asks you a question."

He merely stepped back.

Dara snorted. "See? He be nothing but a ghost. Body be here, but the brain be somewhere else. I always said the sorcerer be up to no good."

All of a sudden, Ruko jumped into action. He flung all of Tandor's possessions inside the trunk and snapped the lid shut hard. Then he heaved it on top of the cart with a thunk.

Ontane protested, "Hey, that be the space for our things."

Ruko didn't react. Without a word, he turned to Tandor—

"Come, old man, the situation has changed. I am real and you are not. I think I'm going to have some fun."

"Ruko, I forbid you—"

"—you're my servitor now." He laughed.

—and heaved him into the saddle of the camel as if he were no more than a small child.

Dara was elbowing her husband in the side. "Go on, stop him. That be the place where we need to put our things."

"Stop it, woman. What do ye think I can do? Have ye seen how strong he be?"

"Oh, ye men be useless!" She stomped to the cart and tried to heave off Tandor's trunk, but she couldn't lift it. "Hey, you! Take this thing off, or we'll have nothing to eat!"

Ruko had been tying Tandor's legs to the saddle straps, but now he wheeled around.

Ontane yelled, "Watch it, woman!"

Ruko pushed Dara aside. She fell bottom first in the straw.

"Ma!" Myra yelled.

Dara screamed, "Did ye see that? He hit me! Do something about that creep, useless lump!"

"There be no time for fights. There be room for our packs to go on top." He picked up a couple of bags, but Ruko had taken the camel by the lead and was leading it towards the door of the shed.

"Hey! Wait!" Ontane yelled, hobbled after the cart and flung the bags on top of Tandor's trunk.

"We still need to get some things from the kitchen," Dara protested.

"No time. You already spent so much time packing. We best move our sorry backsides afore everyone out there wakes up to where we be going and wants to come with us. There be only so much space in the hunting shack."

Ontane lifted the latch and pushed the shed doors.

They would only open halfway, because the refugees had built an igloo outside. Ruko let go of the reins and gave the doors a huge shove, simply pushing aside snow heaped up behind them.

Loriane expected to be swamped with requests for food and shelter, but all refugees were further down the street, staring in the direction of the plain.

Behind her, Myra gasped. "By the skylights."

"What's going on?" Loriane asked.

"The whole sky is crackling with icefire." She gave Loriane a strange look. "You can't see it?"

Loriane shook her head.

"This is like the wall we saw in the City of Glass. The dome of icefire, expanding outwards."

"Can you see . . . anyone?" Loriane asked. Myra had told her that she'd seen her boyfriend, the father of her baby, as a giant figure of burning icefire.

Myra shook her head. Her eyes glittered.

"Is it going to stop when it reaches the edge of the plateau?" she asked.

Ontane shrugged. "It'll stop at the border. Chevakians have barriers."

Ruko turned the camel into the street.

They crossed the village, where refugees hung around their igloos, camped in the lee side of buildings. There were even some Knights of junior rank, trying to organise people into some sort of order. Loriane caught shards of yelling. ". . . and then, once we've registered all your names, you will be given passes for food . . ."

"Hmph. Wonder where he be planning to get food from," Dara muttered.

A man asked where Ontane and his group were going, and Ontane mentioned relatives in some place that meant nothing to Loriane.

"You should tell them about what's coming," Loriane said.

"They'll find out soon enough. We'll have a head start."

As awful as it was, he was right, and she hadn't the energy to protest.

The crowds grew thinner and they left the last of the houses of the village behind. From here, the path sloped constantly down, and soon they reached the edge of the southern plateau where the steep cliffs fell. Far below them spread the rolling hills of Chevakia, looking furred and black in the morning light.

It was the first time in her life that Loriane saw land that was not covered in snow. She understood that what looked like black fur from here were *trees*, even though she had only seen pictures of those strange things.

The terrain plunged off the cliff-side into a tangle of rocks. Ruko led the camel deftly through places where Loriane couldn't see a path. Ontane had been right in that the sled wouldn't have gone down here. At first, there was still a meagre cover of snow, but it was wet and sometimes frozen over. Later, it was just wet.

The cart had enough trouble getting through with all the rocks and the steep slope. Ruko walked at the front leading the protesting, camel, and Ontane at the back pushed the cart when the terrain was too uneven for it to roll across. Sometimes he and Dara both needed to hang on to stop the cart rolling down. Sometimes they needed to lift the cart over rocks. It was slow going, it was wet, and as the day progressed, Loriane grew ever more weary. She was top-heavy, out-of-balance and half the time couldn't see where she put her feet.

Some time in the morning, she stepped on a particularly slippery patch of mud and fell hard on her side.

"Loriane!" Myra called.

Loriane sat there, wetness seeping into her clothes. It had started drizzling and thick clouds of mist billowed up the cliff side, obscuring the land below from view.

That mist now revealed the stumpy form of Dara, rushing back. "Mistress Loriane, are you all right?"

"Think so."

Dara grabbed her under the arms and heaved her back onto her feet. "By the skylights, ye be even bigger than Sinna was with the twins. You must be exhausted."

"I'm all right," Loriane said, but she felt tears pricking in her eyes. "Is it far to where we're going?"

"Oh, if we'd be going where we planned to go, ye'd already be there, but since we can't—"

"What do you mean—can't?" She hated how her voice spilled over. Yes, she had noticed how Dara and Ontane had been fighting, but she had been too busy not falling to hear what they said. "Why didn't you say anything before? Where are we going?"

"Truth be told, mistress, I wish I knew that meself." Ontane came stomping up the path. "But with that spectacle of icefire coming, we'd not have been safe. The hunting shack be only uphill from town."

"Then where to? All the way to Chevakia?" Loriane stared into the mist.

"If that's what it takes, yes."

"I can't walk that far."

"You'll have to, mistress, nothing be helped."

Myra gave her father a furious look. "Can't you at least help her?"

"Child, what do you think we're doing here? It be hard enough getting the cart down this rotten path without you women bellyaching. I wish, too, that we could put our feet up in the shack, but that bain't going to happen, and whether you complain or not, it can't be helped. I'll say it again: it can't be helped."

"No need to be rude about it," Myra said. When her light blue eyes met Loriane's, her expression softened.

"Take my arm," she said.

She held out her left arm. The sleeve of her right arm hung limply below the shoulder.

For some reason, Loriane remembered taking the little bundle of fur from Tandor's arms containing Isandor. A premature baby, his eyes unfocused, his arms and back covered in sparse but unusually long black hair. The stump of a leg withered below the knee. In the first days, she had worried about the frostbite to his single foot, and she had worried about looking after an imperfect child.

Isandor, where was he now? Would she ever see him again?

They kept going.

At first the path was steep, slippery and snow covered. Soon the mist overtook them and turned the world dreary and grey. Ruko led the camel, the beast picking its way between the rocks as if it knew the way. On occasion, it would stop and then everyone would have to lift the cart over some rock or another, but those times became fewer and further in between.

They encountered no other people, although sometimes Loriane thought she could hear voices amongst the rocks behind them, but even when the view cleared occasionally, she could not discern any movement further up the cliff.

When the path allowed, Myra came to walk next to her.

"Have you named the babe yet?"

"His name is Beido," Myra said, and her eyes glistened. Beido was the father of the child, one of those Tandor had gone to rescue, and failed.

"Was his father . . . like Ruko?" She glanced at Ruko's back, at the head of the column, leading the camel.

"No, not like that." Her eyes went distant.

"What happened to him back there in the shed with Ruko? One moment I couldn't see him, and the next, I could."

"When his heart was in the jar, he was Tandor's servitor, his utter slave. But servitors can't exist where there is little or no icefire, so he needed to have his heart back, or otherwise he couldn't flee with us."

"But he's still a ghost."

"I don't know why that happened either. It almost looks like the conversion back was incomplete. Maybe it needs someone with more skill than I . . ." She shuddered.

"I didn't know that conversion back was possible." Loriane had always heard that the king's servitors had died when the Knights killed the king, and that this was the only way to kill a servitor: by killing its master. "I think this icefire is evil. I don't know why Tandor is playing with it."

"There are good things—"

"When you can use it to enslave someone, I don't want to know about good things. Why can't we forget about the whole dreadful business? In the City of Glass, we all lived together, and then Tandor comes in with his talk about Pirosians and Thillei as if there were only two types of people. Things don't work like that in the City of Glass, not at least in the Outer City. The Knights don't have just Pirosians; they have Thillei, too, and all kinds of people in between, other clans, whose names you won't even know. All those clans have intermarried, and all the breeders will have been from different clans." But, she thought with a chill, those with a high percentage of pure blood tended to be more fertile, especially within the Pirosians. And there were legends about the strange occurrences of offspring of two pure members from different clans. She'd seen some crude drawings in the books kept by midwives in the palace. Most of them were very old, and current midwives dismissed the reports of malformed children with six limbs or with *wings* as fantasies. Those children were, they said, badly malformed Imperfects drawn to look more dramatic to justify their sacrifice to the wild bears. If those things existed, the midwives would have preserved the foetuses in jars.

Looking after Isandor, Loriane had changed her views on Imperfects. The Knights liked to picture them as evil demons, but they were just people with limbs missing. She suspected that over time a lot of the palace midwives had come to think the same, so trying to hide their deeds behind demonic depictions of the Imperfect children seemed only a logical step.

Just like the making of servitors was evil, so was the insistence of the Knights on killing all Imperfects.

As they descended the path, Loriane cursed herself, and Tandor, and the camel and the glutinous, slippery substance Myra called *mud*.

Never having seen a ground uncovered by snow, Loriane wasn't impressed by it. It rained—and rain was like snow, only wet—and progress down the rocky slope was slow. Myra helped her, the babe asleep in a sling on her back.

Loriane wished many times that she carried hers outside of her body instead of within it. She was sure that by now the babe had gone well over its expected date. Her legs ached and pressure of the babe's head made her need to seek privacy behind rocks many times. She would re-emerge, just as aching and sore, and having earned another scornful look from Dara. Yes, she slowed down their progress. Yes, they heard voices up there and the horde up there was probably catching up, but she couldn't help it.

By the time they reached the furry mass that Myra called the forest, Loriane was bone-weary.

An odd thing it was, too, this forest. In the City of Glass, little grew outside, even in the high-sun season. On occasions when she had been in nobles' houses, she had seen the "greenhouses" they kept, in which they grew plants. Little waist-high things they called trees that their keepers clipped and kept tidy. Those things were nothing like this. These trees were huge, with straight trunks and feathery branches which flapped in the wind. They made so much *noise.*

And she really didn't like making camp amongst the pillared trunks, where a fire cast flapping shadows into a mass of tangled wood. Anything could be hiding out there, and they would have no means to see it.

At least Tandor had recovered a little. Still strapped to the harness on the camel's back, colour had returned in his skin.

In this forest, they stopped for the night.

What Ontane had called a tent turned out to be little more than a canvas roof. Loriane lay down next to Myra and her babe, under the cover of furs and blankets. But she couldn't get comfortable and couldn't sleep. Her back ached, her belly ached and her legs ached. The babe wriggled inside her, kicking her ribs.

After staring into the darkness for what felt like an eternity, she rose, and picked her way into the forest. In the pitch dark, she crouched for another agonising piss. This time, she sat down on a fallen tree trunk and rubbed her fingers across her wetness. Imagined the pain, the stretching, the sheer hard work of pushing out a child. Nine times, she had done it. Nine times, she had felt the slimy head emerge from her body. Right now, she'd welcome the pain with open arms. She'd do it silently, because no one of the family needed to know what was going on. In any case, there was no need to scream. Screaming was for first-timers. She squatted, her back against the tree trunk, gulping deep breaths as she would do when pains became intense. She waited for tightening aches across her belly, but felt nothing of the sort. She dug her icy hands under her layers of clothing, took her swollen breast in her hands and rolled the nipple between her fingers until it hurt. Previous times she had done this, it had brought on the birth pains. This time, all it did was make her sore. She cried silently up at the stars.

Please, please.

CHAPTER 14

MILLEUS SIPPED his tea, leaning his elbows on the kitchen table. Firelight flickered through the kitchen, making Isandor's hair glisten. He had dropped his spoon by his empty bowl and leaned his head in his hands. For a moment he sagged, then he jerked up and looked into Milleus' eyes, a guilty expression over his young face.

"Oh. Excuse me." He rubbed his face.

"You're tired." Milleus said. It was not a question.

Both youngsters had worked hard all day. Isandor had chopped the entire pile of firewood and had helped Milleus straighten the collapsed fence.

Nila stared into the fire, her look distant. She was also tired, her cheeks red from being outside. She had spent all day in the garden, doing an admirable job for someone who had never seen a plant that didn't grow in a pot.

Milleus asked what they ate in the City of Glass, and Isandor said there were no vegetables, but that everyone drank milk or ate meat, dried, salted or frozen. Nila said people grew some things in greenhouses under the city.

To which Isandor said, "No, not much."

"Yes, people grow things, and eat them."

"Not us. I never had any." He switched to his own language, and they exchanged a few words.

"Not everyone eats vegetables," Nila said, and Isandor nodded, as if it was a consensus summary.

It became ever more clear that the two came from different backgrounds, and this was probably the reason why they had run away.

Milleus said, "Look, why don't you two go to sleep. I'll clean up."

"No, you have been so kind to us," Nila said. "We must help."

"No way. You've done enough."

She had even cleaned up his living room and kitchen with a dedication and precision of someone who did very little of that kind of work. He was almost ashamed of the mess in his cupboards. Mercy, the beetles! Some of the crockery hadn't been touched for years and a thin layer of mould and dust covered the white porcelain. But this morning, she had taken it all out, wiped the plates and put them back.

"Please," he said. "Go to sleep. There will be plenty of work tomorrow. I can take care of these three bowls."

That seemed to sway her.

"Good night." She rose, came to him and gave him a peck on the forehead, just like his daughter-in-law used to do. She smelled of sunshine.

Isandor got up, too, and they both left the kitchen.

Instead of cleaning up, Milleus leaned back staring into the fire. He hadn't seen either of his sons and his grandchildren since he'd come to live on the farm, now a few years ago. He couldn't get his son's angry look out of his mind, that day at Suri's funeral, as if he said, *you killed her.*

Never.

Never would Milleus have thought that Suri would take her own life. She seemed happy, even though they had slept in separate rooms for years. They had come to a silent agreement to make the marriage functional. He brought in the money—she took care of the family things.

That day when he had come home and found her on the couch, white and not breathing, felt like an absurd nightmare. At times, when he thought of Tiverius, he would think that he'd come back to his usual home, the Proctor's residence, and that Suri would be there waiting for him.

Why had she done it? Why?

Because he didn't care about her, the gossip went, because he ignored her.

It was untrue. He did care for Suri; he cared a lot. It was just that she didn't find she could return his care in the way he desired back then: by coming to his bed. She had always been afraid of intimacy, her mother had revealed. At the time, he'd been talking about retiring to a pleasant place in the country. He had sometimes wondered if that prospect frightened her too much. Sometimes she would shut herself in her room and wouldn't come out for a whole day, not even for dinner. She grew thin and gaunt.

These days, there was no use stewing over it. He'd gone over all these things so many times, he couldn't possibly add anything new to it. It happened, and it shouldn't have. He could possibly have helped, but he hadn't seen it coming. In any case, it could never be changed.

He heaved himself to his feet, bones creaking. Mercy, he was too old for all this hard work. Never mind the bowls. He'd wash them in the morning.

He banked the fire and shuffled out of the room. When he walked past the guest wing corridor, he heard a squeaking noise, like a door opening.

Oh, those youngsters weren't . . .

He went back into the kitchen, opened the door as quietly as he could and stalked into the garden. Mercy, it was cold tonight. Most unseasonable.

There's something going on in the south. Sady's words. He wished he'd questioned his brother more.

It was dark in the garden, with the newly weeded beds deep with dark soil that spilled over the top of his boots when he accidentally stepped in it.

Soft light radiated from the window of Suri's mother's room, gilding the tangle of bushes in the courtyard between the main house and the guest wing. Milleus clambered through the overgrown mess and glimpsed inside, feeling dreadful and sure that the kids would be looking back at him, jeering *ha, ha, gotcha!*

But both of them were much too . . . involved with each other to have taken note of any noise Milleus made. Firelight glowed over the pale skin of Isandor's back, half-covered by the sheet. Nila lay under him, legs apart, rocking her hips with each languid thrust, her eyes closed and mouth open in total bliss.

And images from the past rushed up at him.

"A whore?" Suri's eyes had burned with anger. "You went to see a whore?"

The word hurt.

"There were six of us, and she was a dancer. It's the custom in Arania. It's how men entertain important guests. Nothing happened." Entertaining, that was all he seemed to do since entering the doga.

"Milleus, how could you?"

"Suri, I swear, it was nothing. Not important." Not counting the urgency-filled moments he'd spent in the bed in the upstairs bedroom. Sorry, but sometimes he liked to be with a woman who enjoyed his touch, or had the grace to pretend.

He reached out and snaked an arm around Suri's waist.

"You will always be my princess."

A kiss, full on the lips. "Want to be my princess right now?"

She squirmed away. "Milleus, you're drunk."

"Yes, deliciously so."

He guided her down on the bed. She spread her legs willingly enough, and that was an improvement on last year, after she had just lost the baby, but she cried when he entered her.

He bit down a curse. "I won't do it anymore if it hurts you so much."

She said nothing—he knew how desperate she was for a child— but held her breath through much of the action when she lay under him, frozen, while he tried to do the job as quickly as possible.

There was nothing enjoyable about it. He had imagined things so differently.

So different from Isandor's relaxed movements. As if he had all night, and indeed he did. No wonder they had still been asleep this morning when he found them in Suri's mother's large bed, curled up against each other. They could do as they wanted. They were young, they were free and they were very much in love.

Milleus turned away from the window. Nothing he could do about it. If there was any damage, no doubt it had already been done. Who was he to say what the youngsters couldn't do? Were they going to listen to an old bitter man blathering on about marriage before intimacy? What was marriage worth anyway? The girl's parents had probably wanted to marry her off to some dirty old man with money, and she had chosen her lover without money instead.

Isandor worked hard. Nila had cleaned his entire kitchen and sitting room. They were honest, good kids. He'd feed them just as well in the morning, and if they were still here at the start of winter, he'd be standing by to help the girl give birth same as he did with his goats. There was no scandal in bringing into the world the next generation. Heavens knew this house could do with a pair of little feet.

Love was beautiful. There was far too little of it in the world. There had been far too little of it in his family.

He walked back through the garden, cold and alone, wiping a wet trail off his cheek.

If love is so beautiful, Milleus, why did you ignore all those who loved you?

Sady had been kind enough to think of him as someone worthy of support. Fifty signatures. And what had he done?

There was a soft noise, somewhere in the garden. Footsteps, heels on the paving of the garden path.

Someone stood at the front door, a dark shadow.

There was a hard knock on the door, one of those that made the door rattle in its frame.

"Who is there?" Milleus called out, his heart thudding in his chest.

A gasp. The figure turned. "Is that you, Milleus?" A familiar voice: his neighbour Andreus.

"Yes."

Milleus half-ran to the front door, trying to draw attention away from the light in the room across the courtyard, and the activity within. He might not mind it, but this was the country, and people in these parts were old-fashioned.

"I . . . I had to check on the goats," he said. "Wait. Come in."

Next thing he'd be accused of running a shameful house for fallen youngsters. People in the district talked enough about him already.

Into the kitchen. Milleus turned the wick on the oil lamp up. His hands trembled.

"Now what brings you here at this time of the day?"

His neighbour stood on the doorstep, eyes blazing. "Don't hide it any longer, Milleus. You've got them, don't you?" His gaze rested pointedly on the table and the three bowls from dinner.

"Got what?"

"Who, not what, and you know very well what I'm talking about. Those two people that creep on the bird was looking for."

"Mercy, man, what are you talking about?"

For a moment, the man faced him wordlessly, then he said, in a low voice. "This man on a giant bird came to my house. He didn't wear the uniform, but everything else about him said Eagle Knight. Frightened the wife and children. He said he was looking for some people in the district and said I was going to help him find them. I said I wasn't going to do nothing of the sort and that I knew nothing about no strangers in the district, and then he did this to me." He held out an arm, the skin blistered.

"A burn?" Milleus' skin crawled. He'd seen the bird, but it hadn't landed, and now he knew that had been because the rider had seen Sady approach.

Something going on in the south.

The man's eyes flashed. "A burn all right! He had no weapons, Milleus. Fire came from his hand like lightning. But that's not all. I went to the physic emergency practice to have it attended, but I wasn't allowed in the surgery because I set off the sonorics alarm. When the physic held the sonorics meter to me, it went right up into the red. I had to scrub naked and take decontamination tablets. This creep of a man uses sonorics rays, Milleus." He dropped his voice and held his hand to his mouth, and added, in a whisper, "As in the war. It's filthy foreign magic. And here you are: sheltering the people he's looking for. Why don't you just hand them over and let them get out of here? Let them sort their own filthy problems in the south."

"Why should I give refuge to criminals—"

"Milleus, for the sake of the district you proclaim to love, shut up. I know you're sheltering these people, because I don't, and my neighbours don't, and there isn't anyone else to hide them except you."

"They could hide in the forest for all I know."

"And you're feeding the forest three lots of dinner."

Point made.

Milleus sighed. "Can you tell me why you have suddenly become so keen to help a man who has crossed our borders illegally? He *says* the people he's looking for are criminal, but how do you know if that's true?"

The neighbour's eyes flashed. "You're a windbag, Milleus. You can say all these great noble words, but you know nothing of the struggle of the common people. You say these words, but who suffers for them? I don't care what the creep's squabble with those two people is. If we hold out, this man will bring friends and work his magic to harm us. Do you want that? Do you think this foreigner cares who you are? Some has-been member of the doga. He'll be long gone before anyone from Tiverius knows he's here. Give them up. Let him take his trouble home."

Milleus shook his head, while panic filled his chest. He had to protect Isandor and Nila and their young love. Find out who they were, sure enough, but criminals, they weren't. "They're innocent. They're only children."

"Give them up!"

"No."

"And I'm telling you you'll be sorry soon enough, and all of us will suffer for it."

"If that is a threat, you had better reconsider."

"Reconsider what? As far as I know, you're no longer Proctor and you have no power to threaten anyone. I thought, this morning when I heard the rumours that go around the district about you, that you had some guts, but now I see. Get with it, Milleus. You're an old man and no one listens to you."

Red anger flashed before Milleus' eyes.

"Go home, man, before I act on my lack of power to issue threats."

The man glared at him, then turned on his heel and stomped away to his waiting van.

Milleus stood in the doorway, breathing hard.

In his pocket, he clutched the letter. *Fifty signatures . . .*

Who was a powerless old man?

CHAPTER 15

NOLAN LANDED his bird next to Carro's on the dusty farm road. The eagle shook itself and folded its wings. Nolan slid off and gave Carro the knotted rope he used as reins. Carro took it from Nolan's hand. His skin briefly touched Carro's palm. Nolan looked up and met Carro's eyes.

Neither said anything. They knew the drill.

Nolan pushed open the creaky farm gate and crossed a vegetable yard to the door of the house. Such strange houses they had here, too. Walls made from stone blocks and straw roofs.

Burns well, Farey had said yesterday, and had proceeded to demonstrate with an old cranky farmer who wouldn't tell Farey if he'd seen the two fugitives. The farmer's family was hiding behind one of the windows in the house, and when Farey had taken off, he'd flown over the roof and dropped a burning torch.

Woof. The straw burned almost better than the ancient material that formed the roofs of many houses in the Outer City.

Farey laughed.

The old farmer and his family ran for shelter.

They'd frightened a few more families, and with each further house they came to, Carro was more afraid they'd find Isandor and Jevaithi. They had seen the riderless eagle. The beast had been too far away to recognise for certain, but it *could* have been Isandor's. The more he thought about it, the more sure he was that it *had* been Isandor's, because there were only a few wild eagles left, and the books said that in the mountains they didn't grow large enough to carry a man. That only happened under influence of icefire in the City of Glass.

So yes, they would likely find Isandor soon.

Isandor would recognise him, and would plead forgiveness or some such, and Carro didn't think he'd be able to look his former friend in the eye while Farey ran a knife through his heart. There were so many times that Isandor had helped him, or saved him . . .

Nolan knocked hard on the farmhouse door.

After the shoving back of bolts and creaking of hinges, a man opened, holding a sword.

In one movement, Nolan had his staff out and yanked the sword from the old man's hand. It flew through the air and clattered to the ground at Carro's feet.

Carro slid from the eagle, which looked at him as if it wanted to say *Is that all you can get me to eat?* Holding both sets of reins, he knelt and retrieved the sword. The weapon was old and blunt, of the type sometimes sold in the antique markets in the Outer City as having belonged to Chevakian soldiers during the Aranian war. The man was a veteran, clearly.

Meanwhile, the man was whimpering and Nolan shouting in Chevakian. The man was crying, shaking his head. A woman was crying, too.

By the skylights, shut up! Carro wanted to clamp his hands over his ears.

A gust of wind brought a chill.

And Carro's vision faded. He heard, not the cries of the peasants in the farmhouse, but those of fighting youths in the City of Glass. The streets were dark with gloomy pinpricks of light from the odd street lamp. He saw brief glimpses of burning houses and groups of people running through the snow. It had been the night Isandor and Jevaithi escaped.

He tried to banish the memory from his mind.

By the skylights, he thought he'd been cured of the damned affliction.

"Hey, Carro! Carro!" Nolan shouted.

Carro jolted back into full consciousness.

Nolan was running through the yard, pursued by a younger man carrying a powder gun. The peasant stopped, aimed, and there was a loud bang. Something whistled through the air. The eagles pulled on their reins, flapping huge wings over Carro's head. He was almost dragged up into the air.

Nolan flung himself over the fence, scrabbled up, swung himself on the eagle's back and kicked the bird into motion. Carro followed, heading into the icy breeze. Thick smoke billowed up behind him. He tried not to think of the farming family, and what Nolan did to them. Once, when he was young, he had seen his father mistreat his mother—

She was crying and yelling at him, while Carro, about six at the time, hid behind the door.

Carro sits on hands and knees on his sleeping shelf, looking down into the central room of the limpet.

His mother yells, "If you do this again, I will tell my family!"

To which his father responds, "And what do you think they are going do? Admit that their daughter is a selfish sea cow and take her back so she can continue to be a selfish sea cow?"

Carro sniggers, then covers his mouth with his hand, so they won't realise he's listening. It's so entertaining to hear his father yell at someone other than him.

His sister sits next to Carro; she's crying. Carro grins at her.

His mother yells, "My parents will demand to have back their loan. Don't you dare forget what makes you a successful merchant, whose money it is."

"I don't need your damn money, woman."

"No, you just need a sex slave."

Carro clung onto the reins, his hands sweaty.

He had been way too confident lately, had thought that because the visions were gone, he had been cured of them, but not so. Worse, the only thing that could help him, the ichina herb, was not available to him here and the hunters would cast him out if they found out he had an illness. They would tell his father. And his father would disown him, like everyone in his life had disowned him.

So he hung onto the saddle, and peered down to the forest, sweating and feeling sick. He must not give in to these visions. He must banish them.

The hunters' temporary camp was a clearing in the forest big enough for the eagles to land. In the morning, they had piled their camping gear at the base of a tree and put branches on top and covered the fire with dirt and sticks.

It still lay as they had left it; Farey and Jeito were still out.

They went to prepare the camp silently.

Nolan strode to a tree, unhooked a bag from a tree and tossed his bird half a sabre-wolf carcass with the same careless gesture as he had hunted, killed and cut up the animal yesterday. The eagle claimed its prey with a yellow claw. Carro's eagle got the other half of the beast, which Nolan threw with such force that it bounced over the ground and the eagle had to hop after it, only to find that its tether was too short. It gave an annoyed cry. Carro ran to shift the carcass before the bird decided to try chew through the tether. He glanced at Nolan while he did this, but Nolan looked the other way.

While Carro and Nolan relit the fire and uncovered the gear, the birds were ripping up their prey, snapping bones and crunching them in their beaks.

It was so silent that Carro could hear the wind rustle through the trees. Nolan was still not looking at Carro.

Finally, Carro couldn't stand it any longer. He said, "I did something wrong, didn't I?"

Nolan looked up. Oh, his eyes were furious.

"That guy almost killed me. I thought you were there on the lookout! Why didn't you warn me he had a gun?"

Carro had been dreaming, on the verge of getting another spell, but he couldn't say so. He had no medicine for it.

Carro shrugged. "Sorry. I was . . . looking the other way. Thought I saw something."

Nolan's hard stare met his. "I thought you'd look out for me. I thought you cared."

Carro shrugged. "Sorry," he said again.

Sorry was hardly appropriate, and he knew it. You could not say *sorry* so easily to someone who was in love with you. And Nolan was in love. He had said so many times while making love, but Carro hadn't worked out what he thought. Every time Nolan touched him in intimate places, he thought back to the abuse at the eyrie, and he felt the stone under his hands as he clawed at the wall to get away from the tormentors with their cock up his arse. Nolan didn't hurt him as much as the abusers had, and for a while, in the middle of it, he could enjoy the pure sensation. But later, he always wanted to wash the filth off. It was when he crouched near the creek, trying to clean the sticky stuff out of his hair down there, that he felt a seed of hatred grow deep inside him for the way men and women used sex to manipulate others.

He raised the water bladder to his mouth and drank deeply. Nolan was still looking at him, but Carro didn't return his gaze. By the skylights, wasn't it possible for any adult to have *friends* while keeping your clothes on? He finished the water and went to refill the bladder at the spring.

Here, away from the pile of saddlebags, their makeshift shelters and the firewood, the wind soughed through the pine trees. It was a lot colder than it had been yesterday, and the sky was white, rather than blue. Carro shivered. It seemed the cold had quietened the birds.

The grass rustled.

"No, you're not getting away from me that quickly."

He gasped. Nolan blocked his path.

"Looking the other way. That's rubbish and you know it. You haven't been the same all day. Is it because of something I said?"

Carro shrugged. "Back there, at the house . . . I wasn't thinking. We've done so many of these farm calls that I didn't expect the fellow to charge at you. I am sorry." He looked at the ground and felt all the thoughts he had inside seething at him. They were saying *come on, coward, do something.* "I'm probably not very good at saying it."

They were standing on the bank of a creek, and the grass here was green and kept short by animals that came in to graze at night. Farey would set his traps and catch the weirdest creatures. Things he called "hares" with soft fur and long ears and strong back legs with lots of muscle that was good to eat.

"Hey." Nolan reached out and touched Carro's arm.

Carro flinched.

"It's all right. The fellow gave me a fright, but I survived. You were dreaming. Come on, confess, what were you thinking about back there?" His eyes were playful.

"Er—nothing."

"You're sure?" Nolan's hand found its way under Carro's shirt. His fingers caressed the soft skin.

There was just no getting away from it.

When they returned to the camp in semidarkness, Jeito had returned. A fire blazed in the clearing and a cooking pot stood in the flames.

"Smells good," Nolan said.

Jeito raised one eyebrow. The light from the flames lit Farey's face; he stood near the eagles, grooming his bird, listening to every word they said.

Carro didn't know where to look. These men could see straight through him. Even though he had washed in the creek, he could still smell Nolan on his skin. He had no doubt Jeito would know what he and Nolan did at the creek.

Jeito was holding a map and scanning the campground they'd covered so far. Jeito's hair, tied back in a ponytail, flapped with a gust of wind that nearly tore the map out of his hands.

"Oh, fuck!"

Jeito knelt in the grass and spread the map out there, using stones to keep it in place. Not for the first time, Carro noticed Jeito's fine, long-fingered hands. In view of Nolan's clear Chevakian background and Farey's Aranian heritage, Jeito was an enigma. Small of build and southern in appearance, with a fine face, but ruthless with his dagger. Yet, Farey seemed protective of him. Carro got that they were lovers, and had been for a long time, but neither seemed to mind if the other strayed.

"You still think they're in the region?" Nolan said, all business, coming to stand behind Jeito.

When Jeito didn't reply, he continued, "One farmer said he'd been missing things from his garden. That one there . . . The farm with the goats and the big old house. There's tracks in the grain."

"An old man lives there," Farey said from under the trees. "He had a visitor last night. I think it was one of the neighbours, one of the ones we roughed up."

"They're warning each other, huh?" Nolan said.

"Not used to being spied on from the air."

The accuracy of these men was disturbing. Things they picked up he never would have. If Isandor and Jevaithi were in the area, they would surely be found. There were only a few farmhouses left that were yet unmarked by fire. What would Isandor say if he found his friend had been sent to hunt and kill him and the young Queen?

"I've spotted some soldiers on the road, over there." Carro pointed at the map, away from the unmarked farms.

Jeito looked over his shoulder, a hint of irritation flitting over his face. Did he sense the deliberate change of subject?

"I saw them, too," Nolan said. "There were four."

"Four is not an army." Jeito's voice had a *What do you know?* tone about it.

Nolan shook his head. "It's a spying unit. Or a special mission squad."

Jeito raised his eyebrows. "What would they be doing here?"

"Same thing we are?" Nolan said. "They were doing something strange. They had a long section of cloth which they spread on the forest floor. Then they took a crate of silver cylinders from their vehicle. There was a frame attached to it, and they attached the cloth to it. Then there was a burst of air and a flame, and a section of the cloth bulged. And a bit later, it had grown bigger."

"By the skylights, what was it?"

"I think . . ." Carro hesitated, remembering his books; he hadn't seen the thing, but he'd been too busy staying on the eagle. "I think that thing is going to fly. I think it was a balloon."

Nolan laughed. "That a balloon? It was huge and lumbering, and *slow.* Our eagles are much faster."

"They are, but they don't carry heavy weapons." He'd learned about balloons in his books, even though he had never seen one. "You know that Chevakia defeated Arania with an army of balloons?"

"They did not. You're just making things up. Chevakians would be too dumb to think of using things that fly."

"Actually, he's right," Farey said.

Silence was instant. Farey didn't speak much but when he did, everyone listened.

"The Chevakians had hundreds of balloons. In each balloon there were up to ten soldiers. The carried heavy weapons and vats of powder which they dropped on the ground. There were explosions everywhere, and fires, and people burnt to cinders. My father lost many of his cousins that way. The balloons are a great evil. Many people in Arania are still angry about it, and curse at the King who has gone weak and panders to Chevakia."

"But what are they doing here with that thing?"

A moment of silence followed. Wind whistled through the trees. The Chevakians might have had word that the Queen was gone. The Chevakians had all kinds of strange magical equipment to carry their messages.

"We need to warn the Knights."

"You don't think they already know?"

Jeito shrugged. "Question is: do we care if the Chevakians do our job for us?"

"Course we do." Nolan's voice sounded indignant. "No bodies, no payment. Leastways, not for me. Yeah, yeah, I know." He held up his hands. "I still care about getting myself some silver gulls so I can buy things in the City of Glass. I happen to like going back home every now and then."

Jeito scowled.

Carro felt sick. So that was the deal. He knew that the patrol was meant to return the bodies, and he had some idle hope to prevent the killing. They could always say that the remains were too badly burnt to return. But no, it seemed that wasn't going to please the Knights.

"Right, so let's keep an eye on these Chevakian scouts. They know the country better than we do."

He and Farey exchanged worried looks.

"Do you think it had anything to do with the flare we saw last night?" Nolan asked.

Jeito shrugged, but looked worried.

Farey said, with a glance at Carro, "It worries me that we haven't heard from the Supreme Rider, especially since you are with us. I'd have thought he'd be sending us gulls every day."

"How often does he normally contact you?" Carro asked.

"Once every few days," Farey said.

"Why don't we release a messenger gull?" Nolan asked.

"We haven't heard back from the first one yet. We only have one left, and none have come to replace it."

They all looked at the small cage hanging in a tree, holding a white bird with orange legs and a fierce beak.

Jeito shook his head and there was another silence.

"That never happens," Nolan explained to Carro. "Whatever Rider Cornatan thinks of us, he's normally good with his replies. He always sends gulls if we're out. He gives lots of instructions."

"Too many," Farey said, and then glanced uneasily at Carro. "Tends to meddle a lot, telling us how to do our jobs and all that. He says he used to be part of the raiding parties in Chevakia. He'd find the best women, claim them there and then, and take them to the City of Glass, letting the silly noble soft guys think they'd actually sired the children the women bore."

"Quit talking about that, will you?" Jeito said.

An uncomfortable silence fell. Like Nolan, it seemed Jeito had been one of those children. Did that mean Jeito was his half-brother?

"That's right. We were talking about sending out gulls," Nolan said.

Jeito said, "Not much good talking. I think we should send this one. Not much good sitting here yabbering about what might have happened when we have a chance of finding out."

Farey nodded. "Can't argue with that logic."

Jeito had taken a leather folder out of his saddlebag. When he folded it open, it revealed thin sheets of leather and a pen. He went to write a note with a cramped, childish hand. Carro spotted spelling mistakes, but he didn't dare point them out.

Meanwhile, Farey had retrieved the cage with a messenger gull. The bird hissed and pecked at Farey's hand when he inserted it in the cage, but he took it out without the loss of one feather. Jeito gave him the message, rolled up in a tiny cylinder. Farey tied it to the bird's foot and threw the bird up into the air. It gave a single undignified squawk and flew off into the dusk, leaving the hunters in silence.

The flames of the fire hissed. A chill wind made Carro shiver. Shadows trailed through his mind, of the merchant, and a dark cavernous warehouse, but he managed to hold the visions at bay. Not a sound came out of the forest, as if the world waited for a disaster to come.

They sat down and ate, all in silence.

If something had happened in the City of Glass . . . Was this war? Were they now marooned in hostile territory? Or was this just another of his father's silly tests?

CHAPTER 16

LORIANE AND THE family got up early the next morning, all of them miserable and with not much inclination to talk.

A dense mist had settled over the mountainside, dulling any sounds. Loriane kept looking up, expecting to see Eagle Knights searching, or expecting to see hordes of refugees bearing down the mountain, but seeing nothing in that dreadful forest. And she didn't know what was worse: fearing the refugees might come, or fearing they wouldn't come, meaning that everyone up there had been killed.

There were sounds she could not identify. Something was up there, just behind them. She knew they were being followed and sooner rather than later this thing, or these people, would catch up. And it scared her, not being able to see any further than those infernal *trees* all around them.

At first light, Ontane had stoked the fire, and now Dara had put on a blackened pot of water in which she had tossed a couple of handfuls of dried meat.

Branches cracked and Ruko came from the forest with a bloodied animal of sorts. He sat down at the fireside and effortlessly tore a hind leg off the creature and ripped the skin off with his teeth. Blood ran down his chin.

Myra whimpered, looking up from feeding the baby. "That's disgusting."

"He's likely lived like an animal the last few years," Ontane said. "He don't know any better."

"He could be considerate and do it somewhere else," Dara said, giving Ruko a harsh glare.

Ruko ignored her. Loriane wasn't sure if he heard anything at all. Sometimes she thought he did, and sometimes she thought she didn't. If his transformation meant that he was now free, he seemed to be more protective of Tandor.

Dara kept urging, "Ontane, ye must do something about him."

"What do ye want me to do, woman? Ye know he hears us. Ye know he doesn't listen except when it suits him. Ye know I didn't invite him along, and ye know that if he hadn't come, we'd never got the cart down here, over those rocks."

"I wanted no sorcerers with us."

"Jus' shut yer complaining for a change."

Dara rolled her eyes at her husband. She ladled out jelly, a thick, gloppy substance congealed from the extract of the salted meat. It had a stale, rancid smell that made Loriane's stomach churn.

Myra pulled a face at her bowl. "This is like cement."

Dara snapped at her. "Ye be the cook next time, and if it still be too thick, ye can go piss in it."

Loriane was so weary of this family's bickering. She wanted to be alone.

For all the jelly's stickiness, it allowed Loriane to pick up little clumps of grain and shove them between Tandor's cracked and scabbed lips, under Ruko's suspicious glare. Earlier on, he'd tried to feed Tandor pieces of the raw meat, torn off with his teeth, but Tandor refused to eat them.

He seemed a little better; at least, he swallowed the tiny mouthfuls. At times he opened his eyes a sliver. He mumbled a bit, but even when Loriane held her ear to his mouth, she couldn't make out what he said. She didn't think his physical injuries still stopped him speaking. His wounds had scabbed over and, although ugly, they were not life-threatening. His breath still smelled sweet with icefire.

By the skylights, Tandor, wake up and stop this charade.

She met Ruko's eyes, deep black and hollow. His pale face never showed any emotion, but just the look of it made her shiver. Whenever someone came close to Tandor, he would watch. Sometimes she wondered: did Tandor control him or did he control Tandor?

Loriane ate some jelly, too, but spewed it back out moments later. Myra saw her, and looked concerned. Yes, Loriane knew. She was weakening. If this went on for long, she wouldn't have the strength for the birth. With every moment that passed, the child grew bigger; eventually the head would be too large to fit through her birth canal, and when she couldn't pass it, she would have to ask Myra to use Tandor's knife and cut the child up inside her and bring it out in pieces. She had done that a number of times over the years, and only three of those women had survived. And that was when the thing was done by her with all her experience, in the clean surroundings of the palace, and not by a young girl on a dirty forest floor.

They went on. Packed up, tied their belongings to the cart pulled by the camel and descended further down the hill.

Ruko went first, leading the camel, limping on his wooden leg. He stayed with Tandor, attending every step, and wouldn't let anyone near.

Ontane and Dara came next, with Ontane walking next to the cart, and Myra and Loriane made up the rear.

Ontane and Dara's voices carried in the still forest.

"Ye be wrong, woman! I'm not sure what I heard last night, but there be people higher up the mountain. All those poor buggers camping in town be following us."

"That's why we must leave the road. If we go into the forest now, there be a path that goes up from here to the shack—"

"Dang it, woman, don't ye *feel* it? There be icefire all around us. I don't know what happened, but something happened and I'm not going to hang around here to find out."

"We hide and the people will pass."

"And where do ye think *they* be going? They be fleeing the icefire. Nah, I won't stop until we be safe on the other side of the border. I feel it in my bones."

"You remember what happened last time we went into Chevakia?"

"That be twenty years ago. It be different now."

"It bain't. They be the same people. The old folk will remember the raid by the Eagle Knights. They still hate us."

"I say things be different now. Shut up, woman."

"No, because ye be wrong. We go to the hunting lodge, wait until they pass and go back home. There be nothing in Chevakia for us. I don't want to go there."

On and on they went. Loriane closed herself off from their voices, but caught Myra rolling her eyes.

"Are they always like this?"

"Yes, pretty much. Da likes bossing people about, and Ma doesn't like to be bossed about, so whatever he says, she never agrees. He just likes arguing. Are you . . . you're not married, aren't you?"

"As a breeder?" Loriane gave a hollow chuckle. "I have far too many men wanting to use my services."

"Doesn't it ever hurt . . . you know . . . giving away the child that you suffered for? Don't you ever wonder where all those children are? I couldn't imagine giving him up . . ." Her voice cracked and she patted little Beido on the back.

Loriane saw the baby boy in her arms. She saw him suckling at her breast. Felt the despair when a nurse in the palace birthing room had torn him from her arms to give him to some merchant. Since the boy had been born to an Eagle Knight, he would not even have had the joy of living with his natural father. Isandor was . . . not a replacement, but his presence and needs as a child had comforted her. After that first time, it had become easier.

She shrugged. "That's the way it's done in the City of Glass." But she hated how her voice sounded unsteady.

"Whose child is this?"

The path widened and Myra could now walk next to Loriane. The rest of the group was quite a way ahead.

Loriane hesitated. It would be so easy to say *Yanko* but ultimately it wasn't true, and she wanted answers. The time for lies was past. Yanko was probably dead, and her contract with him would never go ahead.

She said, in a low voice, "I don't know."

Myra frowned. "What do you mean? How can you not know? This man is paying for it, isn't he?"

"Well . . ." Loriane hesitated again. "Yes, he's paying." She blew out a breath. "But he's not the father of the child."

Myra's frown deepened. "You were with another man—"

"No, it's nothing like that, because otherwise, if I'd cheated, I'd keep that a secret. I'm not like that. I wouldn't give a man a child that's not his. The truth is, I wasn't with a man for some time before I made the contract, but I was already expecting when I signed it. The only man who came to my house in that time was Tandor. Yes, Tandor sleeps in my bed, and he gives me pleasure. But you know how he is. Damaged."

Myra nodded.

"There is no way Tandor can father a child. Yet, there is no other man I've touched."

"What about any of your patients?"

Loriane shook her head. They were all female anyway.

"Or the apprentice Knight you cared for?"

Isandor? "I would never do such a thing. He's my—" No, Isandor wasn't her son; he wasn't even closely related in blood. Isandor was purest Thillei, and she . . . Tandor had often told her that he was attracted to her because of her pure Pirosian heritage. "I raised him. He's as close to a son as I'll have."

And then she felt chilled. She had never considered Isandor. He hadn't touched her; just the thought revolted her; he was her son, even if only in mind. But such thoughts, of course, did not worry Tandor, and it might well be . . . after all, you did not need to sleep with a man to become pregnant; you only needed his seed, and Tandor always liked to rub her with salves and concoctions which he said he'd bought on his travels.

Slowly, the group made its way down the wet and muddy mountainside.

Fortunately, it had stopped raining and the path was less slippery. It was warmer here, too.

The ground became less steep, and the path wider and less rocky. But the walls of green forest unsettled Loriane, though they offered her handy spots for a pee. The trees made unfamiliar noises in the wind, and there were animals, too, moving in the foliage. She didn't like the idea of animals moving, out of sight.

Myra walked next to her, but since the path was less steep, she needed no assistance. Walking wasn't any less of a struggle, though. She was one big hurt. Her back hurt, her legs hurt.

Myra said little and patted the infant. Like all children born with a lot of weight on them, he was a good baby, asleep most of the time with the rocking of his mother's body, and drinking greedily from her breast at stops. Loriane found it hard to watch the bond between Myra and her son. Out of her children, she had only fed two or three and then only once, after birth. Isandor was the only child she had cradled against her stomach, watching him fall asleep with the nipple in his mouth.

There, she was thinking about Isandor again. *I hope the boy made it out alive.* Her stomach stabbed at the thought.

At about midday, they came out of the forest into a field of green. Sunlight peeked out from between the clouds, and Loraine couldn't get over the amount of colour in the landscape. The grass was so green it almost hurt her eyes. Flowers, which were a delicate rarity in the City of Glass, grew by the side of the road. Animals, not ones she recognised, buried their noses in the greenery, chomping on bits of grass. Their coats were outrageously orange-brown with large blotches of white. They had big wet, pink noses and sometimes one would curl its tongue in to one of the nostrils.

Loriane couldn't have imagined a place like this. Her world, her memories and imagination were white. They passed through forest, and then a few more fields. Some with animals, some with waving vegetation. Grain crops, Myra said. Sheep. Goats. So many new things she couldn't name. For a while, Loriane almost forgot her discomfort. She looked around and marvelled at this strange, intensely coloured world.

Then she became aware that Myra hadn't said anything for a while, and no longer answered her questions. An eerie dense silence had settled over the land. The birds were quiet; the breeze had stopped.

"Myra?"

The girl walked next to Loriane, her eyes hollow.

"Myra, what's going on?"

"Don't you hear it?" Myra's voice sounded haunted.

Loriane listened. If she was very quiet, she could just make out a low hum.

"You mean that noise? What is it?"

"It's horrible," Myra whispered. "It's crying."

Loriane felt chilled. "Is that the thing following us?" She thought people were following them, somewhere higher up the hillside. Refugees.

"Make it stop," Myra cried, clapping her hands over her ears. "Please, make it stop."

"Where is it coming from?"

"I don't know, just make it stop."

Loriane cast a panicked glance ahead, but Myra's parents were out of hearing, although Ruko and the camel had stopped as well.

"Come." She dragged Myra ahead until she came to where Ontane and Dara stood.

"What's going on?"

The sound was much stronger here, not just a low hum but a high-pitched keening.

Ontane pointed. "He be frozen to the ground."

Ruko stood stiff like he'd turned into stone. His eyes wide, muscles straining, staring ahead.

Loriane looked.

Up ahead loomed a thing like she had never seen before. Across the road stretched a row made of huge sheets of metal, each larger than a house. Their mirror-like sides reminded Loriane of the windows in the buildings in the City of Glass. These metal sheets didn't touch each other, but each had been placed upright on a pedestal and set at an angle like shading lamellae. There were hundreds of these things placed in an overlapping pattern, cutting through the forest as far on either side as Loriane could see. The metal plates were taller than trees, and seen from a distance, the air around them shimmered.

"What is that thing?" Loriane whispered.

"That thing be the reason my husband turns to jelly each time he comes here. He be a coward. You feel anything?" It was a challenge, not a simple question, the way Dara turned everything into a black-or-white statement.

"If it's something to do with icefire, people *do* feel it differently." It did have something to do with icefire, because otherwise Ruko wouldn't react to it. Out of all of them, he was probably the most sensitive.

"Pfa," Dara snorted.

"The barrier is singing," Ontane said. His voice had an ominous tone.

Myra's face was hollow. She clamped her arms round herself and shivered visibly. She had stopped in the middle of the road. Her baby cried, but she paid it no attention.

"Myra?" Loriane shook her. Her skin was hot, like she was running a fever.

"It's bad," the girl whispered, staring at the metal wall.

"Bad? How can a—" A dreadful howl interrupted her.

Tandor's face was drawn in a snarl, mad and wide-eyed. Ruko had a hard job trying to keep him restrained.

"Tandor!" She ran to the camel. "Stop it. Tandor, listen to me."

He was having some sort of fit, his eyes rolling. He screamed unintelligible words, kicked out, almost hitting her in the face.

"Stay away." Myra pulled her aside. "He can't hear you. He'll only hurt you."

"What is this horrid thing?"

"The barrier is singing. It hurts."

"But it's just . . . a wall of metal." Thick metal sheets, she could see that now they were closer.

"We have to pass," Ontane whispered, looking over his shoulder. "I know this thing can't hurt us, but—"

Ruko let go of the camel and bashed full-speed into Ontane. They both fell to the ground. Ruko was screaming unintelligible sounds, the first sounds Loriane had heard him make, and Ontane was yelling at him to stop.

"Help! Get him off me, woman!"

Dara took the cooking ladle from the crate at the top of the cart and hit Ruko over the head with it. Ruko crumpled.

"There," she said, her voice full of satisfaction. "That suits him."

Ontane scrambled up. He picked up Ruko, bundled him into the cart and lashed Tandor more securely in the saddle. Dara's face was set like cement. Myra stared ahead, as if she had to do her best to concentrate.

Ontane asked, "Mistress Loriane, do you feel the pain?"

"Not me, but then I can't see icefire even in the City of Glass."

"Good. Lead the camel. Whatever any of us tell you from now on, ignore it, no matter how we scream. Here . . ." He held out a cloth strap. "Tie me to the cart. Myra too."

Loriane did as he asked. Dara refused to be tied and looked at Loriane with suspicious eyes. Her face looked white, though, and when the caravan set in motion, she clutched her husband's arm.

Slowly, they inched towards the sheets of metal. The camel was snorting and tossing its head. It almost yanked the rope out of Loriane's hand.

"Hold it!" someone shouted, and recognised that voice.

"Tandor!"

His eyes had lost the dreamy look and met hers squarely. But pearls of sweat beaded on his forehead.

"Loriane, don't cross this thing. Don't run. Don't—"

His voice spilled over into a scream, hoarse and haunted. Loriane didn't understand a word of what he was saying. Rumours went that in their subconscious, when they were sick or losing their mind, people always returned to the language they grew up speaking. Tandor had grown up in Tiverius. Loriane tried to close herself off from his screams. Tandor was the most fiercely southern man she knew. He hated Chevakia. She didn't want to know that in his nightmares he spoke Chevakian.

Keep going, keep going.

Tandor kicked and screamed. Ontane starting mumbling, his eyes closed. Myra was pulling at the strap that tied her to the cart.

"Let me go. Let me go." Her voice sounded like a shriek.

Loriane kept walking, hoping that the camel would continue to follow. If the beast decided to bolt, she couldn't stop it.

The keening sound grew so loud it hurt her ears. The barrier loomed up ever closer, the sheets of metal towering over her.

"Hurry up, you stupid bitch!" Dara shouted. "They're all going crazy, don't you see?"

By the skylights, even Dara was affected.

What if they all decided to bolt at the same time, or attack her, or whatever it was this dreadful noise made them do.

Stop it, stop it, stop it. She repeated the words with each step, drowning out the shouting.

The sun came out and large shadows of the wall's segments fell over the road. They passed into such a shadow, and then between the metal shields.

On the other side, the sound level dropped quickly, and soon the air became calm. Dara stopped shouting, and then Ontane and Myra, until only Tandor still mumbled. When even he had stopped, Loriane halted and untied Ontane and Myra's hands. They both looked pale like ghosts and neither said anything. Tandor had slid sideways in the saddle. Ruko on the cart was still out cold.

Ontane sank in the grass, his face sheened with sweat

Loriane slipped off her cloak and wiped her forehead. Phew. How could a couple of plates of metal have such an effect on people?

She breathed deeply, sucking her lungs full of sweet air, and then became aware that Myra was staring at her.

"Myra?"

"There is no icefire here. None at all."

CHAPTER 17

I N THE YELLOW-ORANGE light inside the tent, General Finnisius put the map on the table. Sady pushed himself to the edge of the chair so that he could see. The map showed the border regions, from the gentle hills of Ensar, east, to the rough country of Mekta and the rich agricultural region of Fairlight, with the southern platform at the bottom of the paper. The barrier was drawn as a thick black line interrupted only in the most mountainous terrain at the back of the little pocket of civilisation that was Solmeni. It also showed the telegraph line, of which Sady understood some poles had been uprooted by bad weather and that was why Fairlight wouldn't come on the line. Fixing the problem was taking a little longer than he had hoped.

General Finnisius pulled the map so it faced Sady. "If there is going to be a southern attack, we are likely to see birds here, and here." He jabbed his finger at the main railway at Fairlight, and the gently sloping road at Ensar. "As you can see, these are all strategic points where roads and railways provide access to the southern platform to quickly move an army on foot. We have already seen an increase in the number of scout birds reported in the Ensar region."

Sady nodded. Milleus had even mentioned seeing a bird. He should have asked about it when he was there, even though Milleus had said that the bird was without a rider.

"We are as prepared as we can be, without going into full preparation for war. We have balloons ready to counter their eagles. We have nets to protect the balloons from claws and beaks. We have light-weight armour and shields to protect the balloon crew against their crossbows. But one thing I can tell you, Proctor: a skilled Eagle Knight is a deadly weapon. They're quick, frightfully accurate and some of those birds are big enough to wear armour."

Sady nodded while stifling a yawn. Not that he was bored, but he was so incredibly tired. It was cold in the army command tent, and he felt fearfully underprepared for a discussion about military strategy. Milleus knew all about military, having served himself. But Sady . . . he had spent two days going through the doga's financial mess to find money to pay creditors, a mess that was worse than he had expected. Much worse.

"Are we prepared for any weapons they might use?"

"They use crossbows. They also use poison darts, but their range is very much smaller than that of our powder guns. On the ground, they use crossbows and daggers. Those are the weapons we know about."

"Do we need to worry about the ones we don't?"

The general hesitated. "I don't know how much I should mention about this, certainly not to the troops. The southerners are rumoured to have sonorics weapons. They would gather sonorics and somehow shape or bend it into a single destructive beam. But I cannot find anyone who could verify the existence of this kind of weapon. I don't know if the current rise in sonorics has anything to do with it."

The most recent measurement they had was fifty-nine motes per cube at Ensar, but Ensar was further from the border than Fairlight, and Sady feared what he would hear when the line to Fairlight had been restored.

"Do you think . . ." Sady swallowed. "Do you think they're increasing sonorics *in order* to use in attack? Maybe they are trying to break the barrier?"

"I'd like to think not. They've always wanted either food or women, and they're not going to get either of those if they kill us. Besides . . . apart from the border raids, which weren't particularly well-planned strategically, they have never shown any sign of aggression."

"Are there signs that they've established a base in Chevakia?" Sady had received some terse notes from the Lady Armaine to come and see him about unknown southerners in the city, claims which he had been unable to verify, and hadn't had time to chase up.

General Finnisius shook his head. He took a deep breath as if preparing to dive.

"Just between you and me, Proctor, I'm having some difficulty with this situation. A threat may or may not come, but we don't know what shape it will take. My men can prepare for battle, and we're doing our best, but I don't know how we can prepare for an enemy we cannot see. I'm afraid you may need to call in the assistance of people with different skills than mine. Pure military manoeuvring isn't going to solve this."

Sady nodded. "I'm in contact with Alius. We will start distributing his new medicines soon."

Or, more accurately, Alius had better turn up with his wonder medicines. He hadn't had time to chase that up either.

The general stared at the map, chewing his lip for a bit and then he said, "To be honest with you, Proctor, some of the men are scared and there is a fair amount of unrest in the ranks. I cannot, with a clear conscience, send my troops to be the front line of this emergency when I don't know how to prepare them. The men have accepted that to sign up involves risk, but if I ask them to deal with something that looks like *magic*, I'm afraid that there may well be problems."

He met Sady's eyes squarely when he said that, and Sady felt a chill. *Magic.* For years, the Scriptorium had tried to stamp out that word. There was no such thing, they said; everything could be explained, measured and calculated. They thought they understood everything. Their calculations had worked. The barriers had protected the country. But that said, the common people of Chevakia never really *understood* sonorics, and there were those who still called it magic. Those who couldn't afford education and sent their sons to serve in the army.

The warning look in Finnisius' eyes said, *Give me something to tell my men or we'll risk mutiny.*

"I have no reason whatsoever to ask any of our soldiers to enter southern lands," Sady said.

Finnisius nodded.

"I will not ask soldiers to do anything except defend Chevakia."

Finnisius nodded again. "And this medicine? The men have heard the rumours about it."

"The army will get first priority when it becomes available. I will get that distributed to the troops as soon as possible."

Finnisius nodded again. He still seemed to be waiting for more. What else would he want to hear? "Any other problems?"

"Well—I hate to raise this with you at a difficult time, but some of my men have not received their monthly stipend."

Mercy. What was going on? "I will look into it as soon as I get back. The men who defend the country are our utmost priority."

Finnisius breathed out audibly. Were those the words he'd wanted to hear?

What a mess. He hoped that Alius was getting close to providing those magic pills, or there would be real trouble.

He stared at the map and the regions where soldiers might soon have to fight. Declare war. That was his power. Get the people out first. He was glad he'd sent those trains to Fairlight.

"All right, General. I will leave you to your work."

The general bowed and Sady left the tent in company of Orsan and two of the Proctor's guard.

Outside, a cold wind whipped his hair to one side. Sady pulled the sides of his cloak closer around him, and walked back through the camp, past the balloons flapping at their tethers, gusts of wind howling through ropes and loud bursts of fire spewing from burners.

Soldiers greeted him, full of cheer, but he felt uneasy. He hated being unable to give these good men the assurance that they would not be fighting "magic". He had no idea what was happening, other than that, whatever it was, Chevakia was ill-prepared for it, and he was ill-prepared to be their leader.

The camp lay on one of the hills that surrounded the capital, and from here, he could see across the valley. Low grey clouds scudded across the sky, brushing the tops of the ranges on the northern side of the city. In the valley, a grey kind of dust called ghostcloud shrouded the buildings in a soft light. Ghostcloud happened during dry spells in winter, when strong pressure gradients drew winds from the north, and dust from northern deserts fouled the air.

The difference was that it was summer, and that the wind was from the south. There should not be this much haze.

People waited at the entrance to the doga building to see him. Accountants carrying thick books—

He'd have to get to the bottom of the financial problem as soon as possible. It was clear that this budget crisis had been going on for quite some time. No wonder he hadn't been able to get money to travel to the Ensar region; the doga survived by shuffling debt from one account to another; there *was* no spare money.

But first, he went to see Viki, in his old office. It was disturbing how quickly places didn't feel like they were his anymore. Viki had dragged the desk closer to the window so that he could put a large drafting table in the room, and both this table and the desk were full of barygraph readouts and maps, strewn about in disorderly fashion. Some were even on the floor, with indication that they had been there for a while, judging by the dusty footsteps on them.

Viki sat at the drafting table, crunching up his face in concentration while drawing a map. Rolls of paper lay around him and spilled over the edges of the table. Mercy, what a mess.

"Have you seen the increase in ghostcloud?"

Viki looked up briefly before returning to his work. "What do you think I'm doing here?"

Seriously, did everyone have to snap at him these days?

Sady walked to the table and looked over Viki's shoulder. He was drawing an air pressure map, which displayed a large low-pressure cell with closely spaced pressure lines on its eastern side.

"Is that Fairlight?" Sady pointed at the end of a solid straight line, very close to the high-gradient area.

Viki nodded and kept drawing.

So that was where the telegraph poles had blown over.

The winds at the weather front would be southeast, bringing air from the slopes that led up to the platform. Agricultural areas and forest.

"Why the ghostcloud?"

"It's not ghostcloud," Viki said. "There are fires on the slopes to the southern platform. It's smoke."

"*That* many fires that the smoke travels all the way over here?"

Viki spread his hands and met Sady's eyes with an expression of exasperation. "Why does everyone expect me to have the answers?"

Because you're the meteorologist. Having answers is your job, even if you don't. "What about sonorics?"

"Sixty in Ensar, forty-six in Solmeni, nineteen in Twin Bridges."

"Twin Bridges?" That was halfway between the capital and Fairlight.

"That's what I said." He kept drawing.

Filled with worry, Sady went to his office, where he had to wrestle past a long line of people queuing up to see him.

All Chevakian citizens had the right to request an audience with the Proctor, and the queue was more or less a permanent fixture, so that there was even a food vendor allowed to come into the building to sell his wares to those waiting.

In the past, Sady had never taken much notice of those people and what their reasons and demands for speaking with the Proctor were. Back then, he'd known that it wasn't his business and that someone would deal with it. Now that someone was him.

As soon as the people saw him coming, they started yelling.

"Please see me first. I've been waiting for a long time and have small children at home."

"I was here first! The farmers of the city ring need your intervention."

"Proctor, please—"

"But I've come all the way from Solmeni to ask for help with my children's strange illness. Please, I don't know where else to go."

What? Solmeni was in a dead-end pocket of land to the east of Fairlight. Surrounded by the southern cliffs and forest. A railway track went into the town, but the line stopped there.

Sady turned around and looked at the woman. She was thin, wore the long-sleeved garment and colourful head scarf of the type often worn by farming women, adorned with beads made from seeds. Her skin was tanned and wrinkled from having spent much time outside.

Everyone in the queue took the fact that he had stopped as a sign to start yelling more loudly.

"Please, Proctor, see me first."

"No, me. I was here first."

"I have nowhere to sleep. The landlord has kicked me out."

Sady turned to the last speaker, a middle-aged man. "In that case, you'll be better off going to see the housing office." He gestured to the peasant woman. "If you could come with me, please."

"But I was here first! Proctor . . ."

Sady strode into his office, avoiding the protester's gaze, feeling awful and guilty.

A week ago, he would have promised to see all these people, and he would have questioned why Destran didn't do so. Now he knew there wasn't enough time in the day, and that the queue never stopped, no matter how many of them he saw. And that there would always be more people to go back home disappointed.

He shut the door after the woman had entered his office.

"Sit down." He cringed at the mess: the financial books in big tottering piles. Pencils and pencil shavings everywhere.

The woman took the big leather seat opposite his, folding her hands between her knees. Eyes wide, she looked around the office.

"So you've come all the way from Solmeni."

She nodded. "I got a lift with a travelling merchant to Twin Bridges and then got the train from there."

"How long did that take you?"

"Three days."

"Do you know anything about what's going on in Fairlight?"

"Not Fairlight. That's a long way from us."

Not that far, when seen from here, but never mind. "So tell me about your children?"

"Not just mine, but a lot in the school as well. They have been sick to the stomach, sir. Especially the little ones, and all red around the eyes. I took a bundle of them to the clinic in Twin Bridges—that's why I rode with the merchant—but the medic wouldn't see them and won't come back with me. So I got angry and said as physic he has to see them, right?"

Sady nodded. That was part of the physic's pledge, to see every person in need.

"I said they were the town's children. Our future, you know. And he still wouldn't see them. I asked him why and he used a lot of big words—like I never learned. We teach things the kids can *use* at school, not filling their heads with big words, and I asked him to explain, but the physic couldn't make any sense. So I said I'd go and complain. And he said feel free, but I don't think he really believed I would do that. But I did and here I am."

"I am glad that you did."

She smiled a brown-toothed smile.

"Are there any other people in the area with the same illness? Adults?" Why hadn't he heard about this before?

"Not that I've heard, Proctor, but then again, most are in the farms away from the town. Like ours. My man said he liked the hill so he built the house there. You should see the view—"

"Could any adults be sick at home?"

"Could be, why are you asking? All I want is the physic seeing the little ones."

"And he will." Sady slid a sheet of official paper across the desk and wrote a note reminding the clinic of their obligation. As he signed his name, he figured that over there in Solmeni, many people wouldn't even know that the leadership had changed.

He rolled the paper up and handed it to the woman. "I'm going to send someone back with you."

She stared at him. "But that's not necessary, Proctor, much as I appreciate it. Just signing an order for the physic to treat the little ones will be enough. I thank you for that. I know that you and your people are busy and all that—"

Sady rang a bell, and a moment later Orsan came in. In a few quick words, Sady explained that he wanted a small team to return with the woman.

"I want them to take sonorics measurements—and suits," he whispered. "If there's any spare carriages, make sure they get hooked up to the train."

Orsan's eyes widened; he understood. He nodded and, with a quick salute, was out the door.

Mercy. Solmeni was well within the borders. First Fairlight and now this.

What if this evil came to Tiverius? What if the barriers failed? What were they facing?

CHAPTER 18

MILLEUS SLID the truck into neutral and let it coast until the tyres hit the kerb in front of the Town Hall. He glared at the building's facade with its pompous columns. The gentle rolling hills of the town stretched out behind it, with their sprawling timber houses, but the main street was a neat row of solid stone buildings in a mockery of a streetscape in Tiverius. Somehow, it looked even less like anything in the capital. These monstrosities, built from funds squandered by Destran, were all fake.

Mercy, he always grew cranky if he had to go shopping.

But with the youngsters on the farm, he needed decent food, and this morning his second pair of work trousers had come apart and he didn't know how to fix them. He'd grown tired of asking Andreus' grumpy wife and didn't want to ask her after having rebuffed her husband the previous night—she didn't do that good a job anyway. And he didn't want to ask Nila—she was doing so much already and he wasn't sure if she had sewing skills—so he was going to ask the tailor in town. He was, after all, not a pauper.

And that meant shopping.

Despite the pompous façade of the Town Hall, council positions didn't occupy office bearers full-time, so the tailor doubled as the town's mayor, and a visit to have trousers fixed had a second purpose, as everything does in politics. Milleus wanted to know if the southerner the neighbour had mentioned had been elsewhere in town and what the local authorities were doing about it. There was a small army unit stationed at Ensar, and he'd like to know if they had been called or had asked for reinforcements.

Southern Eagle Knights on the loose in Chevakia. If that was true, it was a clear violation of the border agreement. Why wasn't the district swarming with army units? Oh yeah, they were probably still waiting for their supplies.

Mercy, he had sworn never to look into politics again, leave the whole lot to stew in their own mess, but what if the doga just didn't *know*, through collective bureaucracy and incompetence, that there were southern spies foraging around? In his day, they would call in the ambassador, but apparently no one had thought to reappoint an ambassador after the anger over the kidnappings of girls by the Eagle Knights had abated.

Yet he knew there were several southerners in the city. They called themselves merchants, but everyone knew they were spies. If nothing else, he remembered that the lady Armaine had been a gathering point for southerners and their sympathisers in the city. They would certainly know what was going on in the City of Glass. Why didn't the doga—

Pfa, he should stop worrying.

He opened the van's door—it creaked—and slid out of the cabin. His trousers, a sorry bundle of cloth, lay on the bench next to him. He tucked them under his arm, shut the door and crossed the street to the tailor's shop, opened the door, stepped inside . . .

A siren wailed. A high-pitched scream that made him want to clamp his hands over his ears. He stopped, frozen, on the doormat, while the door blew shut after him.

The shop's sonorics alarm.

Milleus just stood there, his heart thudding, like a little boy caught snooping in the pantry.

The alarm quietened. There were yells and shouts inside the shop. Shufflings and clangings. A few moments later, someone burst into the shop through a back door, wearing a full protective suit. Stopped.

"Milleus?"

The voice was that of the tailor, muffled inside the suit.

"Yes, I wanted to have a pair of trousers fixed, but . . ." Milleus stared at his own reflection in the suit's helmet visor.

The tailor walked around Milleus, passing the sonorics meter over his farm clothes. The needle jumped on the dial. Not very high, but it definitely moved.

"Where have you been?" the tailor asked inside the suit.

"Just the farm." Milleus' heart was still thudding.

Andreus had said that something like this had happened to him, but he'd been visited by the mysterious Knights, and attacked. Wait— he had shown Milleus a burn. And where would a burn come from other than some sort of sonorics-based weapon? That wasn't supposed to work this side of the barrier.

He asked, "When have you last checked the sonorics readouts?"

Every day, the meteorology officer drove up to the shack not far from the back of Milleus' farm to read the sonorics levels, which he then telegraphed to Tiverius, and Sady.

Milleus couldn't see the tailor's reaction in the suit, but the man opened a drawer behind the shop counter and drew out a set of hand-written measurements. There was also a sheet of graph paper. He'd seen Sady's work often enough to know how to read it. The highest level of sonorics was sixty-nine motes per cube. Twenty was considered dangerous; fifty was the lowest all-clear level for the barrier. No one knew at what level it would break, but it would do so explosively.

"Look at this." Milleus pointed at the end of the graph, where the squiggly line rose towards the top margin of the paper. The needle on the sonorics meter which lay on the bench jumped when his hand passed it. So much else made sense. The unseasonably cold wind, for one.

"You reported this?"

"All sent to Tiverius," the tailor said.

"Has there been a reaction?" Mercy, why hadn't there been any advice from the capital? "Why are there no warnings up in the street? Why is no one doing anything? Has the army post been notified? Where are the emergency suits?"

The man took a step back. "What do you mean? We were following our normal procedures . . ."

"Even with figures like this?" Milleus gestured at the paper. The needle on the dial jumped as his arm passed. "Someone needs to go and check the barrier. I don't understand why that hasn't already happened. Hasn't the doga's chief meteorologist been here to tell you that sonorics were rising without explanation? And you didn't think to warn anyone to limit time spent outside? You should have rung the bell."

"We discussed it in the council. Tiverius said not to worry, so we didn't. We didn't want panic—"

"No, instead you'll have panic now. You could have started an evacuation before panic hit. Oh—wait—you haven't enough passenger trains available, and the suits are still in storage in Ensar, waiting for authorities to approve their transfer. And half the local army unit is on leave to attend the northern ballooning competition."

The man took a further step back. "Now, wait, Milleus, you can't go accusing—"

"It's true, though, isn't it? You haven't done anything, because the district hasn't the resources and because the politicians are sitting on their comfortable arses pushing documents from one side of their desks to another. They're passing the problem off to someone else, and meanwhile nothing happens. You value your political career over the safety of the people."

"But Milleus, tell me what we could have—"

"What you could have done, with no money? Watch me."

Milleus turned on his heel and strode back out the shop. The alarm started wailing again.

The tailor ran after him.

"Milleus, stop! You have to come inside and—"

Milleus wheeled at him. He felt oddly alive, perhaps more alive than he'd felt in years. "Have to scrub and decontaminate? Never mind that. If I'm contaminated, everyone in town is. I'm an old man, so whatever sonorics is going to do to me, I'll take it. I'll protect the young ones, though."

Mercy, a whole crowd of people had gathered outside the shop, hurling questions at him as soon as he came into the street.

"What's going on?"

"Milleus, I heard you are going back to Tiverius."

"What is the doga doing about those southern spies?"

Milleus held up his hands. "Listen, everyone, listen." And when relative calm returned, he continued, "Everyone please back away a few paces. It seems my farm is contaminated. I have just set off the sonorics alarm."

People stumbled away from him, mothers dragging children. Whispers went around. Milleus picked up his name a few times. The feeling of satisfaction it raised in him was surprising. In his voice, he heard echoes of the past, of a hall full of senators, one by one raising their hands in favour of a general mobilisation of all Chevakian men. That had been one month prior to the Aranian offensive. It had been the most important reason Chevakia had won the conflict. Preparation. His hand went to the pocket of his trousers holding the letter with the fifty signatures. He still meant to burn it. He didn't know, in fact, why he hadn't already done so.

"The sonorics level has risen dramatically near the barrier. Before anyone asks—the barrier is holding for now—but I don't think anyone can guarantee anything in the future. As a way of precaution, I want everyone here to go back home, warn your neighbours, collect your family and most important possessions, including any protective gear you may have, as well as provisions, tents, if you have them, take your trucks, carts and animals and go to Ensar. Make yourselves known to the local garrison and await instructions. By leaving now, rather than waiting for authorities to notify you, you will ensure that nobody needs to panic. But do make sure you tell any family and friends you may be in contact with. Make sure you look after people who are sick or the elderly. Don't leave anyone behind."

A wide-eyed woman at the front asked, "What if you don't have protective clothes?"

Mercy, did they have nothing? The older farmers would have suits to deal with the occasional flare-up, but all these young families would have settled after the barriers were installed. "The suits are made of resin-coated fabric. Substitute anything that is thick, and finely-woven. Winter jackets, truck canopy covers, tents, that sort of material. If you have any, it helps to dip the fabric in paint or wax." Of course they wouldn't have the special resin used for the official suits. It contained metal-dust, which made the suits so heavy and hot.

"Will rain jackets do?" asked a man.

"Better than nothing. The important part is not to expose any part of your body unnecessarily."

There were a few more questions, all asked in orderly fashion, and then, somewhat to his surprise, the first people started moving off. Mercy, people were actually doing what he said.

He watched the crowd disperse.

"Now you'll have panic." The tailor had come onto the footpath behind him, still in his suit. A few women also waited. To buy thick fabric inside the shop, Milleus guessed.

"Panic at this stage is better than the alternative. Any preparation for what may come is better than none. Every step people can put between themselves and the barrier will be beneficial, if the barrier doesn't hold."

Milleus let the threat hang between them. If the unspeakable happened and the barrier shattered, everyone in town would be dead within days, no matter how far they walked.

"Anyway, I'll go back to the farm to get my goats. You better go and serve your customers."

"I can't let you leave like this, Milleus, you really have to come inside with me now."

"And be scrubbed? No thank you."

"You'll endanger the people you live with."

"And just exactly who is that?" They glared at each other for a moment. "I'm old, and if a little bit of exposure to sonorics will kill me in twenty years' time, I'll be dead anyway. So just back off, and let me do my work."

He crossed the street to his van.

The man stared after him through the visor of the helmet, but Milleus felt uncomfortable. *Back off and let me do my work.* Those exact words he had used many times as proctor. They were the words that had led to praise but eventually to his downfall. Too much, too brash, too fast. Not enough communication and consultation with his workers. He liked to boss people around.

Well, sometimes the situation didn't lend itself to endless talks. And anyway, he was no longer in politics, and right now he'd best go back to the farm to start packing.

The youngsters would have no trouble with sonorics, but he wasn't so lucky, and he wasn't sure about the goats. Anyway there was no way he was going to leave them.

He reached the van, opened the furnace door and flung a couple of shovelfuls of coal inside, pumped the bellows a few times and checked the water level in the tank. Steam hissed from the escape valve.

Then he climbed in and drove off. Already some vans were on the road, travelling in the other direction.

People still listen to me. It surprised him every time. It warmed him. It made him think of the old times, when he used to come to the district with his guests, and go hunting, and have good times.

His hand strayed to his pocket.

Oh, curse Sady and his signatures. He was *not* going back to the doga. They didn't want him; they voted him out.

But they're incompetent.

Never mind. Let them stew in their own problems.

There are lives at risk. I should do something.

Milleus' white-knuckled hands tightened on the steering wheel. Curse Sady, curse him all the way to Tiverius.

When he crested the next hill, he noticed a column of dark smoke at the edge of the forested hills. High above it, a few shadows darkened the sky: huge birds circling.

His heart missed a beat. Mercy, the farm, the youngsters, the Knights who had come to the neighbour's house and still had to be somewhere in the area. The neighbour might be a cranky old bastard, but Milleus didn't think the man had lied about those things.

Mercy, mercy.

He slammed the boiler escape vent shut. Pressure in the boiler increased. The pistons of the engine thunked and thudded. The truck's speed increased, windows rattling, the wheels jumping over bone-jarring bumps. This old farm truck was not made for speed. Down the valley. Up the hill. The air became hazy with smoke. The scent of burning wood grew stronger and he was pretty sure that the labouring engine was not the only source. Now he could see clouds billowing from over the hill. Milleus groped on the back seat for the gun. It had to be his house. There *were* no farms other than his.

Mercy, mercy.

The van crested the hill and his house came into view.

Orange flames licked at the roof of the guest quarters. Most of the house was still unaffected, but once that straw roof burned, it wouldn't stop by itself.

He pulled out gears and then let the weight of the van carry it down the hill, honking the horn. Into the driveway, between the paddocks where the goats stood bleating at the fence. He crunched into the pebbled yard, braked hard, spraying pebbles everywhere, opened the door, jumped out, pulling the collar of his shirt over his nose. Smoke drifted into his face. He coughed.

I'm too old for this.

"Milleus!"

The front door of the main section of the house had opened, and Isandor and Nila stood there, white-faced and dirty. Isandor carried Milleus' meat cleaver from the kitchen. Thank the heavens they were safe.

"Come here! To the van!" Milleus called.

Isandor took Nila's arm and they ran across the yard. At that moment an enormous bird flapped up from the other side of the house. As it rose into the sky, Milleus noticed that there was someone in the harness.

Milleus gasped. "Quick! Come!"

But there was no time for them to hide; they were in the open. Surely the rider would see them and come back, and then Milleus would have to fight sonorics weapons he had no idea how to fight. He pointed the gun, keeping it aimed at the bird, not even sure if the measly hunting bullets would bother something that big.

The eagle flapped lazily over the roof of the house. Milleus could see the rider on its back, black curly hair flapping in the wind, his face turned towards the scene in the yard. Surely any moment now . . .

Milleus raised the gun, keeping the point aimed at the eagle. Just a bit closer . . .

But the bird kept rising. The man on its back looked down, but did nothing.

Isandor and Nila reached the cabin and clambered in. They squeezed into the front seat, panting, faces smudged with soot, smelling of fire.

Milleus stared after the bird, now even further out of range, and lowered the gun. It had reached the treeline at the top of the wheat paddock and showed no sign of turning back. Surely the rider had seen the two come out of the house?

"Your house," Isandor gasped. "We have to put out the fire—"

Milleus grabbed his arm. "Nothing we can do. Don't endanger yourself." A gust of wind carried burning straw to the kitchen roof. In the guest wing, the fire had spread to ground level. All his furniture, his memories, all beyond rescue.

Mercy, his library.

"How did this happen?" he asked.

"The men came to the house and banged on the doors," Nila said. Her eyes were wide. "We didn't open for them. Then they broke the windows and climbed in. We hid in the pantry. They didn't see us. They got angry and smashed things. And then they set fire to the house."

"Who were they? Eagle Knights?"

"They were not in uniform," Isandor said.

"Hunters," Nila said, her eyes wide, and whatever hunters were, they had to be something really bad.

"But now they've seen you. Are they likely to send a ground party?"

"The Eagle Knights do not violate the border without the Queen's consent."

Milleus was surprised at the anger in Nila's voice. Her determined, soot-streaked face had an expression that chilled him, and reminded him how much she *wasn't* like Suri.

He turned the van's engine off and let himself slide from the seat. A breeze blew clouds of smoke across the yard.

Over the sound of snapping and burning wood, he became aware of an eerie sound: a mournful keening, something he had hoped never to hear: the singing of the barrier under the pressure of sonorics it was absorbing.

"Come, help me pack whatever we can salvage from the shed. We must go."

He had some stores in the shed . . . and the goats. He was *not* leaving his goats.

CHAPTER 19

NOT LONG AFTER Loriane and Ontane's family passed the barrier, the road grew wider and rutted with tracks. Pools of muddy water covered the road in places, making passage difficult and messy.

Tandor sat unmoving and rigid, atop his camel, and Ruko lay, still unconscious, over the luggage in the cart. Neither had shown any sign of waking up, although Tandor's face twisted in awful grimaces at times, as if he was trying to say something. Loriane hated seeing it, but after a few times, she ignored the horrible faces; they were probably just caused by muscle spasms.

Ontane led the camel. Dara and Myra walked behind, with Loriane following.

The going was slow.

The camel could not be shooed to go any faster. Loriane suspected that the animal was tired. On top of that, the tracks were deep and broad, much further apart than the wheels on their cart, which meant that the cart moved on an angle a lot of the time. Loriane wondered what sort of vehicles the Chevakians used that churned the road up so much.

They passed the occasional house, and a few times Loriane saw vehicles. They were nothing like Ontane's cart. Much bigger, most with four instead of two wheels. Some had harnesses like they were meant to be drawn by animals, but some carts were huge and bulky, with barrels of dark metal, with chimney-like protuberances on top. There would be a covered cabin for people to sit, with chairs covered in fabric. Ontane said that those carts moved by themselves, through fire in their metal bellies and steam.

Tandor had often spoken of the Chevakian engines, but somehow she had never taken him seriously. Back then, his talk hadn't mattered to her. Chevakia was far away and not a place she'd ever visit.

At one house they passed, a woman stood on the doorstep staring after the group. She held a broom and wore a neat and crisp dress, and a clean apron. She had dark hair, and didn't look as Chevakian as Loriane had expected—didn't they have sandy-coloured hair?—but this was clearly a woman from a much more civilised family than anyone except nobles in the city of glass could ever hope to be.

Loriane imagined what they must look like to her: a bedraggled group of travellers, their filthy clothes and their shaggy camel. The camels in the fields were much leaner. Their fur was short and neatly brushed. Most wore colourful harnesses with bells that tinkled as they walked.

Loriane had never felt ashamed of herself, not even in the Outer City, but now she did. Her clothes were dirty and she hadn't washed in days. The machines frightened her, as did the strange animals, and the smells and the colours. There was so much *light* here. More than that, she felt so *backward* and stupid, and the people's expressions only confirmed that.

"People here don't like us much," Myra said when Loriane mentioned it to her. "The Knights used to come and raid this area. They'd kidnap the older girls and take them to the City of Glass to serve as breeders."

Loriane knew. There'd been that year, shortly after she started work as healer, that the birth rate at the palace almost doubled. Many of the Chevakian girls brought in by their masters were closer to death than living. Many had died in childbirth. Others had birthed malformed children before dying soon afterwards. And those were just the ones who had made it to the end of their pregnancy and hadn't died horribly before that time. Chevakians didn't survive long in the City of Glass. Even those who did developed horrible skin sores which eventually crept into their bones. The kidnappings had been nothing but a sad waste of young lives. Not even the surviving half-Chevakian children were entirely comfortable. Many, now Isandor's age, had left, and lived, if not in Chevakia or Arania, on the edges of the southern plateau.

They came among more closely set houses, blocky and painted white. Yards had high walls, and in each grew at least one spreading tree. Children came out of gates to stare, bare-footed in the sand. It was so much warmer here that Loriane sweated under her dress and cloak. She hated the smell of herself. In the City of Glass, there were no smells, but here the earth breathed filth with every breeze. Everything stank, even the flowers on trailing vines by the side of the road.

The road was no longer a dirt track, but paved with smooth stones. Flowers grew in planter boxes, a riot of colour that hurt Loriane's eyes.

Ontane and Dara, ahead, argued as usual.

Dara was suggesting that they set up camp in the field before going into town to get food.

"That's just disgraceful," muttered Myra, glaring at her mother. "You can't expect mistress Loriane to sleep in a tent when there are guesthouses. Even Tandor never wanted me to sleep in a tent once we arrived in the City of Glass. You should say something, mistress Loriane."

Loriane shook her head. "Soon, I'll be taking Ruko and Tandor off your hands and let your parents be."

"What? You're not going to travel like this?" Myra's eyes were wide.

"I don't see what else I can do. I'll sell something from Tandor's chest to buy another camel. Ruko knows how to look after it. Tandor has family in Chevakia."

"But they live in Tiverius."

"Yes."

"But . . . mistress Loriane, do you know how big Chevakia is? We're only in the very southern province. This is the border town of Fairlight. Tiverius is days away from here. Days and days."

Loriane shrugged. "It really can't be helped. I have to go, and your parents have their own concerns. They don't want to come with me."

"Then I will." Myra's face was set. The baby in the sling was starting to stir and make noises, and she patted it. "I'm not going to leave you alone."

Loriane didn't know what to say. It was a nice gesture, but she really preferred to be alone, and people referring to her state as if it were a great illness made her angry. She had given birth alone, twice before. Once in a night with weather so foul she couldn't possibly travel to the palace. Once in her practice rooms when she'd left going to the birthing rooms much too late. Once, too, she had to instruct the sled driver to assist her when the child refused to wait until they were at the palace. She wasn't afraid. Her body was used to it.

They were still bickering by the time they entered the village and had come to what looked like a central town square. Under a collection of trees some sort of market was in progress, a handful of stalls where vendors sold fruit and brown things in baskets. Another sold fabrics. There was also a woman stirring a large pot over a fire. To the right, a makeshift pen held a handful of young camels. The scents of dung, cooking and *people* made Loriane's stomach churn.

The people noticed the group of travellers. Merchants stopped doing whatever they were doing and watched. Children came around and asked questions. Loriane didn't understand them. Tandor sat high on the camel in the bright sunlight. His head lolled to one side and he was drooling over the front of his cloak. Ruko lay like a deadweight on his stomach on top of the bags. Ontane had him lashed down so he wouldn't fall off. The skin on his hands looked blue.

Villagers blocked their path until they were surrounded.

"Get out of the way, ye lot," Ontane called. "We'll not be doing ye any harm."

The people chattered in Chevakian.

Ontane pushed Myra forward. "Ye talk to them."

"What do I ask?"

"Ask them where we can find an inn—"

Dara interrupted. "I said we shouldn't stay in this town. These bain't our friends. If we go in an inn, they'll rob us."

"Please, Ma, stop it. It's not as if we have anything worth stealing."

"Myra! Don't you dare be rude to your mother."

Myra faced her father, eyes blazing. "I'm a mother, too. I need rest. We all need rest."

"We do," Dara said. "And if I'm to cook a meal, I'll need time to buy some things, and I need hands to help me carry things."

"Then what do ye want me to do, woman? Why are ye always bossing me around? I be doing the best I can and you—"

"Stop it, I said! Both of you! I'm sick to death of having such stupid, selfish, bickering parents."

Loriane touched Myra's arm. "Please, Myra, it's all right." She just wanted to be gone.

"No, it's not all right. You need rest."

They continued walking, because arguing was not going to bring a solution.

Their progress across the markets was slow. There were too many curious onlookers.

A couple of women were feeling the fur on Myra's worn cloak. Ontane was shouting at the villagers to leave his daughter alone. Dara glared at them, her arms crossed over her chest. Loriane suspected that her defensive stance didn't help the locals' mood, but at least the villagers left him and the camel with Tandor alone.

Then a couple of men in brown uniforms pushed themselves through the crowd and came in their direction.

By the skylights.

"Tandor!" Loriane clutched his leg, hoping for him to wake up. He spoke fluent Chevakian and would know his way around.

But he didn't wake. Everyone was arguing and yelling around them. Loriane understood none of it, and panic rose in her. It was a bad idea to come here. They were going to be locked up. They would be punished for something they didn't understand they'd done—a sharp pain lanced through her belly.

She gasped.

Oh, little one, not now.

But the pain built, and burned. She had to stop walking. The yelling voices of people around her faded into meaningless noise.

"Loriane!" Myra put an arm around her shoulder, and then there were women all around her, touching her. She panted, chest heaving with deep breaths. Oh, this *hurt*.

One of the brown-uniformed men called out. The crowd parted at his words. Two other men formed a chair linking their hands and heaved Loriane off the ground. In the throng and smell of bodies, she fought not to scream. It was like someone was trying to poke through the skin from the *inside*. She put her hand on the spot and felt a sharp bump. By the skylights, what was that?

"Put me down! Stop!"

The men kept walking, jostling her and yelling at the people ahead, presumably for them to get out of the way. A woman came to walk next to her, holding her shoulders and gibbering words which she took as soothing.

"Stop! Where are you taking me—aaahhh!" Another stab of white-hot pain. Loriane grabbed instinctively for the spot. By the skylights, what was this? The bump had moved to the side.

"Loriane!" Myra came running from behind.

"Tell . . . them . . . to . . . put . . . me down." A surge of bile burned in the back of her throat.

In between fighting to get the words out and struggling not to throw up, Loriane realised she'd screamed, something she'd sworn was for first-timers.

Myra spoke in halting Chevakian; the men put Loriane on her feet, and scrambled out of the way as she threw up her lumpy jelly, and a second time more jelly, bile and blood.

By the skylights.

Cold with sweat, shivering and very afraid, Loriane stared at puddle of vomit. Blood. This babe was eating her from the inside.

"I told you that you needed to see a healer," Myra said, behind her.

"I don't know what a healer can do. I've tried all the things a healer can to make this child move, but it's bewitched. This is going to kill me."

Myra went white in the face.

Loriane swallowed a further surge of bile. "Myra, we need some place away from people. Not a guesthouse, a barn or some such. I'm going to have to ask you to do something very unpleasant."

She retched and coughed. By the skylights, the vomit went up her nose. She coughed, but that only made it worse. Her stomach cramped.

Myra nodded, her face white. It seemed she understood.

Loriane bent over and retched. More blood. Retched again, and again, until it felt her head would explode. She grew dizzy and fell to her knees.

Oh, by the skylights! She leaned over, panting. For a moment her vision went white.

It was a number of heartbeats before she realised the world had stopped.

No one moved to pick her up.

No one moved at all.

No one spoke.

Everyone stood still, eyes wide, staring at the sky.

There was only one sound: the same mournful keening she had heard when they passed the barrier, and it was increasing in volume. A woman screamed.

One of the brown-uniformed men shouted something and all around people started running, hurling themselves at doors.

The volume of the keening increased.

People screamed, crowding before doorways, pushing each other in, scrambling over the fallen, punching others out of the way.

Loriane scrambled up, clamping her hands over her ears, looking at Myra for a clue what to do, but Myra's face was just as bewildered.

Windows shattered, showering glass into the street.

Then there was bright flash of light, a moment of intense silence, a gust of wind and an enormous bang that shook the ground. Roof tiles flew into the street. The entire facade of a house collapsed. A cold wind tore through the street, ripping washing off lines, overturning market stalls and rubbish bins.

And there was silence.

CHAPTER 20

IN THE PLACE between life and death, Tandor shook awake when Ruko laughed. He sat up, a lingering chill of a cold blast still clinging to him.

"What was that?"

"Didn't I tell you we'd win?" Ruko said. "The stupid Chevakians put up their silly walls, but we're much stronger than that."

Tandor tried to look outside that place, and recognised none of the twisted shapes that he could make out. He didn't even see his own body, nor that of Ruko. All he could see was some sort of valley with hills made out of rubble on both sides.

Where were they, and how long had he been asleep?

Had he even been asleep?

He now remembered the pain that made him pass out. They'd passed the barrier, which meant that they were now in Chevakia and the fact that he was conscious in this place meant that icefire had penetrated . . . that the barrier had shattered.

Now he realised what he saw: those were not hills, they were the remains of houses reduced to rubble. Those were not boulders in a streambed, they were dead bodies in the street.

"No." He tried to push himself up, but he was still tied to the chair. "Loriane!"

There was no movement.

"Loriane!"

The child. He needed her child. The hybrid would be the only way he'd be able to control the onslaught of icefire.

If Loriane had been killed, all was lost.

"She can't hear you," Ruko sneered.

"Shut up."

Ruko laughed.

Tandor twisted on the chair, and all of a sudden a rush of icefire found its way into the place between life and death, and ripped the bonds. He was free.

He jumped off the chair and landed in the real world.

The smell of rubble. An overwhelming smell of fire. Moans from people caught under the rubble.

People with burned skin peeling off exposed limbs.

"Loriane!"

Something grabbed him from behind.

"Loriane!"

It was Ruko, pulling him back into that prison. The real world faded. Tandor swung around, and hit Ruko with his clawed arm. The metal went straight through him.

"Let me go!" He had to find Loriane. He had to rescue her and the child. He had to stop her going to Tiverius.

"You will do as I say," Ruko snarled. He tied Tandor back to the chair.

CHAPTER 21

*L*ORIANE UNCURLED herself, sucking lungs full of air with an familiar tang. She was lying on a pavement of a street with tall houses on both sides.

She would have sworn she heard someone call her name. A voice that sounded like Tandor.

A haze of dust hung in the air. The ground was covered in glass and debris and, underneath that, dusty bodies, unmoving. Close to her, a couple of burly men in uniform, eyes open and glassy. Further away, a whole heap of people in front of a door. There was no blood, but no one moved, and the coating of dust made it look like they had turned to stone.

Loriane scrabbled up, awkward and top-heavy, but no longer in pain. Then a fleeting thought: does this child inside me feel icefire? She patted her stomach, but couldn't find the sharp bump anymore.

The breeze that went through the street was icy cold.

Where were the others?

Several houses had lost windows or parts of walls. Straw roofs had been blown off, and the entire town had gone eerily silent.

"Loriane!" That sounded like Myra.

Loriane turned around and almost tripped over a body behind her, half-buried under a piece of wood that had fallen off a shop awning. Every bit of exposed skin on the villager's face and hands was red and covered in blisters. He stirred and moaned, his eyes half open and showing only white. She had seen that before, after the explosion in the City of Glass.

Icefire.

That was the familiar feeling in the air.

"Myra, girl, you be all right?" Ontane emerged from the dust of a collapsed façade of a house, with the camel in tow. Tandor still sat on it, dazed, his hair rimed in dust, but otherwise unharmed.

Myra ran to embrace her father. The baby in the sling made muffled cries in the tight space between them.

What remained of Tandor's hair had turned white with a fine riming of white dust. His eyes were open, and Loriane noticed that the skin on his face had started to peel.

"Tandor? Did you just call me?"

He didn't answer, but when she took his hand, he moved his and squeezed her fingers. His blue eyes stared into the distance.

"Tandor, can you hear me?"

He squeezed her hand again.

"Please, talk to me. Tell us how to find your family."

But he didn't respond to that. His face contorted into frightening expressions. She swore she could hear someone laughing.

On the cart, Ruko sat up. A piece of debris had struck the side of the cart, and the wheels were out of alignment. Ruko glared at her over his shoulder. Somehow, his expression seemed less detached than before.

"Ruko? Do you know where Tandor's family lives?"

But he still wasn't speaking. He was looking at Tandor, though, and she wondered if they had a means of communication.

"We need to get out of here," Ontane said. "Before the Chevakian army turns up and accuses us of destroying this town."

"Where to? That was their accursed barrier that just exploded, dear husband," Dara said. "Haven't you noticed that we live on the other side? We might as well go home now."

"And what do ye think we'll find up there, huh? If the icefire down here be strong enough to kill everyone, it will be strong enough to kill us up there."

She didn't reply, but her face was set, her arms crossed over her chest.

"Be there anything we can do without you arguing about it,

woman? I tell ye now, ye be free to go back home, but I bain't coming."

Dara snorted, but didn't leave either.

Ontane held out his hand to Loriane, not noticing that he stepped in the puddle of blood-stained vomit, and helped her clamber over the debris of a collapsed shop awning. There were several *people* underneath.

With Ontane leading, they picked their way through the street, which had turned into an unrecognisable mess. Stalls had been ripped apart. Houses collapsed. Bodies were everywhere, covered in blisters, some still alive, most of them dead. In fact, apart from Loriane and the family, not one person was walking. A sickening scent of dust mingled with that of burnt meat hung in the air.

"What do we do now?" Myra asked.

Ontane shrugged. His face was haggard. "See if we can find another camel and cart for mistress Loriane, and keep going. Don't ask me where."

Well, damn it, there went her chance to leave this bickering family behind.

Dara still had her arms crossed sullenly over her chest.

Loriane was just so tired. "Please, I want to find a quiet place, away from the town."

"I agree," Dara said. "We wait until it be safe to go back."

"I don't mean that. This child is killing me. It's not normal. I want someone to cut it out."

"Mistress Loriane!" Ontane's face turned white.

"Be that . . . be that really necessary?" Dara didn't look so happy herself.

"It's not coming out by itself, and it won't, because it's too big. I can tell Myra what to do. I've done it a couple of times." More often than she cared to remember. There was a *reason* girls were made to wait until sixteen before being allowed to take part in the Newlight Festival.

"I'm not letting my—"

"Ye can't ask Myra to—"

Ontane and Dara started speaking at the same time, then stopped and looked at each other.

"Congratulations. The first time you two agree on anything is when it's something that has to be done."

"Myra, I don't want ye to do such a horrid thing," Ontane said. "I'll do it."

Dara said, "What do ye know about women's things? I'll do it."

They glared at each other.

Myra stepped between them. "Right then, if we can all agree, let's go and find a safe place."

With great difficulty, they made their way back to the market square. They saw no survivors.

They stopped to consider which way to go and of course Ontane and Dara argued over it.

Ontane said, "I think we keep going that way. The other way's the road we came—look!" His eyes widened.

Loriane turned. Over the rubble of collapsed houses, she could see the hillside that led up to the plateau. She didn't see anything—wait, she did. Higher up the slope clouds of white whirled, covering the green trees. Snow.

There were also clouds of steam, or smoke rising from between the trees.

"Is there a fire?"

"A fire? Can't you see it, Mistress Loriane? The trees be alive with blue flames. It be following us."

Loriane stared up the slope but could not see any blue flames.

"Icefire," Myra said.

"Great, and what now?" Dara said. "So much for all your wonderful ideas."

"You, woman! Ye be full of talk about what to do, but when ye actually have to make a decision—"

"Yes, it be always my fault, of course. It bain't like *you* ever make any mistakes, mister know-it-all! I still think we would have been just fine at the hunting shack, but no, you—"

"Stop fighting!" Myra screamed.

Silence.

Dara and Ontane stood facing each other, both glancing sideways at Myra.

"Hadn't we agreed to help mistress Loriane first?"

Ontane grumbled an unintelligible response. Dara looked the other way.

Loriane just wished they'd stop acting like little children. Honestly, if this was what having a family meant, then she was glad she had never married.

"Look," she said. "I appreciate your help in getting down here, but don't feel like you have to stay with me. I'll ask Ruko to help me." Her child was important to Tandor, and no doubt Ruko would protect it.

"Well," Ontane grumbled, "it looks like there be no time for that nasty business. I vote we be getting out of here as soon as possible."

At that moment, there was a harsh whistle somewhere in the distance, and a sound like Loriane had never heard before.

Myra's eyes widened. "A train! Let's go to the station."

The building Myra called the station was on the other side of the markets. Once it might have been painted white, but half of the entrance had collapsed, showing exposed bricks and timber. Getting there was a struggle. The camel was jittery. Loriane guessed it could feel icefire. The cart was too broken to be pulled with ease; the ground was covered in rubble.

In front of the building, they halted and Ontane untied their packs from the cart. The moment he touched Tandor's trunk, Ruko pushed him aside.

"Hey, you," Ontane yelled out. "Behave yourself, for all ye've been a parasite on us the last few days."

"Let him," Loriane said. What Ontane said wasn't true. Ruko had come along to protect Tandor, and had never eaten from the family's supplies. She added more quietly, "Ruko, we're going on the train here. We'll have to leave the camel, but we need to get Tandor up into that building."

Ruko said nothing, but turned back to the cart and took care of Tandor's enormous trunk

Ontane slipped the headgear off the camel's neck. "We'll turn the beast free. It may find its own way home, if it knows where home be."

Loriane followed the family up the rubble-strewn stairs into the station. She'd be prepared to walk all the way, or ride in the cart. She thought setting the camel loose was a bad idea, and didn't like the sound of the word "train".

After clambering underneath a half-collapsed arch, they came onto a paved area, from where two very straight strips of metal led towards the horizon. Rails, Myra said. For the train, although the train itself was nowhere to be seen. Taking in water, Myra said.

So there was no train at the moment, but there were unharmed seats under the awning of the roof and Loraine sank down gratefully, ignoring Dara and Ontane's bickering over the absence of a train, and whether it would or would not leave. Ruko sat next to her, guiding Tandor. It was the first time he had come close.

She glanced at him and wondered what went through that head of his. He was staring ahead, the light from the field on the other side of the tracks reflected in his eyes. There had to be some secret to speaking with him.

"Ruko, have you ever been to Tandor's family?" Loriane asked.

As usual, Ruko said nothing, but a big tear tracked down his cheek. He reminded her of Isandor and she wondered where her son was. Ruko was just another boy, broken and turned wild by living in the wilderness for years.

Loriane took his hand. It was warm. They sat silently, while Ontane and Dara bickered and Myra rolled her eyes while feeding the baby. Loriane's other hand was on her stomach, feeling the movements of the baby's feet through her belly. The child was facing the right way, and everything felt normal again. One ride in this train, and she would be safe. Maybe everything would be fine after all.

Voices echoed in the entrance of the building, and a group of five young men arrived. Strong and healthy all, with dark hair and wearing fur cloaks. Southern men without a doubt.

They nodded at the family, but didn't approach to talk. Deserters from the lower ranks of the Knights, Loriane thought, and knew that other refugees would have no love for them. They sat in the far corner of what Myra called the platform.

Soon others came in, all southerners. Families, silent children, women with haggard faces, and then the physically wounded. Burns mostly, but also broken limbs and frostbite from those who had fled in the clothes they were wearing.

They talked to whoever wanted to listen.

Their stories were all equally haunting. Some had come from the City of Glass, others from Bordertown. The ones from the City of Glass were mostly nobles or those who had been in possession of sleds. They spoke of a wall of icefire following them and burning everyone who was too slow.

Many had been fleeing constantly without sleep, and had festering sores that needed urgent attention. Loriane did what she could, but without materials, that wasn't much.

The platform filled up more and more. No one seemed to know where they were going, except out of here. Wherever the train went when it came, wherever there was work, wherever someone had some distant relatives or some acquaintance who had long forgotten about them. Most of them had no knowledge of Chevakia, and knew no one, no matter how vaguely, who lived there. It didn't matter, they all waited for the train that still hadn't entered the station. Word came that a second train had entered the town.

Scuffles broke out as some people were trying to leave again, arguing all of Chevakia was dead and there wasn't going to be a train, but the platform was too full and no one knew where to go.

Still the people came. The old and the very young, in a sad, stinking heap of humanity that soon spilled out the station onto the adjacent square.

Ruko had to fight for the bench they had secured for Tandor. He was well enough to stand up, but couldn't do so, or they would lose their seat.

Dara surprised Loriane by bartering some of their saltmeat for a blanket from a group of young men who seemed to be travelling together. When she spread the blanket over Tandor, the Knighthood crest in the corner was clearly visible.

Myra helped where she could. She caught a baby as it slid from the distressed mother's body, while next to her the boy's father succumbed to his injuries. Six more people died before she could attend to them.

There was nowhere to leave the dead. No space, no platforms for laying them out as was the custom in the City of Glass. There were no wild animals to come for their meat.

Fights broke out over the meagre supplies some people had with them.

Then there was a loud whistle in the distance and such hissing as Loriane had never heard before. A few children near the edge of the platform pointed and screamed. One of the children's mothers looked and screamed as well, and a young man yelled, "A train, a train!" Using the Chevakian word.

An older man yelled at him, "Use the right language. We once had trains, too."

A few people gave him suspicious glances, since he was clearly a supporter of the old king.

With much hissing, the huge thing rumbled into the station like some monster.

Mothers drew their little children out of the way, screaming at the older ones to stand back. Children cried and everyone stared at this huge, dark, gleaming and hissing thing.

Loriane felt awed. If this was the technology Chevakia had, then why didn't the Southern Land have this kind of magic? Tandor had even spoken about it. He said he had old books that showed the trains in the City of Glass. He even told her where to look for the remains of the tracks. She had never cared. Why not?

She searched the crowd for the man who had made the remark about trains, and found him surrounded by a couple of others engaged in serious discussion, pointing at parts of the train.

The train came to a complete halt. Despite the refugees' fear of its hissing steam, the boldest ones soon opened the doors and clambered into the carriages where there were rows of seats. Bewildered attendants aboard were pushed aside in the tide of humanity; they were helpless. Healthy and sick, strong and frail scrambled aboard.

Anything to get out of here.

Ontane managed to clamber into a wide door and held out his hand to Myra. In the stream of jostling people, they pushed Tandor up, followed by their luggage, which included Tandor's chest, under close guard of Ruko. Ontane then heaved Loriane aboard and Dara followed.

There were no seats in this part of the train, just a large carriage, with straw covering the floor. Loraine guessed this was how camels travelled. The air even smelled of the beasts.

While others clambered in the door, they secured themselves a seat in the corner of the carriage, and draped Tandor on a heap of straw. He was shivering and mumbling. Loriane covered him with their new blanket, meeting Dara's eyes. A thought crossed her mind that, away from her whingeing husband, Dara might be a successful healer, or merchant.

Still, people were trying to push in, but there was no more room in the carriage, and plenty of people still on the platform. Someone blew a whistle. Steam hissed past the open door. People screamed; a few young men pushed themselves in, stepping and stumbling over the knees and legs.

Men yelled out the door that there would be another train, that they could see it.

The train chugged into motion, and the crowd of people crammed on the platform slid from sight. The screaming and crying for loved ones who had become separated lingered a bit longer.

Silence descended. The only sound was that of the machine that pulled the train and the rumbling on the rails. Loriane had expected to be afraid, but it was much like being in a sled.

Wind blew in through the open doors.

Soon people started asking questions. Where was the train going?

No one knew.

Tiverius, someone said. Others said they had family there, but didn't seem too certain when asked where their family lived.

How long would that take?

Again, no one knew.

The man in black who had known about the trains was with a group of similar fellows in the same carriage. They were explaining to children and anyone who would listen how the trains worked.

"You know anything about this thing of icefire that's following us?" Dara asked them.

"It's power that has escaped from the Heart," a man said. His black clothing looked more clean and unruffled than that of the others, and his white-flecked beard was neatly clipped. "The Knights tried to stifle it, because they wanted to make sure that the people were poor and never understood the riches of icefire. Only because they, themselves cannot see it and cannot feel it or do anything with it. But the Heart doesn't like to be locked up. Its power built and built until it exploded from the earth."

"And before, this power was used for trains?" a young girl asked.

"Yes, that, and much more. The Knights denied us the riches. The Knights wanted the power gone. But you cannot stifle the Heart . . ."

Ontane was making frantic hand movements.

Dara mouthed, *What?*

He whispered, "They be rebels, and we don't want anything to do with them."

"And ye liked the Knights so much?"

"Please—these rebels be dangerous."

"Ye remember how the Knights used to come into Bordertown and rape the women?"

"Shhh."

"I haven't forgotten, husband. I haven't forgotten that the people who called themselves our parents let it happen—"

"Dara!"

She glared. "That be the first time in years ye haven't called me 'woman'."

"Just shut up. We mind our business, and get into nobody's way."

Dara turned away, her face tense. Loriane guessed that had Ontane not been there, she would very much like to join the black-clad men. However did she put up with such a selfish prick as husband? However did he put up with such a prune as wife? How come Myra had grown up as kind and open-minded as she was with parents like them? That had to be the greatest miracle of all. Of course, she'd only lived with them a few years, since Tandor had brought her, but she knew the girl loved them and they loved her, despite all their bickering.

Loriane stroked Tandor's hot forehead. She lifted the bandages. The wound didn't look too bad, but she worried about him. He should have woken up by now. His wounds were healing faster than she had thought possible, and there didn't seem to be a reason for him to remain half-conscious. Unless . . . unless icefire kept him asleep.

Either way, she was uncomfortable sitting cross-legged on the floor next to him. Her back ached. She was sore all the time.

And the train rumbled on.

Some people munched on whatever food they had been able to bring. Men stepped over sleeping bodies to piss out the open door. Women could do no such thing.

Soon, Loriane found herself crouching in the corner, the darkest place she could find, dribbling piss on the straw. Her bowels twisted and churned, ejecting jets of brown, bloodstained fluid, and she wasn't the only one. Many of the weaker people didn't even bother getting up but let it run into the straw where they sat. A young boy close to her was sick. The sound of retching made her cringe. The smell followed soon after.

With that, and the stinking wounds, the vomit and sun baking on the roof of the wagon, the smell became unbearable. Only those close to the door got enough fresh air, but as the train continued, the air became hot, and those close to the door had red skin from the wind and became thirsty. The young men in black organised a rotating scheme so that everyone got a turn at sitting near the door.

Somewhere on the far side of the carriage, a woman wailed when her child stopped breathing. The little boy, covered in blisters and ugly sores, couldn't have been more than a year old. There was nothing to cover him. Nowhere to put him aside so the mother took off his shirt and draped it over his head.

When an old woman died, the young men pushed some straw in the corner and stacked the bodies on top. They were soon joined by the body of the woman who had given birth on the platform. Fever, Loriane knew. The woman's adolescent son clutched the child, but Loriane knew that without its mother, it would soon die. She would offer to feed it, but she hadn't eaten for two days and was desperately thirsty and didn't think she'd have much milk to share.

Myra sat against the wall where they had secured a place, and clutched her baby. No one had any water, and Myra didn't have enough milk either.

The train rumbled on. Steam trailed past the windows.

Forest replaced fields, and then came wide expanses of grass. Groups of camels roamed the countryside. It grew warmer, even as the sunlight turned golden.

Then came night.

Several of the wounded did not stir the next morning. The young men again stacked the bodies in the corner.

A man, who must have done some nursing work, started arguing that they should remove the dead from the carriage.

"What do you mean—remove?" yelled the mother of the young boy, her face stained with tears.

"Well . . ." He looked at the door, over the jumble of dirty and stinking bodies.

"How dare you suggest that!"

"It's in the interest of all of us. If the bodies stay here much longer, they will go bad, and all of us will get sick."

"I will not put my son to rest without a proper ceremony."

Several parents agreed with that.

The man retreated, mumbling about having been to Chevakia before and knowing how quickly things went bad here.

Loriane's belly cramped from sickness and hunger, and the foul smell that grew worse as the sun rose. At night, she suffered another bout of stabbing pains. Same thing as before: strange sharp bumps moving under her skin. She put her hands on the spots, pushed back, and felt the bumps moving, too sharp to be knees, too strong to be hands. She sat like that for a long time, sweat rolling off her back. In her mind, she kept seeing those drawings of malformed children.

There was another pregnant woman in the carriage, and occasionally, they threw each other anxious glances, hoping and knowing that the babes would be better off being born once they got off this train. Loriane was scared. By now, she had to be almost a moon overdue. Not long, and the birth would become impossible.

Tandor, what did you do?

But Tandor had no answers. He sat in his crazy stupor, moving where they told him to go, but not communicating with anyone. Ruko sat next to him, protecting him from people who came too close, and making sure he wasn't hurt. Loriane was glad for that, but the two of them seemed lost to everyone else, and she didn't know what she could to bring them out of their stupor, so that either could tell them where Tandor's family lived. Worse, Ruko had locked Tandor's chest and wouldn't let anyone near it.

The train rumbled on.

How long was this going to last?

CHAPTER 22

IT WAS A GLOOMY circle of faces that gathered around the fire when the sky began to darken. A cold breeze whistled through the pine trees, blowing any heat from the fitful fire away.

It was amazing how quickly Carro had become used to the mildness of the Chevakian climate. He liked it.

"I found this," Jeito said, holding up a wet and bedraggled bird. It had the orange legs and white feathers of a southern gull, and the red paint on the beak to show that it was a bird belonging to the Eagle Knights. A baleful light blue eye blinked, but that was the only sign of life it displayed. "Found it flapping about in a puddle of mud next to the creek."

Carro recognised it as the bird they had released to fly to the City of Glass with messages for Rider Cornatan, and requests for instructions. They had been away for more than ten days now, and not one bird had reached them with further orders or updates on how the Knights coped with the Queen's absence.

Jeito untied the note it had tied to its leg. It was the same note he had attached to the bird a few days ago, except now it was dirty and wet. He crumpled it in a white-knuckled hand, and let it fall in the grass.

"What has happened?" Farey asked, his face in expression of shock. "We've never had any birds fail to reach their destination."

It was the first time Carro had seen Farey worried.

"Maybe the bird was blown off-course," Carro said.

Jeito and Farey gave him dirty looks.

"A few options," Jeito said, his voice low. "Either the bird fell ill, it got lost, or it somehow couldn't reach the City of Glass. Apart from being wet, the bird looks healthy enough, so that leaves the other two."

"I'm not liking either of those," Farey said.

Carro struggled to make sense of it. The birds used icefire to navigate. They were much more sensitive to it than humans, and could detect it even in Chevakia. They always knew their way back to the City of Glass. It was where nature told them to go in summer, after having spent the winter on the Aranian shores.

"What could have happened?" Jeito asked.

Farey shrugged. "Bad weather?"

"Maybe," Jeito said, but they all knew the underlying truth: bad weather of the type that disturbed animals' navigation involved the release of icefire. Not only that, they *had* seen a flare.

"What do we do now?" Nolan asked.

"Stick to our orders," said Farey. "Find the highest in command."

"Go back to the City of Glass?" Carro asked. He didn't want to go back to the City of Glass. He didn't want to face his father, or any of the Knights, or, for that matter, Korinne.

Farey nodded, slowly.

The hunters packed up the camp at first light.

Carro was nervous, looking about him for an excuse so that they could stay. A night of fitful sleep hadn't changed his mind. The obligatory sex with Nolan hadn't changed his mind, nor had the promise of being able to stay in luxury in his father's apartments in the palace. The pool where the hunters held their orgies, the empty-headed girls like Korinne who came only so that they had a chance of securing a good payment for carrying a senior Knight's child. All those thoughts made him sick.

Carro did *not* want to go back to the City of Glass. He did *not* want to face his father. He did *not* want to go back to having visions and having to hide them. And he especially did not want to have to take a girl's medicine to help alleviate them.

But the others were ready to go, supplies packed on their eagles.

"Come on, Carro," Nolan said, and smiled in that leering way of his.

Jeito snorted, already on the back of his bird.

Farey was even less talkative than normal. He was by far the oldest of the group, and his silence unnerved Carro more than anything that had happened so far.

He untied his eagle from the tree and jumped into the saddle. He left his harness dangling. The saddle's leather showed the shine of frequent use. At least none of the Knights would ever tease him again for being clumsy.

Then they were off with a flapping of wings. The countryside glided under him, with its neat fields and forests and burnt-out shells of farmhouses. At least no one would ever question him on the two people he had seen running towards a Chevakian truck from the last farmhouse they burned, one with long black hair and an awkward gait, one with honey-coloured hair, whose Chevakian farm clothes didn't hide her fine figure. Carro had avoided his worst fear of having to witness Isandor's death.

They came to a road which was unusually busy. The vehicles were all travelling in the same direction.

"The Chevakians are fleeing," Nolan said and he laughed. "That's how scared they are of us. This land will all be ours. We don't even have to fight for it."

Carro felt sick, remembering the flames and Farey's murdering of people whose only crime was not to reply to questions.

Ahead lay the area the Chevakians called the wastelands, forested hills that slowly climbed to the southern plateau. From up here the hills didn't seem so tall, and in the distance the cliffs of the plateau were already visible. It was strange, Carro contemplated. He had never thought about it, but the plateau was as if a giant had cut out a section of land, and pushed it up from the earth. He wondered if in history before human memory icefire had anything to do with this strange layout of the land. After all, the City of Glass was said to have been built by an ancient civilisation and destroyed in an evil war. The machine sometimes referred to as the

Heart was said to be a construct of that civilisation. Living with his stepfather, Carro had learned not to believe everything—his stepfather distrusted everyone—but surely there was a reason for those rumours to exist? Even if they were spread by old Thilleian books. It couldn't be coincidence that his father had approved of him reading those books.

"By the skylights, look at that cloud," Nolan said, pointing at the horizon.

Carro looked.

At the horizon, sitting atop the plateau was a huge black roiling mass of cloud. Lightning arced across the top.

"Some bad weather, that is," said Farey.

"Do we have to go through?" Carro asked. There was an uncomfortable chill in his bones and he felt a strange disconnect between what his eyes saw and what he experienced, as if the world wasn't real.

"We may have to shelter until it blows over."

Nolan had his hand above his eyes to shelter them from the biting wind. He squinted at the cloud. "I've never seen anything like this."

"Agree it's not normal for this time of year." Farey's voice sounded far off.

Carro shook his head to banish that disconnected feeling, as if he was about to get a vision, but the cloud morphed into vaguely human shapes, and one had the face of his stepfather.

By the skylights, already those damn visions were returning. He glanced aside at Nolan, who looked at him. "You all right?"

Carro nodded, his face stiff like a death mask. He noticed his dangling harness and knew he should clip it on before a full-scale vision struck, but Nolan was watching and would think him a weakling, having learned how to ride without a harness just recently. A tough hunter didn't use a harness, storm or no storm.

But as they came closer, it turned out that the blackness wasn't just a cloud. Along a long storm front, the trees were on fire. Entire trees exploded, spraying embers everywhere.

The embers whirled and formed human-like figures made solely of fire threaded with lightning.

Carro shook his head. He was surely imagining things.

"Stay together!" Farey yelled somewhere in the distance.

Next to Carro, Nolan struggled to keep control of his bird. It flapped and bucked, threatening to throw its rider off.

Farey steered his eagle into the cloud and disappeared from sight. Jeito followed, but Nolan's eagle refused to obey its rider's command.

Carro went in after Jeito. The moment his bird plunged into the roiling mass, something hit him that made his entire body tingle. All around him, human-like figures roiled.

"Stop," he yelled, fighting to keep visions at bay.

But he couldn't see Farey or Jeito, and he couldn't see Nolan behind him.

He yanked at the eagle's reins. But the bird was plummeting down.

Carro knocks on the door and walks into the room.

Standing by the window, Rider Cornatan turns. "Do you bring me the fugitives, son?"

"Yes," Carro says, and somehow he's come in carrying a stretcher, and on it is a hunk of bloodied meat. It barely looks human except dangling from it is a ponytail of black hair.

"How do I know that this is him?"

It is Isandor, because of the hair clip.

Isandor. He and Jevaithi had been staying with the old farmer. He hoped they were safe. The south would gain nothing from their deaths.

Smoke trailed past him. Still, the eagle was going down.

"Up, up!" Carro pulled the reins, but the bird took no notice.

Carro knocks on the door and walks into the room.

Standing by the window, Rider Cornatan turns. His face twists into a sneer. "Do you bring me the fugitives, son?"

"They escaped," Carro says. "I think we know where they are."

Within a heartbeat, Rider Cornatan's face twists into a snarl. "You *know*? What good is knowing alone? If you know, what are you doing here and why don't you bring me their bodies? I thought you would do me proud, but you're as useless as the rest of those weaklings."

His hand flicks out and slaps Carro hard in the face.

Ow.

Carro ran his hand over his cheek. It burned like fire. He looked down his tunic to see a trail of black. He must have been hit by an ember.

The eagle was still descending in slow circles. The mist had become acrid smoke from the flames below. A strong breeze carried the sound of exploding trees.

"Carro!" someone shouted in the distance. "Carro, what the hell are you doing?"

Carro gave up trying to control the eagle. Some strange voice in his head told him that the bird knew the way and that whatever fate awaited both of them, it was inevitable.

He squinted through the shards of smoke and when a breeze cleared the air, he could see the burning forest. Amongst the exploding trees walked a huge, human-like figure made entirely of fire.

The moment Carro saw it, the figure turned its head up. It pointed a flaming hand and a bolt of lightning shot into the sky. It missed Carro and his eagle. The bird swooped, leaving Carro to clench its labouring body hard to stay in the saddle.

He laughed and punched the air.

"You can't get me!"

The figure on the ground ripped a tree out of the ground and swung it in a great arc while fire spread over the crown. Then it let go of the tree, which flew into the air, but rose far short of Carro's eagle. Again, the bird swooped.

But as Carro hung onto the saddle, he noticed two more flaming figures plundering their way through the forest. One was smaller than the first one, the second one much bigger. His laugh fell flat.

He yanked the eagle's reins again. "Up, you stupid bird!"

Too late. The large figure pointed, lightning gathering around its outstretched hand.

Carro dug his heels into the eagle's sides. "Up, up!"

Carro's vision went white. The reins slipped from his hands.

Carro knocks on the door and walks into the room.

Standing by the window, Rider Cornatan turns. His face is triumphant and his smile chills Carro. "Are the fugitives dead, son?"

"Yes," Carro says, and somehow he's come in carrying a stretcher, and on it is a hunk of bloodied meat. It barely looks human except dangling from it is a ponytail of black hair. The carcass is a Chevakian goat's and the hair is Carro's own.

Rider Cornatan walks around the stretcher. "How do I know that this is him?"

"Look at the hair clip," Carro says, clutching the dagger behind his back.

Rider Cornatan bends over and at that moment, Carro jumps, plunging the dagger deep into his father's back, so that the point comes out the other side.

Rider Cornatan staggers, a surprised look on his face. He tries to speak, but blood oozes from his mouth. His eyes unfocused, he slumps forward over the goat carcass.

He whispers, "Why, son, why?"

Carro was flying, flying, like an eagle. He spread his arms and legs and the wind flapped past him, roaring in his ears.

The thought crossed his mind *I'm falling, and I'm going to die,* but he didn't care. He'd done his duty and rid the world of a great evil.

He was a hero.

Historians would sing his name.

He was dead.

"What the *fuck* were you doing?"

That voice sounded far too real and it sounded far too much like Nolan.

Not dead, then.

Carro opened his eyes with a great effort.

He was on the ground in a forest clearing where dark pine trees rose around him. Directly above him was a face, the features blurred, but clearly Nolan's.

Carro tried to speak, but he couldn't. Everything hurt, even breathing.

"You would kill us all trying to rescue you from that fire?"

Carro shook his head. He didn't honestly remember what he had done. He only remembered his father's eyes as he stabbed the dagger into his heart. He remembered his father's rasping voice. Why indeed?

"That was the stupidest thing I've ever seen anyone do in my life," Farey said. He poked into the fire, sending sparks flying.

"Where . . . where are we?" Carro's throat hurt.

"Well back into Chevakia. We can't get home that way."

"At least now we know why the gull came back," Nolan said.

Farey glared at him.

"Did you see those fire devils?" Jeito asked. He had his arms clamped around himself.

"Yeah, what are they?" Nolan said.

"Fire devils are constructs of icefire."

"But those things looked human."

"They *are* human."

"You're kidding me."

Jeito shook his head. "I've read about the old king's creatures. He had servitors, but he had ones that were way worse than that. There were beings that could change their shapes at will." He stared into the fire. "They could fly. Some people said that eagles were descended from these creatures."

For a while the silence lingered. Carro wasn't sure what to say. A few months ago, he would have laughed at such tales. The fact that they were in the old books meant nothing. Books were full of stories; but now he had seen the working of icefire, shown to him by his father, and he had seen human figures made out of fire. There might be some truth in those old tales. There were other things in those books: shape shifters, crossbreeds, living ice. Who was to say what was real and what a myth?

"Well, since it's clear we can't go to the City of Glass, what do we do now?" Nolan said.

Jeito gave him an irritated glance. "Is that all you worry about—what do we do now, what do we do now? Can't you think for yourself?"

There was a haunted expression in his eyes. Worried about family, Carro guessed.

Farey reached out to his lover and squeezed his shoulder. "We'll find a road of some kind," he said. "There are a lot of people travelling. I'm not sure where they're going, but they'll be going somewhere. Meanwhile, stick to our orders: try to find the fugitives and kill them. Also, follow where everyone is going and find any of the senior command. We'll confiscate one of these vehicles and send the eagles to roam. They'll attract too much attention. If we travel by road, we can remain hidden. One of us goes with the eagles each day."

CHAPTER 23

THE LIGHT HAD turned orange, and the pine forest cast long shadows over the road. The haze amongst the trees shrouded the straight trunks in a veil of purple.

Milleus drew a hand over his eyes while steering the van with the other. Up ahead, the van they'd been following since the last village crested the hill and became a silhouette sharp against the yellow sky. The van that had followed them had already stopped for the night, and they'd passed a few camps along the way, where people were making fires and children huddled in blankets against the biting southern wind.

"I'm tired," Milleus said to no one in particular. He cast a glance over his shoulder, where Nila lay across the back seat, half asleep, a slice of bread still on her lap. She had been hungry; he had given her the bread, and she hadn't eaten it. He didn't know what to think about that, which only intensified the feelings of unease in his own stomach. He had been contaminated with sonorics. With less severe contamination, it always took a few days for the effects to show. Was he feeling nauseous because of that, or from the worry about his health? Rumours of the barrier having shattered were coming in too frequently for them to be untrue. The same was true for the many reports of huge birds circling the sky.

He had tried to contact Tiverius in a few of the villages they had passed through, but the lines were either busy or out. Or there were huge queues at the few stations that did work; he was too impatient to wait his turn. Meanwhile, he looked for signs that people were falling ill from sonorics poisoning and found no evidence.

The only one who seemed off colour was Nila.

On the seat next to Milleus, Isandor unrolled the map and traced his finger across the line that represented the road. "There's a village a bit further down the road. We can stop there."

Amazing, how quickly he learned. Milleus would have sworn that the boy had attended some form of tuition in Chevakian. "No, we stop here. There's a glade on the other side of the hill. There's a spring nearby and plenty of firewood." He knew the place from his hunting days.

Isandor threw him a sharp glance. "Why you always stay away from people?"

"I'm not staying away from people. We need grass for the goats."

But the boy was right, and by the looks of things, he knew it. Two days they'd been on the road, travelling in a loose convoy of trucks. Normally, it only took a day to get to Ensar, but they had to stop frequently to let the animals graze. Isandor would collect handfuls of grass and heap them on the floor of the trailer. The goats had to be milked by hand. It took a lot of time, more than he wanted, and people passed them on the road.

Nila would set up a roadside stall to sell milk to other travellers. Milleus would stay with the goats, avoiding the looks people gave him.

They *recognised* him. Closer to Tiverius, that happened more often. Old men came up to question him about politics.

"Are you going to fix things in the capital?"

"The doga should send the army across the border."

"Why isn't anyone doing anything?"

Milleus made non-committal responses, going over excuses in his mind. He was too old to become involved. The rumour that he was returning to the city, however, travelled faster than he did, and he felt like he was caught up in an unstoppable wave that was outside his control. It seemed people expected him to return, whether they wanted him to or not. He still hadn't burned the letter in his pocket. Damn Sady. Return to Tiverius.

Well, he'd do no such thing. They were merely on their way to

Ensar to get out of immediate range of the border. When they got to Ensar . . . what then? He knew no one there. His only family was Sady —in Tiverius. Well, the only family still talking to him, that was.

The van reached the top of the hill and the turnoff to the glade, where he had camped so often in his younger days, with Sady and some senators, or with foreign ambassadors. He could still hear the laughter and the baying of the dogs. He could smell roasting meat over the fire, he could hear the Aranian ambassador telling his tall tales. Memories.

Milleus killed the engine and leaned on the steering wheel. Rest. Food. Sleep.

Isandor pushed himself out of the van. The grass was knee-deep and lush green and Isandor left a track when he limped out of sight to the trailer.

The goats must have seen him coming. They were bleating and jostling each other, making the van rock.

Isandor opened the tailgate with clangs of metal and then the whole herd rumbled out, with much bleating and jingling of the chains that held them together. Isandor whistled and they quietened.

Mercy, the boy was good with animals.

Milleus pushed himself out of the driver's seat. He'd best make a fire for cooking while Isandor set up the tent. In his hunting days, they always left a pile of firewood under the trees. He wondered if it was still there.

Nila emerged from the van, rosy-cheeked and with mussed hair. "Sleep well?"

She looked better now.

"Yes. I'm hungry. Do you want me to get water?"

Milleus pointed her in the direction of the spring and, for a while, everyone went their way, Milleus making the fire, unpacking the cooking pot and peeling vegetables, Isandor milking the goats. He had learned this trick yesterday and seemed to enjoy it; his young hands were certainly much better suited to it than Milleus'.

Nila was just coming back from the creek for the second time, with bottles to fill the goats' water trough, when the putter of an engine disturbed the peace.

The last rays of the sun glittered in the window of another van entering the glade.

Oh mercy. Milleus didn't want company.

The van stopped on the other side of the glade. A young man came out, followed by a toddler and a woman. The man greeted Milleus briefly, but then went about his business of setting up a tent.

Well, that was fine then. They were nice young people, looking for quiet.

But while he was lighting a fire, another van came down the road. This one with four passengers, youths all. They stopped on the far side of the glade, almost amongst the trees. They had no tent, but unrolled bedding on the forest floor. Three of the youngsters had glossy black hair and one curls which glowed golden in the light of the fire.

Foreigners. That was fine with Milleus, too. No one who would pester him about his plans to return to Tiverius. He didn't point the group out to Isandor. At least two of those youths looked awfully southern, and one Aranian. But Isandor must have seen them, too, and made no move to talk to them. In turn, the foreigners kept to themselves and mostly sat behind their van where they made a fire out of sight of the glade.

Mercy, I'm a coward. Yes, he knew. In a way, he was afraid to find out what the youngsters' crime was. He liked them. He didn't want anything to happen to them. If he found that they'd stolen things or harmed people, he would feel betrayed. Yet, something in him told him that he really *should* find out why they were important enough to warrant search parties.

Pfa—Nila was probably just a rich man's daughter. And children were valuable enough in the City of Glass.

But, the little voice argued, the rich nobles of the City of Glass don't control the Eagle Knights. Each were a class of their own; he knew that much about their strange society.

The Lady Armaine used to wrangle invitations to doga functions; she used to shadow him at dinners, holing him up in dark corners while pressing her ample cleavage under his nose. Yeah, no goddess, that one. A power-hungry snake, more like. No doubt she revelled in all this renewed attention on the south. He could almost hear her voice. *I am a southerner. I know what is going on in my country.* No, she didn't. She'd left over fifty years ago, and hadn't travelled there since her son ended up spending some time in a southern dungeon as teenager.

He only shivered at the thought of what she would do to Destran, the spineless gasbag. What was she telling him now? *Oh, it's only a temporary flare. No need to do anything. Knights in the border provinces? Don't worry, they're just looking for some dangerous criminals. No harm will be done to anyone.*

Why wasn't this district crawling with Chevakian soldiers?

Mercy. He should go into the towns and do something, instead of hiding here with the refugees and the outcasts.

They'd been travelling all day and had seen not a single official or soldier. The people could be forgiven to think that Tiverius didn't care.

In fact, Milleus was sure the doga didn't care. From what Sady had told him, they were far too busy fighting for their political survival. The people of the district would be disgruntled and support him, ride all the way to the capital with him and march into the doga . . .

Pfa, what nonsense. You're an old man, Milleus han Chevonian.

They ate and Nila announced she was going to sleep. She looked tired, too. Milleus still couldn't shake the feeling that she wasn't well.

Isandor got up to accompany her to the tent, his arm around her shoulders. She leaned into him and let him caress her. Milleus guessed Isandor would probably not come back to the fire either. Last night, Milleus had gone to sleep in the van trying to block the soft noises from the tent.

But soon after the youngsters had gone into the tent, the flap moved and Isandor came back out. The flickering glow from the fire danced over his face. Was it a trick of the light, or had the ungainly black hairs on his chin increased? Maybe he should lend the boy his barber's razor.

Milleus held out an empty cup, for tea, but Isandor shook his head. "You watch when we sleep. I get up in the night and watch you."

Milleus frowned.

Isandor cast a quick glance at the van with the southerners.

"It's all right," he said. "I think they're just refugees. None of them look like full-blood southerners."

"The Eagle Knights use elite teams called hunters. They're mostly half bloods and other outcasts from the City of Glass. They are the most dangerous soldiers the south has."

The intensity in his eyes made something click for Milleus. All of a sudden, he understood what Isandor had done. "You're a deserter."

Isandor squinted and let the silence linger for a few long seconds. Then he said, "Of a kind, yes."

Milleus thought he knew the kind. He was well-familiar with armed forces and what superiors sometimes did to men they didn't like. With his wooden leg, Isandor would fit the bill of someone these tyrants loved to pick on. He fought to repress a shudder.

"Is that why they're after you?"

"They want to kill us," Isandor said.

"These foreigners don't look dangerous."

"No." Isandor's eyes were intense; they said *I think they could be.*

"All right. I'll watch them."

Isandor nodded in that intense way of his and went back into the tent.

Milleus sipped from his tea and stared into the fire. One piece of the puzzle put into place. Isandor had been an Eagle Knight apprentice, or whatever they were called. That's why he knew so much about military strategy.

The thought again crossed his mind, *What if he's a spy?* But he discarded it just as quickly as he had before. Certainly a spy would never flaunt that type of knowledge. Nor could he see any government, not even the dictatorial south, appointing mere teenagers as spies.

That left the enigma of the girl. Because Nila wasn't her name. What did she have to hide?

Their voices and rustling of blankets were soft in the tent. They really were very considerate. And anyway, how much did you need to hide that you were in love?

He sighed. Saw Suri at the dining table a few days before she took her own life. One bright look, a smile. Not at him, but Sady. What was going on between them? He'd asked her.

So it's fine for you to see prostitutes and it's not fine for me to have a friend?

It was not the same, and she wouldn't see that. If she wanted a playboy, whom she paid, that was fine, but his own unmarried brother . . . she refused to say whether or not she ever slept with Sady. "That is just such a ridiculous question, Milleus. You don't understand how ridiculous." His best guess was that her refusal to answer the question meant that she had.

And Milleus had . . .

Jealousy was an ugly emotion. There was no excuse for what he had done, for what he would have to forget. The marriage had been bad from the start. He should have known the moment she became reluctant to be touched. He should have let her go, but he'd never wanted to push her. He should have . . .

He'd expected her to run out on him, find another man, but *kill* herself?

"Mind if we join you?"

Milleus started at the sound of the young male voice.

The young father stood there, holding a lute. The young woman, the toddler's mother waited just behind him.

Milleus shrugged. "Sure. Sit down. Want some tea?"

The young couple sat down and introduced themselves. They were from one of the towns they had passed through and underway to Tiverius, because the man had family there.

"It's much safer to go there than stay in Ensar," the young father said. "If anything happens, do you think the doga would let it happen to the capital?"

His eyes met Milleus' and Milleus felt uncomfortable, but there was no suspicion on the man's face. He was possibly too young to have remembered the glory days of Proctor Milleus han Chevonian.

Milleus shrugged. "Politics don't interest me much." *Liar.*

The subject changed to travel experiences, and then goats. The young man played his lute, and the music drew three of the foreign youths to the fire. There was a lanky young man with olive skin who had to be Aranian, an adolescent youth with curly golden hair but hazel eyes who had to be a Chevakian half-breed. The third person turned out to be a young woman with silky black hair and intense blue eyes. Under a too-wide shirt of thin material, her figure was thin, androgynous. She moved with the grace and stealth of a sabre-cat. Milleus didn't doubt the strength of those corded muscles. But her eyes were wide and held a kind of innocence that only came with youth. She was gorgeous in every way.

The young father sang and the foreigners shared bottles of a heavy, sweet liquor. Milleus felt drawn back to the pleasant memories he had of camping in this glade. In those days, there had never been any women, but the southern woman seemed to fit in perfectly. She laughed with the boys, she swore enough to colour the ears of a soldier, she drank like them—straight from the mouth of the bottle—and her deep sensual voice carried a promise of living fast and dangerously, like a man, like a soldier. The golden-haired youth had a huge store of bawdy jokes, and in between passing the bottle they laughed themselves silly.

The more he drank, the more Milleus looked at the sleek-haired beauty. She returned his glances, secretly, over the shoulder of her hawkish Aranian friend. Milleus wasn't used to drinking so much anymore, and somewhere in the back of his mind a voice told him to get out before there was trouble and go to sleep. The voice sounded like Suri, who used to be angry with him when he was drunk. Mercy, when he was drunk he used to do stupid things. Like force her into his bed. It was a wonder those two useless sons of his weren't born with alcohol in their veins.

He rose, so unsteady on his feet.

"Look, I better go to bed. 'S a long day t'morrow." He couldn't even talk properly anymore.

He stumbled to the van. Remembered vaguely that we was supposed to stay awake to guard the tent. What for? These half-southern youngsters were just louts.

They haven't told you who they were and where they're from, the little voice in his head said.

"Ow, mercy, sh . . . shuddup." He put his hand on the door of the truck's cabin. All right, he'd guard the truck. He'd just sit in the cabin and—

—the pale-skinned woman slipped next to him, bottle in hand.

"Don't go yet." Her voice was deep and sultry, unlike any woman's he had heard before. She leaned against the truck and tipped the bottle to her mouth. A rivulet of moisture ran from the corner of her mouth down her chin, over her neck.

The firelight gilded her thin blouse and the merest of curves underneath. A nipple, hard and erect, pushed the fabric.

Something stirred in him.

Milleus tried to shake himself out of his stupor. *You're seventy-one years old and you're drunk.*

"Why don't you come with me?" She flicked a glance in the direction of the forest.

Beyond the glow of the fire, tree trunks stood as dark sentinels.

A few moments of unattached passion. He had plenty of money, and she needed it. Come to think of it, that was probably how the four of them survived. She'd been scouting him out all night. Since the young father made an unlikely customer, she had set her eyes on him.

Mercy.

He should go to bed if he knew what was good for him. Go to bed and listen to Isandor and Nila's lovemaking for much of the night.

He shook his head. "I'm an old man, twice the age of your usual customer, I bet."

She gave a crooked laugh. Her blue eyes were intense.

"You'd be surprised," she said. She trailed her fine-boned but wiry hand over his arm. He shivered, feeling the blood stir inside him.

"I think you had better go and bother a younger man."

"Really?" She raised her eyebrows.

"Don't fl . . . flatter me." His voice was unsteady from the drink, but his crotch glowed pleasantly.

"I like older men. I think you could show me a thing or two."

Oh woman, where do you think I've been the last ten years?

On the farm with the goats, that was where. He hadn't been near a woman for a long time, had no idea if his body was still up to the task; but it might be, it just might.

Who would care, really, if he spent his own time and own money on a bit of pleasure? The goats wouldn't eat any less, and Isandor and Nila wouldn't know. He was meant to watch the southerners, and he was just watching them very closely. Even if the youngsters did find out, they might realise that not just young people had fun.

"Come." She pulled his hand. Milleus stumbled a few paces, swaying, and then regained his balance. Mercy, it had been a long time since he'd been this drunk. She draped her body cat-like against his. Warm and smelling of female perfume. It wouldn't take long, oh no, it wouldn't, he could feel it, he still had some fire in him.

"Ow, let's go, then."

She gave him a mischievous smile.

He hooked his arm in his, and drank another good swig from the bottle. She offered it to him; he took it and gulped the burning fluid. Oh, his whole body was throbbing *most* pleasantly now.

But somehow, in his drunkenness he registered that she was pulling him towards their van, and he vaguely remembered that he vowed to keep an eye on Isandor and Nila.

"No, no, Lady. I have a nice van. There's a lot of . . . room inside . . ."

"I have all my oils in the wagon. I'll give you a good rub."

But Milleus wasn't interested in a rub. He wanted to . . . hell, he wanted to fuck her hard, not care about decency, and wake up the youngsters with the noises they had plagued him with.

"Let's just go in the forest." From there, he could keep an eye on the tent; he'd promised Isandor.

"All right." She gathered up her shoes.

Holding her hand, he led her between the trees. He stopped a few paces in, pushed her against a tree trunk.

"No," she whispered. "Not here. I don't want my friends to see. They can't know what I am."

Oh, rubbish. Everyone knows what you are. "Your friends are drunk as anything. Just stay still. I won't take long."

In one movement, she pulled her shirt over her head. "Catch me."

She jumped a few steps and he chased after her, and managed to get hold of her arm.

He pulled her into a close embrace in the shadow of the tree trunk. She panted, arching her back, undoing the fastening of her trousers. He slid his hands over her skin, breathing the scent of her hair. The muscles on her belly were firm, her breasts soft. Blood roared in his ears. It had been so long . . .

A branch cracked behind him.

Milleus gasped, suddenly wide awake.

Hang on.

Somehow, her *catch me* game had taken him far enough in the forest that he could no longer see the tent, where his two southern fugitives lay asleep.

"Wait."

"What?" she said. She was stark naked, and the firelight gilded small breasts. "Come on, I'm waiting for you." She pulled his arm.

"Gotta check something." He shouldn't have left the fire.

He yanked himself free, and ran, half-stumbling through the forest.

The tent was silhouetted against the firelight. He couldn't see anyone near it, but a shadow stood beside the foreigner's van—the fourth member of the southern group, the young man who hadn't come to the fire.

Milleus ran, all effects of alcohol banished from his mind.

"Isandor, Isandor!"

He reached the tent, at almost the same time as a dark figure rushed out. The man crashed into Milleus and swore, or so Milleus presumed, because he didn't speak Chevakian. Milleus thought it was the Aranian youth.

Then there was Isandor's voice, also not in Chevakian. A knife flashed. Someone screamed and a second figure ran from the tent, his head wrapped in a headscarf. An engine started up.

Nila came to the tent entrance holding a flapping candle. "Milleus? Who was that?"

Isandor scrambled out after her. He opened his clutched fist in the pool of light cast by the candle. There was a handful of fur in bloodied his palm. "Knights."

Nila clasped her hand over her mouth. "They cut you."

"It's nothing." Isandor wiped the fur on his trousers. His gaze was on the edge of the forest where the foreign van no longer stood. "They were not here to capture us. They were here to kill us. I woke up because there was a noise. I saw the knife."

"Who were they? How did they get in?"

Isandor met Milleus' eyes.

Milleus felt heat rise to his cheeks. Yes, he was supposed to have been watching. And just as well one of the foreigners stepped on a branch. "I was in the forest—" And then he felt like he needed to explain. "Taking a piss."

Isandor frowned. "With a woman?"

Milleus looked over his shoulder. The foreign woman was gone, of course, but Isandor would have seen her.

Isandor's blue eyes met his. Then he gave a wolfish smile. "Oh."

Oh indeed. Milleus didn't know whether to feel stupid or victorious. Had he been near the fire as he ought to have been, nothing would have happened.

"It's not safe here," he grumbled. "I'll sleep in the tent with you."

He went to get his mat and lay down, after stopping for a good spew behind a tree. Mercy, he'd feel like a wet dishrag tomorrow morning.

Somewhere in the dark beyond his vision Isandor and Nila kissed and whispered to each other. Milleus pulled his bedding over his head, irritated that the itch inside him had not been stilled.

He lay staring into the dark until silence returned and still couldn't sleep. His mind churned.

He'd been stupid. Not just about a silly pair of pretty eyes, but about everything he cared about, and everyone who cared about him.

And he had grieved over his sour marriage and Suri's death far too long. He might well have another twenty years of fire left in him. Seventy-one was old, but he wasn't dead yet. If he was still up to misbehaving himself, he could be useful to someone. He would have to go and fix the mess Destran had made, find out what foreign spies were doing here, and why there had been two attempts on the youngsters' lives. When all that was sorted, he would go to a matchmaker to find himself a woman. Not too young, mind because he didn't want any more children.

Tiverius then, it was.

Damn you, Sady.

CHAPTER 24

CARRO STARED at the hunk of meat in his hand. The yellow light from the fire glistened in fat dripping down the bone over his hand and down his arm.

He had taken a few bites of the leg from the animal Nolan had shot, but was no longer hungry. This life sickened him. The way Jeito and Nolan had held up a family of refugees and confiscated their van and their food, and shot the father when he protested too much, the way Nolan enjoyed stealing from others on the road.

Why couldn't they even leave refugees in peace?

The whisper of voices in the back of his mind had almost become constant, an itch he couldn't scratch. It had whispered at him while they ran back to the van after having been disturbed, and during the mad ride through the forest, and the lonely drive on the dark and deserted road and the hours no one had said anything in the cabin. Farey drove like an idiot, and now that the sky was turning blue in the east, they had finally stopped.

Jeito and Farey sat on the other side of the fire, casting him occasional glances. If they hadn't known about the fire in the house and how Carro had ignored the two people fleeing from it, they knew now. Nolan had settled between them and Carro, as if he couldn't make up his mind who to support.

No one told any jokes now.

"So . . . straight to Tiverius from here?" Nolan asked into the silence that had lasted too long.

"No point hanging around here now they're all on alert," Jeito said, with a sharp glance at Carro. "Remembering that both of them can use icefire, and if the barrier has really broken, they'll burn us to ashes if we try again."

"We almost did it," Farey said, staring into the fire.

Again, Jeito glanced at Carro. Carro shivered in a breeze of cool air. So that had been the secret. Jeito was a woman, or could be, if he wanted to. Or maybe he was one of those confusing people who were born both.

"Clumsy pup," Farey snarled. "Stepping on a piece of wood. Why did we ever agree to take you?"

"It's not fair," Nolan said. "Carro has never been here before. He doesn't know how there are branches on the ground that can break and how much noise it makes when they do—"

"Oh, just shut up," Farey said. "We had our chance. We've blown it, thanks to him, deliberate or not."

The haunted grey eyes met Carro's. Carro looked away.

And the strange thing was: he didn't feel sorry. He hadn't planned to do it, but Carro could still see it before him, a dead piece of gnarled wood. He could feel himself lifting his foot, and stomping down on the twig.

Crack. Deliberately, as far as he had ever done anything deliberate. Which, admittedly, wasn't often.

Why?

To make up for the fact that he had betrayed Isandor? Because he still called Jevaithi his queen no matter what Rider Cornatan—his father—said? Because the merchant, his foster father, had despised her and therefore Carro must adore her?

Because Isandor was my friend.

Isandor and Jevaithi weren't doing anyone harm. They were fleeing with the old man, fleeing something that they, with their southern blood, didn't need to flee. They could have taken the old man's farm, and they didn't. They were helping him and his flock of noisy animals. And the old man, a Chevakian if there ever was one, seemed to care about them.

Care. That was the key word. Had he ever cared about anyone?

Not his stepfather, certainly not his stepmother or his stepsister. Not Korinne. Not the Knight Apprentices, not even the man who had claimed to be his real father. And here, Farey scared him shitless, Jeito scared him more if that was possible, and Nolan was just an innocent bumbling idiot who happened to be good with a blowpipe and dagger. Carro found his proclaimed love increasingly wearying.

Could he care for anyone or had this horrid abnormality of his mind robbed him of that, too?

He'd watched Isandor and the old man from a distance, talking to each other, laughing, smiling. A pat on the shoulder, a hand getting out of the truck. Caring for each other, even though they were not related, total strangers as little as a moon ago.

By the skylights, Carro, you're jealous.

Carro threw the bone and remaining meat in the fire and rose to go into the forest for a piss. To clear his mind and consider what to do now.

"Yeah, that's right, walk away when things get hard, that's how you live, isn't it?" Jeito shouted.

Carro froze, met Jeito's eyes and felt cold at the naked fury in them.

"You're a coward. You need some balls. Come on, tell me. Why did you do it?"

"I did nothing," Carro said.

"Too right you didn't. You've been nothing but a burden to us ever since we let you come along." When angry, Jeito looked more female.

"I had to stay behind. We all agreed on that. They would have recognised me."

"So instead, you betrayed us." Jeito rose. The firelight glinted on the boning knife in her hand. Yes, her arms were thinner than his, but corded with muscle.

"Whoa, Jeito." Nolan stepped between them. "Calm down. It was an accident."

"You know nothing about accidents. Get out of the way, oaf. I'll kill him!" Jeito pushed Nolan aside with far too much ease, grabbed Carro by the collar of his shirt and drew him up. Muscles quivered. The firelight shone through Jeito's thin blouse. She had breasts. But muscles, and a face with angles and planes like a man.

Carro tried to pull his shirt loose, but Jeito's grip tightened; he could barely breathe.

"You just fucked up my chance at getting back to the City of Glass with the Knights. I've been waiting for this for years, and you come along, you little creep. . . and you fuck it all up. You hear that? You fuck it up!" She screamed in his face and shook his collar. "Fuck, fuck, fuck! That's what you are, a little fuck! I'm going to kill you."

"Stop it!" called Farey.

Jeito froze. Licked her lips and gave him a sideways glace. Farey was the only one who had any kind of influence over her, even if only because he was much taller. Maybe he fucked her, but Carro had no doubt that was only because Jeito let him.

"Calm down," Farey said. "There's no point in fighting over what has already happened. The damage is done, and we won't get a second chance. It's not our task to deal with Carro's stupidity. If we do, we'll only be punished. Remember who he is. Let his father take care of it."

He looked at Carro, his dark eyes full of hatred.

A chill made Carro shiver. His father. His father who wanted him to kill the only friend he'd ever had.

Maybe he should just . . . vanish, become a foreign spy in another country, like Farey. Run away.

That's how you live your life, isn't it?

"Yeah, you're right." Jeito chuckled and let Carro's collar go. "I think I like that. Let his father take care of it."

"All right, so if we've decided that, let's quit fooling around with this stupid van, take the eagles and go to Tiverius," Farey said.

Nolan raised his eyebrows. "You know something we don't?"

"There was a bird. We've been ordered to join up with the other Knights either in the west or Tiverius. Tiverius is closer."

"Why didn't you say so?"

Carro was glad Nolan had turned his anger on Farey.

Farey flicked his eyebrows. "Why should I tell you anything that you might let slip out while you're fucking the traitor?"

Nolan's eyes grew wide with indignation. "Hey, have I ever betrayed you in all the time I've been with you?"

Neither Farey nor Jeito spoke.

"Come on, really?"

Farey rose, leaving Nolan standing there, still without an answer. Carro didn't know where to look. Because of him, people got into trouble. Because of him, people died. Maybe he would be better off dead, too.

Farey let out a long whistle.

Jeito walked to the fire. While whooshing wingbeats of the approaching eagles disturbed the predawn silence, she pulled out a log that burned on one end. Carro realised what she was going to do just before she threw it, trailed by a stream of embers, into the truck. The canopy burst into flames almost immediately.

"There," she said, rubbing her hands. "Never liked that Chevakian devilry anyway." She wiped her hands on her trousers—a very female gesture now Carro knew the secret—and scratched her eagle's neck. The bird bent down and rubbed itself against her shoulder, to which she responded by ruffling its feathers. The bird stretched out its head at a weird angle, presenting more of its white-feathered neck to her.

"Oh, you stupid bird," she muttered, and scratched, sending a cloud of down into the air.

Even Jeito—murderous, evil, two-faced Jeito—cared about something.

One jump, and she sat on the bird's back, face aglow with the light from the burning truck.

"Come up, pups, hurry up. I'm not waiting for the Chevakian army to turn up to investigate the fire."

Carro lifted the harness over his bird's head. It snapped at the straps and hissed while he attached his bedroll.

Yes, I know you hate me, too.

Then they were off into the predawn. Farey knew of an abandoned shed where they'd sleep until dark, and from there on, it was straight to Tiverius.

Even Nolan was giving him looks that said, *Don't you dare trying to sneak off.* And where would he go anyway?

He had no home.

Tiverius was bigger than the biggest city Carro had ever seen. Even in the dark, and from a distance, the spread of lights dazzled him. There were no tall buildings, like in the City of Glass, but there were so many of them. Street after street with neatly planted trees and regular streetlights. He'd read of Chevakia, of course, but had not appreciated just how many people would live there, and how impressive and peaceful it would look.

Farey had made the hunters wait until dark before approaching the city, so no one would see them. He even knew where to go. Farey had probably been here before. He had not shown the note he was said to have received to anyone, but somehow, neither Jeito or Nolan questioned the order. When Carro asked Nolan about it, he said something about Farey having skill with tampering with the Chevakian *telegraph* whatever that might mean. It seemed the hunters *did* have a post deep in Chevakia, and had a base in Tiverius. Maybe they'd always had it, but none of the hunters was answering Carro's questions anymore.

After skirting the city's outer edges, they flew over hilly terrain where the ground was dark with trees and dotted with lights from the occasional farm.

It was in such a farm that the eagles landed, a low arch-shaped building of the type he had also seen near the border. The open end of the arch was blocked with a number of open sheds. The courtyard was bare and it was here that the eagles landed.

A young stable boy came out of the nearest shed to take the eagle's reins. Now Carro saw that there were more eagles under the canopy, at least ten birds, none of them familiar.

Under the balustrade that surrounded the courtyard, a senior Knight waited, also someone Carro hadn't seen before. He greeted Farey with a single nod of his head, and a hand sign that Carro didn't recognise. Farey mumbled something.

"The eastern road, he told me," the senior Knight said.

"What, now?" Farey spoke in a low voice.

"Immediately."

"Tell him to go fuck himself," Farey snarled. "They won't arrive until daytime. I haven't slept for days. These soft Chevakians don't do anything at night."

"Then send one of your sissy-boys—aaah!"

Jeito stood very close to the senior Knight. Carro couldn't see much by the soft dawn light, but if he wasn't mistaken, Jeito had the man by the balls.

"See what these sissy-boys can do?" she said, her voice menacing.

The man's face glistened with sweat. "Go. Do whatever. But don't come to me when he gets angry."

"The fuck he won't. Come, let's find a bed," Farey said and stomped off. Jeito followed—the senior Knight took a step back—and then Nolan, but when Carro walked past, the senior Knight held him back. "No, not you."

What? Carro stared after the hunters' retreating backs, his heart thudding.

"Your father wants to see you."

Oh, by the skylights. "He's here?"

"Not right now, but I've been ordered to give you some work that you're said to be good at. Something he needs done urgently."

Carro wanted to say, *It's all a lie, I'm not good at anything*, but he only nodded, so the Knight preceded him into the building.

Carro sees his mittened hands atop a wall. Isandor stands behind him in the alley.

"Can you see anything yet?"

Carro peers between the limpets ahead, pointed roofs half-hidden in thick roiling smoke. The breeze blows some of it his way. He coughs and shakes his head.

"Must be a warehouse on fire."

He hopes it's his father's. He hopes his father is inside the building and that the door is locked—

The house was a dark affair with high stone halls in which all noise echoed relentlessly. A few Knights sat to eat in a room with long tables. Carro didn't recognise anyone in this room. Several Knights sported injuries, especially faces and hands.

"What exactly happened in the City of Glass?" he asked.

"What, you don't know? Where have you been?"

Carro opened his mouth and then remembered that hunters never spoke of their missions.

"Just came in from regular patrols in the countryside."

The senior Knight chuckled. "Those hunters are quite fearsome, aren't they?"

Carro almost reminded the man that the fact that he still had his balls had nothing to do with his senior Knight rank, but he didn't. "Wherever I was, it wasn't in the City of Glass."

The Knight let a pause lapse. Then he said, "No one knows what caused it, but there was a huge explosion under the palace. The entire city has been destroyed. Many died. The people were talking about huge ghosts made out of steam."

Another senior Knight walking behind them broke in, "I reckon the sorcerers did it. Those evil ones in black."

"There have always been Brothers of the Light in the Outer City," Carro said. "They're idiots, with all their formulae and calculations."

That earned him a lot of harsh glances.

Carro was going to say that the Brothers never hurt anyone, and that no one would have as much knowledge of the old King without the Brothers having preserved some of the books, but he didn't think these men would appreciate that. So he just kept walking.

Visions niggled at the edges of his mind. Snow-covered plains and sleds made from pieces of rubble they found in the back alleys of the Outer City.

A man, shouting at him, probably for coming into his yard to filch bits of rope or pieces of dried fish.

The constant fear of running foul of his foster-father. Knowing that whatever he did and whatever time he came home and whatever the state of his clothing, the merchant would be angry anyway. Seeing Isandor being led away by his mother, her arm on his skinny shoulders.

. . . and all of a sudden, they arrived in a large room where old furniture had been shifted to the side to make place for a couple of dining tables of varying height, shoved together and surrounded by a mismatched lot of chairs. An ornate, high-backed chair stood at the head of the table. Heavy curtains covered the windows, faded and frayed, and the room was lit only by smoking oil lamps on the walls.

For some reason, Carro thought of that black stone room in the palace where he had first met Rider Cornatan.

Another, less-senior Knight came from somewhere at the back of the room, frowning at Carro.

"I'm supposed to do some work for Rider Cornatan," Carro said.

"Your name?"

"Carro."

Eyebrows shot up. Another glance up and down his dirty uniform.

Carro was sweating under his shirt. Any moment now and he was going to be challenged about the veracity of his name, about his mission, about the state of his clothes—

"So, you're the famous boy, eh?"

Carro cringed.

"Your father's not in, but he left you some work to do. Sit here."

Carro sat. He clutched the medallion through his clothes. Maybe he should just give the damn thing back. Surely Rider Cornatan had other sons.

"Here you go." The man had returned with a pile of books.

Books? "What am I supposed to do with them?"

"Check them. The Supreme Rider tells me you're really good at that."

Carro took the top book off the pile and opened it.

It was a ledger.

What? They were kidding, right?

"You might wonder why we worry about finances while there's a war going on?"

"Um—yeah." His mouth had gone dry. He fought the visions clawing at his awareness. Of his father carrying a big pile of books. Of his hands aching with cold. Of his father dousing the flames in the hearth, *Heat is for soft boys*. Of lines and lines of numbers dancing before his eyes.

"Well, money in Chevakia is important, and we need money to buy things so that we can survive here. The caretaker of this house has run off, leaving the books in a mess."

CHAPTER 25

To SADY, the afternoon session of the doga—the important debate to discuss the vital tightening and redistribution of the budget—felt like stepping in tar. As soon as you thought you'd crossed it safely, it turned out there was some sticky residue on the sole of your shoe that kept leaving its mark all over the floor.

Sady seemed to have stepped in a patch of northern railways and had so far been unable to wipe the contamination from the afternoon's debate.

Yes, the north would support spending on distributing suits to the southern regions, if the promised expansion of the northern railway remained unaffected by the budget cuts. Yes, they would sign for the injection of non-existent funds into the balloon industry, if the old trains got new carriages. Yes, they would vote with the central regions in favour of Sady's proposals, providing that—you guessed it.

An eastern senator summed up Sady's feeling. "And I would like my honourable colleague to elaborate on how we are going to finance this railway."

Unlike the other senators, Sady couldn't yell and shout; and he wanted to, because with every hour that passed, he discovered more financial mess. The latest disaster he had uncovered was that someone appeared to have taken a number of the doga's finance record books from the treasury office, and not only didn't anyone know where they were, but no one had missed them.

The doga was wasting valuable time with this kind of nonsense, time they should have spent discussing what to do about the unfolding crisis in the south.

And Destran, at the back of the hall, looked like he was enjoying himself. The debate about railways went around in circles, and Sady kept glancing at the door, wondering what held up General Finnisius, who was meant to address the doga on the progress made by the army on the balloons, and was running late. The general had always been very punctual in previous meetings.

The thought clawed at the edges of his mind, *something has happened*. It was about the time that the trains from Fairlight would be expected back, and he hoped that the majority of Fairlight's citizens had taken the warning to get on.

And then this stupid meeting . . . Sady leafed through his documents, which detailed the agenda for the meeting that wasn't happening in any orderly fashion, but which he couldn't steer because the proctor was not allowed to interfere in the debate; the speaker was meant to be doing that, except the speaker was a central senator who had voted for Destran, and was obviously still sore about that. Every time someone mentioned an important point, he ever-so-subtly allowed senators to derail it with trivialities, like the stupid northern railway.

Sady had the documents with measurements from his trip to the border towns all done up, but there had already been some rumbles about who funded his trip, because he'd had to declare Lady Armaine's sponsorship, and this was causing all sorts of political spot fires about southern spies, about her loyalty and about whether or not she could possibly be called Chevakian. And that was just amongst his own office staff.

Never, ever, trust this woman.

Sady hadn't seen her since his trip and now wished he'd had nothing to do with her. Nothing of what she'd said about the south had been verified through other channels.

The scout he had sent with the peasant woman to Solmeni sent an alarming report from Twin Bridges this morning. The town's lines to the south were all out. The town was shrouded in smoke from forest fires, but it was unseasonably cold.

A vicious storm, Viki said, and showed him the crowded isobar lines having made their way into southern Chevakia.

Sady had asked Viki to contact the border stations on the telegraph, but he had received no new data. He wasn't sure Viki knew how to get the most out of the automated barygraph network, and wished he could do it himself, but writing new code for the machine took time, which he no longer had, having to discuss railways to the north instead.

And he hoped Viki would have the sense to keep trying. If his awful premonition was true and the barrier had shattered, sonorics in the city wouldn't increase for a number of days. Those days were crucial, since they could find out how far the menace would travel and how strong it would be. The city did have some defences. There were guidelines, a plan to keep people indoors, and, if necessary, an evacuation.

But he needed data to justify taking those measures.

No one knew what had happened. Not a word from the City of Glass, although Sady had made sure that messengers had finally been despatched. His trip to Milleus to seek out his wartime experience had been in vain, and none of the data he had gathered could convince the doga of the urgency of the threat. His support margin was too small to allow him to push through hard decisions. He was a leader without a real mandate.

Milleus, old goat, you let us down when we needed you.

Someone tapped Sady on the shoulder.

"Proctor?"

He turned to see his office boy behind him.

He mouthed, "What?" The office staff didn't usually come into the doga hall. His heart skipped with the nervousness that had never left him these last few days.

"There's a soldier in the office, Proctor. He insists that you come with him."

"We're in the middle of a session. Can it wait?"

The boy shook his head. "He said it's urgent."

"Is the message from General Finnisius?"

"He says the general has a problem. Please, Proctor, he was most insistent."

Sady heaved himself out of his chair. Senators fell quiet even before he hit the dais with the hammer. "You are going to have to excuse me. I have to adjourn the session. Something has come up."

There was some unhappy grumbling in the hall, mainly from northern senators.

At the back of the hall, Destran said, loud enough for him to hear, "Adjourning the session won't save your arse."

Some senators laughed.

Sady gathered up his documents and left, feeling chilled. His term would be a short one, he feared, having achieved nothing, and leaving the doga in more upheaval than it had been when he came to power—was that only a week ago?

In his office, he found that "the soldier" was the Proctor's personal guard Deri, who was normally stationed in the guard's post on the building's ground floor, but performed other tasks while the Proctor was in the building.

"What's this about?" Sady asked.

"Major Orsan asked me to come and get you. It's an emergency. The escort's down the corridor. Orsan says to bring your monitoring gear."

"But General Finnisius—"

"Is already there, Proctor. Please."

"What is going on?"

Deri didn't know any more, except that it was an emergency. Orsan was not someone prone to theatrics and neither was Finnisius, so Sady collected his cloak and his field box of sonorics measuring gear and followed him into the corridor.

A breeze came in through the open window, biting and cold.

In the courtyard of the doga building, two lines of soldiers faced each other in a changing-of-the-guard ceremony. The tassels on their epaulettes flapped in the wind. Soft green leaves that had grown on the trees with the beginning of spring now lay on the ground.

A young member of the city guard waited at the top of the stairs, his face anxious. He fell into step, taking up position on Sady's other side.

"Any report on what's happening?" Sady asked him.

"About midmorning, a train with what appeared to be refugees turned up at the station."

Mercy, the people from Fairlight. Finally.

"Stationmaster needs your advice urgently on what he should do. Thinks that you should make a decision because they're contaminated. Major Orsan is there, trying to keep them under control. It's not easy, Proctor. These people are in a bad way, and they're angry. They're not in the mood for being friendly, and we're still trying to find someone to communicate with them."

"Communicate?" Rebelling refugees? Certainly not the citizens of Fairlight.

"Yes. They're all southerners, sir, and we haven't found anyone who speaks Chevakian."

Sady turned to the man, his heart thudding. "Southerners?"

"Yes, I thought you understood that."

"Surely there must be some of the citizens of Fairlight on the train."

He shrugged. "If there are, we haven't found them yet."

"How many people are there?"

"Oh, I don't know. The train was packed. Many of them. Many are injured. They look like they've been burnt. There's dead people, too."

"Have you measured them for sonorics?" Sady felt his grasp on the situation slip from under him.

"Off the scale, sir. Station's been sealed off pending your advice."

Burn injuries meant extreme exposure to sonorics. Southern people, too, who were supposed to be resistant. The scale of this disaster made him feel numb. Was this what the Lady Armaine called rebellion?

He forced himself to focus on immediate needs. He could not have these people loose in Tiverius contaminating everyone else. "How many injured?"

The man shrugged, but he read the answer in his eyes. A lot.

"Well, let's see what we can do." He certainly sounded a lot more confident than he felt.

While they walked, he found some strands of reason. There was a field on the south-eastern outskirts of the city that was used sometimes by travelling troupes of artistes or cheapskate merchants. He would ask the army to set up tents there. The only trouble was, he would have to close the main road to Ensar because it went through the field, but they would have to set up diversions.

The marketplace bustled with the normal kinds of activity, which seemed surreal after his recent experiences. A young man and his wife or sister pulled a heavy cart full of fresh glistening fish. The man interrupted his work for a cheerful, "Good afternoon, Proctor," and other merchants echoed the greeting.

Sady had the feeling that soon, all normality would be blasted out of everyone's lives, that something was brewing the likes of which Chevakia had never seen.

The station was on the other side of the marketplace. There were soldiers at the station entrance, blocking the way in. A few confused passengers carrying bags of shopping waited and argued with them.

"But how can I get home?"

"I paid for the ticket."

Beyond the blockade, the steps into the building were empty.

The soldiers would not let Sady through until a man in a protective suit came down the stairs. He pushed up his hood. Orsan. His face glistened with sweat.

"Sady, I'm glad that you're here."

"How many people are in there?"

"Hundreds. The train was crammed."

Sady glanced into the dark maw of the station building, where he saw no one, but heard the murmur of many voices. A breeze carried a stink such as Sady had never smelled in his life. He gasped. "What's that awful smell?"

"Sorry, sir," said a man in station attendant uniform. "There was nothing we could do. We had to let them out of the trains. They're all on the platform at the moment, but many of them were dead, and the wagons . . . The line master says there's another three trains coming —" His eyes were haunted.

They were the trains he'd sent all right.

"Any citizens of Fairlight on the trains?"

"Not that I've seen," Orsan said. His eyes went distant.

Sady shivered in a cool breeze. He had never seen Orsan dishevelled like this. "What happened to them?"

"Your guess is as good as mine, sir, and at the moment I'm not sure I'll like your guess any better than mine."

Dead. The barrier shattered.

"Where is the stationmaster?"

"In his office, sir, with the driver." The station attendant continued, "What do you want us to do with these people, sir? They're anxious and nervous and I don't know how long we can keep them here. We need more guards."

"Already notified and on their way," Orsan said.

"Let me talk to the people," Sady said.

"No, sir. No one should go between them. These people are desperate. There's hundreds of them. They're hungry and sick. They'd rip you to pieces. They crackle with sonorics, all of them, and I don't know that any speak Chevakian."

Sady breathed in deeply as a waft carried fresh air across the marketplace. He scoured in his pocket. Found a handkerchief and pressed it over his nose. "Then find me a suit. I'm going to talk to the stationmaster."

What else could he do? He had to get this mob out of here somehow, in a way that didn't make them angrier than they already were, and after a three-day train ride from Fairlight in that stench, he guessed that would be pretty angry. "Where is General Finnisius?"

"Gone to mobilise the troops, sir."

Good. At least someone was getting a measure of what the situation required.

Someone handed him a suit. Sady pulled it on over his clothes. He hadn't worn a suit for a while, and the musty smell reminded him of his trips to the City of Glass. But even while the weather was unusually cold, Tiverius was much warmer than the City of Glass, and he was sweating inside the suit as soon as he'd done up the helmet.

"Come," he said, keen to get out of the suit again as soon as possible, because a proctor who'd fainted from heat stress was no good to anyone.

A heavily armed guard of four accompanied Sady up the stairs.

People crammed on the platform behind a barrier of armed guards in protective suits.

They were clearly southern people, with a dominance of dark hair, pale skin and blue eyes, and the latter were rare in Chevakia. Many carried packs and blankets of dirty fur. The people were dirty, too, sweaty, greasy-haired, red-faced.

Even through the suit, the stench was incredible. Sweat, dirt, vomit, excrement and overriding all that, the all-pervasive smell of decaying flesh.

A woman screamed and tried to run past the guards. The crowd surged and pushed. Soldiers struggled to keep them on the platform, guns levelled at the people. Civilians, all. Frightened out of their senses. Hungry, desperate. Contaminated. They had despair in their eyes, weeping sores on exposed skin. Horrific injuries.

Three more trains. Mercy, what were they going to do with them all? There were at least . . . he let his eyes roam the heaving crowd . . . at least a thousand people here, if not more. Yes, probably far more than that. Three more trains?

Sady swallowed nausea.

Then, in the middle of the seething crowd and between the suited bodies of two guards, his eyes met those of a woman sitting quietly serene. She wasn't exactly young—early middle age—but she was hideously pregnant. She wore a plain brown dress and had a mass of black curly hair tied at the nape of her neck. Her face was pale, her cheeks red and incredibly alive. She saw him, and her gaze held his. Her expression didn't radiate despair; it radiated hot anger. A woman having fled for her life, crowded onto a train, a woman proud and dignified even after all this hardship. A woman who didn't deserve this.

Just a moment, and then he'd lost sight of her.

The guards led him up the stairs to the stationmaster's office, which overlooked the platform.

The stationmaster stood at the receiver behind his desk, talking to the mayor. Both wore suits but no helmets. Sady entered the room, shut the door and lifted the helmet off his head. After exchanging greetings, he asked, "Someone told me the train driver was here?"

"Gone," the stationmaster sighed out. "Sat here not two counts and spewed all over the floor."

Yes, there was a wet patch, recently cleaned.

"Sonorics illness?"

The stationmaster shrugged, then handed Sady a printout from the station's sonorics reader. A wriggly line tracked over the paper, rising slowly, until it jumped off the edge of the paper. One hundred and fifty motes per cube. Mercy.

The stationmaster pointed. "That was when the train came in." The figures were clear enough. "Driver said the refugees were on the platform when he pulled into Fairlight, and there was nothing anyone could do about them boarding. The Fairlight station was completely overrun. None of them paid for their tickets. None of the train attendants could stop them coming in. The attendants are all amongst the dead, with their clothes soaked with shit and vomit, and blood running out of their eyes." He didn't need to say *sonorics illness*. "Story's the same for the other trains."

"Where are those trains?"

"We managed to stop them at Curly Loop. Waiting for your orders as to what to do with them, sir."

What to do? What *could* they do? Send the army and shoot all the passengers?

"Are there any citizens of Fairlight amongst them?"

He shrugged again. "Driver said he didn't see any, but he said that there was a lot of smoke in the area, and shortly before he entered Fairlight, there was a bang loud enough to shake the ground."

That bang would have been the shattering of the barrier, and the locals couldn't flee—because they were dead. If they had somehow survived and made it onto the train, they would have died on the way. How many people lived in the Fairlight region? He hardly dared add up the numbers. Thousands dead. Tens of thousands. All people Chevakia needed for food production.

Then another horrible thought: Milleus. Some of those towns down Ensar way hadn't responded recently either. He wiped sweat off his forehead. When he had a moment, he must make more of an effort to get in touch with Milleus, brotherly grudges be damned.

"I want to speak to General Finnisius. I also want a team in there to take out the dead and select the most desperately ill and their families."

"We tried to collect the bodies, sir," one of the guards said. "But they won't let any of their relatives out of their sight, even if they're dead. Some people say . . ." He swallowed. "Some guards say that these southern strangers eat their dead."

"Oh, nonsense. You don't believe that, do you?"

The man looked away. "None of them appears to speak Chevakian, sir."

"Then get an interpreter."

The man's eyes widened. "But where do I find—"

"Go and get Lady Armaine or one of her daughters. Don't pretend to me you don't know where she lives."

"Yes . . . yes, sir." The man bowed, put his helmet back on and trotted out of the office.

Never, ever, trust this woman.

Sady heaved a sigh and turned to Orsan, and noticed with satisfaction that General Finnisius had come in. "The army is at your service, proctor."

"Thanks, Finnisius. We need to establish a contact, a leader, and we need tents to house them. I want the army to set up a camp on the field on the Ensar road. We need vehicles to take them there and we need men to put up the tents. I want the route to be fenced off for citizens."

"What about the people who want to use the Ensar road?"

"Put up signs that they should use the Mekta road instead."

"Yes, sir."

"I want drivers and anyone working with the refugees to wear suits. I want all army personnel out of the camps before the refugees move in. We need to process the refugees first by decontaminating them. No one is to deal unsuited with anyone before decontamination. We need a temporary hospital. We need food."

"We can deal with the tents and decontamination," Finnisius said.

"All right, arrange it."

Finnisius left.

He turned to the mayor. "Could you ask the hospital to send a team, and for food for these people? Report to Orsan."

"I can do that, proctor." The mayor met his gaze squarely. He was a tall man, with short-cropped curly hair, quite handsome in his late middle age. "What account do I use to pay the merchants for that food?"

It was a valid question, and probably made out of innocence, because Sady didn't think the mayor of the city had much of a reason to be aware of the financial woes of the doga, but it chilled him to the core. What account to use to save thousands of *foreign* lives?

"Use general expenditure."

"But—"

"I'll make sure there will be extra funds to cover this event." He hoped he sounded confident, because he didn't feel it. He really needed to find those missing books and get someone to get to the bottom of this financial mystery.

"And wait."

The mayor stopped with his hand on the door.

Sady undid the chain he wore around his neck. On it dangled a small key that would unlock a cabinet in the town hall. He gave it to the mayor, whose eyes were wide.

"Do you want me to ring the bell, sir?"

"Yes. Once only, at this stage."

"Yes, sir." He bowed and left, leaving behind silence and the murmur of the crowd downstairs, the residual hissing of the train's engine, the shouts of soldiers, all muffled by the presence of a floor between them and the platform.

"Ringing the bell? Is that really necessary?" asked Orsan.

"Precaution." Or so he hoped, but if whatever the City of Glass had unleashed made its own citizens flee, then what hope did Chevakia have?

Then he turned to the stationmaster. "Do bring the other trains in here as soon as you clear the platform. We'll process the refugees at the station. Also, cancel any inbound trains. Keep Westside open, and the Curly Loop as well. Close the main line."

"But the people going to work—"

"When the mayor rings that bell, no one will be going to work. I want this part of the city sealed off, together with a corridor we will use to take the southerners out of here."

The stationmaster nodded, feebly.

"We'll need some help from the refugees themselves, but I want to wait until we have some interpreters who can talk to them—"

"Two young men have just come in to offer their services as inter-preters, proctor."

"Excellent. Take them to the platform and let them explain what is happening. Now, excuse me. I'll go back to work."

He rose and picked up his helmet.

Sady and Orsan went back down into the station hall, where it was noisy, hot and smelly. Most of the people were still seated, but there were some pockets of disagreement, people yelling at the guards who kept them on the platform.

"How are you coping?" Sady asked a guard, and his voice sounded muffled in the helmet.

"Only just, sir. Ideally, we'd need a lot more people. And someone to talk to them."

"We're working on that. Meanwhile, keep them occupied and show that we're doing something. There should be some young men to work as interpreters soon. Start by organising these people into groups so they can be transported to the camp we'll set up. I want you to select any that are severely ill or injured . . ." He hesitated. ". . . or very young or pregnant."

He looked over the crowd, but couldn't see the pregnant woman.

CHAPTER 26

IN THE MORNING, Isandor still sat huddled under his cloak at the tent entrance. His legs were stiff from sitting in this position all night, and his arm ached from clutching the dagger.

He didn't think Jevaithi, in the tent, had slept much. He had heard her cry and he'd ached to comfort her, but he didn't dare leave his post. She'd been right; they weren't safe. He still shuddered at that moment of panic, when the shadow had loomed over him, the horror of feeling the shorthair cloak under his hands. By the skylights, these were *Knights*. Not only that, they were hunters.

But when the light grew from blue to white to pink, he was happy to see that the rogues with their van had indeed gone. He'd heard an engine after the attack, but it had been too dark to be certain. Additional vans might have appeared in the night.

Time for breakfast.

He stretched limbs stiff with sitting in the same position, huddled up under his cloak, and finally slid his dagger into his belt.

He checked in the tent, and found Jevaithi still asleep, her hair fanned out over the pillow. His heart ached to touch her, but he didn't want to wake her.

Next, the goats. They already stood in the corner of the pen closest to him and when he collected the bucket from the back of the truck, a few let out plaintive bleats. Their udders were swollen with milk, and they jostled each other to be first in line.

Isandor got the stool and bucket and sat down with the first animal, its warm smell all around him.

Milking had become an easy, relaxing task.

Milleus said that they were on their way to Tiverius. Apparently, he had a brother there, but Isandor wished they didn't have to rely on Milleus. He couldn't muster the courage to tell Milleus that they were going their own way. He didn't even know if he wanted to go his own way. Alone, he and Jevaithi would be so much more vulnerable.

But by the skylights, Tiverius.

There were a lot of people in the city and people meant danger. He couldn't imagine that Tandor would be the only southerner ever to travel to Tiverius. There had to be other southerners who regularly crossed the borders. They would recognise Jevaithi.

Isandor wanted to find somewhere safe for them to live, not to keep running, but for now it seemed everyone in Chevakia was running. Maybe people in Tiverius were running, too. Milleus had explained why they were running, but Isandor still didn't quite understand how an increase in icefire had everyone in such a panic. Yes, he knew that icefire was lethal to Chevakians, but somehow deep inside he didn't really *understand*. Chevakians were people just like southerners. They even had Imperfects. Yesterday he had spotted an old man on the road, pushed in a chair with wheels by a younger woman.

How could Chevakians be killed by icefire? They looked just like him.

By the time he finished milking, the sun had gone and grey clouds were rolling in. A gusty wind tore at the trees around the clearing, making them whistle and sigh.

The young mother from the family they had met yesterday came to buy some milk. Isandor poured the rest into a container and sat down with a cup of the frothy, tangy liquid.

Isandor stoked the fire and fed it some wood. Meanwhile, he put out the plates and then judged it safe to go to the creek to get water.

When he came back with the pot, a man he hadn't seen before stood at the fire watching him. He was middle-aged, dressed in a rough woollen jacket, loose trousers, wearing a scarf on his head against the sun. A typical Chevakian peasant.

"You can share some of our water for tea." Isandor nodded at the man and went on with his business, pouring a bit of water in the teapot and scrubbing it out, and then adding tealeaves.

When he looked up, the peasant had come right up to the fire, squinting at Isandor.

"You are from the south?"

Isandor straightened. "Yes, I am."

The next moment, the man took a swing at him. Isandor saw it coming and ducked.

"Hey, what are you—"

Another punch missed his head.

Isandor managed to get hold of the man's arm to stop him punching again, but he had the strong arms of someone who worked in the fields.

"What have I done?"

"It's because of you that we have all this trouble," the man said, spitting between his teeth. "You're filthy, raping savages, that's what. You're ruining our country."

"Hey, calm down, let him go." This was a new voice. Milleus pulled the peasant's arm, and he let go of Isandor, but continued to glare with hatred in his eyes.

"These young people are refugees just like all of us," Milleus continued.

The man spat on the ground. "They're southerners. They are raping savages, the lot of them. Why do you defend them, mister? Even as we're all running for our lives because of them. They burned my farm. They killed my animals."

Milleus snorted. "What—these youngsters?"

The man squinted at Isandor. "I don't care which of them did it. They came on their damn birds and set fire to the house. They killed my father-in-law in front of my eyes. Ran a sword right through him, like that." He made a slashing motion. "And you . . ." He pointed a trembling finger at Milleus. "You dare come here with a pair of them. Protecting them. Letting them touch our food."

"One southerner isn't the same as another."

"They're all the same to me. Evil *magicians*. Much as the idiots in Tiverius tell us that there is no *magic*."

"There isn't. The Scriptorium has explanations for everything."

"Oh, there is no magic, huh? Then tell me mister, how come we're all running from this non-magic we can't see but that kills us nevertheless? Are you going to tell me the south doesn't control it either? Are you going to tell me that those vile southerners are doing this to us by accident? Are you telling me that the southerners are not doing this so that they can send rampaging hordes into our land to take our farms? And that while this goes on, we should smile kindly at any southerner we meet?"

A deep anger welled up in Isandor's chest. "The City of Glass wants none of your land. They wouldn't even know what to do with it—"

"Raping savages, the lot of you!"

"I've done nothing. We have fled ourselves—"

"Isandor." That was Milleus, a steady presence behind him. "Ignore him."

"But this man is saying untrue things about us."

"Leave it. He's angry and hurt. Arguing will not change his mind about southerners."

"Too right, Mister. I will *never* change my mind about southerners."

"But they're lies," Isandor called out. "No one in the City of Glass wants your farms. They don't even know what a farm is."

"Then tell me: why did they come to our farmhouse and burn it? Why are we all running from this menace? Why did the barrier break?"

Isandor shrugged. He thought he knew why the hunters—those who had tried to kill him last night—burnt the farms: to mark the ones they'd searched. And the reason they were searching was Jevaithi. But he couldn't tell anyone that. As for the barrier, he had truly no idea. He hadn't even known Chevakia *had* barriers.

"Oh, give the boy a break," Milleus said. At least twenty curious onlookers had gathered. "I found the two of them in my barn before any of this happened. They are young lovers having eloped from their families, fleeing an arranged marriage. They know nothing. They are innocent and can answer our questions just as much as you or I can. If you want answers, you should look at your local authorities."

Several people laughed at this.

A man said, "Destran's probably too busy covering his own backside to look out for any of ours."

Another said, "What have the authorities done to keep us safe? None of them warned us of this magic."

"They did talk about it a bit, but no one ever said it was urgent."

A strange expression came over Milleus' face. He straightened his old back. "Did they ever send suits?"

Several people laughed at this.

A woman shouted. "They promised they'd send some ages ago. They finally sent twenty, for a town of thousands. And they were all a huge size."

Another chimed in. "Yeah, like all their promises. Has Destran put in the road he promised? The school? The hospital? All the things that made the district vote for him? Of course not."

"So why didn't you vote out your representative?"

"He's all right. A local man. In the job for years. We couldn't vote against him. There is no one else, really."

"No? But your mistaken loyalty has consequences. Because you vote for him, the local representative gets away with doing nothing, because he knows that he doesn't have to work for your votes."

Milleus looked like he had grown, and shed ten years in age. Like this, he was formidable, nothing like the old man on the farm. An echo of something he used to be, Isandor thought. Something he no longer wanted to be, but couldn't help breaking through at times.

A flutter of movement stirred the air at Isandor's back. Jevaithi had come out of the tent, her hair mussed, her skin still warm from the blankets. She took his hand behind his back and rested her head on his shoulder.

"Let me guess," Milleus went on. "The council says that in order to get these things approved, they need to be signed by the doga, and in the doga, with all the regional factions bickering against each other, your road, your school, your hospital becomes unimportant, because they are debating other problems in districts more important to them than yours. Because you re-elected your representative, who is a long-time supporter of Destran. I tell you something else . . ." Milleus now discarded the farm jacket he'd been wearing for the past few days. They had gathered quite an audience. Women, men and little children had come out of the vans and watched. "The money that goes into paying your council, and paying their trips to Tiverius, and paying their meals and their work clothes and the buildings they sit in—that money—where do you think that comes from? Tell me where? Out of Tiverius?" He pointed at the peasant, who took a step back and mumbled something.

Milleus continued. "No, it comes from your pockets, and you should determine what is done with it."

Jevaithi looped her arms around Isandor's waist while standing behind him. In a way, he was glad that Milleus had diverted attention away from him and the issue of southerners. On the other hand, something strange was happening.

One woman on the other side of the fire elbowed her neighbour and whispered in her ear. The other gaped, and then elbowed the next one.

"They know him," Jevaithi whispered.

Yes, she was right. And Isandor thought of the library and all the books on warfare he had seen in Milleus' sitting room. "Do you have any idea who he is?"

She shook her head. "It's been a long time since we had any visitors from Chevakia at the palace. When they still came, they'd have to come to the palace all suited-up. Mother wouldn't let me be there when she received them, anyway. I was too little."

"Could he be a retired army general or something?"

"Could be, but I truly don't know any of their names."

And Chevakia, Isandor remembered reading, was governed by a large council of representatives chosen by the people.

But there was the fear and the stories. Things he had been told in his brief time as Apprentice Knight. Chevakia had resoundingly defeated Arania in the year he was born. A few years later, Chevakian weapons made mincemeat of Knights who had been caught in the border villages. Apparently, Chevakians didn't like the idea of Chevakian girls being offered the chance to be well-respected breeders in the City of Glass. The girls had *volunteered*, never mind the whole thing had been a mistake with results none of them could have foreseen. The Knights had reduced icefire to a point it hardly existed, and still it killed Chevakians.

Milleus finished talking and a good number of bystanders cheered, before moving back to packing their tents.

Milleus, Jevaithi and Isandor went to do the same. Milleus put his jacket back on and changed back into a farmer.

Isandor rolled up the tent. Milleus rounded up the goats, chased them up the ramp onto the trailer. Jevaithi packed away the dishes.

When Isandor carried the tent to the van, he found Milleus leaning on the trailer's railing, scratching goats between their ears. He looked deep in thought.

"I thought, Milleus, when you were talking to those people. I thought you said that really well."

Milleus sighed. "Yes," he said, patting a goat's furry back. "I think they liked it. That's the trouble."

He stood silently for a while. No, he wasn't going to say anything; Isandor would have to ask.

"Milleus?"

"Yes."

"Were you ever an important person, when you were younger?"

"Don't know that you'd call it important."

Guess that meant yes.

"What happened?"

"It doesn't matter. What happened was that for all the work I did and the lives I saved, I wasn't wanted. I was discarded. That's when I went to the farm, and I wanted to ignore people. I guess . . ." He shrugged, and fiddled with something in his pocket that sounded like paper. He blew out a heavy breath. "That time can never come back. I made mistakes, bad ones. I can never take those back, either." He lifted his head and met Isandor's eyes with his clouded brown ones. "I want you to remember, if you have a passion, and you believe you can make life better for everyone, don't wait until someone comes to ask you to fix it. Because by that time, it's too late."

By the skylights, fleeing the City of Glass had been the biggest mistake he made in his life. Taking Jevaithi, handing the power to the Knights, who only abused it, who seemed to have used it to unleash the biggest disaster the City of Glass had ever seen. They'd been looking for a reason to kill the Queen, and he'd just given it to them.

And they were now doing something that could be felt even in Chevakia.

"I know," Isandor said, the truth on the tip of his tongue. *Nila is Jevaithi, the Queen of the City of Glass.* He felt like he wanted to say it, because he was sick of hiding.

"You can't know. You are what you are, Isandor. What have you been, other than a teenager who ran off with his girlfriend?"

Actually . . .

Isandor hesitated, but the moment for confession slipped.

CHAPTER 27

SOMEWHERE, IN a place between life and death, a voice said, "Tandor."

It was a female voice, and one he knew well.

He turned around on the chair; his head was the only part of him he could move.

She was coming into the room behind him, a mere ghost of a form, barely visible. Everything about her was white, from her dress —which he recognised and definitely wasn't white in real life—to her hair to her hands.

"Tandor, some Chevakian soldiers just came to the door. They wanted me to come and speak to a large group of refugees that are at the station. Apparently, these people have fled a large explosion and destruction in the City of Glass. I thought your stupidity had harmed only you, but now it seems you have taken down the entire country with you. Why did that happen?"

"I don't know, mother." He'd done all the calculations, and should have been able to control the Heart with all his children there. Why had it possessed them? Why had icefire taken their corporeal beings and turned them into evil beings of light? Why had Ruko stopped listening to him?

He added, "Because the Knights meddled with things they did not understand."

"You should have seen what they were doing. Compensated for it."

"I couldn't!" Without his children, he hadn't even been able to get into the palace until it was already too late.

"I am not happy," she said. "You are stupid and incompetent."

Ruko laughed somewhere in the room. "I've always said that."

Lady Armaine gave him an irritated glance. "You have destroyed everything we have worked for all these years. Now I have Chevakians accusing me, and if I were to show my face amongst those refugees, they would surely rip me to pieces. Tandor, these people were meant to see the *splendour* of what can be done with icefire, not its deathly force."

Tandor wanted to say, *Maybe you cannot have one without the other,* but he kept it to himself.

"If you'd only used your brain, we could have won already. We would have been on our way to show the people the glories of the past, show them how the Knights repressed all that was wonderful in our land. Because of you, people will now be saying that the Knights were right in trying to stifle icefire, that it *has* to be used for evil. And as we all know, it does not."

"I couldn't—"

"You have caused this to happen, son."

"But it wasn't possible . . ." He thought of that moment when he'd stood there watching the enchanted children walk from their prison towards the Heart. He'd yelled at them to listen, but they couldn't. He'd known what the Knights had done, and he had been unable to do the only thing that could have averted the explosion: kill them. He couldn't kill the children. He cared too much for them. Because it was too dangerous to show affection for his own two children, he cared for the ones he had saved.

"You're the biggest failure of my life. I don't understand how the Thilleian royal family could have birthed such a weakling. All the conditions were right for us to take over. People loved Jevaithi; people hated the Knights. We had support from the Brotherhood. Think of it, Tandor, the biggest and richest independent organisation in the entire world. Not just in the City of Glass—I've worked hard for their support right here in Tiverius. And what can they do now? What can we tell them? They cannot continue to defend the good of icefire when people start to die. The Knights have arrived in Tiverius. The doga will trust them, because we cannot give them anything positive. It's all your fault, Tandor. We spent years planning this. There will not be another chance."

Tandor had nothing to say to that. She was wrong. It was not his fault, and he was sick of her continuous taunts. But unless he was released from this in-between world, there was nothing he could do about it.

"I think we'll take over from here. We are lucky that at least the hybrid child is safe. We must have the child, Tandor. If you cannot control its mother, we will be forced to send someone who can."

"She is Pirosian. You can use all the icefire in the world on her, and it won't have any effect." He felt victorious saying that.

Dear Loriane, good, down-to-earth, Pirosian Loriane, the Pirosian princess his mother's minions had exchanged for the baby Maraithe. He saw her smiling face, the crinkling skin around her eyes and his incorporeal body flooded with warmth. He'd loved Maraithe, of sorts, out of duty to his family. He'd been young and at that age, any beautiful woman would have captivated him. Loriane was different. She was neither pretty nor impressionable, but for that, she owned his heart.

"There are ways to control Pirosians that don't involve icefire."

"Don't you dare touch her, mother!"

She laughed. "You are giving me orders?"

"She is innocent. She doesn't know anything."

"Ah, I think we've found your soft spot. Keep an eye on this lady, Ruko."

"As you wish, mistress."

"No, Ruko, listen to me. You're my servitor. Keep your hands off Loriane!"

But Ruko approached him from behind, and the cold of his touch froze his movements. He returned to the crowded platform amongst the press of people. He was on the ground and Ruko was holding his head in his lap, stroking the ravaged skin on his forehead. What a mock gesture. The very person who kept him imprisoned. Tandor wanted to scream but the icefire that flowed from Ruko's fingers made his muscles stiff.

CHAPTER 28

LORIANE SAT dazed, crammed on the platform amongst the press of stinking bodies. The Chevakian leader had come and gone. He had spoken with some of the soldiers, gesturing as if telling them what to do. He had gone upstairs, where she could still see him through a window. He took off the helmet that made him look like a bug. Underneath, his hair was curly, short and greying at the temples. Loriane liked his face; he looked like someone who would care.

But now he was gone, and one of the Chevakian soldiers yelled, and some semblance of quiet fell in the crowded hall. It looked like something was about to happen.

A suited Chevakian came up the stairs in the company of two young men without suits. One was tall and lanky, with long black hair hanging down both sides of a narrow face, the other was broader and shorter, and wore his hair short.

Someone seated close to Loriane muttered, "Who are they? Were they on the train?"

"No way," someone else said. "They're too clean."

"They're Knights," someone else said, and someone else made a shushing noise.

"How do they dare to show their faces? The Knights caused this trouble. They should hide in shame," Dara said, a bit too loud for Loriane's liking.

Ontane said, "Shut your trap, woman, if you want to survive."

For once, Loriane agreed with him. Because surely, the Knights had fled the City of Glass on their eagles, and they only had to wait at the end of the train line for all the city's surviving citizens to show up, and they would look very carefully for supporters of the old king. Who knew how many of the Knights had survived?

"I don't care who they are. I just hope this means we can get out of here," Myra said, patting little Beido on his backside.

Beyond her, Ruko cradled Tandor in his lap, his hand stroking the ravaged skin. There was something eerily mechanical about the gesture. Loriane didn't think Ruko had ever done something like that before. His eyes were distant, focused on the two southerners, and the expression in them chilling.

"Ruko?" Loriane said.

He turned towards her, and she thought she saw a glint of fire in those black eyes, something that said, *don't interrupt*. He went back to staring at the two men, one of whom was now clambering on a chair which a Chevakian guard had brought.

"Citizens!" he called out. "Citizens, listen to me."

There was more grumbling in the audience. Citizens was a word most often used by Knights when speaking to the public.

"I have a message from the Chevakians."

"When will they let us out of here?" someone at the front yelled.

Someone else added, "We don't want speeches. We want food!"

People close to Loriane stirred. Someone muttered, "We were hoping to get *away* from the Knights, not to be bullied by them again."

A number of people agreed with this, so Loriane couldn't hear what the man at the front said.

"... The Chevakian army is setting up a camp for everyone here. They have food. They have medicines. They will take care of you. Shortly, they will send some vehicles and will need us to divide into groups of about thirty people each so they can be transferred in orderly fashion. Please give consideration to the ill and feeble first, to wounded, elderly, pregnant and the very young. Any of you who have places to go to in this city, relatives or friends they can stay with, let us know. The Chevakian authorities have informed us that resources are stretched and that they will do their best to help us, but the fewer of us need help, the better."

"Who do you think you are?" a voice sounded from the back of the audience. Everyone turned around.

One of the men who identified himself clearly as Brothers of the Light had risen.

Someone closer to him yelled support.

"We've come here all the way to be free of the tyranny wrought upon us by the rulers of the City of Glass. We don't need the Knights to tell us what to do. Think for yourselves, people, and accept what you think is fair. The Chevakians are providing tents for us, but they don't know who we are and who our leaders are. This is the chance, do you realise, to get freedom from the dictators who have ruled us for so many years. They . . ." He pointed at the two young Knights, who were making their way towards him. "They want us to obey. They want everything to continue as before. They want us to meekly submit to their regime of secrecy and misinformation. Do you want that? Don't you, like most of us, think that it is time the Knights came clear about what actually happened back there in the City of Glass? Don't you think it is time for the people to have a say in how the City of Glass is governed?"

Most of the grumbling had died down. The people were staring at him. Someone at the front yelled, "I don't care where it comes from, as long as we get food."

A woman close to Loriane said, "You mean, he thinks there is a chance we'll be able to go back home?" She was a noblewoman, in her middle age, who had somehow ended up caring for a group of six adolescents who couldn't possibly all be her children.

Loriane had wondered if Tandor had been the only Thilleian descendant to have collected children with abilities to see and bend icefire. He might have collected the most, but he was not the only one. Were they organised through this Brotherhood? She had thought that all they did was collect books and educate orphans.

On her other side, Ontane muttered, "They better be quiet, or there be trouble, I tell you. If they go against the Knights—"

The noblewoman turned to him. "Maybe then it's time to go against the Knights and tell them we won't stand for this anymore." Her expression was fierce.

"I agree," Dara said. Her voice was determined.

"But . . ." Ontane turned to his wife, an astonished expression on his face. "Dear, don't you think . . ."

"Don't ye 'dear' me, husband. Ye've been calling me 'woman' all these years, and I've had to come with you all the way to Chevakia to see what a selfish coward ye really be. Back home, when they came to our door, I wasn't allowed to give any of our food to these people. We had to hide. We had to get out so they wouldn't follow us. And you know what? Here we be, surrounded by them anyway. These people be our family. The Knights have ruined the lives of all of us, and I'll no longer stand for it."

"Dara!"

Myra stared at her mother, her mouth open.

"The man be right. We should do something, or the Knights will just treat us like they've treated us before. They will not speak to the Chevakians on our behalf."

"And you want to make an example of your family?"

A man in front turned around and said, "Look, I really don't care about politics right now. I'd rather hear what the fellow is saying so we can get food."

Many others agreed with him.

The two Knights were making their way through the audience, but people were deliberately getting in their way.

The man in black still stood there, defiant. He yelled, "Remember, you do not need to do what the Knights tell you to do. This is not the City of Glass. Demand to see the Queen."

"Yes," someone yelled. "Where is the Queen?"

"Show us the Queen," a woman yelled at the Knights. "If she is safe, we'll believe you."

"The Queen, we want the Queen."

Other voices took up the chant. "Jevaithi, Jevaithi."

The Knights gave each other a nervous glance.

"Jevaithi, Jevaithi!"

One of them reached for his crossbow. The other put a hand on his arm to stop him.

"Jevaithi, Jevaithi, Jevaithi."

A couple of refugee men rose, much closer to the Knights. The crowd was chanting so loudly now that Loriane could no longer hear what they said, but the Knights backed away, first slowly, and then faster as the men followed. Under loud jeers and chants, the two disappeared down the stairs.

People cheered, including Dara, who rose and jumped around with the noblewoman and her six foster children.

It took a while for the crowd to calm down, but eventually, some Chevakians in suits came up the stairs and moved onto the platform. They pointed and waved, stepped over legs and luggage, and picked people out of the crowd and helped them towards the front. A couple of people with injuries, a few elderly nobles, all dirty and dishevelled, the young woman Loriane had seen on the train who was also pregnant. Many people needed to be carried.

"Get out of the way," someone yelled. "They're taking out the people most in need."

People shuffled aside so that the Chevakians could walk between them.

"You go sit at the front with the sorcerer, Mistress Loriane," Ontane said, while pushing Loriane in the back.

Soon enough, a soldier approached the area where Loriane and Ontane and the family sat.

He took one look at Tandor and flinched.

He said something, which sounded funny inside the suit, and beckoned forward.

Ruko rose, and picked up Tandor.

Ontane rose as well.

Dara hissed at him, "It be just the injured they want. Can't see anything wrong with you."

Ontane pointed. "The others be bringing their families."

That was true.

"We're not family," Myra said.

"He be my brother," Ontane said.

Loriane felt like shouting, *You selfish liar!* but she liked Myra and didn't want to embarrass her in front of the crowd, or lose sight of her. In a way, they *had* become family. Besides, little Beido needed fluids and Myra's milk was drying up.

"Come on, women, let's go." Ruko and Tandor were already walking down the cleared path.

Myra's eyes met Loriane's, apologetic. Loriane shrugged. Not that Myra could help having such a selfish man for a father.

Dara held out a hand to assist Loriane up. There was thunder on her face.

"No matter what ye be thinking about us now, in your city ways, mistress, I did *not* choose to marry him."

"It's all right, Dara, really." Loriane cringed with embarrassment.

Dara grumbled, "No, it bain't."

Ontane whirled. "I heard that, woman. Can ye for once do what they say and stop making me feel stupid?"

"Yeah?" Dara turned to her husband. Her cheeks were red and her eye the most alive Loriane had seen. "Ye *be* stupid. Ye be an embarrassment to me. Ye be a coward, a selfish prick and a petty whinger. If this be time for a change, let's have a change: I will no longer be bullied by ye, and I will no longer call ye my husband."

Ontane looked like someone had slapped him in the face. "Dara, please stop being ridi—"

"I mean it."

"Stop it, you two!" Myra yelled. All around them, people were staring.

"No." Dara folder her arms across her chest. "I've had enough."

"Shut up. You're making me feel ridiculous." Myra's voice cracked.

Ontane said in a low voice, "Your mother be just angry. She'll forget this when she calms down."

"I'm serious."

"Dara, dear, please stop—"

"I'm serious."

"Can we just keep walking?" Myra said. "We're holding everyone up."

Ontane gave a glowering look and stomped off. A few women gave Dara victory signs.

Dara balled her fist. And Loriane felt a pang of jealousy for this woman, who had the courage to do what she herself should have done long ago: tell her lover to fuck off. In a way, she felt the explosion was her fault, because she had provided Tandor with a safe place to stay in the City of Glass.

They made their way to the front of the crowd, where a broad set of steps led out of the station. A flimsy barrier had been erected, and on the other side Chevakian guards paraded in neat brown uniforms.

The square outside the building was completely empty. Loriane gaped at the amazing buildings made of stone. There were carved columns and sloping roofs, wide stairs, ornate railings and paved courtyards. Trees grew in little square bits of ground that had been left uncovered, in neat rows.

They waited.

Then, from the other side of the platform came a vehicle Chevakians called a *truck*. It was a big thing, much bigger than any of the farm vehicles they had seen so far, but smaller than the train. The cabin, with window, sat in front of a large barrel, from which rose a chimney belching smoke, and behind the barrel was a covered trailer. Both its metal surface and the cloth cover were dark as the night.

The vehicle came up to where the refugees were waiting, and stopped. A suited soldier got out and spoke to the soldiers who had been waiting with the refugees. One went and opened the back of the canopy. He beckoned.

The line of soldiers opened up and the first injured refugees shuffled towards the truck.

Two more suited figures in the truck helped the refugees climb onto the loading tray.

When it was the family's turn, Ontane went up first and helped Myra; he tried to help Dara, but she refused his hand and climbed up herself, and then held out a hand for Loriane.

As Loriane stepped onto the narrow ladder, a stab went through her belly worse than she had yet felt. She cried out and stumbled back.

Gloved hands stopped her falling.

She stood there, clutching her belly, swaying and panting. *Oh, by the skylights.*

"What is it? The babe coming?" Myra asked, looking down from the truck.

Loriane couldn't reply for the pain. She clamped her teeth to stop yelling out. Was it possible to forget how much this hurt? Two Chevakians in suits picked her up and wrestled her up the ladder. By the time she was in the truck, the pain had abated.

There were mattresses inside the trailer for the worst injured. Ruko had put Tandor on one of them, and he sat at the edge, again stroking Tandor's forehead.

Someone in a suit, a woman by the sound of her voice, guided

Loriane to a bench that surrounded the perimeter of the trailer and indicated that she should sit down. Two men shuffled aside, looking at Loriane as if she had the plague.

There was no room for Ontane, Dara or Myra to sit.

Soon all the mattresses were taken by wounded.

A Chevakian pushed up a panel that closed the bottom half of the opening at the back of the trailer.

The vehicle growled and jumped into motion, which set off another stab to her belly. Loriane grabbed onto the edge of the bench waiting for it to pass. Sweat rolled down her face into her neck.

By the skylights, she wished that this truck would hurry up.

WHEN SADY CAME back to his office, a long line of people was already waiting there. Not just citizens, but senators and city administrators, and—mercy—the doga's treasurer.

Sady gestured at the man, and he stepped out of the line to follow Sady into the office.

As soon as Sady shut the door behind him, the man started, "Proctor, I implore you, before you make any plans, you really need to consult with me about the mo—"

"No. You need to bring me the missing books. Now."

"I'm working on that. We think we know where they are."

"Here. In my office. Now."

"But I can't—"

"Now." Sady was getting enough of this weaselly man. "Or tell me what has happened to them. If you really know. Which, frankly, I'm beginning to doubt."

The man swallowed visibly. "I had hoped you were going to be reasonable about this."

"Tell me what is reasonable about this crisis and suddenly having thousands of extra people to feed and no money to do it."

"Well," he said and didn't meet Sady's eyes. "It was like this: Destran wanted to check a few things, so we lent him—"

"You let the financial records leave the building?" That was completely against regulations.

"Um—yeah. It was only for a little while."

"Before or after his defeat?"

"Um . . ."

"Answer the question, or I'll assume the worst."

He said nothing, because it seemed there was nothing he could say to improve the situation: that somehow Destran had managed to get damaging records out of the building after his defeat.

Sady spoke slowly to control his emotions. "Do you have any idea what corruption and blackmail looks like? Destran wants to cover the mismanagement that he's presided over for the last ten years, so that he cannot be punished for corruption, so that the senators—and I bet they were northern senators—whom he paid in exchange for their support cannot be found out and persecuted. If you care one bit about your country, and care about any of the thousands of sick and injured people out there, bring me back those books, so I can personally find and throttle the people who took money that wasn't theirs."

The man said nothing, just moved his mouth.

"Don't sit there like that, go!"

"Yes, yes, Proctor."

He rose and went to the door.

"And make sure that with the books, you hand in your letter of resignation."

The man nodded, nervously and scuttled from the room. He left the door open, and to Sady's surprise no one came in.

Well, what the . . .

He pushed his chair back from the desk and went to the door, where he was met by circle of stunned faces.

"Anyone else?"

Several of the administrators shook their heads. Others were suddenly very busy talking to their neighbours. Fancy that. He had scared complainers away.

"It's the han Chevonian blood," Orsan said, weaving his way through the people in the foyer. Sweat glistened on his face from being inside the helmet. "I think they were in doubt that you had it."

That hurt Sady more than he wanted to admit. He didn't want the job. He was just warming the seat for when Milleus returned.

"Anything to report?"

Orsan sighed. "Do you want the bad news or the worse news?"

"Start with the least bad."

"The refugees didn't like the two men who offered to interpret. They were lucky they didn't get lynched before they made it out of the station. So now we are again interpreterless and clueless about what made these people come here."

"Who were these men?"

Orsan spread his hands. "I don't think that anyone checked."

"Right, we're not doing that again. Future applicants will have to identify themselves. Any report on Lady Armaine?"

"The men went to see her, but were told she wasn't home."

"Oh, that's rubbish. She likes playing hard-to-get." He would have to chase the cranky old toad up himself. "What's the worse news?"

"The hospital administrator wasn't keen to send people. He said what if Chevakians need the hospital? I don't know how many he had to spare. I don't suspect he has nurses walking around doing nothing in the first place. I guess we have to make do with what he's willing to share."

"Yes. I know."

"He did eventually agree to send a few people, but it's nowhere near enough to help them substantially."

And that would only add to the anger of the refugees.

"And—"

"There is worse news still?"

"I'm afraid so. Finnisius reports that a large batch of the suits in army storage have deteriorated and no longer offer protection. He wants to know if we have any other stores, or his ability to help will be limited."

"Other stores?" It came out as a shout. "He knows what we have, and he already has it."

"He knows that. I think he was trying to put it politely."

Sady blew out a breath of frustration. "Seriously, Orsan, is this entire country falling to bits?"

Orsan's face didn't betray any emotion. He let a silence lapse, and when it became clear that Sady expected some kind of reply, he said, "That's up to the politicians to decide, sir. Not my place to comment."

"Well, maybe not, but promise me, if you see any sign of anything untoward happening, like people having access to things they shouldn't have, removing things that aren't theirs, or being paid for votes, please tell me."

"It's part of the doga guard's pledge to protect senators current and past. I'm afraid I am not authorised to comment."

"But if there is criminal conduct . . ."

"That is for the doga and the courts to decide. It is my job to make sure no one gets murdered in the process." He was very closed about this. Sady wondered what prompted this behaviour. Orsan had only come into his service when he became chief meteorologist. Before that, he had worked for the proctor's office . . . at the time Milleus was deposed, as a young guard maybe? And had, in his enthusiasm, stepped across the line?

Sady blew out a breath and leaned his head in his hands. A waft of sweat-laced air surrounded him. Mercy, he stank.

Then, in that defeated and frustrated silence, he heard a sound he'd thought he'd never hear: the clear stroke of a bell. Once, then, after a couple of heartbeats, again, and again. It seemed like all the sounds in the building and in the square below fell quiet but for that eerie clear sound. *Ting.* Two breaths' silence. *Ting.* Two breath's silence. *Ting.*

Sady met Orsan's eyes. The expression on Orsan's face was haunted. "Sady, the whole country is looking at you to help us through this."

Sady stared at the clouds scudding across the patch of sky he could see through the window. Right then, he could not have felt any more desperate and alone.

Sady hurried through the corridors of the Scriptorium. Across the mosaic-tiled floor of the tower, up the stairs to the mezzanine gallery, where soft carpet muffled his footsteps and handcrafted bookcases lined the curved outer wall. A student scurried past carrying a pile of books. A few others sat reading on leather-covered chairs.

While the ringing of the bell had put a stop to normal activity in the streets, it seemed life within these solid stone walls went on as if nothing had happened. Coming in from outside, Sady was still in the suit that the proctor's guard insisted he wear—although he argued it was overkill—his helmet under his arm. It was warm in here and the suit felt restrictive and hot. He felt like a creature from a different world. Hot, smelly and bone tired.

"Alius!" Sady knocked on the familiar door that brought back memories of his time as student here. Sadly, he never had the time to pay more than a fleeting visit to this venerable institution these days.

He heard voices inside. People stopped talking. There were footsteps, and a moment later, the door was opened and Alius appeared in the doorway. He looked tired and harassed. "Proctor." He looked surprised. "How did I earn this honour?" He kept the door close to his body, and Sady couldn't see who his visitor was.

"I presume you've heard about the trains," Sady said.

"I have indeed."

"We have thousands of refugees from the City of Glass who are contaminated. Finnisius tells me that many of the army's suits have deteriorated to the point where they no longer offer protection, and the army will be hampered in dealing with this emergency as a result. The southerners are desperate and angry. We need people to keep them under control. We need your medicine. Urgently. When can you have it ready?"

Alius glanced over his shoulder as if looking into the room, except the door was behind him.

"Look, is it all right if I come to your office a bit later? I can explain to you where we are at and how long it will take. I'm in a meeting right now, and—"

"No need to spend much time on explaining. The only explanation I'll need is when the medicine will be ready."

"Yes. Yes, sure. I understand. I will come to your office as soon as possible, and I'll show you the work we've done. I know it's important and would like to prepare a bit and get all the data out. It's going well, but . . ." He laughed. "We're *extremely* busy and we're not in any state to receive important visitors or make coherent presentations."

Sady's courage sank. "You're not ready at all, then."

"No, no, proctor, don't misunderstand my words. We're very close, but very disorganised at the moment."

"I understand. I will expect you later today, then."

Alius retreated back to the visitor Sady still hadn't seen and Sady turned to walk back to the stairs. The door of Alius' office shut with an audible click.

Very close, huh? Who was that visitor Alius had been so keen for him not to see?

Orsan, bearing arms and thus not allowed into the Scriptorium's tower, waited in the room provided for that purpose. He was chatting to a guard Sady didn't recognise and probably belonged to a private family, but he couldn't see which one. A guard would only wear family colours when stationed at the gate to the family's estate.

Orsan rejoined Sady and they left the tower through the ornate columned entrance.

"Whose guard was that?" Sady asked when they were well out of the building.

"Young fellow used to work at the doga, but he's gone private. I don't know who he works for. I didn't ask." Because that was again part of the code of honour, but Sady was beginning to feel that it was this code of honour that was stifling Chevakian politics. Don't ask, don't tell. Protect the back of the person next to you, because next time the lions might be after you.

Mercy, that was the way things had operated in Chevakian politics for a long time, but it seemed to have become much worse under Destran's rule. He was well aware of unwritten rules not to stab any other family of power in the back, but since when, he wondered, had that come to mean cover up for each other's crimes?

Even this late in the afternoon, the foyer of the proctor's office was in chaos, with more people than ever lining up to speak to Sady. He bypassed all of them, to increased shouting of *See me first*, and *I've waited here all day*.

He turned to Orsan, "We must really do something about organising this circus. If this is the only way the common people can make themselves heard, it's dire indeed."

Past Orsan's uniformed body, he spotted a boy much too young to have any kind of political interest. He carried a lute. A skinny lad he was, and he was the only one not shouting.

Sady half-stepped into his office and said to Orsan. "Get me that boy over there."

He went inside, sat at his desk and the boy came in, wide-eyed.

"Sit down," Sady said.

"Thank you so much for seeing me, proctor." He bowed awkwardly.

"What is your name and how old are you?"

"I'm Perin, sir, and I'm twelve. My father has broken his leg in a building site and cannot work, sir. The builder says it's my father's fault and will not pay. I am really good at playing the lute, so I was wondering if any of the senators, or you . . ." His face turned red. ". . . have any parties. I can play for you—"

"You play on the street sometimes?"

"I do, sir, but not today. I've been waiting here."

"All day? To play the lute?"

The boy nodded, his expression eager. "Thanks so much for seeing me, sir."

"I'll give you a job, and it's an important one." Sady had to stop speaking to stifle upwelling emotion. This boy, and children like him, looked to the proctor to save the country. Many of the people outside his door expected the same. Much as he felt without a clue of what to do, he could not fail these people. He could not wait for Milleus, who might never come. The people of Tiverius looked to him, Sadorius han Chevonian, to guide them.

He cleared his throat. "Listen. In the guard room of the tower of the Scriptorium is a guard waiting for his master. I want you to wait outside the building, in a place where this guard won't take any notice of notice you, and tell me who leaves the building with him. You think you can do that?"

The lad's eyes widened. "Yeah, I can." He half-rose. His eyes shone. "Does that make me a spy?"

Ouch. The boy was probably too young to be handed this responsibility. "No. And I want you to be extremely careful. Just go and play somewhere like you would normally do. Watch. Don't talk to anyone."

"I won't. Thank you so much. I will do my very, very best." The boy clutched his lute.

"And, Perin, did you hear the ringing of the bell?"

"Yeah, I did, but nothing's happened, has it?"

"You can't see sonorics. If you're outside, you might want to wear a suit."

"We have no money for a suit, sir."

"Being inside a building will give you some protection. Find a covered courtyard or a hall to keep watch."

The lad's eyes went wide. "I know just the place, sir. The music sounds great in there, too."

"Good. Then go, before the man has left."

The boy grabbed his instrument and scurried out the door.

Sady groaned. Mercy. He couldn't expect Tiverians to have suits. There was no money to give everyone suits, and besides, producing them for the entire population would take too long.

And, meanwhile, the bell rang every hour, and the people of the city had questions, and the southerners had questions but no one could understand them.

He hoped by all that was dear to him that Alius would turn up with the medicine soon.

CHAPTER 30

HE TRUCK WAS moving much too slowly, and Loriane's pains were fast getting worse.

She let Myra pull her into a sitting position, leaning against the outside of the truck. The bench was hard and too narrow, so that she hung on with the hard edge of the metal biting into backside, because her stomach got into the way of her sitting, and there was not enough room for her to spread her legs and lean forward. Loriane's neighbours were both men casting her nervous looks. Loriane swore they would feel the sheen of sweat over her skin each time they bumped into her, which was a lot. There was just no room. Myra stood wedged between the mats on the truck bed floor and those well enough to sit on the benches. She hung onto the metal frame over Loriane's head and tried not to step on Tandor, who lay on the mattress at Loriane's feet.

Loriane dug into her thighs when the pains came. It hurt so much that she didn't know what was happening down there. She couldn't move and couldn't see through the forest of legs and knees. For all she knew, she'd already peed all over the floor.

Three agonising pains later, the truck stopped. In her state, her vision blurred by sweat that was running into her eyes, Loriane couldn't see much beyond the standing passengers other than a barren field. There were some trees and a fence.

"What are we doing here?" she asked, her voice hoarse. She wanted out of this damn truck.

"I don't know," Myra said. She was patting little Beido on the backside, but he was squirming and muttering in the sling. "He's hungry." And of course she couldn't feed him like this, standing up in a moving truck. That was if she could feed him at all. More often, Loriane had taken him, but she couldn't possibly do that now—

The pain returned. She clutched onto the edge of the bench and stared at her knees, trying to control her breathing, and trying not to make any sound. Sweat rolled between her breasts.

When it passed, the truck still hadn't moved, and two Chevakians in their weird suits stood at the back.

"It seems we've arrived wherever we were going," said someone near the back of the truck.

"Can you see anything?" asked another man.

"There's tents," the first man said. "And there's Chevakians in suits."

"Hey you," someone else shouted at the Chevakians. "We want to get out."

A Chevakian said something that sounded like a muffled order.

The next moment, the engine let out a huge hiss and the truck jolted into motion again. Loriane could see glimpses of white tents before another pain overwhelmed her. The child wormed around inside her, a sharp bump tracking across her stomach. It felt like a knife cut her there. By the skylights, what was this thing?

They stopped again, and now a Chevakian came and let down the back panel of the truck. He spoke and pointed, and the first people climbed down. More suited Chevakians waited there, and they led the passengers away. Soon they ran out of people who could climb unassisted, or who would leave their loved ones. The Chevakians came into the truck and handed people down to a couple of others, who carried them away.

Ruko would not let them touch Tandor, and one icy look from those hollow eyes was enough to make the Chevakians back off. He put Tandor down near the edge of the trailer bed, jumped off and heaved Tandor onto his shoulder. The Chevakians stepped back when he passed.

What if . . . Loriane got a strange idea. What if Ruko wasn't trying to protect Tandor, but was keeping him in his dream-like state?

She called out, "Myra!"

But Myra was at that moment being led away by the Chevakians.

"I'm not leaving you."

"Myra, we need to get Ruko away from Tandor. Maybe he'll wake up then."

"What?"

Two Chevakians lifted Loriane up. The movement set off another pain. She dug her fingers into the strange texture of their suits, feeling the arms of the people within. Every bump lanced through her belly and back like a knife. She fought not to scream.

They handed her down to two other people.

Outside the truck was a grassy field with tents in neat rows. There was a broad zone without tents and then a fence. Behind the fence, a forest. The field sloped down towards the city where she could see the roof of the buildings poked through the haze.

All the truck's passengers were being taken into a large tent.

There were benches and mats lined up inside, where other suited people walked around and attended the sick. At the far end was a partition screened off with a curtain.

The Chevakians put Loriane down on one of the benches, in between Myra and Dara. Ontane sat on the other side of Myra, trying to make the point that he was not looking at his wife, but glancing from the corner of his eyes anyway.

A Chevakian was going through the room, examining the wounded one by one. Loriane caught a glimpse through the helmet's visor, and thought that this person was a woman. She held a slate with a piece of paper, and wrote something on the slate every now and then. When she had finished with someone, this person was led or carried to the screened area out the back.

People only spoke in soft voices. Sounds of trucks and hissing steam came in from outside the tent.

When the suited woman approached Tandor, Ruko rose and placed himself in front of his master. He was pale—Loriane did not recall seeing him eat anything—but he towered over her. She stepped back, clutching the slate to her chest. She called out something to another Chevakian in the tent.

"See?" Loriane said to Myra next to her. "There is no reason that Tandor should be mute like this. I think it's because Ruko is keeping him that way and he needs to be close to do it."

"Maybe, but who can scare Ruko?"

Loriane didn't reply, because another pain was building. She grabbed the edge of the bench and squeezed it as hard as she could, aware that a lot of people were watching her. She wanted to move around and see if she could find somewhere comfortable where Myra could assist her with the birth. She also really needed to pee.

She wished this woman with the slate would hurry up, but she was still a couple of patients away from her.

There was a commotion at the tent's entrance and a couple of Chevakians came in. They spoke to one already in the tent, who pointed at Tandor. The newcomers marched between the mats. Loriane noticed belts and weapons when they passed her. They stopped at Tandor's mat. Ruko faced them, his arms crossed over his chest. One of the Chevakians spoke; Ruko didn't react at all. The Chevakians waited, but after nothing happened, two of them went to either side of Tandor's mat. One grabbed the bottom corners, the other the top two corners, and they lifted the mat.

At that moment, Ruko whirled. With a roar that sounded like it came from a wild animal, he swung at the Chevakians, hitting one in the head with his elbow. The man dropped the mattress. Tandor fell. The Chevakian tumbled on top of him, while the other Chevakian had pulled a weapon. There was a huge bang. People screamed, and whoever could move, scrambled away.

"Quick, get Tandor," Loriane called to Myra. She tried to get to her feet, but her legs wouldn't cooperate.

Ontane yelled, "Don't be stupid, Myra." But Myra was already pulling Tandor away.

Dara got up to help her.

Ruko had fallen, and all Chevakians were now struggling to hold him down and tie him up.

"He been shot," Ontane said, his eyes wide. "And he just keeps on living."

"You can't kill a servitor unless you kill the master," a rasping voice said.

"Tandor!"

He looked terrible, shiny new skin stretched taut over his face and half his head, but his eyes were alive.

"Loriane . . ." He panted. "Loriane, have I ever told you how much I love you?"

"I sure as hell don't love you." All her anger rose to the surface. If only she could get off the chair, she'd go and wring his neck. All the problems in her life were because of Tandor.

"Loriane, please . . ."

"No, Tandor, the game is over. What did you do to me? Where is Isandor?"

"It's all wrong," he said. "Ruko, my mother . . . watch them. They'll want the child."

"And what am I supposed to do? Protect this hideous creature? Have you ever thought what it would do to me, carrying a child like that? You betrayed me, Tandor. I hate you, and I'll always hate you. When this child is born . . ." Another pain was building. "When it's born, I'll kill it."

"No, listen . . ."

"I hate you." She panted.

"Loriane, you are my princess, the only one I've ever loved."

"I don't love you. I fucking hate you!" The wave of pain built and built. She screamed at him. "I hate you. I hate you. I hate you!"

"Shut up." He grabbed her wrist in a surprisingly strong grip. "Don't draw attention to us."

She struggled. "I hate you!"

"Behave yourself." He slapped her in the face.

She spat at him. Tangled her hand into his remaining hair and pulled. "I hate you!"

He slapped her again, harder this time.

Loriane spat, and screamed, and howled with the pain that felt like she was being torn apart.

Two of the Chevakians came and lifted him under his arms. Tandor struggled, and yelled at them in Chevakian, but they picked him up and carried him out the back. His screams became progressively weaker. Ruko still stood, bound and gagged, in the corner. His eyes shone. As if in slow motion, he ripped apart his bonds, tore off the gag. Two remaining Chevakians rushed to tie him back up, but he mowed them aside, and ran for the exit. The Chevakians ran after him, and their shouts faded, too.

The pain ebbed away. Loriane slumped onto the bench and sat in dazed silence.

Myra said, "Well, that worked. Tandor is talking again. I'm not sure if abusing him was so smart. I thought you needed him to get a place to stay in Tiverius."

Loriane felt like saying. *You don't know what pain like that is like*, except Myra did know, very well. Whatever this child was, it was just another birth, and nine previous births really did not make it any easier. You could have all the experience in the world, but whenever the next time came, it was just as painful, as scary, as tiring, and just as much sheer physical, sweaty hard work as the previous one. She didn't know why she had ever allowed herself to forget that.

The Chevakians came for her next.

They carried her out the back entrance into a second tent, this one not as busy, with a series of cloth-walled rooms on one side. Going past the entrance of one, she got a glimpse of a child being washed by a Chevakian in a suit. The cubicle where the Chevakians brought her had an examination table and a chair. There was also a Chevakian woman in a suit. She indicated for Loriane to undress and get onto the examination table. But Loriane couldn't walk, so she had to call for someone to help Loriane up and assist her. Cold suited fingers undid the buttons on her dress.

"Sorry, is there anywhere I can piss?" Loriane asked

The nurse shrugged and pulled Loriane's dress over her head, eyes widening at the dreadful red marks that criss-crossed her belly. Even her thighs were bruised now.

She made Loriane lie down on the table and proceeded to prod her belly. Loriane clamped her jaws. *Hurry up, hurry up.* By the skylights, if this lasted any longer . . . Then the nurse pushed Loriane's legs apart and slid a cold gloved hand inside her. A stab of pain made her gasp. Warm fluid dribbled onto the table.

The nurse called out.

I told you so, sea cow.

Another woman in protective clothing rushed into the cubicle. The two of them dragged Loriane into a sitting position on the table. One tried to shove a metal bowl under her, but it was much too late.

A pain built and Loriane lost all sensation. It was a bad one, and she closed her eyes and breathed in and out slowly. The cloth under her grew sopping wet. Drops plinked onto the floor.

When she opened her eyes, both Chevakians were gaping at the table.

Loriane looked. Her piss was nearly black.

What was this about? What was going on inside her body?

She yelled, "Tandor!"

She stumbled off the table, out of the cubicle, naked as she was, the Chevakian nurses yelling behind her.

But then a pain started building, stronger than before. She couldn't walk, couldn't move. Purple spots danced in her vision.

A number of white-suited Chevakians caught up with her, dragged her back into the cubicle and one of them directed a stream of hot water at her, while another held her from behind. One rubbed a sharp-smelling substance all over her that made her skin burn. Then they hosed it off. Pains lanced through her like hot knives.

Loriane struggled. "Let me go! Let me go! I'll kill this thing as soon as it's born!" She could feel the pressure building. It hurt like nothing had ever hurt before.

"Tandor, I hate you. I FUCKING HATE YOU!" And then the building pain exploded into agony.

Somewhere in the middle of all that, the nurses finished hosing her down and lifted her. Like some sort of out-of-body experience, she was aware of people running into the tent, looking at her. She was aware of being carried. She was aware of the tent flap opening and a couple of important-looking people coming in.

The Chevakians were rubbing her dry. The pain subsided, but the pressure grew worse. And the Chevakians were trying to put some sort of nightgown on her. She hit at them.

"Let me go." She was going to give birth right here.

More Chevakians were still coming in, and held her arms behind her back so that she couldn't move and this stupid woman was trying to put this stupid garment on her. She trembled. Drops of fluid trickled down her legs. The nightgown went over her head.

The Chevakian nurses—now without suits—were talking to each other in calm voices. They lifted her onto the examination table.

Two nurses held her motionless while a third stuck a needle in her arm. There was a thin hose attached to it and attached to that, a fluid-filled balloon.

"What are you doing to me? Leave me alone!"

One nurse spoke in harsh Chevakian. She tapped a few times against the balloon and turned away.

"Hey, where are you going?" They were still holding her. Another pain was building and she really wanted to get off this table.

But the nurse paid her no attention. The pain built and built. It wasn't just pain anymore. She could almost feel the child's head inside her. If this kept up, she was going to embarrass herself and give birth on this stupid table. Very soon.

Help me!

The Chevakian woman put a blanket over her.

Help me!

A wave of dizziness came over her.

The roof of the tent twirled and circled. Oh, by the skylights! She closed her eyes. And then she knew no more.

CHAPTER 31

WHEN THE FIELDS became smaller, and the houses closer together, Milleus found it harder to concentrate. His mood swung wildly between melancholy and fear. He hadn't been here for so long, and all these people who might recognise his face made him nervous. What if they booed him and chased him out of the city? The peasants might listen to his arguments, but the folk in the city would be more cynical. They were, after all, the ones who had cheered when Destran had deposed him, and at times, especially at night when he lay in bed staring at the ceiling in the van, he could still hear that cheering.

He fell into a brooding silence, but the youngsters didn't seem to notice. They found so much to look at or express their wonder about.

Then they crested the last hill of the plateau and came to the lookout. From here, undulating country sloped down to the city. Tiverius lay stretched out before them.

Row after row of blocky buildings made from pink stone crowded rolling hills. Trees lined the roads, which were straight and lined out in geometrical patterns.

In a strange way, he felt relieved. Tiverius was still here. It looked like it always had. Life here went on as normal.

Seated in the back of the van, Nila leaned over his shoulder to look. She pointed ahead at the golden dome. "That is where the Chevakian Doga sits."

"Yes, very good. Do you know the building next to it?" All that was visible of the building in question was a squat round tower four storeys high. There were arched windows all around, which you couldn't see from here.

She frowned.

"It's the Scriptorium."

"That is the place where . . ." Her frown deepened. "You keep books."

"Yes and no. The books go in the library. The Scriptorium is where people work to further their knowledge."

He remembered spending much time in a room on the top floor of that tower. His friend Alius' office.

From the crest of the hill, the column of vehicles snaked down the slope that led into the outskirts of the city. Forest on both sides was used for firewood. Here and there farms dotted the landscape. There were many fields with sunflowers, all pointed in the same direction where the sun, at that moment, wasn't.

Isandor whispered, "Wow. It's beautiful."

"Pretty," Milleus said. "A woman is beautiful." It would be a lot prettier if it were sunny. But the sky was grey with low scudding clouds.

"Isn't a city like a woman? You have to care for her, otherwise she ceases to be beautiful to you?"

That comment hit him in the gut. Like Suri.

Milleus swore that sometimes that young man said things that would be more appropriate to come out of the mouth of someone three times his age.

Like Suri indeed. While he was here, he should go to her grave and bring her flowers, and hope his sons didn't come chasing after him.

What are you running from?

Mercy, the voice of his conscience was starting to sound like Isandor's. He had no time for family business. Most likely, his sons wouldn't have the time either. He wondered if Markian was still with that silly woman—oh, mercy, what was her name again?—and wondered if Parto and Lyvia had their much-wanted girl yet.

"Where are the goats going to graze tonight?" Isandor asked, shaking Milleus from his thoughts.

"We'll bring them to a commercial stable at the edge of the city. You'll see."

The van rolled down the hill, following the column of refugees which slowly made its way down. It grew very crowded here, and progress slowed further and further, and came to a complete stop.

Ahead, the motionless column stretched around a bend.

People were hanging out the windows trying to see what was going on. Others had left their vehicles and stood on the side, or sat in the grass. Some people piled up wood for fires.

Isandor gave him a worried glance. "What is going on here?"

"It looks like the road is blocked further on," Milleus muttered. That was something he hadn't considered, that the doga would simply block the city to keep any refugees out. They wouldn't be that stupid, would they?

He opened the door and slid stiffly from behind the wheel.

The van rocked with the movements of the goats in the trailer. They were bleating and pushing each other. Panicked by all the noise and the barking of dogs and smells of too many people.

He walked down to the trailer and banged his hand on the side. "Oy. Quiet, you."

The familiar voice did seem to calm them some.

When he turned around, a man stood behind him. "Do you sell meat or milk?"

"Yes, I have milk."

The man rummaged in his pocket and produced a fat purse. "How much?"

Milleus frowned. "Not now. At milking time."

"Please," the man said. "The wife has twins to feed and we've travelled for three days without food."

"There will be milk later." Some other people had turned to him. "But I'll need feed, for the goats."

A woman said, "That's no problem. We'll get hay. You give us milk."

A queue had already started forming, and two boys were running towards the forest, presumably to get grass.

"Hey," he said. "I said this afternoon. There is no milk right now. Goats are not machines you can turn on and off at will."

But no one was listening.

Mercy, milk for this many people? He'd never have enough. There were hundreds of people here. Hungry, thirsty, annoyed that they had to wait so close to their destination.

Isandor stood on the truck's doorstep, looking over the chaos from his point of vantage.

Milleus said to him, "I'm going to see if I can find out what the hold-up is." Would it be worth waiting for? "You better keep an eye on the animals."

Isandor nodded.

From the other side of the truck, Nila said, "Can I come?"

"Sure," Milleus said, and then he looked back at Isandor. "Is that all right with you?"

Isandor glanced over the crowd. "I'll be fine."

Milleus saw through his veneer of carelessness. Isandor didn't like this seething mass of people any more than he did.

"You know where the gun is . . . if you need it."

Isandor nodded.

Milleus and Nila went on their way through the chaos of vehicles, campfires, tents, yelling people, screaming children. At the bend in the road, where there was a small glade, several people were trying to turn their vehicles around, but once they were turned, there was nowhere for them to go, because of all the people still arriving from behind. Men were shouting at each other to get out of the way.

Knots of young men had gathered on the roadside, glowering at everyone who passed.

There was a fence across the road ahead, blocking it off completely.

A couple of uneasy city guards stood sentry on the other side of it, in the field where normally circus troupes or travelling merchants would camp if they didn't want to stay in the city. Now there were rows and rows of army tents. Milleus could see some people walking between them, but they were too far away to see who they were.

"Hey!" Milleus called out to the guards.

They didn't react.

"Hey, you! I want to talk!" he yelled again.

"It's no good. They won't talk to us," said a man next to him, a middle-aged fellow who had the clean hands and finely-cut clothes of a small-town administrator.

"What's going on?" Milleus asked.

Nila pressed her nose against the fence and stared in the distance.

"I've been told they are setting up a camp for refugees."

"Why are you all waiting here? The road is blocked."

"We're waiting to be let in."

"Let in?"

"Yeah, they're setting it up for us, surely. We got nowhere else to go."

A lot of things started to make sense now. "How long have you been waiting?"

"Most of yesterday and today. I hope they hurry up. People are getting very impatient back there."

"Have they said anything about how long it's going to take?" Would there be a way to get out of this queue and contact Sady? "I have a brother in Tiverius. I don't need to get into any camp."

The man shrugged. "I can't help you there."

Nila was still staring at the tents down the hill. He touched her shoulder. "Come, we're going back." He was surprised by how angry he felt, a sensation he remembered well. He needed to get really fired up about something to act, but once he did, there was no stopping him. Yes, he would march into the doga with his signatures and face Destran, if only it could mean that his countrymen could be properly helped.

Nila came without speaking a word. He noticed how tired she looked. He'd promised them they'd sleep in a real bed, safe from the world, safe from their countrymen.

Around the corner, the attempts to turn some vehicles around had escalated in full-scale shouting matches between families.

A woman was shouting, "Oh, I didn't? And then what about you, fat cow. I saw you take two loaves of bread yesterday . . ."

More young men had gathered to watch. They stood with hands in pockets or arms crossed over their chests. They watched Milleus and Nila walk past with suspicious looks.

Nila said, "We shouldn't get involved." As if she felt that he was on the verge of doing just that.

"I don't like this," Milleus said. "People are angry. I don't understand why those soldiers don't let anyone into the camp. There's going to be grief if they don't."

"Soldiers in a position of power don't care about anything except maintaining that power."

He glanced at her sideways. Mercy, where did she learn things like that at her age?

Back at the truck, a huge queue had formed. Many people were sitting in the grass, prepared for a long wait. Many were holding buckets. Isandor sat on the railing of the trailer, holding Milleus' gun.

He said nothing, but Milleus saw in his eyes that he was glad to see them return.

"We can't get through," Milleus said. "The army is setting up a camp in a stupid place, and there is an idiotic fence across the road. No one knows when they're going to let people in. Ridiculous."

Isandor flicked his eyebrows. "Can we turn back?"

"That's not so easy." Milleus looked up the hill, where the long line of refugees completely blocked the road.

Whoever's stupid idea it was to block the road. Did they *want* the people to start fights out here? Was this the way Destran thought to control who came into the city?

Mercy, the doga had no idea, absolutely no idea at all. Who ever could have approved of such a *stupid* idea—

Isandor was still watching him, eyebrows raised as if he wanted to say, *What's the matter with you?*

Oh, mercy. The kid couldn't understand. He stomped away from the truck. "Right, people, listen to me."

A few people gave him strange looks, but many gathered around, probably for the lack of anything else to listen to.

"It's pretty clear that no one's getting through this way. And some of us have families in Tiverius and don't need this camp, so let's organise for everyone who wants to turn around and get into the city by some other road. I want this path . . ." He waved at the right side of the paved road. ". . . cleared of all vehicles so those who want to leave can do so." He waved at a truck which blocked the road. "Move aside, please, sir, so people can get past. Move aside, move aside!"

The truck's owners, and extended family, started pushing the vehicle aside. Others also moved to make room for them.

"Move aside, move aside, so people can get out!"

More trucks moved.

Milleus progressed further up the road, but there, people had made a huge fire right in the middle of his intended path.

Someone had caught an animal that looked suspiciously like a goat—mercy—and which was now roasting over the fire. On both sides of the road were trees and fenced paddocks. People had set up tents. There was no way any trucks could get through.

Milleus let his shoulders slump.

"Pity. Good try. We'll try to keep going tomorrow," one of the drivers said. He had a young family and didn't look entirely unhappy to have found a place where people had food.

Well, important things first, huh?

Milleus went back alone, still burning with anger inside, and fearful for Isandor and Nila, and his goats.

Isandor was making preparations to start milking. Most of the goats were inside the pen, watched by Nila. He had put grass on the feed trough, placed his stool on the trailer bed. The animals were pushing each other to be the first to be milked. Their udders were fat and swollen, some already leaking milk.

A male voice behind him said, "Are these animals yours?"

Milleus turned around. Behind him stood a soldier in uniform. "Yes, I took them all the way from my farm." What did he mean *are these goats yours?* Didn't he have anything better to do than harass people?

The man's eyes narrowed. "There have been reports of theft from farms."

"That's what happens when you let people wait for too long. They run out of food. They start getting it wherever they find any."

"We've told people that there is no point in waiting here. Everyone should clear this area as soon as possible."

"Let me tell you, I'd love to get out of this mess, but we're stuck here because no one can turn around, and there are still people coming. Why do you even let them come here?"

"We're dealing with that right now. We'll start at the back of the column tomorrow, so we can have everyone on their way to the processing posts tomorrow."

Processing posts. What a load of rubbish. Why block a major access route unless the intention was to keep people out of the capital?

"I don't need processing. I have family in Tiverius."

"You'll have to verify that at the processing post."

Milleus clamped his jaws. Oh, for mercy's sake.

They turned back to his van, where Nila was handing out the first cup of milk to a young boy. The queue had grown, but for now, was orderly.

Milleus went into the truck to find something for their own dinner.

Apart from hay, Isandor had collected donations of blankets, some jewellery, a coat, boots, a set of cups and a small heap of coins. Whereas earlier in their trip, there had been eggs and ham and fruit, it seemed people had no food left.

There was some bread and cheese and a few eggs left in the store, but that wouldn't last them more than a day.

A glance out the back window showed Isandor and Nila still handing out milk, and the queue growing longer. There was no way there would be enough milk for all those people.

Milleus cut up the ham, balancing the cutting board on his lap. He would normally take it outside, but he was afraid that he'd be mobbed.

There were clangs of metal from Isandor shutting the goats back in the trailer. He climbed up on the railing and sat there, the gun in his lap.

Nila opened the door and climbed into the cabin, her face harrowed. "Those people are crazy."

"They're hungry."

He passed her the bread and she ate, quietly.

Milleus cut bread for Isandor and then left the cabin.

It was starting to get dark, earlier than normal because of the heavy cloud cover. A cold wind made the trees whistle.

The line of people wanting to get milk had dispersed, but several people had put up tents in the space Milleus had planned to use as corridor to get out tomorrow morning.

Mercy, he was powerless against chaos like this. Where were those soldiers? Why weren't they organising the crowd?

"You go inside and eat," he said to Isandor in a low voice. "I'll watch here."

Isandor stiffly climbed off the railing and handed Milleus the gun.

Milleus took position on the trailer, and sat staring into the darkening sky. Campfires burned everywhere. On the other side of the road, people were chopping up fence posts for firewood, the animals inside the paddocks already stolen or eaten. Mercy, what a mess. Wasn't this typical of Destran? How could he contact Sady?

He wanted to do something, but needed help. The more he thought about it, the more he concluded that if turning people around wasn't practical, there was only one way get out of this mess: by using the road that was intended for that very purpose. Even if that meant destroying the stupid fence. The camp didn't look particularly well-patrolled, and as a farmer, he never went anywhere without a pair of wire-cutters.

CHAPTER 32

THE GUARD at the gate waved his hand, and the truck entered the camp. From behind the glass, in the sheltered environment of the truck, Sady studied the neat rows of tents, most still unoccupied, since the first of the refugees had only just been decontaminated and were being shown their tents.

Mercy, he was tired and annoyed. It was starting to get dark, and normally, he should have been home long ago.

But problems multiplied. For once, Orsan's scout had not been lied to. The Lady Armaine was *really* out, as were her daughters, and of course the guards wouldn't say where she had gone and how long she would be.

On top of that, the station guards had reported fighting on the second of the trains. Not angry citizens trying to smash their way out of the carriage, but people fighting *each other*. It looked like the refugees were from two different factions, and he might have to separate them to keep the group under control. Except he didn't know who was who, and needed the interpreter worse than ever. And Lady Armaine wasn't helpful by disappearing at this crucial time.

Meanwhile, the young musician he had sent to spy had come back from his task and caused him worry by reporting that Alius' secret visitor was none other than Destran. Yes, he understood why Alius wasn't happy about the timing of Sady's visit, but what did he have to discuss with Destran, who continued to serve as senator?

There was still no sign of the missing account books. And, as predicted, Tiverians lined up in front of his office grumbling about money being spent on housing the southerners. He didn't know which of those things worried him most, but he resolved to tackle the easy problems first. Part one: since he could find no Chevakians who spoke the southern language, he had to find southerners who spoke Chevakian. Southerners who were respected by those in the camp. He'd already made the mistake of not checking people who offered themselves once, he was not going to make it again. So that was why he was here, at the camp.

The truck stopped at a tent where a number of soldiers waited.

Sady climbed out of the cabin to salutes and nods.

"We have five people for you," a soldier said.

"Five? Is that all?"

"Sorry, sir. We asked everywhere, but only five responded. Either people are too scared to come forward or there are only a few people in the south who speak Chevakian."

Wonderful. Just what he needed: people too scared to speak out. Scared of what or whom? "Let's go and look at these ones, then."

Sady and Orsan went into the tent, which was an administration post. A Chevakian officer scurried from behind his desk. "Ah, proctor. We have the people here, as you requested. . . ."

The five sat on a bench, three men and two women, all clad in southern fur cloaks, not talking to each other. Only two met Sady's eyes. One of them attempted a clumsy greeting.

"Thank you. I'll talk to them now. I'm very busy."

"I understand, proctor. Please, use my desk."

Sady sat down.

The first person to join him at the table was an elderly man. He was dressed in a black shirt that had smears of slime or some other goopy substance over the front. His hair was thin, greying, and tied together at the nape of his neck. He had a straggly beard that hadn't seen a barber's knife for a long time, with the long pointed end hanging down from his chin yellow with dirt.

He bowed deeply.

"I understand that you speak Chevakian?"

"I have learned a bit your language," the man said.

"Where did you learn it?"

"I learn as young man. When travel to your country."

"As merchant?"

A blank look.

"Were you selling things in Chevakia?"

"No. I was in army."

Mercy, that would go down well with the doga. One of the men who had raided the border regions. Probably had done his fair share in raping and pillaging.

The next person was a young woman with wide eyes, who gave confused answers to Sady's questions. She had her well-endowed bosom half hanging out of the shirt and fixed his gaze with wide eyes. Whatever she wanted, being an interpreter it was not.

The next person was a young man with intense eyes. Although he seemed to understand Sady well enough, he answered with mono-syllables.

The fourth person was an older woman, a favourite auntie type, rotund and smiling. At least she didn't appear to have an ulterior motive, but her Chevakian was worse than that of the others.

The last person was a middle-aged merchant who, when Sady asked questions, came up with a huge jumbling theory about market advantages of *something* that Sady didn't understand.

Sady cut short the torrent of incoherent babble and turned to the administrator, who stood by the door.

The man gave him an apologetic look. "These were the only ones who applied."

Sady sighed, and put a hand on the man's shoulder as apprecia-tion. They were doing their best, all of them. "It's not your fault. I think they're spooked, afraid that if they speak up, they'll be singled out. Understandable, although not helpful. Do you think it would be safe enough for me to walk through the camp and ask for volunteers informally?"

"In that part where people have been given beds and food, yes. Don't go near the processing area, because some of them get pretty violent."

Sady nodded. He could understand that being asked to remove their clothes, being scrubbed with soap and hot water while they didn't understand why, could make people angry, especially if they were tired and hungry.

"Tell these people I may need them later. I'm going for a walk."

Orsan raised his eyebrows, but followed.

"Honestly, I cannot use any of them," Sady said to Orsan when they were well out of the tent. "It seems like the only people who volunteered are at least mildly disturbed."

Orsan said, "The guard mentioned that he thought the people might be scared. I think he's right. Everyone comments on how subdued these people are."

"Well, we'll see if any come forward if I talk to them directly."

They went into a few tents where refugees lay on mats, and where no one replied to Sady's greetings, and Sady was cursing himself for having been part of the government that allowed this country to become so isolated that no one spoke each other's language.

Then, as they were about to enter the next tent, there was some sort of commotion behind them. A woman was screaming and people yelled out in Chevakian, "Stay here!"

Another called for assistance.

Orsan glanced at Sady, who nodded, "Let's go."

Orsan and one of the guards went first, then Sady and another guard.

In the tent, the found the woman he'd seen at the station, stark naked, her belly like a balloon, screaming and fighting two nurses, who held her. Her belly was vividly coloured with bruises and red lines. Mercy, he had never seen anything like that.

Orsan didn't have time to help before she collapsed, and the nurses heaved her onto a bed.

Sady felt a little queasy. He was a politician, not a physic.

Mercy, he'd never had a wife, let alone witnessed a woman grow with child—except Suri, hidden under her clothes. Were those marks and bruises normal? No wonder women hated it so.

The woman now lay on the bed. Sady walked to the table, trying to focus on something other than her hideously swollen belly.

The woman was not what you'd call beautiful, but her face had strong angles that made her look like she would put up a good fight. Her black curly hair was tied in a loose ponytail. Curly wisps had escaped the tie and danced around her head. She was older than he would have guessed, with faint wrinkles around her eyes and greying hair at her temples.

"Can someone please cover her up?"

"Sure, Proctor." A nurse rushed over with a sheet.

"What are you going to do with her?" he asked the physic at the table.

"We're waiting for a midwife to come. We hadn't envisaged dealing with these sorts of problems."

"How long will it take before she's here?"

The physic shrugged. "Hard to tell. There is so much work to be done, we need all our people."

Sady glanced at the mound under the sheet. "Is she having twins?" He could not remember Suri having looked anywhere near as big as that. If anything, he remembered her looking rounded and cute, but that brought the uncomfortable thought that he wished the child would be his and not his brother's.

"No, a single child."

Mercy. "I didn't know that women could get like . . . this." He felt like squirming.

"It won't be easy," the physic said. "She's going to need a lot of help."

Sady felt goosebumps crawl over his skin. Even he had heard some stories that made his hair stand on end.

There were voices behind him in the tent. A man said, "Proctor, excuse me. We've located someone who claims to speak for the refugees." The sheets of the temporary barrier rustled.

"Yes, I'm coming," Sady said, started to turn, glanced at the woman again, and asked, "What kind of help, exactly?" Not really wanting to hear the reply. The subject made his skin crawl.

"Well . . ." The physic hesitated.

"Not pretty." Sady filled in the blanks.

"No. The child is too big to be born the normal way."

Sady shuddered at the thought of what had to be done. He'd heard stories about that, too. Many women died horrible deaths.

"Proctor, please—" the man at his back insisted.

"Wait. I'm talking to someone!" It came out more sharply than he intended. Yes, he knew that following the disaster with the previous two interpreters, it was important that they find someone else.

The physic raised her eyebrows. "No help needed, proctor. We have everything under control here."

Sady said, "About this woman, I've heard that there is this thing, where you can cut out the child without killing either it or the mother ..."

"Yes. We do that for our women, but I honestly think we're going to be far too stretched to extend the procedure to refugees. It's very expensive—"

"I'll pay."

The physic's eyes widened. "But—"

"From my own personal funds. That's allowed, isn't it?" He couldn't quite say what possessed him. Maybe the chance to save one person from a horrific death, the chance to make a difference. He had never seen injury and suffering on this scale. This looked like a problem he could fix, with a happy outcome.

"Um—yes."

"Well, then, what are you waiting for? Take her to the hospital. Bring the physics you need here. Whatever. Get it done."

"She can't go to the hospital, sir. We have an exclusion zone in place around the camp. Until we've decontaminated everyone, taking anyone outside would place the citizens of the city at risk."

Mercy. He'd been so caught up he'd forgotten about the exclusion. Mercy. He wiped his face with his hand. The skin of his palm scratched over his chin. Since when had he last shaved? He was so tired.

"Proctor?" the man behind him insisted.

"Yes, I'm coming." Sady sighed. "Is there anything else we can do? Anywhere else she can be treated?"

The woman lay there, her face peaceful, unaware that her fate was being decided. Sady knew he could not let her die. He could also not leave her child to be killed by the hands of butchers.

"If we took her into the city, she would need to be in an isolated place, possibly underground, or with thick walls, away from any other people."

A place where other people were a long way away. The solution was crystal-clear. "My house."

"What?"

"It's huge, and mostly empty." *Ever since I failed to marry.* "We can put enough stone walls between me and her, and her family. I'm hardly ever there at the moment. Take her and her family to my house and let the physic come there."

The woman raised her eyebrows, but started to make arrangements.

As Sady left the tent, he looked over his shoulder. The woman lay peacefully, as if she was asleep, her dark hair draped over the side of the bed. She looked tough. Someone who wouldn't have time for nonsense. He hoped she and her child would both survive.

He and Orsan left the tent . . .

. . . and walked into a menacing circle of people, all facing the tent entrance.

Sady found himself shoved aside by his guards. Orsan, a head taller than him, stepped in front, protecting him with his sheer size.

"What's this?" Orsan said, in his most intimidating voice.

Between the guards' bodies, Sady could see the faces of men. More than the occasional few had beards. A lot of them were dressed in black, like the man who had applied to become an interpreter.

Sady's guards drew guns.

"Who are these people, and what do they want?" Sady asked.

The woman he had seen earlier, the one with the suggestive clothing, came out of the group. "I see what people want."

"Who are they?"

"From the Outer City."

Sady remembered having seen the community referred to as the Outer City on his trips. No one went there, his hosts had assured. The workers lived there. It was full of criminals.

And those would have been the people most likely to survive a disaster. If anything, they were used to surviving. Living in the southern land was about surviving.

"Tell them that if they threaten me, it is unlikely to impress the Chevakian doga."

She spoke. Sady had no idea if what she said was anywhere near accurate, but there were protesting grumbles.

"They say they want bodies of their dead. They want . . . ceremony." Someone in the crowd commented. "Funeral," she corrected.

Sady wasn't even sure where the army had taken the bodies of those who had died on the train. It was a horrible thought, to have lost a loved one, and then not to know what happened to the body.

He raised his voice, hoping that at least someone would understand. "Select a couple of representatives, make a list of which bodies you need, age, gender, clothing, and we'll speak tomorrow."

"Today," a man said, in heavy accent. He also had a beard. This was not someone who had come forward as interpreter.

"Tomorrow. It is late. We need interpreters. Why didn't you come forward when we asked?"

"When we do that, everyone can see us."

Another man yelled something in a loud voice.

Several of the black-clad men yelled back at him.

The guards raised their guns.

"Stop," Sady called. "I will meet with you. Both groups. I'll meet with anyone who feels they should have a voice in his camp. Tomorrow. You're safe, fed and you have beds. There is nothing that can't wait until later."

Several of the black-clad men still protested, but others calmed them. Who were these people in black? Mercy, he needed a crash course in southern politics and culture.

With that, Sady's guards cleared a path and Sady walked through the group who formed a strange kind of honour guard all the way to the truck. There were a lot of these black-clad people. With a disturbing feeling, he noticed their age, too. Many young men. Angry young men with beards.

Into the truck. The door shut, and while the driver fired up the engine, Sady felt safe enough to remove the hot suit. His clothes underneath were sweaty and dusty. Outside the window, the groups of refugees lined the road. There were so many, and the Chevakians so few.

"What's with the black and the beards?" Sady asked.

"Apparently, they call themselves the Brotherhood of the Light. Those guys are trouble," Orsan said.

"Yes, and I have no idea who they are and what they stand for," another guard added. "There seem to be a lot of them in the camp, but I don't know that they would speak for many of the refugees. I don't even know that anyone speaks for any of the refugees."

"We have to ask Lady Armaine." Orsan again.

"No," Sady said.

Orsan frowned.

"Lady Armaine offered to help us. She was much too keen to give me the money for my trip. I think she might be part of the problem. The south is not at war with us. It's a civil war, and we have the two groups here, or whatever is left of them. Something done by one of the groups caused the explosion. As outsiders, we don't know who the groups are and what they stand for. We don't know who did what. And we don't know who, if anyone, we should support."

They had arrived at the gate, manned by two Chevakian guards. Far too few, Sady realised, to contain a conflict within the camp. But the army was already stretched. Finnisius had sent units to Twin Bridges, and to help ready the balloons, and to manage the camps, and to patrol the curfew imposed by the bell.

The doga wasn't just running out of money; it was running out of people.

CHAPTER 33

CARRO SAT at the desk, and leafed through the book, his hands trembling. The columns of numbers danced before his eyes. He was back in the warehouse. He felt the biting cold. He heard his stepfather's footsteps.

So that was what his father thought of him?

Death by accountancy.

The Knights in the room were all busy at work, reading through Chevakian documents, or writing notes on tiny pieces of paper to be carried by gulls. The squawks of those birds drifted in from the courtyard.

No one took any notice of Carro. He could make a scene about how much he hated this work, but no one would care. So he opened the book.

The account book was Chevakian. He claimed a bit of knowledge of the language, but a lot of lines had long words that were unfamiliar to him.

Someone thunked another book onto the desk.

Carro slid it towards him and read the Chevakian text on the front sheet. *Planned and actual expenditure of farm operations.*

By the skylights.

He turned around, glaring at the back of the Knight who had brought it. "Hey, what the fuck am I supposed to do with this?"

"Check it. The Supreme Rider says you know about this stuff."

Carro turned the first page. Crops, fences, many words he didn't recognise. He let his shoulders sag. "What is this? A farm budget?"

"You got it. Didn't think this place ran on thin air, did you?"

"So . . . it belongs to us?"

"Smart boy."

A few men laughed.

"Anyone got a dictionary?"

"You're smart, you make it up."

Carro cursed silently. "Why do you need me to do this?"

A few quick footsteps, and the man leaned over him, menacing. He wore a Senior badge. "Look, pup, I don't care who you are, but in this room, we shut up and work."

The figures at the end of the page do not add up. Carro sits and stares at them, through eyes gone teary with cold. His hands hurt and his feet hurt and his father is waiting outside the room. But he knows his numbers, and these ones do not add up.

His father yells, "Hurry up, the tax collectors are nearly here."

"But something is wrong," he says. In fact, it's more than that. The numbers are very wrong, and to check them, he needs a lot more time than his father is willing to give him. There are so many stupid mistakes.

"Then make the numbers right."

Carro squeaks, "I can't." The tax collectors will notice. He knows these men and they can add up better than he can. They will notice that there is a huge sum missing from the books.

But his father grabs his collar and shakes him. "Make it right."

So Carro does the only thing he can think of: he rubs out a few lines and a few numbers. He makes expenditure higher, and income lower. Quickly, he adds the amounts until the columns balance, and hopes the tax collector will not ask to check the money in the safe.

Carro worked, his pencil scratching over the paper. Sweat rolled over his back. He didn't want any of these Knights to notice that he drifted off; he didn't want these visions. He wanted nothing to do with this book.

The draft that went through the room was cold, reminiscent of the warehouse. There was no fire, also like in the warehouse. The Senior Knight was pacing like his father used to do. With every step he heard his father coming closer.

Add up numbers.

No, that was wrong. He rubbed out his calculations.

Add up again.

The result was wrong. The two columns didn't match, like in the warehouse. Any moment now and his father would come and scold him. He was no fighter, not much of a spy, no hunter, and he'd also fail at accounting.

"Why are you all blue around your neck?" Isandor asks.

Seated on the lid of a rubbish container in a narrow alley, Carro sips his soup and tells Isandor of the columns of non-matching figures. He tells Isandor of how he rubbed out and changed the numbers, with his father watching over his shoulder. He tells how his father grabbed him around the neck as if he was going to choke him to death, but then shoved him in the cold cupboard and left him there while the tax collector went over his father's books, saying things like, "Your business hasn't done very well this year."

And all the while his father was explaining about how he was robbed and how his wife's family was asking for return of a loan they had given only a few years earlier.

"It was all nonsense," Carro says and looks into Isandor's blue eyes. There's despair inside him, bursting to come out.

"Maybe your father doesn't want to pay his taxes," Isandor says.

"But he should. He makes a lot of money."

Lies are the worst thing in the world.

Yes, Carro remembered that. He'd been ten or so, just a little boy.

And now all these figures danced before his eyes. They didn't add up either, far from it. Someone had made a big mess of this book.

The touch of a hand on his shoulder made him gasp. He whirled around and looked into the face of Rider Cornatan, smiling.

"I'm glad to see you made it, son."

Carro didn't know what to say. What had his father heard from the hunters? That they hadn't killed the Queen? That he'd let her escape?

Finally, he said, "I'm glad that you're safe, too."

His father laughed. For all that he was a refugee, he was extraordinarily well groomed. His uniform was as crisp and clean as it had been in the City of Glass. Not like Carro's which had stains that didn't come out no matter how much he scrubbed it.

"We managed to get away just in time."

"But . . . what happened in the City of Glass?"

His father's face went serious. "There was a huge explosion. Some saboteur blew up our experimental installation, and it set off a chain reaction."

"The Heart?"

"No longer there, I'm afraid."

Carro thought of the cellar where his father had taken him, where he'd seen the merchant treated with that machine. He remembered the table with metal implements. The eerie feeling as he hesitated to touch anything. The metal of the staff going cold in his hands. It seemed such a long time ago. Back when his life had been innocent.

"Much of the City of Glass has been destroyed. There is too much icefire even for us. It will take a long time before it is safe for anyone to go there again."

"What about . . . all the people?" His father—no, not his father—the merchant, his snarky wife, his sister, Isandor's mother. By the skylights, would he ever find ichina to cure his infliction now?

"Many of the Knights got away," Rider Cornatan said.

"And the other people?"

Rider Cornatan's eyebrows went up, as if surprised Carro should even ask. "The Outer City was destroyed in a fire. I don't know how many got out."

Carro stared at him. *What, are you saying that they're all dead?* His eyes pricked, and that made him angry. He'd always said he didn't care about the merchant and the rest of the family. But . . . all gone?

His neighbours, and Isandor's mother, and the girls he'd eyed in the marketplace, and . . . all gone?

Rider Cornatan's voice came from far off. "I understand that you didn't find the Queen."

"No."

Carro sat stiff, with his hands clasped in his lap and waited for his father to speak, for punishment.

But Rider Cornatan said nothing.

Hatred burned in his father's eyes, but Carro didn't know who was the object of the hatred. So he sat and waited to be punished.

Then his father said, "Come."

Carro stands in his father's study. By the light of the fire, his father sits at his desk. His face looks old.

"Why are you so late?"

"I was out with friends."

"You don't have any friends. Only that cripple boy and if I see you with him again I will come and chop off his other leg. He gives you ideas."

"What ideas? I only want to play." Isandor comes from a poor family, but he still has more toys. He has a box of colourful blocks made from real wood. He has no father, but Isandor's mother cares a lot about him.

Rider Cornatan went out the room, a little way along the dark corridor, and in through another doorway. The room on the other side was huge, with dustsheet-covered furniture towards the far end. The windows were dirty, with lots of cobwebs in the corners.

Carro's footsteps echoed back from the ceiling.

"Nice mansion, isn't it?" Rider Cornatan chuckled. "This is the country house of the old southern ambassador. While the people starved in the City of Glass, the King's cronies lived in luxury."

In the far corner of the room, near the window, the sheets had been pulled off two couches and a low table between them. On a cabinet against the far wall stood a selection of bottles.

Rider Cornatan gestured that he should sit, so Carro sat, the muscles in his legs stiff with tension.

"And, what have you found out so far?" said Rider Cornatan while settling on the other couch.

"What do you mean?"

"You've been checking the accounts, as far as I know."

"Yes, but why—"

"With what's happened in the south, we're going to be here for a while. The icefire bubble is still expanding. This place has been allowed to become run-down, and I'm aghast at how poorly the caretaker has looked after it. I had hoped there would be a nice little bit of farm income for us to buy essentials, such as food. But the caretaker fled as soon as we turned up here, and the books are not up-to-date. At this rate, we can't support the troops still coming from Arania. We need money, and we need to obtain it in such a way that is not going to anger the Chevakians. Your work is extremely important. You need to find us that money."

Carro nodded, but his inner voice squealed, *But what if there is none?*

Rider Cornatan continued, "Of course, it could well be that it could take us a while to retrieve that money. In that case, we'll need to look for opportunities to get some."

"Why don't we hunt our own food?" The Knights always did that.

"There are too many of us here. The Chevakians would be upset. There are not enough large animals in this country anyway."

"Why don't you offer to help the Chevakians? Then they might give us food or money?"

Rider Cornatan smiled. "That's exactly the idea. Except that damn upstart of a new proctor is too suspicious. I sent two men to act as interpreters for the camp of refugees, but the refugees didn't like them and now the Chevakians are suspicious. We need to work harder at gaining their trust. Us, over the Brothers. But the people in the camp can't be allowed to see who we are. I must remain hidden. I want you to be the face of the Eagle Knights."

Carro's father says, "Don't be afraid. They only ask stupid questions."

But Carro feels very small and scared. His father leaves the room and goes to open the door.

Carro sits at the desk in the chair where his father never allows him to sit. He can hear the footsteps in the warehouse. The voice of a man. Laughter.

"Go and see my son, sir. He does the accounts."

Carro glances at the books, and counts the steps. One, two, three.

Any moment now and the tax collector will knock on the door.

Carro turned to the window, feeling chilled and sweaty at the same time. He was no prince, and he was no leader, and he had no intention of becoming the person to blame if things went wrong. Forcing the common people of the Outer City into accepting Knight rule was wrong. Knights did not rule, they protected. The queen ruled.

"Pour us a drink, son, and I'll tell you our plan."

Carro crossed the room to the cabinet against the wall, where dusty glasses stood amongst an assortment of jars, carafes and bottles. He wondered why the ambassador had left all those years ago, and why he had such a wild range of chemicals in his drinks cabinet. A jar of salt, all gone hard and stuck together. Lumps of an unidentified white crystal in a bottle of oil. Carro opened the lid. A sharp scent made him cough. Phooey. What was that awful stuff?

A tiny glass vessel with an ornate glass lid contained something he did recognise: light blue cyan crystals. Weren't they used as a crude method of assassinating your political opponents?

What sort of man had this ambassador been? Maybe his departure had less to do with the south's involvement in the border raids than with his own behaviour.

"What are you doing over there, son? The carafe of bloodwine is on the shelf," Rider Cornatan said.

Carro hesitated, the jar of cyan crystals in his hand. Drop a crystal or two in someone's drink and they would die a painful death. He imagined the merchant writhing on the floor, but got no satisfaction from the image. Everyone in the City of Glass had died.

This was not about him and his petty problems; it was about the people of the City of Glass. It was about the City of Glass not existing anymore, and all its citizens being forced to live here.

Rider Cornatan had known what was happening and had not warned the people. Rider Cornatan wanted to destroy the royal family, and anything that was outside his control. Rider Cornatan didn't care about the Chevakians, the ordinary people who had done nothing wrong.

"What's keeping you, son?"

"Um—nothing." Carro set the jar of crystals down, hidden behind two larger bottles. "It seems you expected something like this to happen."

He picked up the carafe, poured two drinks, and handed one to his father. Rider Cornatan drank deeply, then breathed out satisfaction.

"Always be prepared for everything, son. Now let me tell you what we're going to do. I'm going to send you to talk to the Chevakians."

A Word of Thanks

THANK YOU very much for reading *Dust & Rain.*

As author of this book, I would appreciate it very much if you could return to the place where you purchased this book and leave a review. Reviews are important to me, because they help readers decide if the book is for them.

In book 3 of the Icefire Trilogy, _Blood & Tears_, the saga concludes, as the Chevakians scramble to defend their homeland against an ever-expanding cloud of icefire, and the refugees fight against the power of the Eagle Knights.

Also be sure to put your name on my mailing list, which I use to notify subscribers of news and new fiction. For everything else, please visit my website at _pattyjansen.com._

ABOUT THE AUTHOR

Patty Jansen lives in Sydney, Australia, where she spends most of her time writing Science Fiction and Fantasy.

Her career started in earnest when her story *This Peaceful State of War* placed first in the second quarter of the Writers of the Future contest and was published in their 27th anthology. She has also sold fiction to genre magazines such as Analog Science Fiction and Fact, Redstone SF and Aurealis, before making the move to independent publishing.

Patty has written over fifty novels in both Science Fiction and Fantasy, including the *Icefire Trilogy* and the *Ambassador* series.

pattyjansen.com

BOOKS BY PATTY JANSEN

For a complete list of books, scan the image below with your phone.